MY X HEART
L.A. WAYWARD

ISBN Paperback edition: 9789083074436

Editors: Lauren Clarke and Sali Benbow-Powers, CREATING ink
Copyedit and Proofreading: Sarah Plocher, All Encompassing Books
Cover Design: Lori Jackson, Lori Jackson Design
Cover Photo: Michelle Lancaster, model Chase Cassels
Formatting: Stacey Blake, Champagne Book Design

Thank you for buying my book and respecting the hard work of this author. Yeah, happy dance. High five to all you babes!

Visit my website at www.lawayward.com

ALSO BY L.A. WAYWARD

The Nashville Outlaws Series

Make It Burn #1

Stand-Alones

Ranger Danger
Thirst

Coming Soon

Just Shred
The Page In Between
Firestarter
Moonlight

X MY HEART

Love isn't clean. It's messy, and sometimes it's as dirty as BMX. Hunter, BMX's number-one bad boy, has everything he needs: money, fame, gold medals, and girls between his sheets to fill the constant ache in his chest. He doesn't need anyone to mend the hole in his heart, and certainly not someone like Sky Alexander.

When Sky, his trainer's long-lost daughter, comes into his life, she screws up his plans to never let a girl distract him on his way to the number one spot.

Sky doesn't need a tattooed BMX wild boy to mess up her plans. There is only one race she still needs to ride, and it doesn't involve falling for the BMX champion with enough problems and vices to fill a whole arena.

X My Heart is a story about love, loss and taking on every hill life has to offer. True love doesn't have to make sense for it to be real or for it to change the path you are on.

It doesn't matter how many wrong turns you make, or how many times you crash. The only thing you have to do is chase the ride till the end.

Fuck Forever

X MY HEART PLAYLIST

"So Far Away" by Agust D (feat. Suran)
"Bad Mother Fucker" by Machine Gun Kelly ft. Kid Rock
"Once In A Lifetime" by The Night Game
"On To The Next" by Tyler Bryant & the Shakedown
"Scream" by Avenged Sevenfold
"Ocean Eyes" by Billie Eilish
"Who Says" by John Mayer
"Feel Good Inc." by Gorillaz
"Born To Die" by Lana Del Rey
"Novacane" by Frank Ocean
"Sweet Child o' Mine" by Guns N' Roses
"Deep Inside" by Trevor Something
"Live Forever" by Oasis
"Black Hole Sun" by Soundgarden
"Until I Bleed Out" by The Weeknd
"To Be Alone" by Hozier
"Once" by Liam Gallagher
"I Fall Apart" by Post Malone
"Driving Rain" by Slash ft. Myles Kennedy & The Conspirators
"Always" by Bon Jovi
"Times Like These" by Foo Fighters
"Free Bird" by Lynyrd Skynyrd

BMX

BMX is my life, the one true love I chase down the tracks.
The only one who will have me as the broken man I am.
Climbing higher to chase a dream.
The closest I ever get to truly being free.
It isn't pretty, it is a violent and dirty ride I race.
I got enough gold to chase the light when darkness is my only fate.
I count the seconds, waiting for the starting gate to come down.
Got blood on the frame, closing my eyes for the truth that remains.
My hands are blistered like my soul, no reason to live because the end is my only goal.
I got a mean reputation and dope coursing through my veins, numbing my pain.
Going the wrong direction, losing every part of myself along the way.
When I look in the mirror mine is not the face I see.
Every mistake has led me to the man I want to be.
I chase the hurt, the pain, the broken bones to feel again.
Finding comfort only on the track.
Not enough to last.
Mad I can't shake my past.
I got the will others crave.
I got a name tied to a past I want to keep locked away.
I'm nothing, I deserve even less,
still the gold keeps me obsessed.
I keep holding out for someone to help make this part of me die.
Getting anger in return, more reason to fly.
Blindness when I want to see a love who will set me free.
A mistake is what I am and she will agree.
It doesn't matter how many wrong turns I make, how many times I crash, I will chase the ride till the end.

PROLOGUE

Sky

Present day

"I love and hate you for giving me forever," I whisper in Hunter's ear, leaning against the pillows, I trail my fingers over the tattoos on his back.

Holding the letter against my heart, I watch him sleep. I smile, kissing the place between his shoulder blades before I let the shaking pen touch the paper again.

There are so many things in life I took for granted. Every hour, every minute, every damn second. I barely made it through the day without feeling like shit. I was scared to fail, scared of success. Love and happiness were some distant dream I couldn't remember when I woke.

You changed everything. You remind me every day to live life in the moment. You make me remember; you give me strength I didn't even know I possessed.

Babe, you inspire me, and you see everything every color, every light, and every shade. The best and the worst. You see all the pieces of myself I lost along the way, the pieces you helped me put back together.

He rolls over onto his side, resting his head on his tattooed bicep. Clutching the pen more firmly between my aching fingers, I adjust the notepad and push through the pain in my chest before I can't write anymore.

I'd never met anyone who lived his life exactly how he wanted, screw the consequences, until you. You don't care about other people's opinions, or what they say or think about you. You face life head on with a big "fuck you" smirk on your face. You live life with no regrets, taking credit for every success and every failure that's led you here. How many people can say that? Truly say they did it all? You can, and you will.

You once told me you were a mistake. Babe, you are the best mistake I've ever made.

You are my home, my life.

My love. My once-in-a-lifetime.

You made me lose myself and helped me find what was missing.

I love you from now until forever,

Cross my heart.

I put the letter in an envelope and slowly place it on the night-stand. Turning around, I tell him, "I love you," and softly brush his hair out of his eyes before I kiss his forehead.

I press my lips against his, and the corner of his mouth hikes up.

"No one told me holding on would hurt more than letting go," I say, the tip of my nose touching his.

"Don't let me go, babe." His voice is a hoarse whisper.

Tracing the line of his jaw with my shaking fingers, I smile through my tears.

"Love can make you believe anything—even in a fucking forever," he says, his voice groggy as he scratches his unshaven cheek before he locks eyes with me. His sad smile tears me apart.

"I guess it does," I tell him, slowly moving my fingers through his long hair to the stubble on his jaw. He closes his eyes, the side of his mouth curling up the tiniest bit.

I've been watching him sleep for hours, his strong body moving with every breath he takes. It's like I'm seeing him more clearly with each passing day. He closes his eyes again, and turns on his front, pushing both inked arms under his pillow. I skim my fingers over the tattoos on his broad muscular back, to his sleeve, and try to smile through the tears moving over my cheeks.

I kiss the skull tattoo, then kiss every line of the letters on his shoulder blades and lower back, all the way around to his rib cage. He shivers under my touch, and butterflies take flight in my stomach. Hunter slowly opens his sapphire eyes, taking my breath away. An ocean of tears is reflected in those bright blue depths. There's love, anger, hate and everything in between. They're eyes to get lost in forever.

"What are you thinking about?" he asks, turning on his side.

"About our forever." I smile, dabbing away my tears with the sleeve of his black shirt I'm wearing that swamps my small frame.

"Fuck forever," he whispers, pulling me into his arms and kissing the top of my head. His lips linger on my skin. I love how he tries to hold on, making a memory out of every touch, each moment. Burying his nose in my hair, he links our fingers together. Tears blur my vision as I stare at the new *free* tattoo on his knuckles.

"Promise me you'll stay." His voice breaks.

I kiss his temple, laying my hand on his heart, trailing a path over his chest.

"I'll never leave you," I tell him, skimming my fingers over the stubble on his jaw. Leaning forward, he kisses me softly, his calloused thumb caressing my cheekbone.

"I don't know what to do," he whispers, voice strained.

"You will, babe," I tell him, staring into his eyes. "You will."

"I don't know how to live without you," he rasps, his hurt underlined in every syllable. "Fuck I love you," he says, closing his eyes. "So fucking much," a sob escapes him.

"Cross your heart?" I ask, caressing his cheek. Blue eyes find mine. He shakes his head and tries to smile as I brush away his tears. With trembling fingers I trace his lips, eyes, his freckled nose. Memorizing every line, every laugh wrinkle. Every beautiful part of him.

"Cross my fucking heart," he whispers, pulling me into him.

When his lips touch my own I know what it means to love without fear. True love isn't pretty; it is messy, layered and sometimes plain dirty. It hurts, makes you feel alive, and destroys you in the best possible ways. And, for the first time in my life, I'm not afraid to lose this race I'm in anymore.

I know I've already won.

When you love,
love all the way,
like it's your dying day

OK, riders, random start.
Riders ready!
Watch the gate!

—BMX gate start announcement

CHAPTER 1

Sky

Four months earlier

"Fuck, I'm on a highway to hell," I huff, looking in my rearview mirror as I change lanes.

"That's not funny, Sky," my mom warns, her beautiful voice echoing through the speaker of the car I rented at San Diego Airport. I took the afternoon flight out from New York, and if I'm lucky it will still take me about another hour, with traffic, to get to my father's BMX compound in the middle of freaking nowhere.

A wave of nausea hits me, and I skid to a halt on the side of the road. Grabbing the steering wheel, I squeeze until my knuckles turn white. "I don't know if I can do this, mom," I say, locking eyes with her over FaceTime.

She lets out a deep breath, and walks onto the balcony of our Park Avenue penthouse, the dark skyline of Manhattan glistening with a thousand lights.

She takes a cigarette out of the pack and blows me a kiss. "I know you can, baby girl."

"I thought you didn't smoke anymore?" I ask, laughing, through the tears that threaten to spill over.

She rolls her eyes. Sometimes she looks so much younger than forty. She winks, and says, "Don't tell your stepdad."

A small smirk tugs on her lips, and I can't help but snicker thinking about Conrad's reaction, the man adores my mom.

We are both quiet for a while.

"Mom ..." My voice breaks.

"You can do it, kiddo," she whispers.

"What if Jay doesn't want to see me," I sob, trying to sound strong, but breaking all over again. "I...I...need..." I can't even finish my sentence through my hiccups.

She covers her mouth with a trembling hand and starts to cry. "You're strong, baby. If anyone can do this, you can."

"I don't know what's going to happen," I say, brushing away a tear with my sleeve. I clutch the necklace Jay gave me in the palm of my hand. "It's been years."

"I know, but he misses you, just as you miss him," she tells me.

Our eyes meet. "Why didn't he love us enough to stay? Why does he only call once a year? Why did he never come to get me?"

"Oh, honey," she whispers, tears streaming down her pretty face.

"Mommy."

"Give yourself some time, it's going to be good for you both. And then you can come home to us, and your brother."

"Okay," I smile, wiping at my nose. "I googled Jay's info on the plane. The itinerary on his website said he will be home tomorrow when the tour ends."

"I just don't want you to get hurt. BMX was Jay's life; it still is. I don't know how much he's changed."

"I don't care, and you know why?" I ask as she looks up, and brushes a stray lock behind her ear.

"Why?"

I run my fingers over the necklace. "Because you taught me to be strong," I whisper, kissing the screen.

"Promise me you'll come home to us. I'm not ready to lose you. But I also know you have a strength inside of you," she says, placing her hand on her heart. "I know you need to mend things with Jay, and maybe there are still parts of yourself you need to find as well. I love you so much," she tells me.

"I love you too, and I'll come back," I promise, ending the call, never wanting to let go.

My father bought some land in Chula Vista, one of the number one training areas for BMX, and started his company not long after the last time I visited. I turned fifteen that summer, five years have gone by, and I tried not to think about him or his life here.

I put the car in drive, pull back on to the highway and focus on the road ahead, slowly breathing in and out until the lump in my throat disappears. Turning up a Metallica song blaring through the speakers, I pull in a tight breath and blink back my tears. "Get it together. I'm strong. I can do this." I try to convince myself.

It is getting darker by the minute, and I'm tired and anxious at the same time. I stop at a motel a couple miles from Jay's house to crash for the night. I'll knock on his door in the morning. At least if I surprise him, he won't be able to run away.

Staring in the dirty bathroom mirror, I take a deep breath. My ringtone, "Free Bird," a song by Lynyrd Skynyrd, echoes through the bathroom. My best friend's picture pops up on the screen, making me smile.

"Hey, honey," Tim says as I answer the FaceTime call.

"Hey," I return, walking into my room and plopping down on the bed.

He brushes a hand over his buzz cut. "Can't believe you

went through with it," he says, but I pick up on the concern in his voice. I try to give him my best fake smile, but the moment I see his red-rimmed eyes I break, and the floodgates open.

"Oh, Sky," he whispers. "I'm taking the first flight out."

"You don't have to. I'm busy having a pity party over here," I joke, trying to smile through my tears.

"I'm coming anyway, so don't try to convince me otherwise," he promises.

"Thank you, Timmy," I say softly.

"Call me if you need anything. I'll be there by the end of the week. Need to go to a couple of business meetings first. I've been talking to a guy from Nashville who's been experimenting with a new strain of medical marijuana," he explains.

"I'll text you the address." I tuck my long hair behind my ear. "Can't believe I'm back in California. I was never interested in Jay's dreams. Maybe I should have listened to him instead of being an uninterested asshole teenager."

I grab my iPad and tap on dad's website I've still got open, and scroll through the pictures on his site of the riders he trains.

"Don't be so hard on yourself. Things fell apart. Hell, life happened. I'm proud of you for taking the first step," Tim says.

"Maybe he doesn't even want to see me." Spotting a set of the bluest eyes I've ever seen in my life I stop scrolling.

"You okay? You're biting your lip like you do when you see something you like." Tim laughs.

I quickly scan the guy's bio. Apparently, his name is Hunter and he's been defending his champion title for a couple of years. "I'm looking at Jay's website," I murmur.

"Checking out the merchandise?" Tim asks, excitement ringing through his voice, while he boots up his laptop. "Let me get with the program."

I stare at Hunter's picture some more. *Damn, the guy is hot with his dark hair falling in front of his eyes and tattoos covering the better part of his neck.*

"Wow, hon, you didn't tell me that Drew guy was hot," he drawls, the dimples in his cheeks popping. "The bad boy isn't half bad either."

"What bad boy?" I ask.

"The dude with the tats and crazy shaved hair. Maybe you should reenact one of those romance novels you like to read, and fuck the stepbrother you never had?" he replies drily.

"Screw you," I laugh. "I'm here to reconnect with Jay, not get some fling going." I shut my mouth, biting on the inside of my cheek.

"Sky, come on," he says.

"I need to go, Tim, I'm beat," I say wiping my eyes with my sleeve. "Talk to you later, okay?"

"I'm here for you," he whispers.

"I know." I smile, blowing him a kiss before I end the call.

Scrolling through the pictures of Jay and his riders, I twirl the necklace around my finger. I pull it over my head and hold the pendant in the palm of my hand. He used to tell me the silver bird reflected all his dreams, the promises he couldn't keep. I grab my phone and press play. "Free Bird" fills the room. I've been listening to the track for the last couple of months. First, I hated the song because each line reminded me of Jay. I spent months, no years, waiting for him to visit, or pick up the phone, not counting the five-minute calls on my birthday. He was always on the track or traveling the world, creating this whole other family, and forgetting about me.

Leaning against the headboard, I close my eyes, singing along with the lyrics and cradling the necklace in my hand. I stop singing, and my face is wet from my tears. And I know I made a big mistake coming here, because no one can ever change.

CHAPTER 2

Hunter

Earlier that day

Burying my face in the pillow, I try to cancel out the constant banging on the door. Whoever it is can go and fuck themselves into oblivion. I swear under my breath, turning on my side.

"Hunt, open the fucking door. I know you're in there. You changed the passcode again, you bastard," Drew yells.

I cover my head with my arms. "Let me sleep," I grit out, while the two girls I have with me in my bed moan.

My best friend's swearing intensifies. "Hunter!"

Growling, I sit up, almost hitting my head against the bunk ceiling. "Fuck. Yeah, I'm coming. Sorry girls," I huff, stumbling out of the tiny compartment and leaving them alone.

There's more knocking from Drew.

"Okay, fuck," I yell, my toes getting caught on a pink lace

G-string. "I'm on my way," I roar, pulling on my sweatpants and stumbling to the front of the bus.

"What do you want?" I grunt, yanking the door open, rubbing the sleep from my eyes. Drew is shaking his head with an angry scowl on his face.

"You're late, man," he says, tapping his fingers impatiently on the door.

"Dude, not this shit again," I let out a low growl, brushing my hands through my tousled hair. "Leave me the fuck alone on my day off." I fall back onto the black leather couch and throw a purple lace bra on the floor. Putting my feet up on the table I light a cigarette.

"What are you talking about?" Drew asks, looking around the bus, his eyes lingering on the empty beer bottles, pink lingerie and used condoms. "Fuck you're disgusting," he laughs, throwing a condom in my direction.

I duck, damn the guy has good aim. I grab the rubbers, and drop them in the trashcan under the sink. "Fuck you, dude, you're just jealous."

"We leave you alone for one night, and this is what happens?" he asks, exasperated, flinging a neon-green thong in my face.

"Will you relax? You're bumming me out." I blow the smoke out through my nose. Brushing my hair out of my eyes, I scan the trailer for a shirt. "Don't pretend you didn't have a good time with what's-his-face after the party last night," I mumble.

Drew swears under his breath.

"If you think about it, this," I joke, flapping my hands around the bus, "is actually your fault. You know I don't thrive when I'm alone," I drawl, laughing and coughing at the same time.

Drew rolls his eyes and flips me off. "My dick isn't complaining, have you seen his ass? And, judging by this mess, you shouldn't bitch either," he replies drily.

"Please don't," I say, covering my ears with my hands, giving him a playful push with my shoulder. "TMI, dude." I take a deep drag, and blow out the smoke, the cigarette still in my mouth. Grinning, I watch him move through the aisle of the bus.

"Where is your gear?" he mutters, checking the beds. He opens the curtain of my bunk, and the girls whine in protest.

"Get out," he orders. They look to me for support, but I just shrug, I'm done with them anyway.

Drew throws my BMX shirt, pants, shoes and gloves in my direction. He clears his throat. "Come on, asshole. Jay is going out of his mind. Get dressed."

"Why? Dude is always going out of his mind about something he thinks *I've* done," I grumble, changing into my gear. "Why the hell do I need my race outfit, do I have some photoshoot I forgot about again?"

"You have ten minutes, dipshit," Drew says playfully. "Or, if you want to give up your number-one spot, that's fine by me," he teases, holding up his hands in mock defeat.

I balance my cigarette on the edge of the kitchen counter. After pulling my shirt over my head, I take one last drag before stamping the smoke out in the sink.

"Before what? This is our day off, ain't it?" I ask, and brush my teeth. *I did all my interviews yesterday. Flirted with a female ESPN sports commentator and talked to the Red Bull guys. What is his problem?*

"For the race, asshole," he bites out, shoving his phone in my face.

"Fuck," I swear, looking at the date I spit the toothpaste into the sink, and stare at the time.

"Hunter? Why don't you come back to bed?" the platinum blonde whines, stumbling out of my bunk in the back of the bus, and clutching the white bedsheet to her body.

I can't help but roll my eyes at my best friend. Drew snorts, and I wipe my mouth with a dirty towel. Fuck, I can't remember her name—it's Ashley, Ainsley or something.

Drew picks up some clothes from the floor and hands them to her. "Get a move on girls, you can change in there," he commands, pushing her into the back lounge.

"You too." The brunette whose name I can't remember either, whisks her dress from his hands, and pouts.

I stick my tongue out at Drew and he pushes my face away. "Don't look so smug asshole," he smirks.

After they change, Drew guides them like a pro to the front of the bus while I grab my shit.

"Later, sweethearts. Duty calls," I say, giving them a mock salute. "Had a great time," I tell them as they walk away. The blonde looks over her shoulder, and purses her lips as if I've insulted her—faking it, no doubt. The two of them fuck everyone on the circuit. *I'd better stop screwing these chicks.*

My gaze zeros in on her tits.

Then again, maybe not.

They leave but not before flipping me the bird, and Drew and I burst out laughing.

"Got everything, fucker?" Drew asks, looking around the bus, pushing me outside.

"Yeah, I guess," I answer, still grinning as Drew and I sprint through the backstage area. We both run as fast as we can toward the grounds before getting stopped by a couple security guards.

"Passes?" one of the guys asks.

I search my pockets for my credentials. "Come on, Andy, we do this almost every damn day."

He flashes us an evil grin. "And each day, you boys are late, have forgotten your creds, and take too many girls backstage, or in the pits. This is not some circus."

"Andy," Drew pleads. "Give us a break."

Andy sighs, shaking his head. "You guys are lucky I'm in a good mood right now," he says, and steps aside to let us pass.

"Later, dude." I laugh, running to our rig with Drew not far behind.

"This is the last time I let you get away with this," Andy yells after us.

I turn around, making a jerking off motion with my hand.

"Back at you, Cole," Andy roars, laughing.

Drew snickers. "Hunt, you never learn."

Shaking my head, I grin. "Half the fun, baby." Still running, I say hello to a couple guys I know; we've been competing together for years. I've been bringing home the gold the last couple seasons, and they hate me for it, but we still like to throw back a couple of beers after the races.

We come to a full stop at our black trailer with my name, and all my sponsors' names printed in big white letters on the side.

"Where the fuck have you been?" Jay bellows, jumping out the back of the truck.

"Hey, Hunt, nice of you to join us," I say, mocking. "Glad I came, Jay. My pleasure."

Jay balls his hands into fists, shaking his head. "One day, you're going to get fucking burned for your antics."

The old man is already starting to count to ten. I grin. I do it too; it doesn't work for me all the time though. But Jay's good people. I don't mind the guy; I tolerate him even. Hell, he's like a father to me, but most days, he's a hall monitor on steroids.

I spread out my arms. "I'm here now, aren't I?"

"What the fuck?" he says, examining my face more closely.

"What?" I ask, trying to feign surprise.

"In your fucking lip," he roars.

I flash him a big smile. "You mean this new lip ring is a problem?"

He shakes his head, brushing both hands through his hair. "Get ready, you piece of work," he orders, inhaling sharply.

I give him a wink while I take out my other piercings, handing them to Drew. Jay mutters a couple of swear words under his breath. I ignore him and inspect the bike Mac fixed after I crashed it during a practice run back home.

"Looks good, Mac," I tell him, paying attention to what he

has to say about the new frame and the adjustments he made to the handlebars for improved grip.

Mac hands me my helmet, shaking his head. "Damn, boy. One day your luck is going to run out."

I take the helmet from him. "Don't need luck. Maybe I will one day, right now my pure talent will earn us all some green," I snicker, bumping fists with Drew.

"God help us all." Mac laughs, peering up to the heavens.

We head to the starting gate. The music and the commentators get louder as we walk past the stands. I don't know how many people came out today—a couple thousand is my guess.

The starting gate marks the beginning of the three-hundred-meter track. I make my way up there, nodding to a couple of fellow competitors. Crouching next to my bike, I inspect the frame one last time. I may be a fucking slacker in some areas but not this one. This is my life.

I'm checking my pedals, and a guy bumps into me. "Watch it," I warn him, turning around.

Ryan takes his place next to me. "Ready to start losing?" he asks. Fucker has been getting on my nerves ever since the season started. I mean, I did beat him at the world championships. And I fucked his ex-girlfriend after I won, but he shouldn't be this fucking anal about it.

"What's up, Ryan?" I ask mockingly, taking a seat on my bike. "Are you ready to bite the concrete like you did last time?" I waggle my hand, making the shaka sign. A couple guys laugh.

"Fuck you, Hunt," he bites out.

I roll my eyes in response.

"Do you ever get tired?" Ryan asks, flipping me off.

"From what? Fucking your mother?" I say, keeping a straight face, sliding my helmet over my head.

"You fucking ass."

One of the referees grabs his arm. "Watch it," the man says to both of us.

I shake my head and peer around the track. I've memorized each hill, every bend in the road, every steep angle. Before a race, I usually walk the whole track to get the lay of the land. To get a sense of the layout, the concrete, the gravel, the dirt, locking it all in my mind. Luckily, I did that yesterday morning. Fuck, I hope I still remember everything.

Standing at the edge of the hill never gets old. I'm like two or three stories high and when I ride in a couple of seconds I won't think of anything but the experience of the wind against my skin. With winning on my mind, I'll be flying over the hills, and bringing home the gold.

The commentators introduce all eight of us one at a time. The men's booming voices echo through the air. Some riders are from Australia; there are a couple from the Netherlands and Canada, and the rest are from the States. I know them all. We've trained and competed against each other for as long as I can remember. "And here is Hunter Cole, everyone, the twenty-two-year-old reigning world champion. Can't wait to see what the bad boy of BMX has in store for us," he yells.

Girls are screaming my name and the audience applauds. I raise my hand to acknowledge them. Without fans, I wouldn't get paid, get sponsors, or get laid. Grinning, I scan the crowd and notice Jay standing next to Drew and Mac. Jay crosses his arms, scowling at me. I flash them my tongue. Drew shakes his head but smiles anyway. Jay flips me off, and takes out his cell phone. Weird. He never answers a call when I'm about to race. He grabs the railing for support. I stand and watch him leave the side of the track. *Strange as fuck.*

Cracking my neck, I slam my hands on my legs. I need to focus on the task ahead—the thirty to forty seconds it takes to get to the finish line, toward my number one spot. I make sure my helmet is in place. The gate moves up, everyone else stands with me and we balance on our bikes.

"Catch you on the other side," Ryan yells over the roar of the audience. Closing my eyes, I take a deep breath, focusing on my body placement.

"Okay, riders, random start," the referee says.

I grab the handlebars of my bike so tightly my hands hurt.

"Riders, ready! Watch the gate!" the voice says over the speakers. The beeping starts and as the gate drops down, I'm off, flying across the track. I drown out the commentators, the roar of the audience, and focus on the path in front of me.

I'm in shared first position with Louis, the guy from Canada. There is a crash behind me and the commentators yell. Probably lost a couple of riders on one of the hills.

The cheers from the stands get louder. I grip the bars even tighter, angle my bike in the air and jump over the first three hills.

From the corner of my eye I see Louis falling behind, but then Ryan is gaining momentum. I pedal harder and take the last jump, the highest of them all. The finish line is just up ahead. I want to win with a bang, and show the crowd what I'm made of.

I sense Ryan next to me, and I misjudge my jump. Asshole gives me a push with his shoulder, and I wobble in the air.

"Fuck," I grit out, trying to maneuver the bike in a straight line, but I lose my balance. My helmet makes contact with the concrete.

Everything fades to black.

"You need to watch yourself, Hunter," Amy, the smoking hot nurse tells me, while she binds my beat up ribs with a compression wrap. "Try to restrict your activities."

"All activities?" I ask, winking at her. I wince from the pain, fuck even making a joke hurts like hell.

She laughs, and pushes me carefully down on the workbench in the trailer. "Rest your eyes for a bit, lover boy, I need to talk to your trainer," she says while I close my eyes.

"I'll be right here waiting, Amy, just so you know," I chuckle and swear under my breath, I feel like I've been hit by a truck.

"He needs to take his rest, Jay," she says, and the man in question grunts a response. "You know I can't keep vouching for him, or you," she warns.

"He's been trying, Amy," Jay bites out. "Bastard is working on it."

"You have to promise me, if he shows any signs of a concussion or swelling you will take him to the hospital. I can't have him OD again on my watch."

"Okay, damn it, let him crash for a while, then we'll see," he murmurs, his deep voice slowly fading away.

Why the fuck is someone slapping me? Damn, my cheek hurts.

"Hunter! Hunter, can you hear me?" Jay's voice sounds miles away.

"What the hell? Stop it, man," I grumble. Trying to sit up, I squint, hoping the spinning will stop soon. The bike parts hanging on the wall of the trailer are a slap in my face. I really fucked it up this time. I try to open my left eye, fuck, the swelling has gotten worse.

"Damn, what the hell happened?" I rasp. I lean forward. My stomach drops, and I puke all over the floor.

"Shit, Hunt," Jay mutters, stepping around my vomit before he jumps out the back of the rig.

Drew is leaning against the side of the trailer. The sun shines in through the open door; it's probably late in the afternoon. I think—really, I've got no idea how long I was out. I wipe my mouth with the back of my hand. Could be the next day, for all I know.

"Give me a second, before you fucking yell at me again," I mumble, getting my bearings. Mac shakes his head in my direction, pulling apart what's left of my damaged bike piece by piece, and I grimace scratching the back of my neck.

"Probably the last time I'm riding that thing ever again." I try to laugh but grab hold of my ribs. "Shit." The bile rises up again, and I cover my mouth with my hand, swallowing it back.

Mac mutters under his breath, "This is the fifth time this season you've driven a bike into the ground."

I roll my eyes—no, scratch that. I try to roll them. Shit, it hurts.

Jay hands me an icepack for my eye and leans against the trailer, before he says, "Amy checked you out. She wanted to take you to the hospital. But, lucky for you, Drew told me you'd been drinking last night, and I convinced her to let you sleep your injury off."

"Fuck, but in my defense, counselor," I say, trying to make a face, as I press the icepack against my eye, "I thought we had a day off."

"Damn, Hunt, you know you can get fucking banned if she checked your blood," Jay roars, sounding worried, but the guy looks even worse than I feel. His hair is tangled and he has blood on his shirt. My blood? His knuckles are raw and busted open. And his eyes are bloodshot red.

"Man, are you okay?" I ask, motioning with my chin toward his battered hands.

"Yeah, I'm okay," he bellows. His eyes glaze over, like he's miles away. Then he focuses his angry gaze on me again. "Why the hell did you jump so high on the last hill? You don't fucking jump like that right before you finish. Have I taught you nothing?"

"Hell, Jay, take a chill pill, will ya?" I say, holding in a laugh. I try to shrug, but it's not happening with the pain in my side. I sit, dangling my legs over the edge of the wooden bench used to fix the bikes.

Jay grunts a response, scrubbing his face with his hands.

"Ryan has another thing coming for pushing me," I tell him. I wobble a little as I stand, careful not to step in the puke, and crack my neck. "Fuck," I swear. "How long is it going to take this time for my ribs to heal?"

"With your track record, probably a couple weeks; you're lucky this one was the last of the first run," Jay tells me, helping me out of the trailer. He motions to Drew to clean up.

Giving me an angry scowl, Drew brushes past me. He gets a bucket to clean up my shit, muttering a couple of expletives under his breath as he does.

The big white bandage I have wrapped around my ribs is making it hard for me to breathe, and I've lost my shirt somewhere. Girls are waiting around, gaping at my tattoos and probably my nipple piercings. I give them a little wave.

"Damn, boy, and put a fucking shirt on," Jay murmurs, before he answers his phone and walks away.

I try to smile, taking my seat on one of the cardboard boxes my sponsor sends us. I let out a deep sigh and the girls giggle. After slicking my long hair back, I scratch the shaved right side of my head, and throw the lukewarm icepack on the ground.

"Are you okay?" Drew asks, setting the dirty bucket at my feet. I spit on the ground; the sand turning red with my blood.

"I will be, once I get my hands on that piece-of-shit Ryan," I groan, holding the side of my waist.

Drew hands me a bottle of water. "He won, you know," he says, staring at the track in the distance.

"Figured as much."

"Thanks, Drew, for cleaning up my shit in the rig," I say, letting out a slow breath, motioning with my chin to the trailer.

"Don't sweat it. I'm always cleaning up your mess. Damn, Hunt, you're like a house plant that needs constant watering, and has to stay out of the sun. And by sun, I mean pussy," he says, his grin pure evil.

"Ha. Hilarious," I say sarcastically, "but I'm sorry, dude. I know I fucked up."

"Here. Hold up your arms, pretty boy," he says, helping me

pull a long-sleeved black shirt from one of the sponsor boxes over my head.

We're both quiet for a while. A couple of other riders walk by, we ignore the girls hanging around and they bolt probably looking for greener pastures. I take a sip from the water bottle. "Man, I feel like roadkill."

"You have to keep yourself focused and lay off the booze, the smokes and the women, even on your days off. Jay has all these extra costs, and with me not riding anymore, it's hard for him to meet his payment deadlines," he says, handing me another water bottle. "And I thought your NA sponsor said you shouldn't drink?"

"He did. Trust me, I'm scaling it back, but sometimes I want to escape, and I fuck up," I confess.

Drew snorts. "We all want to escape, dude. Try not to lose yourself along the way."

"I know, okay? I fucking do, and I'll try," I promise.

"Heard that one before, asshole. I love your sorry ass, but you need to get a handle on things. This shit is not going to last," he says, waving his hand around the backstage area.

"I know," I murmur, staring at the trailers parked all around us. "We really need the money, and I probably should stop destroying so many bikes."

"Don't hurt yourself." Drew laughs, pushing my face away, and I wince from the pain. I rinse my mouth with water and spit on the ground again, gazing over at Jay who's talking to Mac and surveying the damage.

Ryan walks by, flipping me off.

"Motherfucker," I growl out. Jay heads in the direction of his trailer, probably to talk to Neil, Ryan's manager. A real piece of work. Him and Jay used to fight it out on the track; now, they do it verbally.

Ryan wraps his arm around the same brunette I had in my bed this morning. Turning to me, he asks, "Did you have trouble getting off the track?" He pulls the girl closer, and she rubs her manicured hand over his chest. Fuck her and his cronies, hovering behind them. I stand. It takes me a lot of effort, but being face-to-face with the son of a bitch is worth it.

"What did you say?" I ask, mockingly laughing.

"Your winning streak is over, Cole," he spits out. He lets the girl go and gets right in my face.

"What? I couldn't hear you over all the proverbial shit leaving your mouth," I reply, looking him dead in the eye.

"Your days are numbered. Yours, and your handler over there," he sneers.

"Don't fuck with me, Ryan," I tell him, doing everything in my power to hold it together. I ball my fists and count to ten. *One, two, three ... One, two, three, I keep repeating over and over.*

"Jay's a wash-up, like you. I've won, bitch. Deal with it," Ryan says, pushing me.

Okay, ten.

I clock him right under his eye. He loses his balance, and I'm on fire so I keep punching him. I hear nothing except the ringing in my ears. I ignore the stabs of pain coursing through my body; anger and adrenaline take over, and I keep punching the son of a bitch.

Ryan gets a couple good uppercuts in; fuck, the guy can still throw a mean right hook. I taste blood on my lips, and it brings back too many fucked up memories.

Jay pulls me from Ryan, who's bleeding as much as I am. Before I can blink, Ryan punches me in the jaw, and my teeth clatter in response.

"Fuck you, Ryan," I tackle him to the ground before Jay drags me off him again.

Neil points a finger in my face. "We are going to report your ass."

I spit on the ground, wiping the blood from my bust-up lip. "Fucking try me, old man," I grunt, holding my ribs.

"Oh, I will," he says, helping a pissed off Ryan off the ground, but Ryan pushes him away.

"Fucking hell, Hunt," Jay chimes in.

"Leave me alone," I hiss, shrugging Jay's hands off me.

Jay lets me go. "What the fuck were you thinking? You probably have a concussion," he says, sounding worried and angry at the same time.

"Nah, man, it's all wood." I shake my head. "Good, I mean." I scrub my hand over my two-day stubble and my forehead. Shit, it hurts. And, apparently, trying to walk in a straight line is not so easy with everything spinning like a motherfucker.

"Hunter," Jay warns.

I shake my head. Fuck, this is not good. I stumble over my own two feet, or is that four? Shit, I'm losing it.

My beat-up bike is the last thing I see before my forehead makes contact with the dirt, and I pass out.

CHAPTER 3

Sky

I wake up early, pack my suitcase and am on the road, biting my nails the whole ride to Jay's house. I've been nauseous and dizzy since waking up. I stop to get a coffee, and swallow down a couple pills.

Following the last exit leading up to his training facility, I try to get my nerves under control. I don't know what I'm hoping to find once I get to Jay's house. The last time I was here it was only his trailer he lived in, and nothing but barren ground.

Entering the driveway I spot a sign, with *Jay Alexander BMX Training Center* in big black letters on it.

"This is it," I mutter.

Nothing could have prepared me for this. The grounds are huge—even bigger than I remember. Grabbing the steering wheel more firmly, because my hands are sweating like crazy, I swear under my breath. "Damn, Jay."

Driving onto the tree-lined road leading to his house, I can't believe what I'm looking at. It's like an oasis. Luscious green plants, trees, and the bright colors of sunflowers surrounding the property are not what I expected to find.

I stop the car in front of a garage, next to a couple large pickup trucks.

"Jeez, this is big," I mumble. I step out of the rental, even this early the sun is blasting down in full force. Taking in the land, I sigh, blinking back my tears. I lean against the side of the car staring up at the house. What the hell am I going to say to him? *Hi Jay, long time no see. Can I crash here until…*

"Fuck," I whisper. My hands are clammy and I feel dizzy all of a sudden. Maybe I shouldn't have come, he hasn't been a father to me the last couple of years, what the hell is going to change now? Do I really believe he's going to welcome me with open arms? Taking a deep breath, I shake my head, and what about his riders? Drew seems like a nice guy, judging from the pictures on his website, but how's the blue-eyed bad boy who's also been living with Jay going to react with me invading their space?

I straighten my spine. "Whatever, you can do this," I whisper, taking in the beautiful white ranch-style California home. There is a small condo with two doors and another huge garage not too far from the main house. I leave my suitcase in the trunk, and head to the front door. My fingers hover above the doorknob.

"Get it together," I tell myself, and knock.

No response.

My heart is racing so fast, that my hands begin to shake. I knock a few more times. Great, I had this whole speech planned for when he opened the door, the only thing I can remember is '*Hi Jay*.' Pushing back my anger I knock again, still, no one answers the door. I take my seat on the steps of the house and wait. Humming under my breath, I tap my feet restlessly on the wood. I'm nervous as hell.

Maybe I'll go explore before I chicken out.

I grab the railing of the porch for support, and make my way down. Taking in my surroundings, my anxiety subsides a little bit. Jay's place is beautiful, the sunflowers next to the house, and the Adirondack chairs overlooking the driveway are not what I expected to find. I imagined some bachelor compound, definitely not this.

I follow a path next to the house, and pass the garages. There are a couple of surfboards hanging on the side of the house like works of art. Mom told me Jay loved to surf when they were younger. The stories she let slip always involved her and Jay going on some road trip. He loved the outdoors and spent most of his free time either on the track, in the water, or on his dirt bike exploring the rough terrain around San Diego.

I spot the training facility in the distance—*big* is an understatement. He has built a whole BMX track behind the house with a starting gate and all. Probably so his boys can train here without any onlookers. I run up one of the hills, and my breath catches. Damn it.

"Shit." I grab hold of my knees. I'm done already. I can't imagine doing this every day.

Straightening my spine, I'm in awe as I take in the beautiful view. Everywhere around me there are mountains, and beyond them must be the ocean. The colors in the sky are a mix of yellow and orange; it takes my breath away.

An engine rumbles from my left. I turn my head to a car coming up the drive. After slowly walking down the hill, I make my way to the front of the house, trying to suppress my nerves with each step.

A bus parks in front of the garage with a pickup truck and big trailer behind it. Shielding my eyes against the sun, I watch a blond guy, and an older man I don't recognize getting out of the bus. They are both talking and laughing.

"Yo, Drew, I'll take the bikes into the garage," the man with a long gray beard says.

"I'll help you." Drew smiles. With his blond hair, he could easily pass for a professional surfer. Jay gets out of the driver's side of the pickup truck, and I take a couple of steps. His hair is long, and he's wearing a baseball cap. "I guess one of your fans decided to show up," Jay says, pointing in the direction of my car.

Another guy hops out of the passenger seat. "What the fuck are you talking about old man," he drawls. Leaning against the truck, he winces holding onto the side of the door for dear life. He has a swollen black eye, and raises his shirt to scratch his inked stomach revealing a white bandage wrapped around his ribs.

"Hunter," Jay yells, "we need to talk." He slams the driver's side door shut.

"Can't it wait? I'm this close to passing out," rolling back his shoulders the guy moans. He is covered in tattoos. They stop just below his jawline, and disappear under his shirt. He's trouble waiting to happen, and searing hot at the same time.

The black shirt hugs his broad shoulders and his biceps—to a mouthwatering effect. One side of his head is buzzed short; the rest of his dark hair reaches below a pierced earlobe. His *Vikings*-inspired haircut should be ridiculous, but it works for him.

I spot the tattoos covering his arms, even his neck is inked, and my stomach does a back flip. The piercings decorating his handsome face give him an undeniable edge. *Damn, the guy is hot.*

Hunter flashes Jay a pained grin. "We'll talk after I make it to my bed, fucking crash for twelve hours, and work on my social skills," he says, baring his white teeth in a mocking smile.

Jay shakes his head, grinning he throws him a phone. "Oh, yeah? Some girl called—said you're going to be a father in nine months. How's that for a good night's sleep?" He flips him off.

I stifle a giggle. The look on Hunter's face is priceless.

"It's called humor, Hunt. Look it up," Jay deadpans.

Drew laughs. "Wouldn't be the first time he missed a punchline."

Hunter flashes him a toothy grin. "Fuck you, Drew. Once I get the feeling in my hands back, I'm going to punch your lights out."

"I'd like to watch you try. You remember last time?" Drew taunts, poking his tongue in his cheek. Hunter gives him the finger in response.

"Hey, guys, are we expecting company?" the older guy says exiting the garage, and points with his thumb in the direction of my car.

"Not me, probably one of Drew's good night fucks," Hunter drawls, and Drew's cheeks turn pink.

"Jealous, asshole?" Drew counters.

"Damn we're home two minutes and I'm already dreaming about pussy," Hunter whines, scratching the side of his shaved head.

Jay chuckles and says, "Behave yourself, son."

"Guys, but for real whose car is that, are you expecting someone, Jay?" Drew asks. "I don't want to kick some other poor chick out just because Hunt can't keep it in his pants."

"Fuck you," Hunter drawls, "maybe that guy from the gas station finally decided to make a move," he whistles, a smirk playing on his lips.

"No, I don't think so," Jay answers, looking in the direction of where I'm hiding behind a tree, like a damn coward.

Taking a deep breath, I tell myself, "Let's do this," and I walk up to them.

"W-what t-the..." Jay stutters, taking a step away from me.

I give them a wave. "Hello, Jay," I say, locking eyes with my father.

He opens and closes his mouth, like he can't believe I'm actually here after all these years. The other guys hover by the truck, staring at me.

"Is it really you?" Jay asks, wiping at his forehead. He hobbles a couple of steps closer to me. He crashed his bike during the world championships when I was ten, and could never ride or walk normally again thanks to his busted up ankle.

"Hi, Jay," I say, fumbling with the silver bird hanging around my neck. His eyes fly to my hand, and I immediately let go of the necklace.

"Kid," he says, his voice cracking. Before I can blink, he hugs me tight to his chest. After a couple of awkward seconds he lets me go, and takes off his baseball cap. He runs a shaking hand through his hair. "Sorry, I wasn't expecting you so soon. If I had known, I would have, you know, been here."

I can only stare at him, my father, who I haven't seen in five years.

Wait.

He said he wasn't expecting me *so soon.*

"I want you to meet my guys." He motions with his chin for them to come over.

"Fuck, kid, you've grown," Jay whispers, staring at me as hard as I'm staring at him.

The bad boy walks over. *Shit the guy is even hotter up close.* His ice-blue eyes running over my body ignite a secret thrill deep inside.

"This is Hunter," Jay says.

"What up?" Hunter drawls, giving me a two-fingered wave.

He keeps checking me out from top to bottom. "I'm Sky," I say, ignoring the way my heart skips a beat at his obvious appraisal.

"I know. I recognize you from the pictures Jay has on his mantle," Hunter answers, running a hand over his stubble, sounding not the least bit interested. Definitely no lip biting on his part.

"I'm Drew," the blond guy says, flashing me a sweet smile before he hugs me.

"Nice to meet you," I say, letting him go.

"I'm Mac," the older man says, shaking my hand. He winks

noticing Jay is still staring at me. Mac drapes his arms over Hunter's and Drew's shoulders. "Come on, boys. Let's give them some space. Nice to meet you, Sky," Mac says, before pushing the guys toward the truck and leaving us alone.

"So," Jay says hesitantly, clearing his throat.

"So," I repeat, not knowing what to say now I'm here.

"Want to grab a coffee on the deck, you must have had a long trip?" he asks, wiping a hand across his forehead.

"Sure. Lead the way," I answer, following him up the porch steps.

Walking around Jay's living room, I try to picture myself staying here. It's nothing like I expected it to be. I thought he would be spending his time in a real bachelor pad, not in this family-style home. It's cozy with pictures on the wall of Jay riding his BMX bike or catching a wave. I pick up a picture from the mantle of Jay and me on the beach holding hands, taken when I was a toddler. Setting it back, I explore some more, listening to Jay make coffee in the kitchen.

I gaze out one of the big windows; Drew is busy getting the BMX bikes out of the trailer with Hunter's help. Something falls on the kitchen floor, followed by Jay's swearing.

I peek around the corner and ask, "Everything okay, Jay?"

His cheeks are flushed, and he has his baseball cap on backwards. Being with him now, up close, he doesn't look forty-two at all. Wearing a faded Metallica T-shirt, camo shorts and flip-flops, it's like he's reliving his twenties all over again. Jay's sporting a short beard, and his big brown eyes tell me he's scared shitless of me being here.

"Jay," I begin, leaning against the doorframe.

He flashes me an awkward smile. "Yeah?" he asks, brushing a free hand through his long hair.

"The coffee?" I reply, motioning to the coffeepot he's clutching in his hand. Seeing Jay is as nervous as I am is actually a little comforting.

"Shoot, you drink it black? Or milk and sugar?" he asks, opening the fridge and peering in.

I smile. "Black is good."

"Okay great, good, milk it is," he replies, filling two large cups, and spilling the milk. "Let me get a tray."

"Jay," I say, chuckling.

He mumbles some expletives. "Yeah?" His eyes dart around the kitchen, not meeting my gaze.

"Relax. I'm not here to rob you or anything." I pick up a cup, trying not to make a face looking at the creamy substance. He's probably freaking out right now; five years is a long time not to see each other, minus the short calls on my birthday every year.

"Rob me. Good one." He laughs and coughs at the same time, taking a sip from his too hot coffee.

Smiling, I follow him out onto the porch overlooking the training grounds. I take my seat in a big white chair. We don't say anything, and just stare out across the backyard to the BMX track. *Uncomfortable* is the understatement of the century.

"Fuck kiddo. I can't believe you're here," Jay tosses his baseball cap on the table in front of me.

"I know." I flash him a half-smile.

"I feel like I'm dreaming, with you sitting here," he rasps, locking eyes with me. "How did you know we'd be here? Fuck, I sound like an asshole; it's great, don't get me wrong. Damn. I should probably stop talking now."

"I checked your itinerary online," I confess, hiding my smile behind the coffee cup. "You're still the same as I remember. I can't say the same for this place," I glance around the lawn spreading all the way to the track, there is even a skate ramp, and a fire pit. "Your place is great, Jay."

A lopsided grin warms his face. "Thanks, I never did get the grownup memo, and those boys certainly aren't helping," he says, shaking his head, but I pick up on the love in his voice.

"They seem nice," I say softly.

"They're both pains in mine and Mac's asses, but their hearts are in the right place." He taps his fingers on his knee, not saying anything for a while. "You okay?"

"Getting there, Jay," I say, my voice small.

He stretches his long legs out in front of him, rubbing at the back of his neck. "Been a long fucking time," he says quietly, taking a shaking sip from his cup, and his eyes go hazy.

I nod. "Do you remember the last time I was here?"

He rubs his thumb over his bottom lip, like he's trying to find the right words to say. Clearing his throat, he says, "I do; I showed you the building plans. It was a couple months before Hunt and Drew came to live with me here I think, before I started the company. You were this angry fifteen-year-old kid, you reminded me of myself the whole time you were here." He grimaces, before running a hand over his beard. He can't even hold my gaze.

"I still feel like that kid sometimes," I say without thinking about it.

He looks at me, eyes guarded.

"How's the business?" I ask, trying to change the subject.

"You mean with the guys?"

"And with you," I mutter. Hating how his job took him away from me and Mom.

"We're on a roll. Hunt's been winning a ton and he's training kids with Drew. They'll be here tomorrow; I can show you around if you want. I mean, if you'd like that?"

"Why not? I'd like to see what you've been up to." I want to say *without me*, but I quickly close my mouth.

He only nods, and taps his knuckles on the armrest of the chair.

"Jay," I mumble. His eyes find mine, and I lay my hand on his, but quickly pull it back again. "Can I stay here a while? I know it's beyond weird, after all these years," I tell him, and blow out a breath. "I don't even really know if I should have come. I can go back to the motel if you want."

He cuts me off. "Kiddo, I'm glad you came. And of course you can stay here."

I almost lose it. I've been fooling myself these last couple of years thinking I don't need him. I have to bite the inside of my cheek so I don't break down right in front of him. "Why?"

He frowns, probably waiting for my response. "I've missed you," he tells me, "more than you know."

"I don't know what to say."

Jay is quiet for a moment. "I know." He swallows hard, his Adam's apple bobbing. "Are you passing through?"

I close my eyes for a moment, when I open them back up I catch him watching me. "Yeah, just passing through." Brushing my hair out of my face, I flash him a weak smile. "Don't know for how long though."

He nods, glancing around the porch. "We have a couple weeks off before the tour picks up again. You can stay in your room. Enough time to catch up if you want?"

I raise my brows in response, "You made a room for me?"

"Yeah, why not? I didn't know when you were coming and I wanted you to feel comfortable," he says, the smile on his face falls.

We don't say anything for a while, and I drink my coffee in silence. There is a chill in the air. I close my hoodie and he sees it. Tapping his fingers on the armchair again, he says, "Do you want to get settled upstairs?"

"Lead the way," I reply.

He puts his barely touched coffee cup in the sink, and I follow him up the stairs.

"Hope you like it," he says, sounding almost nervous opening a door.

The room is amazing. The walls are painted a beautiful soft yellow. There's a queen-size bed with pink covers and a lot of trinkets, a skateboard, and paintings decorate the walls.

"Got that stuff on my travels, I didn't think you'd want me to send them to you in New York, so I kept them here," he says.

I take a seat on the mattress and run my hands over the soft fabric, I'm already tired from walking up the stairs, and tears fill my eyes.

"This is all mine?" I gasp.

Jay sets my luggage in the corner, and awkwardly looks around. "It's always been yours," he says quietly.

Silence fills the room, "Jay..."

"Right, so through this door is a deck." He points to the French doors. "You can sit out there if you want." He opens one. Cool air blows into the room and I smile, spotting two comfy chairs on the big balcony.

"If you squint, you might spot the ocean on a clear day between those mountains," he says, with a proud look on his face.

I stare at him, not saying anything.

"And right through there," he says, pointing to another white door, "is your own bathroom." He stuffs his hands in his pockets. "And here you can hang your clothes if you want and..."

"Jay," I say, standing, "it's perfect."

He clears his throat, and takes me into his arms. He kisses my hair, surprising me. After an awkward grunt, he lets me go. "If you need anything, I'll be outside getting shit organized with the boys. See you downstairs in a couple?" he asks, walking to the door.

Smiling, I sit on the edge of the bed. "Sure."

"We usually have dinner together after a tour ends. Drew is a great cook, but I thought with you being here, I could light up the barbeque, say, around seven?"

"I'd like that," I answer.

He nods, putting his hands in his pockets again. "I'll be downstairs if you need me." He gives me a small smile and closes the door behind him, leaving me alone.

I fall back on the bed. Turning my head, I take one last look out toward the training ground, and close my eyes.

After a couple of minutes there is another knock on my door. "It's open," I say, sitting up.

"Here's the last of your stuff," Hunter says, dropping my bag on the floor with a thud.

"Thanks."

"Don't mention it," he drawls, and shoves his hands in his pockets, staring at me.

"You want something?" I ask, taking a deep breath to get my racing heart under control.

"Yeah, I don't know what your fucking deal is, but we have a good thing going here. We don't need someone to stir shit up," he warns.

"I'm not here to stir *shit up*," I tell him as he turns his back to me.

The asshole stops in the door opening and flashes me an angry glare over his shoulder. "Whatever," he spits out. "Just stay the fuck out of my way, and we'll be good. Jay is the best fucking trainer in the game, and he doesn't need you to reserve a seat for him at your pity party table."

I gasp, "This has nothing to do with you. I don't even know you."

"Whose fault is that Park Avenue?" he asks, raising one brow like a dare.

"Fuck you," I spit out.

"Good one. You know, you could have come here many times over. That's why you're here now isn't it, to even some fucking score?" he says, and turns around. "Guess what *Sky*, we've all had a shitty past, you ain't special."

"I think you need to leave," I warn, *what a fucking asshole.*

"Stay out of our way, and we'll get along fine," he repeats, glaring at me.

Standing, I stride to the door. The fucker stands his ground, the side of his mouth twitches, like he's enjoying our little back and forth, and doesn't move an inch. I place my palm flat on his chest and push, taking him by surprise. "Get the fuck out. And for your information this is between me and Jay. Certainly not between some lost puppy he took in to make a buck off," I say, the moment the words leave my mouth I want to take them back.

If looks could kill, this guy wouldn't have a problem knocking me out.

"Remember what I said, *Sky*," he says, spitting out my name.

"Fuck you, Hunter," I say, slamming the door in his face.

CHAPTER 4

Hunter

"Fuck her," I drawl walking into the garage. Drew is busy opening my sponsor boxes, *asshole* likes free shit even more than I do. I open the fridge and hand him a beer, looking at the label I grimace, fucker stocked it with zero percent drafts."So, I just had a nice chat with that chick." I try to sound like I don't care, but fail miserably.

"What about?" he asks, holding the cold bottle against his forehead.

Taking my seat on a chair in the corner, I put my feet up against the workbench.

"I told her she shouldn't stir shit up. Newsflash, she can handle her own."

He takes a swig and winks at me."She's Jay's daughter after all, and that's rich coming from you," he says, rolling his eyes.

I stare at my black Vans."Fuck you," I joke, waggling my eyebrows.

"You wish," Drew counters, cracking his knuckles.

Picking at my shoe, I continue, "She's kind of hot, isn't she?"

"And you say I'm a manwhore," he says, opening another box.

I snort, shaking my head. "Better give me a heads up when you plan to screw a guy against the workbench again," I say flipping him off.

"You're just jealous."

"Fuck you, man. I get enough from those girls on tour," I say, giving him a cool look.

"Yeah, STD's," Drew answers, pushing his tongue against his cheek.

"Damn, don't make me laugh. I'm injured."

He shakes his head. "Play nice, Hunt, you know how much Jay cares about his daughter," he says, throwing me another beer I catch midair.

"This shit tastes like piss by the way," I huff, knowing he's right. "Why is she here, after what, five years?"

He raises a brow and I smile.

"You could just ask her, Hunt."

Grinning, I take a slow swig from my bottle. I'm quiet for a moment, debating my next move. "And how long do you think she's going to be here for?"

He slams his beer on the table giving me an eye roll that says, *how the fuck do I know?* "Why did you get into it with her? I saw the look you gave her before."

I almost choke on my drink. "What look? And she slammed the door in my face," I reply drily, feigning innocence.

"You know what I mean, you never go after a girl. Certainly not with a look that says, 'Let me FUCK YOU. PLEASE FUCK MEEE.'" He drops to his knees on the floor, laughing his ass off.

I raise my eyes to the ceiling. "I'm gonna really punch you later on."

Getting up, he slowly shakes his head. "Your come-hither stare."

"Fuck you, I don't have a come-hither stare. That's fucking ga..."

He chuckles. "Gay? Lucky I am."

I start to laugh. "Aw, man, don't hurt me." I clutch my ribs with both my hands.

"Admit it, Mister *Lords of Dogtown* extra," he jokes, opening another box.

"That's a compliment and I'll take it," I tell him, standing, strands of my hair fall in front of my eyes.

"You're intrigued by her, admit it," he states, pointing a Stanley knife in my face.

My lips turn up slightly, "I'm not intrigued. I don't even know her. She's hot, I'll give her that. And she already pissed me off."

He chuckles, and I shove him away. "Dude, this girl conversation has already lasted longer than any before."

I throw some fake beer in his face to shut him up.

"Motherfucker," he grunts, trying to take the bottle from me. I make a run for it but stumble over a couple stray dirt bike tires. "Fuck." I laugh, clutching the door with both hands.

Jay walks up to us. "Stop horsing around," he orders.

"Yes, Jay," Drew says, and starts stacking boxes to the side of the garage.

"Yes, Jay," I mimic his voice.

Drew raises his eyes to the ceiling in exasperation.

"So, your daughter," I say, crossing my arms in front of me.

Jay balls his hands into fists, shaking his head. The message is clear. *Don't even think about it.* I hold up my palms in surrender.

I grin. "Don't forget to breathe, Jay, but I think your daughter..."

"Don't even think about it, Cole," Jay warns, pointing a finger in my face.

"I wouldn't dare," I tell him, shuffling out the door.

"I mean it, Hunter," Jay warns. Him threatening me is a daily occurrence so I don't even take it personally.

"Later, guys!" I chuckle. After walking to the training ground, I kick my Vans against a loose screw lying on the ground. Damn, I can't get her dark eyes out of my mind. Last time Jay mentioned his daughter, he said she was living it up in New York. But she carries herself like a Californian surf girl, with her beachy hair, and that damn body hiding under her oversized shirt. I groan, brushing both my hands over my face.

Passing Mac working on his longboard, I whistle. I really need to go surfing with Drew again.

"Heading to the track?" he asks.

I salute him. "Just making sure everything is in order for the kids tomorrow."

"Oh yeah, did Jay tell ya we're having a barbeque later tonight? Thought I'd give you a heads up now in case you were planning on going to a meeting," he says, his hands sliding over the surface of the board.

I shake my head, running my thumb across my bust up lip, "Jay didn't say anything." *Interesting*.

"Around seven," Mac tells me.

I spread out my arms, "Thought about going to a meeting, but Jay's daughter being back is going to be much more entertaining than sitting in a circle talking about our problems."

"Play nice, Hunter," he returns, continuing to sand down his board. "Might be good to have a female touch around here."

"You know that's not my style," I joke, and he sighs. "Later, Mac," I say, still thinking about those chocolate-colored eyes of hers. Perhaps the next couple weeks are going to be entertaining after all.

Sky

I don't know how long I've been sleeping. I check my messages on my laptop; there's a couple from my mother and even one from my little brother, asking me if there are a lot of insects here. He's obsessed with the scary creatures, any critter really, and probably figured California would be filled with them because Jay's compound is pretty off the grid.

I answer their messages and go through my emails. I have one from Peter, my ex-boyfriend and Tim's brother, who's studying to become a neurosurgeon, asking me how I'm doing. I reply and let him know I'm okay. Immediately, my screen lights up with a smiley face. I also have a message from Timothy asking how I'm holding up, and letting me know he's coming to visit soon with his best friends, aka lots of green buddies.

Closing my MacBook, I sit up. I'm a little bit dizzy—probably because I haven't had anything to eat since this morning.

Voices travel up through the open patio doors of my room. Slowly, I head downstairs. I enter the kitchen, and Drew is already busy making a salad. He smiles at me in greeting.

"Need any help?" I ask.

He nods. "If you could take the salad out you would make me a happy man."

"Sure thing." I take the bowl from him.

His fingers skim mine. "You find the house okay?"

"I did. Thanks for being so welcoming."

"You're family," he whispers, winking at me. "Planning on crashing here a couple of weeks?" he asks, washing his hands.

Staring at my beat-up All Stars, I take a deep breath. Should I be honest with him? The guy seems nice enough. "Yeah, I am."

"Great. We could use a woman around here to change things up. I'm always the one cooking," he says. "Fuck, that was a sexist thing to say."

I giggle. "I'd be happy to help you. My best friend, Tim,

taught me how to cook, since my mom can only make a grilled cheese sandwich." I laugh.

"Must be a special guy," he says, leaning against the kitchen counter.

"He is," I show him a picture of us together on my phone.

"If he's single let me know," he jokes, checking out the picture. "Damn, he's hot."

I chuckle. "He actually is. And he's coming to visit in a few days. I think he would love to meet you."

"Well, count me in then." He flashes me a shy smile, while the bad boy swaggers into the kitchen.

Hunter's eyes dart between us. "Don't mind me," he says, holding up his palms, "only getting a *real* beer."

"Do you think that's wise?" Drew asks, handing me back my phone, crossing his arms. "Damn, Hunt, your eye is starting to swell. Put some ice on it."

Hunter opens the fridge. "What are you? My Obi-Wan?" After grabbing a beer, he twists the top off and throws it in the trash. "Boom, nailed it," the idiot says, holding the bottle against his swollen eye.

Drew shakes his head. "You need to take better care of yourself, man."

Taking a long gulp, he burps. "Yes, mother."

What a jackass.

"You're a pig," Drew says.

Hunter raises his beer in the air, and heads outside.

"See you out there?" I ask Drew, watching Hunter swigging back his drink, leaning against the porch railing. How can he be so incredibly sexy but such a dickhead? Our eyes meet, and I quickly turn my head away, before my cheeks heat even more than they already are.

Drew nods. "I'll be right out. And I'm usually stuck in the office here, if you want to talk or hang out." He motions to a closed door next to the living room.

"Thanks, Drew. I appreciate it," I answer, before opening the screen door and putting on a brave face.

Jay lights the barbeque, and it doesn't take the guys long to eat everything he puts on there. The conversation flows easily with Mac telling me about his surfing days in Hawaii, and how he came to work as head of material for my father. Drew tells me about the public relations and advertising side of the business, and how they are trying to get more kids interested in the sport.

"Tell her about the kids you're working with," Drew says to Hunter. I focus on the man in question, and he immediately stops staring at me like he has done all evening. The way he's sitting in the chair, balancing on the back legs, is fitting for the whole devil-may-care attitude he has going on. Sitting back, he spreads his legs wide, the black denim straining against his thighs in the best possible way. My heart is hammering, and my mind wanders while I drink him in. He is angry, that much is clear from the way he's grinding his jaw. He flicks open his Zippo and holds his head to the side, lighting his cigarette. Our eyes meet and he lifts up one eyebrow, it's almost like a dare. Like he wants me to fight with him, the bastard probably gets off on it. Well I'm not giving him the satisfaction of knowing I like this back and forth we have going on. What the hell is wrong with me? I need to keep focusing on why I'm here—to mend things with Jay. I'm not interested in a stupid fling. Certainly not with a guy like Hunter.

Hunter shakes his head. "No."

"How old are the kids?" I ask, turning to Jay who has his eyes fixed on the track.

"Huh?" he asks, not looking away from the setting sun behind the mountains.

"They're teenagers," Drew chimes in, saving the conversation from destruction.

Hunter stares at me some more for the better part of the evening. I do my best to return his cocky smile with my death stare, which only seems to spur him on. *What an asshole.* I can't stand the way his eyes seem to look right through me, and it has only been a couple of hours. I keep reliving the conversation we had in my head. I should have told Hunter to mind his own business. Once I talk it out with Jay, I'm out of here.

He and my father are quiet while Drew, Mac and I keep chatting on about everyday stuff. Jay gives me curious eyes every now and then like he can't really believe I'm here. Hunter's grunts and his eye rolls make me want to punch him in the face. He's one big distraction I don't need. And the comments he makes most of the time are downright irritating. He obviously doesn't like me. Well, buddy, the feeling is mutual.

After dinner, the guys leave me and Jay alone on the porch. I'm grateful Drew dragged Hunter back to one of the garages. I was starting to get agitated with Mister-Grunts-A-Lot. Something about him makes my blood boil, and my heart race.

"Kid?" Jay asks.

"Huh? What?" I reply.

He smiles. "Where did you go?"

"I was thinking," I say, stretching my legs a little.

"About?" he asks, taking a long gulp from his beer.

"About Mom, Stevie and Conrad," I lie, and avert my eyes.

He clears his throat. "How is your mother and her husband?"

"He has a name, Jay."

"What's the Conrad guy like?"

"Mom loves him," I answer. My stepfather adores Mom, and has made it his life's mission to make her happy. "He's a good guy. He's been great to me, and loves my little brother," I tell him, showing him a picture of us in Central Park on my phone.

"He has your mother's eyes," he whispers, staring at the photograph of us.

"He's a great kid," I say, putting the phone in my pocket.

Jay nods, not saying anything more. I look up and my breath catches as I follow the path of the stars above the house. "Wow," I breathe.

"What?"

"I forgot how many stars you can see out here," I say, pointing upwards.

He chuckles.

"What?" I ask, turning toward him.

"You always loved to sit outside and look at the stars when you were a kid," he murmurs, leaning backwards and scrubbing his face with his hands. His sad eyes catch my gaze. "Kid, I know..."

"I'm really tired, Jay, I'm going to bed," I croak, and quickly stand.

He gets up as well, pushing his hands in his back pockets. "Maybe I could take you on a tour tomorrow." He hesitates. "I would like to show you my life here. And we could talk some more, if you're up to it."

"Sure, Jay. See you tomorrow," I say, opening the kitchen door.

"Kiddo?"

"Yeah?" I answer, hovering in the doorway.

"I'm glad you're here," he rasps, his eyes misting over.

"Me too," I reply, quickly turning around before he sees my tears.

CHAPTER 5

Sky

During the night, bursts of pain shoot through my body. I take a pill and try to sleep but I can't seem to relax. I keep tossing and turning in my bed. Everything hurts. I'm nauseous, dizzy, and angry at the same time. Biting back my tears, I groan trying to turn on my side.

I focus on the clock on the nightstand. Five-thirty in the freaking morning. After throwing the covers off me, I put on my skinny jeans and a black long-sleeved shirt, and head downstairs, careful not to wake Jay.

The rising sun warms me as I make my way toward the track. After slowly walking up the gravel hill, I sit and watch the sun come up. I close my eyes and let myself fall back against the sand. I love the warmth on my body, my fucking beat-up body. I stare at my hands, praying they're not going to shake or cramp up. The necklace is hot against my throat and I listen to the wind, the birds chirping. I focus on my breathing, and the beating of my own heart. It's peaceful, lying alone on the track soaking in the sun. Peaceful, calm.

"Watch out!" someone shouts.

I open my eyes. A wheel is coming straight at me. I scream and close my eyes, rolling my body to the right just in time for Hunter to divert his bike. He stops inches from my head.

I stare at the man in question, who's looking at me with an angry scowl on his face.

"What the fuck were you thinking?" he yells. He takes off his helmet and places it on the ground. He brushes his sweaty hair out of his face, piercing me with his hard stare, still straddling his bike.

"I…I," I stutter, peering up at him, squinting my eyes against the sun. He is drenched in sweat, his white T-shirt clinging to his six-pack.

"I…I…" he mimics, tossing his gloves on the ground. "Dude, what were you thinking, lying on the track? Some of us have to train."

"I thought no one would be here this early, and aren't you injured?" I stare at his face, and his piercing in his freckled nose. Damn, the man is beautiful, even with the dark blue swelling around his eye.

Shit, I shouldn't be checking him out like this. I should definitely stop staring at his six-pack. Spotting his nipple piercings pressing against the thin fabric of his shirt, heat creeps up my neck.

He swings his leg over the bike as I sit, hugging my knees to my chest. Angrily shaking his head, he throws his bike on the ground, the muscles in his arms flexing. "I thought I would get a couple easy laps in. That almost went to shit with you sleeping here," he growls, grabbing his ribs. "Fuck, and yeah, it still hurts like a motherfucker."

"Shouldn't you be the one lying down?" I ask, and I want to kick myself in the head.

"Are you inviting me, *babe*?" he asks, flicking his lip piercing with the tip of his tongue.

I shake my head and flip him off. "Definitely not after you told me to fuck off."

He gives me another death stare, and I actually blush as his eyes zero in on my cleavage. Shit, what the hell is wrong with me?

"Wanna do it, Shorty?" he asks, with a smile in his voice.

"Yeah, I want to do bad things to you, like punch you in your smug face," I bite out as I stand.

The left side of his mouth hikes up, and my cheeks heat. He towers over me, and I quickly cross my arms over my breasts, hoping he doesn't spot my nipples poking against my shirt. Fat chance. His mocking laugh gives him away.

"What the fuck is your game?" he asks after a couple beats, raising his brows like he's intrigued.

"My game?" I ask. What is he talking about?

"What are you doing here, Skylar?"

"It's Sky, and it's none of your business," I say, averting my eyes from his plump lips.

He takes a step toward me. "It's my business if you decide to take a nap on the freaking track."

"I wasn't taking a nap."

"Sure you weren't?" His mouth parts slightly, trailing his tongue over his pierced bottom lip. He swallows hard, not saying anything as he stares at my necklace, then looks up to my mouth.

"N...n...no, really. I wasn't."

"Looked like you were," he drawls.

"God, do you have an off switch?" I snarl.

A lopsided grin warms his otherwise stoic face. Hunter chuckles, running both his hands through his damp hair. "I'm messing with you. Man, you're just like Jay when he's pissed. Couldn't resist to rattle your cage."

"You're a dick," I state.

"I'm being a dick? You're the one calling me names, sweetheart."

"Leave me alone and we'll get along fine." I raise my voice. "I'm not here to make friends," I say and start to walk away from him.

"Friends? Why do you think I wanna be your friend?" he asks, coming after me. I turn around and he raises one brow, eyes dancing with laughter. "A little full of yourself, aren't you now?"

I roll my eyes. "I'm not."

He shakes his head. "I thought I was in for a boring couple of weeks. Guess I was wrong," he declares. A slow, smug smile spreads across his lips as he takes another step closer to me. "I did like the way you kept checking me out last night during dinner when you thought I wasn't paying attention. Turned me on like you wouldn't believe, *Shorty*."

"You're so full of it," I say, "and don't call me Shorty."

"Fuck, you do have a little Jay in you. But I'm just messing. Admit it—you like it," he says, his eyes crinkle at the corner, amusement evident on his face.

"Like what?" What is the guy talking about?

"Me," he drawls, waggling his eyebrows.

"Go screw yourself." I raise my voice, letting my arms drop to my sides, this guy is unbelievable.

"As a matter of fact, I did that this morning in the shower." He lifts up his hand like he's jerking off. "Twice."

"You're disgusting," I yell, trying not to laugh.

Hunter swallows hard, running his tongue over his lip piercing, and I feel my cheeks heat. Stupid hormones. He places both fingers in front of his mouth.

"Don't you dare," I warn him.

Slowly, he pokes his tongue in and out. Oh my God, he really is disgusting, but then I spot the silver metal in the middle of his tongue. *Is that a tongue piercing?*

His chuckle tells me he's totally messing with me, and enjoying it. *Ass.*

With burning cheeks I rasp, "Get away from me." My mouth twitches while I try to fight the smile playing on my lips.

He snorts. "You still like to look, so don't judge what you want to taste." He laughs, giving me a once-over. "But this is a place of business, not your local nap spot."

I clear my throat. "Work? Don't make me laugh. You probably party, and ride your damn bike all the time," I grit out. Shit, why am I even having this conversation with him? *Shut up, Sky. Don't give him more ammo to shoot you down with.*

My eyes travel from his face, to his chest, to his flat stomach, and south to his sweats. *Don't stare at his package,* I scream in my head. *Don't!*

"I also ride my skateboard up and down the road if you wanna hang. You know, babe, if you're looking for someone to pass the time with, I'm your man. Never had any complaints," he taunts as he towers over me. It's like the guy is vibrating with pent-up sexual energy.

"I'm not going to hang out with you," I counter, my voice a little hoarse.

"You're doing it right now, Shorty," he says, grunting as he adjusts the front of his sweats. "For someone who says she isn't interested, your actions say otherwise." He bursts out laughing, waggling his eyebrows. "If you want to pass the time, night or day," he says, matter-of-factly, "I can show you how to ride, or catch a wave." He waits a couple of seconds before he says, "Or you could ride me."

Immediately, heat spreads between my thighs.

"I'm joking. Relax," he says, a roguish smile tugging on his lips.

I open my mouth and close it again. "You are unbelievable, you know."

"Tell me something I don't already know," he adds, a little smug. "Jay told me once you used to surf," he says like a challenge.

"Haven't done it in years," I tell him, remembering how much fun Jay and I used to have on our boards and skateboards, but that was a long time ago. I'm not that person anymore. Or that's what I try to convince myself.

Not saying anything, Hunter nods and licks his lips, his tongue piercing poking out. What would it feel like if we kissed? My stomach drops, and lightheadedness takes over. I stumble backwards. He quickly reaches out and grabs my waist but I keep falling, taking him down with me. The cold sand of the track hits my spine, and I pin his arm between my body and the sand. He hovers over me, a pained expression on his face.

He swears under his breath. "You okay?" he asks, sounding worried.

"Yeah, you?" I whisper.

He turns his head toward mine, squeezing his eyes shut for a moment. "Give me a sec," he says, his husky voice rolling over me.

His breath mingles with mine, and a shiver runs through me.

"Sure you're okay?"

"I will be, damn I like it rough, but this is next level," he says, leaning forward. Hunter places both his hands on either side of my face, holding me captive between the cold sand and his body. I can smell his sweat, and my mouth dries. Gazing into his blue eyes, I try to focus on my breathing. *In and out.* I still inhale his scent, my nerves making me shiver. I fist his shirt in my hands trying to give him a little push, but my hands betray me, the way I'm holding him in place so he can't escape. *I'm pathetic.*

"Why are you here, Sky?" he whispers in my ear, his nose skimming my earlobe.

My head falls to the side, giving him fantastic access to my neck. His stubble scrapes over my feverish skin as he traces the line of my jaw with his lips.

"I..." He pulls me upright, and the rest of the sentence gets stuck in my throat.

"You were waiting here, to give me a piece of your mind, weren't you?" he whispers in my ear. I pick up on the humor in his voice.

"I wasn't. I'm here for Jay. Nothing else," I tell him, my voice stern.

He traces the line of my jaw with his lips again, and says, "You'll warm up to me eventually. They all do." He hums, dragging his stubble over my jaw. I glance at my hands, still clutching his tank top. I quickly let him go.

He pokes my stomach with his finger. "Admit it, you do need a friend." He bursts out laughing. He's totally screwing with me and loving every minute of it.

I grit my teeth, my anger building to the point of combustion. "Do not touch me," I bite out.

"Sure you don't want me to? Might loosen that stick you've got up your ass, *Shorty*," he says, teasingly. His eyes sparkle with mischief and a wild look that makes my heart skip a beat.

I blink a couple of times, and start counting to ten, balling my fists.

"Counting to ten?" he asks, his eyes gleaming.

"No," I growl, pushing him away from me before making my way down the hill. I almost stumble again, but he grabs my arm, keeping me upright.

I shake his hand off. "Let me go," I say, with a threat in my voice.

"A 'thank you' would be nice. I protected your pretty face from eating dirt," he grunts.

Giving him one of my best fake smiles, I tell him, "Thank you so much." There's sarcasm underlying each word.

"Come on. That wasn't so difficult. Now say my name."

I turn around, walking backwards toward the house. "No."

"Come on, you can do it. Say, 'Thank you, Hunter.' Scream it, so you can practice when I take you there," he replies drily, and winks at me. I open and close my mouth, not knowing what to answer. He blows me a kiss and I flip him off. He laughs and I turn around, rubbing my hands over the goose bumps covering my arms.

Drew walks out of the garage, BMX bike in hand. "Hey," he says to both of us.

"Is he always such a pain in the ass?" I ask him.

Drew nods. "Hunt, play nice man."

Hunter puts his arm around Drew's neck. Turning around I head to the porch. "See you at breakfast," Hunter yells after me.

I stop in my tracks. "Breakfast?" I ask, turning on my heels. Hunter waves at me, a stupid two-finger wave, grinning from ear to ear. My cheeks heat up, and I basically run into the house and up the stairs to my room. I'm such a damn chicken. Leaning against the closed door, I try to catch my breath and not think about how his lips brushed over my jaw, just missing the corner of my mouth. The sooner I talk to Jay, the quicker I can go home and forget about the bad boy outside.

Heading downstairs after a quick shower, the kitchen is buzzing with activity. I recognize a song by the Foo Fighters playing in the background, and Drew is making pancakes, by the smell of things. Mac is reading the newspaper at the dinner table, his glasses perched on his nose.

"You know when the article is coming out?" Hunter asks, leaning against the counter next to Drew, taking a sip from his cup.

"I talked to him a couple days ago. He said sometime next week," Drew says, sounding proud. "Can't believe we're going to be in Rolling Stone."

I hover in the living room, not knowing what to do or wanting to intrude. Jay walks through the front door holding a couple of grocery bags in his hands. "Hey kid," he says in greeting, closing the door with his foot. "Want some breakfast?"

"Sure," I mumble, following him into the open kitchen.

Hunter pulls a chair back for me.

"Thanks," I say, and our eyes meet. The side of his mouth hikes up a little. *Okay, that was kind of nice.*

"Don't mention it," he drawls, carrying on with his conversation with Drew.

Drew hands him his pancakes and he immediately digs in, stuffing two in his mouth.

"Damn, Hunt," Jay says, laughing. He puts away the groceries in the refrigerator, and hands me some yogurt without asking.

"I'm hungry," Hunter mumbles, talking with his mouth full, eating the last bite of his pancake. "Burned a lot of calories because I almost ran someone over at the track," he says, waggling his eyebrows at me.

"For the last time, I thought everyone was still asleep," I reply, locking eyes with the troublemaker.

Jay clears his throat, and Hunter winks at me.

My father places a bowl of granola in front of me. "Here you go," he says, giving Hunter the stink eye.

"You remember what I eat for breakfast?" I ask, looking at Jay.

"Jay, here," Hunter begins, "loves to go on and on about..."

"Before you open that big fat mouth of yours, Cole, the kids are waiting," Jay huffs, motioning with his chin to the door.

"And that's our cue," Hunter sighs dramatically. "See you guys later. *Shorty*," he taunts, heading out to the porch with Drew on his tail.

"I'm going to Home Depot after I catch a wave," Mac says, pushing back his chair. "Need anything, Jay?"

Jay fills a cup with hot, steaming coffee, and hands me one as well. "No, I think we're good."

Mac waves at us. "Later, kids," he says before leaving the two of us alone.

"Did you sleep okay?" Jay asks, leaning awkwardly against the kitchen counter.

"Yeah, I did," I tell him and finish my yogurt.

After a while Jay asks, "Ready for the tour?" He sounds a little nervous.

"Let's do it."

We finish our coffee in silence, and I follow him outside.

"Your place is different," I say, while we slowly make our way to the track.

"The last time you were here we only had the trailer. The track came a couple months later, and the guys' digs as well. I hope we're not coming on too strong," he says chuckling under his breath.

"Yeah, no, I didn't mean..."

"I know. It's all a little too picture-perfect with the white house, those plants, trees and shit. I even have a white picket fence leading up the road," he says, shaking his head as if in disbelief.

I grin. "Hadn't pegged you for a gardener."

"I'm not. Mac is though, and he wanted a little Hawaii here since he wasn't able to do that when he was in prison."

"Prison?" I ask, incredulous.

"Yeah, did five years in Oahu for tax evasion. I knew him from his surfing days before he got locked up, and we became good friends. Kept in contact throughout the years. One thing led to another and he started helping me with the upkeep of the bikes."

"Nice of you," I mutter.

"Nice has nothing to do with it, kid. The guy is good at his job, and most importantly, he keeps me on my toes on a daily basis. I need it. As you know, I can do stupid, impulsive shit."

"He seems great, Jay. They all do." *Even Hunter,* I want to add, but I don't.

"So this is where we train," he says, motioning to the enormous track spread out in front of us. Drew and Hunter stand at the top of one of the hills, a group of kids around them with rapt expressions on their faces as Hunter speaks. A couple of parents are watching the training from the stands on our left.

"What about Drew and Hunter?" I ask, motioning with my chin to the guys.

Jay takes off his baseball cap and runs a hand through his

long hair before putting it on backwards again. "Drew was the first who started training with me. His parents are in the Navy and traveled a lot. When he turned eighteen, he asked if he could live here, and help out with the company. I was swamped with work so I said yes, and he's been living here ever since. I think he moved in a month after the last time you came over," Jay mumbles, looking at me sideways.

I swallow hard. Leaning against the fence, Hunter grabs the side of his hip, biting on his lip like he's in pain, before he continues with his speech. "And Hunter?"

"He's our champion, and a certified pain in my fucking ass," Jay mumbles, tapping his knuckles on the fence. "Kid has collected more black eyes than medals."

"I can imagine," I snort.

"What about you, Skylar? Are you still going to New York University?" he says, sounding proud.

"I was. I'm taking a little break right now," I state, "and it's Sky, has been for a long time."

He doesn't say anything for a while. "What are you going to do, Sky?"

I shrug. "I don't know yet, and that's okay."

"You need money?" he asks, nudging me in the shoulder, and I can't help but smile.

"No, I'm good—perks of having a stepfather who works on Wall Street. He knows how to set up a trust fund. Do you need money?" I tease, trying to lighten the mood.

He grins, rubbing at the back of his neck. "I always need money. But don't worry, we're doing okay."

"Hasn't Hunter got a lot of sponsor contracts? At least, that's what I got from your website."

"Yeah, he does. Vans, GoPro, and Red Bull, amongst others," he explains.

"Isn't that enough?"

"It should be," he answers quietly.

"What do you mean?"

"A lot of things happened. And, fact is, people don't want to pay for poor kids to have a life. With his pro-bono tendencies, the upkeep for the track, and him using his money to pay for every hospital bill or school supplies request getting thrown his way..." Jay sighs. "Let's say what he earns isn't enough to keep this place running. Makes him a freaking saint in many books. But Hunt has part of the devil in him too."

We are quiet for a while, and I keep thinking about what Jay told me, watching the boys as they make their way up to the starting gate. Maybe the BMX rebel isn't that bad after all?

"Hey, Hunt!" Jay yells.

Hunter looks over his shoulder. "Yeah?"

"When you center them like that make sure you double check their feet and body placement," he explains, "before they head down the hill."

"Will do," Hunter shouts back, giving Jay a thumbs up.

"What's Drew doing?" I ask. He has ten kids sitting on the ground in front of him while he talks, gesturing to different parts on a BMX.

"He's showing them how they should do a final check on the bike before you race, making sure everything is screwed in nice and tight," he says, crossing his arms in front of his big chest.

"You really found your place, didn't you?" I say, leaning against the fence.

"This has always been my life."

I turn my head away. "That much was clear the last couple of years."

"Fuck, Skylar. Sky, I didn't mean it the way it sounded," he pleads.

"No, it's okay. I know what life was like before you and mom got a divorce and you were still competing," I state, swallowing back the emotion in my voice. I remember all the times they fought and screamed at each other, the tears and broken promises.

Grabbing the railing his knuckles turn white. "I was still a kid back then. Your mom just turned nineteen when she had you. Man, I was barely legal myself."

"And that was the reason you let us go?" I ask, raising my voice.

"No, fuck, it wasn't. I should've known better. I should have fought for you like I did on the track," he says, holding my stare.

The kids look in our direction. Hunter whistles and they turn their attention back to him.

"Known better and done what? Not marry mom, then leave when I was still a kid?" I ask, turning around and walking away.

"Fuck," he swears, going after me, "Sky, wait."

"Wait for what? You know how fucking long I waited for you? Do you?" and I can't help it, I cry, tears stinging my eyes.

"Kid," he says, trying to grab my arm.

I pull my hand away. "No, dad. I had this whole plan on how we were going to do this," I say, motioning between us. "I had a plan, and now I don't know what to tell you, how to tell you..."

"Tell me what?" he asks, his voice cracking.

"You are being so nice about letting me stay here for fuck knows how long, with your stupid yogurt and granola," I blubber.

He starts to smile. "I hear myself when you say shit like that," he says, sounding proud.

I swear under my breath. "This is not funny," I grit out, stamping my foot. But I can't help but smile as well. "I missed you, Jay, do you know that?" I ask locking eyes with him.

"I missed you too, kiddo." He laughs, but the side of his mouth turns down.

"Just not enough to visit." He cringes at my response. "I just need some time, before I go back home," I say, taking a step away from him.

"This could also be your home," he whispers, his eyes pleading.

"Could it really?" I ask, motioning to the track. "BMX was always number one, why would it be any different now?"

He opens his mouth like he wants to say something, but changes his mind at the last moment. "I'm here whenever you feel like talking," he tells me, taking a step back.

"Just give me time, Jay," I say, turning around, not looking back.

CHAPTER 6

Sky

I rap my knuckles on the garage door. There is a grunt from behind the raised hood of the Ram truck.

"Jay, I'm sorry for what I said," I begin, trying to find the courage to say what should come next.

"Jay went out," Hunter says, closing the hood of the truck with a thud.

"Shit," I mumble. I didn't expect *him* to be here. "Do you know where he is?" I ask, leaning against one of the workbenches.

Hunter grabs a dirty rag, and wipes the black grease from his hands. His hair is tousled, and his white shirt is stained, like he's been working on the truck for hours.

After my conversation with Jay, I went for a drive. I needed to clear my head, and figure out what I should tell him.

Hunter shakes his head. Walking to the workbench in the

corner, he starts rummaging through a toolbox, swearing under his breath until he finds what he's looking for.

"He and Drew had to go to a meeting in the city—should be back after dinner I guess," he mumbles, walking back to the car. "You don't know anything about truck engines, do you? Usually Jay helps me with this shit, but since he's out, I'm fucked. I need to see someone later tonight," he says, opening the hood. "Ahh, forget it."

"No, let me check," I say, walking toward the front of the pickup.

He keeps staring at me.

"Hunter?" I ask, smiling up at him. I should try to get along with the guy. "Before I stopped coming here during the summer, I helped Jay with his car, mostly because he didn't have any money to pay a real mechanic," I say, grinning. "I picked up some skills here and there."

"I wanted to start the truck, but it stalled on me for no particular reason," he says, exasperated, peering into the engine block. "I checked everything, and nothing I do seems to work. I usually work on my KTM," he says, pointing to a dirt bike standing in the corner of the garage. "Much easier, once I get the damn thing to work as well. Give me a BMX bike any day of the week."

"My mom used to hate it when Jay rode," I tell him, checking out the engine. Shit, why am I even telling him this?

He nods. "He told me. He doesn't really ride anymore. We usually head out to some trails together for fun if we have time off, which isn't often, but I love it," he says, standing next to me.

"Did you check the fuel filter?" I ask, changing the subject. It looks clean, but you never know.

He furrows his brows at me. "Yeah, I did. I changed it because it was clogged last week. I even put in a new battery before you walked in because the other one was fucked." I stifle a giggle, staring at the problem.

"And you reattached the battery cables?"

"Of course I reattached them," he says. "Damn! I forgot." He leans forward and plugs in the black cable. "This can't be it."

"Why don't you start the truck and see?" I ask, grinning up at him. The guy really isn't that bad.

"If you're right, I'm buying you a drink," he says, getting in the driver's seat. "Here goes nothing." He starts the car, and the truck rumbles to life. I close the hood and he hollers.

"Glad I could help," I say, walking to the garage door.

"Hey, wait up. What about our drink?" he asks. I can't really place the look in his eyes, is it hopeful? "I need a pity party because apparently I know nothing about trucks."

"You sure Jay and Drew aren't going to be back soon?"

"Nah, we could grab something to eat as well," he offers. "To make up for the fact I almost killed you at the track."

"And?" I ask, fighting against a big ass smile.

"For being a certified asshole," he deadpans.

I pretend to think about it, and say, "Why not?" getting in next to him.

"Come on, dude. A little more enthusiasm next time," he teases, backing out of the garage.

"So, where are you taking me?" I ask, while he makes his way down the driveway, and onto the main road.

"Best Mexican food in a fifty-mile radius," he replies, flashing me a lopsided smirk.

We are both quiet the fifteen miles it takes him to get to the beach. Somehow it isn't as uncomfortable as I thought it would be. It gives me enough time to check him out. He winks catching me staring at his tattoos, I try to hold back my grin as I quickly stare out the window again.

"Shouldn't take long," he says, grabbing the steering wheel firmly, his knuckles turning white.

"What do you mean?" I swallow hard, rubbing my sweaty palms on my thighs.

He follows the movement before our eyes clash. He shifts

and turns his attention back on the road. "For you to leave," he mumbles under his breath.

"You might be right about that," I whisper, not wanting to show him any more pieces of myself. I don't need a friend while I'm here, the guy seems nice enough when he's not being his asshole self at the track, or staring at me during dinner. Still, actions speak louder than words, and he seems to be trying, maybe I should do the same.

I look at his profile, his straight freckled nose, the tattoos covering the better part of his neck. The black ink, and his piercings scream 'back the fuck off,' so why do they keep drawing me in?

He parks the car and motions in the direction of a food truck. "You hungry?"

"A little," I confess, swallowing back the sudden lump in my throat.

"Wait here. I'll be right back," he tells me, handing me the car keys. I get out of the truck and a soft warm breeze picks up. I lean against the grill of his Ram, looking out over the ocean, waiting for him to return.

"I've got the stuff, so get up there," he orders.

"Get up where?"

"On the hood," he says, motioning with his chin. "Here. I'll give you a hand." He sets our food and drinks down on the ground, helps me up and hands me two drinks and the wrapped food. He hops on the hood and gets comfortable next to me.

"You come here a lot?" The smell of the juicy burrito reaches my nose, and I moan.

The side of his mouth hikes up. "Yeah, sometimes Drew and I hang out here after catching a wave. They've got the best street food."

I take a sip from the drink. A rich and full flavor bursts into my mouth. "What is this?"

"That, my friend, is horchata," he explains, sucking on his

straw before digging into his burrito again. The palm of my hand cramps, and a sharp pain shoots through my fingers. The cup almost slips from my grip, but he reaches out and catches it before it falls in my lap.

"You okay?" he asks, looking at the way I'm stretching my fingers. I take the drink from him with trembling hands.

"I'm okay," I whisper.

"I'm sorry, Sky, for acting like an asshole before. Jay is like a father to me, and I got…"

"Possessive," I finish for him.

"Yeah," he says grinning.

Three girls walk by the truck and stop next to Hunter.

"Hi, Hunter," the blonde says.

"Hey, Lauren. What's up?" he answers.

She gives me a hostile look, and runs her pink manicured hands over his knee. "Nothing much. Missed you these last couple of weeks," she purrs, taking a step closer to him. Her two friends stay back, and watch her while they chat with each other.

"Been on the road a lot," he mutters, rolling back his shoulders while she lets go of his knee. "This is my girl, by the way," he tells her, jerking his chin in my direction.

What the hell? His girl? And why does that give me a secret thrill?

"Hi," she says, without even looking at me.

I give her a wave she ignores.

"I'm throwing a party later if you want to come by," she says, her voice hopeful. She gives me an angry glare while pulling down her shirt to expose more of her ample cleavage. Hunter doesn't seem to notice since he only has eyes for his food.

"We're good, but thanks anyway," he answers, taking another bite, giving his burrito more attention than her.

"You know you're an asshole, Hunter Cole," she seethes. "If I were you," she says, looking at me, "I would run." She turns around and walks away with her girlfriends in pursuit.

Hunter shrugs, like nothing happened. "I'm sorry I called you my girl. She has a tendency to latch on and never let go, and she's the third chick who's called me an asshole this week," Hunter confesses, swallowing hard.

"They will, if you keep calling us chicks," I offer.

He flashes me a pained smile. "I don't know, Shorty. Sometimes it's easier to create some distance between the chicks I..."

"Fuck?" I prod, trying to hold back my grin.

"You got me there. But don't change the fucking subject, what's going on with you?" he asks.

"What do you mean?"

"I recognize the look in your eyes."

"What look? I don't have a look," I say, turning my head away.

"I was the same when I moved here. I was angry, mixed with I don't know what. Jay would preach some shit about me being hurt, but I'm more like a let's-beat-the-problem-to-a-pulp kind of guy, if you know what I mean," he says, his voice serious.

I set my drink and food down, and run both my hands through my hair to buy me some time. "I don't really know what I'm doing here to tell you the truth. You do know I haven't seen Jay in years?" I ask. "To say it's awkward is the understatement of the century. I have no idea how to talk to him."

He scratches his stubble. "If it makes you feel better, he doesn't either," he says, making a face. "Just tell him what you need to say, and get it over with. I'm used to being the grumpy asshole around here."

"I don't know how," I reply honestly.

"Shorty, we're talking, aren't we? And here I thought you kind of hated me, judging by our little run-in at the track."

The side of my mouth hikes up into a full-blown smile.

"See? You're warming up to me," he teases, all seriousness gone from his voice.

"What about you?" I counter. "Why is it easier to behave like an asshole?"

"You want the honest answer, or the politically correct one?" he asks, his expression dark.

"What do you think?" letting out a slow breath while the muscles in my feet and legs start to hurt.

"Because then I never have to show them who I really am, I don't have to be..." he says with his mouth full.

"Vulnerable, yourself?" I chime in.

He takes a moment to swallow and clears his throat.

"Fuck, I don't know, maybe you're right. Easier to keep parts hidden I guess."

"You're showing me parts aren't you, even the asshole ones," I tease.

He looks out toward the ocean, furrowing his brows while he takes his time to answer. "I know I'm an asshole, Shorty, but I'm so much more," he says, still not looking at me. It comes out as a confession, a promise. "I'm showing you all my cards, and I don't even know what game we're playing."

"I know what you mean," I mumble, taking another sip from my drink.

He cocks his head. "About what?"

"Before Mom and Jay got a divorce, when I was six, I loved it on the West Coast. We didn't have much but we had each other. At least, that's what I like to believe. It all went to shit when dad started winning more and traveling the world for his races. He forgot about us. I guess it was an easy decision for him to leave when he had all this."

"All what?"

"Trophies, money, fame," I say, eating the last bite from my food.

"That didn't mean shit to him," he rasps. "I think you have it all wrong."

"About what?"

"That it was easy for Jay to leave you. He talks about you every day. Fuck, I remember when I came to live with him, he showed me pictures of you. I even helped him paint your room."

"You did?" I ask, trying to hide the jealousy in my voice. He's had this whole other life with Jay. A life I wasn't a part of, and it hurts.

"Don't sound so surprised," he answers, dimples popping. "He always held out hope you would come back, but I think New York was much more interesting than watching a bunch of teenage dudes and your old man train?"

I lock eyes with him, not knowing what to say, because he's right.

"You like living in New York?" he asks, and sucks on his straw.

"Yeah, I do. It's always busy; you see something new each time you step out the door. Me and my best friend, Tim, used to go out and party almost every day."

"I guessed you had some party in you," he teases, nudging me in the shoulder with his elbow.

I laugh before I take the last sip from my horchata. "I did. I had a lot of friends, or so I thought. Turned out they only liked to party if there was enough booze involved. It just came to a point that I couldn't remember why I was friends with them in the first place," I say. I quickly bite on my lip. Shit, why am I telling him this?

He turns to look at me. "What do you mean?"

"Tim is the only real friend who stuck around, I don't really party anymore. It was fun for a while, but …" I give him a look, "… it didn't mean shit."

"I think we are going to get along great, you and I," he drawls.

"If you say, 'This is going to be the start of a beautiful friendship,' so help me," I joke.

"Nah, I think I'll leave that one to Bogart," he answers, laughing softly.

"So you're a movie buff?"

He leans back against the windshield, locking eyes with me. "Got a lot of time on my hands when we're traveling."

I stretch out my legs, and get comfortable next to him. We are both quiet, looking at the sky and the setting sun.

"I probably won't watch *Bambi* ever again though," he dead-pans, and I burst out laughing. "Hey, don't make fun of me. That shit was the first ever horror movie I saw. Someone shot his fucking mom," he tells me in a serious voice.

"It was kinda sad," I admit.

Shaking his head before he looks me straight in the eye, he says, "Babe, it was brutal. My old man put that on when my mom..."

He doesn't finish his sentence. Leaning his elbows on his knees he sits up, and I do the same, waiting for him to continue with his story.

"After she died, my childhood was challenging, as my NA sponsor would say," he sighs.

"You mean Narcotics Anonymous?" I ask, trying to hide the surprise from my voice. I know the guy is a bad boy, but drug addiction is a whole other ballgame.

"Yeah, the one and only," he says, his voice light like he's trying to make a joke out of it.

"What did you use?" I ask. "I'm sorry, I shouldn't pry. It's anonymous for a reason."

He takes a deep breath. "What didn't I take? But my preferred poison was oxy. Mom was a heroin addict, she overdosed when I was ten," he tells me, cracking his neck. "Fuck, haven't told a chick this before, sorry *girl*. You're taking this friend thing to a whole other level, Shorty."

"I'm sorry, Hunter," I say, meaning it.

"I beat it. No, correction, I'm still beating it. Life's too short to go through it fucked up."

"I guess it is," I say, staring at the waves crashing on the beach.

He shrugs. "Shit happened. My dad got mixed up with some bad people, which led to doing some time, and I found myself on the street dealing."

"When you were a teenager?"

He looks at me, eyes guarded. "Yeah. Don't act so surprised. You do what you got to do to survive. Haven't talked about this in a very long time, but I promised Bill, my NA sponsor, I would open up to strangers," he says, his voice hoarse.

"I thought we were friends?" I chuckle, nudging him in the ribs.

"Hey, watch it." He fakes a wince. "I'm still injured."

"*Right.*"

Our gazes meet, and he's the first to crack a smile. "As I was saying, what was I saying?"

"You were talking about your sponsor," I tell him.

"Oh, yeah. I used to live with my dad in a trailer park, but it was easy to sneak away. Later when he was doing time, I stayed with his motorcycle buddies at the clubhouse. My dad's brother got custody of me. But he was a nomad so he was either running shit on the road for the club or partying. There wasn't a lot of parental supervision, so I took to the streets. The older guys who were dealing liked me because I was fast and I looked rather innocent." He snorts.

I frown, highly doubting his last remark.

"Wipe that look off your face," he scoffs, and I laugh. "I didn't have the tats and the piercings back then," he mumbles, and grins at the same time. "They asked if I wanted to earn some money. I used to ride a BMX bike at the downtown skate park when I wasn't going to school, which was a lot. I wanted to get the hell out of Dodge. In order to earn some quick, easy cash, I started trafficking shit all over town, which led to dealing, which led to using when I was thirteen."

I stare at the darkening sky. In the distance, lightning flashes. "What did you take?"

"Pills, cocaine. When I switched to fentanyl, shit went south," he admits.

"Wow," I whisper.

"Man, you're your father's daughter with the one-sentence conversations," he says.

Chuckling, I ask, "How did you come to live with Jay?"

His expression darkens. "I knew what I was doing was fucked up. I'd met Jay a couple times. He came to watch me ride at the park when I wasn't too strung out, and we sort of became friends. I didn't turn up one day, and he tracked me down and stepped up. I got busted with too much on hand, and the judge gave me a choice—stay in juvenile detention or Jay could take over custody from Abel, my dad's brother, and 'pay my debt to society,'" he says, making quotation marks in the air. "I chose Jay in the end. Hey, doesn't that make us step-brother and sister?" he asks, winking.

"Hell no," I laugh shaking my head.

"Probably for the best, shit could get weird very quick."

"What was it like?" I ask, trying to ignore my beating heart.

"You mean if we would, you know," he says waggling his eyebrows in slow motion. "Or living with your dad?"

"The last one, *asshole*." I nod, and right on que my voice trembles. His ice-blue eyes pierce mine. He doesn't say anything but as my heartbeat starts hammering in my ears, he casts his eyes down and the right side of his mouth hikes up a little bit.

He slides the pad of his thumb over his plump bottom lip, like he's debating his answer. "It was hard. Luckily, Drew was already staying there on and off. I helped Jay with the house, even Mac with the fucking garden, and I started dealing with my addiction and anger-management issues."

"How's *that* going?" I ask, staring at the purple coloring next to his nose.

He touches the place below his eye. "I try. Some days are better than others, hence the shiner."

He makes a face, and I giggle.

"I go to NA meetings every week. I still enjoy my beers, which I should probably fucking cut back on."

"Jay wrote the textbook on that," I mumble, remembering the bottles stashed around his trailer when I was still a kid, and the times mom had to help him get inside because he was too drunk to stand on his own two feet.

"Yeah," he says, taking a lighter out of his pocket and flicking it open and closed. "Jay gave me purpose though." I cock my head, and stare at the guy sitting inches away from me. He looks tough, but there's something broken underneath his rough exterior. Like he's searching for something, or someone.

"By the way you're raising your eyebrows, you probably think I'm full of shit, giving you some sob story to get in your pants?" he asks, joking, but judging me too. My stomach does a little back flip. A part of me wants to believe that's true.

Thunder booms in the distance. "I don't think you're full of shit," I whisper, leaning my chin on my knees, and stare out to the ocean and the rainclouds forming above the water.

"Is it working though?" he asks, his voice low.

The wind picks up, blowing my hair back.

"I don't know. Maybe," I offer, leaning into him, our mouths a breath away. His cheeks flush a bright red color, and he quickly pulls back.

I start to giggle while he rests his palms on his jean-clad thighs, rolling his eyes at me.

"Got me good, Shorty, friends it is," he admits, giving me a roguish smile.

"I'm just sad I never visited Jay earlier," I confess, swallowing back the lump forming in my throat.

After a beat, he asks, "Why are you here, Sky?" He holds me captive with a determent look. "You can tell me the truth. I might be an asshole, but I'll listen."

"I wanted to see Jay," I state.

"Yeah, I know, but why now?"

I shake my head, not wanting to tell him anything more than I already have. And I'm sad, and so damn angry at Jay, at myself, for not having more time. *I need more time.*

"Shorty," he says, laying his hand on my shoulder. "Whatever it is, you need to tell Jay."

"Why?" I bite out, the breeze picks up and I shiver a little. He takes off his hoodie and hands it to me.

"Because he loves you," he tells me, jumping off the hood of the car while I put on his oversized sweatshirt.

I slide off the front of the car, and lean against the grill. In the distance, the sky is getting darker, and after a couple of seconds, lightning flashes across the horizon again.

"I don't know what's going on, and frankly, it's not my damn business, but I know secrets can tear you apart. It did with the people I loved." Hunter throws away our trash in a garbage can.

"Why are you telling me this?"

His lopsided smile makes my heart skip a beat. "That's what friends are supposed to do, aren't they?" he says, flipping his hair out of his eyes. "Now get in the truck. I think the storm they talked about on the news this morning is going to hit."

I stare at the black sky before getting into the car. "I guess it is."

Hunter

The drive home is filled with silence. Fuck, maybe I told her too much about myself. I focus on the road ahead, the soft rain pelting the car soothing me a little. I have no idea why I'm nervous whenever she's around, and I start talking way too freaking much. I've only known her for two days. I don't know anything about her other than what Jay let slip. I wasn't kidding about the friend part; she looks like she could use one. Hell, I could use one. I'm not going to screw up whatever we have by sleeping with her. The guys all see me as this fuck-'em-and-leave-'em guy, hell *I am* that dude. But there is something about her I've never experienced before. Maybe this girl is different.

The light for the tire pressure flickers on, and I swear under my breath. "This shit is getting better and better," I mutter, checking the rearview mirror before I hit the turn signal. "Fucking piece of shit truck."

"What's going on?" she asks, while I park the truck on the side of the road.

"Probably something wrong with the tire, but I should check nonetheless because we're still a couple miles out."

"Should I help?" she asks, looking out of the window while big fat raindrops attack the car.

"Thanks, babe, but with the storm and all I can handle it myself," I tell her, and shut the door behind me. Taking one step, the rain drenches me to the core. I check the two front tires; they're okay.

Damn, the right rear tire is almost entirely flat. "Fuck," I mumble. I let my fingers run over the side and feel the gash where air is escaping.

"Need help?" she asks, hopping out of the truck, zipping my hoodie up. Immediately, my dick takes notice, and I swear under my breath. A chick—fuck, a girl wearing my shit shouldn't give me this reaction.

"Got a flat," I reply, opening the truck bed, thanking the Lord I always carry a spare tire and a jack.

She kneels down and looks at the tire, and I can't tear my eyes away from her face. Damn, the way the rain is hitting her body and her long hair makes her even more beautiful than she already is.

"Do you have a wrench?" she asks, smiling up at me. I'm momentarily speechless.

God, she really is beautiful, why didn't I see that before?

I shake my head. Jay would kill me if he knew I had these thoughts about his only daughter. I don't care if she never looks at me the same way, as long as I can be close to her. Growling, I shake my head, what am I doing? I kneel as well, and start cricking the jack before I turn the nuts loose. I push up the sleeves of my shirt, blinking rapidly as the rain runs down my forehead and into my eyes.

She sways a little and grabs the side of the truck for support.

"You okay?" I ask, over the roar of the wind.

"Yeah," she says, her voice a little hoarse. I push my hair behind my ears, she glances at my tattoos and her eyes widen. The way she licks her lips has my dick twitching in my pants, and I swear.

The wrench slips from my grip and lands on my foot, "Fuck." She chuckles, and I can't help but smile at her. I hope she likes my ink. I catch myself grinning like a fool. *What the fuck is wrong with me?*

She stands, leaning against the side of my truck and closes her eyes. The wind moves through her hair and the rain runs down her face while I push the bolts in my pocket. "Let me get the tire off," I mumble. Standing, pain shoots right through me. My damn ribs still hurt like a motherfucker.

"Need help?" she asks, laying her hand on my shoulder, and I feel it through my wet shirt. I never thought you could get burned by a touch alone, but my shoulder's on fire. She quickly pulls her hand back, like I've burned her as well.

Sky keeps staring into my eyes. She bites her lip, and I have trouble holding onto the tire. It would be so easy to get involved with her; she would be like any other girl I fucked—a way to pass the time. Or would *she* be different? *And what about Jay,* echoes through my mind.

"No, I've got it," I mumble, and she takes a step back while I work on the tire. "Can you hand me the wrench?" I ask, trying to speak over the roar of the wind and rain.

She hands it to me, and our fingers briefly touch, her lips curling into a smile I haven't seen on her before. I catch myself staring into her brown eyes, hoping the tingling feeling in my body will subside. My heart rate kicks up, and my throat tightens. What the hell is happening to me? Color creeps up her neck, although she's drenched from head to toe. She breathes in and out through her mouth, and I watch her warm breath mingling with the cold air.

"Sky," I begin, damn it, why do I suddenly feel shy, like some sixteen-year-old kid who's got a new crush.

"What?" she asks, still looking at me with those innocent doll eyes, as I stand and tower over her. A gust of wind makes her lose her balance, and she stumbles forward, right into my arms.

I hold her up. "W-w-a-a-tch out," I stutter. Without thinking, I caress her cheek.

"I'm trying," she whispers. I think she's going to push my hand away, but instead she covers it with her own, keeping it against her face. Shaking from the cold, I hold her tight and stare at her pink lips.

What am I doing? "I can't," I whisper, more to myself than her, before I do something stupid like pin her against the car with my body and kiss her.

She takes a step away from me, guilt sliding across her face. "I know," she says before she gets in my truck.

I close the truck bed, and look up at the ominous sky.

"Fuck my life," I mutter, hoping those brown eyes aren't going to haunt my dreams tonight.

We don't talk the whole way back. I park the pickup next to Jay's in front of the garage, focusing on the rain slamming on the roof of the car.

"Thanks for this," she says, taking off my hoodie and handing it to me.

Before I can answer, she leans in, and kisses me on the cheek, then bolts out of the car. I'm stunned; the girl's got balls. I caress my face, somehow still feeling her lips as if they grazed my stubble. I hop out of the truck and she walks into the main house, swaying her hips and ass in those tight jeans that leave absolutely nothing to the imagination.

After a minute, Drew walks into the garage. "Damn, dude, you're all wet."

"Turns you on, doesn't it?" I counter, laughing at my own joke.

Drew shakes his head, smiling. "You're a crazy motherfucker. One who's gonna get his ass kicked if you go there," he says, motioning with his chin to the house.

"Ah, fuck off. Nothing is going on," I reply, getting the flat tire out of the back. "There was a moment though," I mumble, rolling it to the corner of the garage.

"A moment?" he asks, leaning against his truck.

"What about you? Did you hook up with the interview guy while you were in the city?" I make kissing sounds.

Drew shakes his head, pushing my face away.

"No, but I did pick up a stack," he says, handing me the *Rolling Stone* magazine from the pile.

"Damn. I made the cover?" I ask, flipping through it.

"Sure did. I think I went a little overboard though," Drew says laughing. "I'm gonna frame and hang them on the walls. Damn dude, do you really like her?"

"Is that the new model?" I ask, changing the subject and motioning to the bike.

"This is the prototype. What do you think?" he replies, staring at the black bike in the back of his truck.

I keep stealing glances at the back door like there's a chance she might miraculously reappear, but judging by how much I behaved like a horny asshole, my chances are next to nothing. We lift the bike out of the back, and I check out the new frame. "I like it but maybe we could ask Mac to sand it down a little." I motion to the bar.

"I was actually thinking the same thing," Drew says, squatting beside the bike, his hand traveling across the straight lines.

"You know what they say, don't you?" I ask my best friend.

"Don't fuck your sort of stepsister?" Drew smiles. "Or great minds think alike?"

"Fuck you," I laugh, changing into a semi-clean long-sleeved Henley I find on the workbench. I smack the end of my wet T-shirt against his ass, he chuckles, and I drop it in the washer in the corner.

"Sweet dreams, princess," he jokes. "Hey, you want to go surfing tomorrow, before we work on the bike with Mac?"

"Yeah, why not, say around five?"

"Better bring your A game," he drawls.

"You bet your ass I will. Later asshole," I wave, heading for my room.

It's not even light out when I meet Drew in the garage. Handing him a coffee, he rubs the sleep from his eyes, his yawn a mile wide, leaning against the table.

"You ready?" I murmur. "The storm from last night is bound to bring in some good waves."

Nodding, he pushes himself from the workbench. "Yeah, let's head to the beach," he says, stretching his arms high above his head.

I slam my hands on my legs. "Hustle, let's go, grandpa," I say, walking toward the boards in the back of the garage. I need to clear my head and the best way to do that is to go out into the ocean. I spent the better part of the night tossing and turning, thinking about Sky.

"Come on, dude, we still have a couple hours before the tourists storm the beach," I say, picking up the longboard and heading to his pickup truck.

"What really happened between you and Sky yesterday?" he asks.

"Nothing," I answer, and he gives me a look. I shake my head, "I don't know what I'm doing."

He comes after me with his board tucked under his arm. "Why don't you ask her out or something?"

"Ask her out? Are you crazy? Jay would kill me," I say, as he helps me load the boards in the truck bed.

He smirks. "Yeah, but when did Jay getting angry ever hold you back? She's probably leaving in a couple of weeks," he says, crossing his arms in front of him.

"My point exactly."

He raises his brows, like it's a dare. I fucking hate it when he does that.

"What are you saying, Drew? Screw her a couple times and move on?" I ask while he hands me the keys to his truck.

"You're driving, and no. Take her out to dinner, try to get to know a girl before you screw her over," he says, getting into the passenger seat.

"I intend to do just that, the screwing part I mean," I joke, slamming the door shut.

"I should be keeping you out of trouble, not pushing you over the edge."

Snickering, I turn the ignition. "Eat shit."

"Take her out. I dare you." He laughs darkly.

"That's never going to happen. The screwing part? Maybe in my dreams," I mumble, glancing in the rearview mirror. I'm totally lying and judging by the look he gives me he knows it. "I'm kidding. Relax will ya, I can't go there, and I don't intend to. Jay's blood, can't vouch for her though, did you see the way she looked at me?" I reply drily, trying to keep my face in check.

"You're an asshole," he says, rummaging through the glove compartment.

"You're not the first who's called me that this week."

Drew smirks, shifting in his seat, and balancing his feet against the dashboard. I look over my shoulder to check if the wetsuits are still where we left them. Putting the car in drive, I hit the gas pedal.

"She only needs a friend. She has those lost puppy eyes going on," I yell, trying to speak over the rock music. I glance at Drew. The son of a bitch is smirking, like he doesn't believe I can keep it in my pants. My dick twitches against my zipper, thinking about the way my hand tingled as I touched her cheek. Turning onto the highway I push up the volume of a Motörhead song.

"The way you're trying to convince yourself she only needs a friend says it all, dude," Drew tells me.

"Hey, don't we all?" I shrug.

He narrows his eyes. "Maybe the cold water will do you some good."

"Damn right it will." I grunt, praying the ocean will give me some perspective when it comes to the brown-eyed girl back at the house.

We spend a couple hours in the water before we head home. I love the beach. There are no problems in the water. It's just you and your board. My father used to tell me, before he got sent to Afghanistan, before the drugs, before his arrest, that the water washes everything clean. Maybe my old man had it right all along. Could Sky being here be a new start, for everyone? I park the car in front of the garage, Drew jumps out, and hangs our wetsuits on the wash line outside.

"Can't believe you talked me into working on your shit, I'm tired man," Drew mumbles, as I follow him into the garage. He heads straight for the coffeemaker and empties his cup in three large gulps.

I place our boards against the wall, and catch the towel he throws my way. I dry my long hair and slam dunk it in the overflowing laundry hamper.

"Come on, dude, where did your happy fucking demeanor go?" I chuckle.

He flips me off. "It went out the window when I got a text from that interview guy when you were in the water, basically saying we're not going to fuck again because he's getting back with his model boyfriend. That's where."

"I'm sorry, dude," I tell him, and I mean it. He deserves someone real, not like those fuckers he keeps bringing home. His scowl never falters, and I press my shoulder against his trying to lighten the mood. "You know I'm here for you, I may not suck your dick, but you'll always have my heart." I wrap my arms around him, pulling him against my chest. He takes a deep breath and relaxes.

He kisses my cheek, and says, "You're an asshole, Hunt, but I love you anyway."

Grinning, I help him put the new bike onto the workbench. "I'm sorry, man, he doesn't fucking deserve you. And I always pictured you with some military type dude, someone who doesn't take shit from anyone. And judging by your porn habits I guess I'm right," I say, trying to bite back my smirk.

"Yeah, dipshit, I may go for the strong silent types, now get to work." He grins, bumping his fist against my shoulder. He turns on the Spotify list on his phone as Mac walks in. Some country tune blares through the speakers, and the early morning hours pass by in a heartbeat.

Running a hand over my sweat soaked forehead, I lean against the open door and light a cigarette as Sky walks onto the back porch and grabs the railing, looking in the direction of the track. "What do you think brought her here?"

Drew shrugs, and Mac shakes his head not saying anything. "Don't know," Drew mumbles.

"Don't you think it's weird she's here?" I pause. "I tried to ask her why she came when I took her to the beach yesterday, but she shot me down."

Drew shakes his head. "Dude, I think it's weird how obsessed you are with her. You know she's only visiting, right?"

"Fuck you, asshole, and of course I know," I reply.

"If you like her so much, take a chance. Try and act like a normal guy. That might do the trick, instead of almost running her over at the track," he says, and Mac chuckles.

I hold the cigarette between my teeth, and brush both my hands over my stubble, the bristles scratching my palms. "I took her with me to get a burrito, and you were the one who told me I should make new friends," I say, ignoring his last comment.

"You want to be her friend now?" he counters. "Have you ever had a girl as a friend?"

"Umm never," I tell him, stamping the cigarette out.

Mac lets out a slow whistle while I'm putting the screws in their designated boxes; I'm not the Marie Kondo type, and he knows it.

"You're scared, aren't you?" Drew asks.

"When have I ever been scared?" I scowl, a lock of hair falling in front of my eyes.

His grin is pure evil.

"Better make up your mind, son, before you start courting," Mac drawls, "I'm going to Jay's for lunch, can I get you guys anything?" Mac asks.

"No thanks, man," I say, and Drew shakes his head. He gives us both a wave, and heads to the main house leaving us alone.

"What?" I ask Drew, crossing my arms, and leaning against one of the many work tables.

He dips his chin at me. "Mac's right. I've never seen you look at someone like you look at her."

Shaking my head, I say, "She doesn't need my shit. And judging by my track record, she is better off alone," I tell him. "Facts, man."

"Maybe this time it could be different," he states.

"I love your silver-lining thinking, bro, but this is my life and I can't screw it up like I already have. It takes everything to stay off drugs, I don't need another distraction," I say, throwing the screwdriver on the table overflowing with other crap. "She doesn't need that in her life—waiting for me to go off like some ticking time bomb."

He narrows his eyes. "Why do you do that?"

"Do what?"

"Punish yourself," he answers, his voice soft.

"Don't," I warn him.

"Hunter, come on."

"Forget it. I'm going to answer some emails," I say, leaving him alone.

I spend the rest of the afternoon in our homemade gym to do some stretches, and ride around the track until my ribs can't take it anymore. After I'm satisfied with my progress I head back to my apartment and microwave some leftover pasta. Later, Drew and I settle ourselves behind my PlayStation before he calls it a night. I take a shower, and don't bother putting on a shirt, instead I pull on my sweatpants and walk into the kitchen. The couple hours Drew and I spent in the water, and my session on the track helped me clear my mind for a while. That all went to shit the moment I started to think about the way Sky touched me, and I decided I needed to do something about the blue balls I was sporting. I've never come that quick in the shower before thinking about some chick, one I haven't even seen fucking naked.

The knock on my door wakes me from my daydream. "It's open," I yell, pouring myself a cup of coffee.

"Are you busy, Hunt?" Jay asks, closing the door behind him.

"Want a coffee?" holding the pot in the air.

"Sure," he says, looking around my room like he's nervous.

"You okay, Jay? You look kind of tired," I say, pouring him a mug and take my seat on the couch.

He sits down in a chair opposite me and runs both his hands over his face. He looks at me, and takes a deep breath. "I need you to stay away from my daughter."

"What do you mean?" I frown and slide his cup across the table.

"I'm asking you to back off," he states.

"Nothing happened. I only took her to the beach, and you always tell me to make new friends," I say, forcing a smile.

He shakes his head, taking a large gulp from his coffee. "Trust me. I'm not asking this to piss you off."

"So, you're ordering me to keep my distance?"

"Fuck, Hunter," he says, raising his voice, "promise me you'll leave her alone?"

"Why?" I ask, sarcasm ringing through my voice.

He gives me a cool look. "We both know why."

I lean forward, resting my arms on my knees. "I thought you were starting to warm up to me after almost ten years?"

He hangs his head. "I'm not joking. Back the fuck off or else," he warns me, clearing his throat.

"Why do I have to stay away when nothing is going to happen?"

He gives me a pained look. "I don't want you getting hurt, son," he says, laying his hand on my shoulder. "You're like my own kid, and you can't be distracted right now—not with your NA meetings, and certainly not with the last leg of the season."

"I haven't had a drink in two days, Jay. And I don't even wanna get high anymore," I confess, my voice small.

"Heard that one before," he replies.

"Thanks for the vote of confidence." I shake his hand off my shoulder. "I'll stay away, okay? But I can't promise she'll do the same."

He takes a deep breath, balling his hands into fists and narrowing his eyes at me.

"We're both adults here," I begin, not really knowing how to respond, because Jay is right.

He holds up his hand and I shut my mouth. "And she's my daughter."

I stare at my ink-filled hands. "You just don't want me around her?"

"Son, that's not it. She's ..." he begins, but doesn't finish his sentence.

"Whatever. I need to go to bed. I have physical therapy for my damn ribs in the morning and training after, so let's call it a night," I mutter.

"Hunt," he says, opening the door.

"Yeah?" I ask, looking up.

"I'm only saying this because I love you. You know that, right?" he asks, sounding sincere.

"Fuck, man," I groan, "you don't trust me, is that it?"

"Not even a little bit," he says, winking at me.

"Fuck you, Jay," I say, smiling.

"Right back at ya, kid." He closes the door behind him.

I settle against the couch cushions, putting my feet on the table. What the hell just happened?

"Fuck," I whisper, staring at the ceiling, covering my eyes with my arms. Jay is right. I have to stay away, but I don't know if I can, or if I even want to.

CHAPTER 7

Sky

A couple days later

It's almost five in the morning when I hear a knock on my door, "Yeah?" I croak out pushing the covers from me.

"Hey, kiddo," Jay says, opening the door wider. "Want to come downstairs with me?"

I can't help but laugh, "Jay, it's five in the morning."

"I know, but I want to show you something," he mutters, leaning against the doorframe. "And you can call me dad by the way, I mean you don't have to. I understand if you need some time, or..." he says rambling a little.

"I know you're my dad, but you were always Jay to me, and I need..."

"Time," he finishes for me.

"That too, give me five minutes and I'll change," I tell him.

"I'll be waiting on the porch," he says, leaving me alone again.

I jump into my yoga pants, pull a sweater over my head, and meet him on the back porch. "What did you want to show me?" I ask, stifling a yawn.

"That," he whispers, pointing to the purple and pink canvas painting the sky.

"It's beautiful, Jay," I tell him, and I mean it.

"I love it here, Sky. I'm proud of the life I've created for the boys and me," he says, adjusting his camo baseball cap. "But I'm not proud of the way I left things between us. I…" he begins, leaning his arms against the wooden railing.

"You don't need to explain," I link my arm through his, and rest my temple against his shoulder. I know we need to talk, and I keep pushing the inevitable conversation we need to have out in front of me. It's easier that way, to pretend everything is going to be all right.

His lips brush my forehead, "I should, you are my kid and I didn't try hard enough to keep you in my life."

"You're trying now," I whisper, watching the vibrant colors paint the morning sky. "That's all that matters."

"I'll keep at it, baby girl," he promises. "I'll try with you till the end."

I park the truck at the water's edge. I spent the morning with Jay; we chatted about everyday things. I want to get to know the man he has become. We didn't talk about the reason for me coming here, and I want to keep it that way a little longer, because once I tell him, I'll break. Checking my rearview mirror, my mascara is smudged. I try to wipe it from my cheeks with a paper tissue. "Darn it," I growl, and put my Wayfarers on. Staring at the steering wheel in front of me, I grab it hard with both hands.

"Fuck!" I scream with all my might. I slam my hands against it. My knuckles hurt like hell but at least I feel something. Why did I come here? What the hell was I thinking? I couldn't expect Jay to open up to me immediately. I don't even want to tell him what is going on. I don't know what to say to him half the time. And why can't I stop thinking about Hunter? He's nothing like I expected him to be. He's scary and exhilarating at the same time. Tim's voice echoes through my mind, *why not have a good time?*

Letting my head drop, I honk the horn with my forehead and I laugh. There are not many people on the beach except two families with small children playing in the sand. Climbing out of the truck, I take off my shoes and walk to the shore.

I toss my Vans on the ground and plop down, staring at the little kids playing near the water. Curling my toes, I lean back, letting my hands disappear in the warm sand. The little girls laugh and scream in the distance.

Pushing my sunglasses up into my hair, I take the prescription out of my pocket, staring at the little piece of paper until my eyes start to water.

After Drew helped me return the rental earlier, I dropped him off back at Jay's place, and headed to the pharmacy. I want to be alone. I know Jay suspects something is going on. The way he's been asking if I'm all right the last couple of days, hovering over me all protectively, is a dead giveaway. I don't want to deal with the inevitable conversation we have to have.

The sun is warm. I take off the black sweater and watch the waves roll in, clutching the list of medicine and medical marijuana between my fingers.

My hands are getting numb. I stretch my fingers but I can't feel them for a couple of seconds. I close my eyes and concentrate on the wind brushing against my skin. Even lifting my hand hurts.

Listening to the kids screaming as they run after each other, I try to find my center. I focus on the sound of waves crashing on the beach, and Hunter's blue eyes flash in my mind. I relive the way he touched my cheek, and the secret thrill that ran through my body. The way my hand tingled when I covered his has me breaking out in goose bumps.

Taking a deep breath, I stretch my fingers and gaze out toward the ocean.

A pair of big boots stop next to me. The peaceful, easy feeling goes to hell. I glance up and close my eyes again, fighting against the threatening tears.

"Are you following me?" I ask, not even smiling, because how can he ever fall for someone as broken as me. "Please go away, Hunter."

Hunter

I stop at the beach and recognize Jay's truck immediately. What the hell is she doing here? She slams her fists against the steering wheel and yells so loudly I can hear her even with the doors to the car shut. *What the actual fuck?*

I want to run up to her, then she hits the horn with her forehead and laughs. My lips curve up in a full-blown smile as I watch her moving out of the truck. She stretches her fingers as she walks with her shoes in her hand, her short black dress hugging her curves.

Placing my helmet on the bike, I walk across the beach, running both hands through my hair, not knowing what I'm doing. My boots disappear into the white sand with each step I take. Girls with little pigtails are busy building a sandcastle, and stop the minute they notice me walking toward them. They gape at my arms, then at my neck, probably debating what to do—scream or keep staring at my tattoos and piercings. I flash them a smile, and wave.

"Hey, kids. What's going on?"

The youngest points to the sandcastle. "The princess has to cross the bridge, but it's falling apart," she says, pouting.

I crouch next to them and fix their bridge, and their mothers smile reassuringly.

"Here. Now the prince can rescue the princess," I tell them, wiping my hands on my jeans.

They both start to giggle. "No, the princess has to save the prince," the younger one tells me, their little faces serious.

One of the mother's laughs.

"You raised them well," I tell her.

She nods. "Thank you for helping them."

"Anytime, girls," I say, tipping my imaginary hat, I grin while they continue playing.

Sky stares at her hands, before they disappear in the sand and I take my sunglasses off to get a better look. A couple of guys around my age walk by and check her out. Not noticing them, she keeps staring out toward the ocean. *Damn,* she's beautiful sitting there, wearing all black. But she's also lonely and sad. I have no idea what to do—turn around or go and sit beside her?

My feet have a mind of their own. I stop right next to her.

"Please go away, Hunter," she says, her voice hard as she brushes away her tears. Tugging a piece of paper in her dress pocket, her hands tremble. She's clearly doing everything in her power to give me a back-off vibe, but in the process, she's only drawing me in.

"I'm not going to do that, Shorty," I state, sitting next to her. She can't hide the smile on her face when I call her Shorty. Sky slides a little away from me, I can't blame her. I probably smell awful, like sweat and motor oil. I lift my arm. Yep, definitely bad.

"I wasn't following you, by the way. This is my beach," I tell her.

She raises her eyebrows. Fuck, she's cute. "Your beach?"

I give her a smile she returns although it's a little small. "Yeah. I come here to think, and stuff my face with Mexican food."

"A BMX guy who can think, Jay must be so proud," she taunts, stretching out her feet, her toes disappearing into the sand.

Chuckling, I actually like this back and forth. "Yes he is," I say, smiling, but I want to add *I think about you a lot.*

She turns away and stares out toward the ocean, watching the waves roll in.

The little girls leave the beach with their mothers. "Bye!" they yell.

I wave at them. "Bye, girls."

I grin at Sky and she frowns.

"Hey! I can't help it if the kids like me," shrugging unapologetically.

"You pretend to be such a bad ass, but you're one big softie, aren't you?" she asks, nudging me in the ribs.

Laughing I run my thumb over my bottom lip, rubbing my tongue piercing against my teeth. She focuses her stare on the silver in my mouth, our eyes meet and she quickly glances away.

"Are you okay?" I ask, taking off my leather jacket.

"I'm getting there," she mumbles, her voice tender. "I'm in a fucked up mood, Hunter, I'm sorry."

"You don't have to apologize," I offer, "I wrote the fucking manual."

She snorts at that, and my heart slams in my chest. This girl fucking gets to me without even trying.

I shake my head. "Are you avoiding me or something?"

She closes her eyes and takes a shuddering breath. "Maybe I am," she whispers.

I sit up again, brushing the sand from my hands. "I guess we both have roller coaster personalities, don't we?" I say, giving her a gentle nudge, needing an excuse to touch her.

"Roller coaster?" She chuckles.

"Up one day, down the next," I tell her, flicking my tongue over my lip piercing.

She rolls her eyes but the corners of her mouth hike up a little. "I don't know what I'm doing here. I came here for Jay, and then I met you guys and everything feels different."

"Good different or bad different?"

"Good different," she answers, her eyes shining with mischief.

"I didn't know what to expect either when you crashed our party. I thought you were some stuck up Park Avenue, New York, bitch," I tell her, meaning every single word.

"Some days I am," she says, her voice all serious. "Other days I just want to scream, and I don't know, just *live*."

I lift my brows. "Live?"

"I feel so alone," she whispers, letting her tears fall.

I drape my arm around her shoulder, and after some hesitation she melts into me. "I could really use a friend," she says, her voice barely audible.

"I could do that," I say, giving her a lazy smile. "I can be your friend."

"You sure about that?"

"No problem, Shorty," I answer a little smug.

She opens her mouth and closes it again. I want to lean forward and trace the curve of her bottom lip with my tongue to get a small taste. I hold back a groan while my hungry gaze zeroes in on her mouth.

"Don't," she mutters.

I hold up my free hand. "What?" I turn my head, and let my eyes burn through her.

She shifts away from me, and I let her go. "You don't want me."

"What are you talking about?"

"Forget it," she growls, trying to stand.

I place my hand on hers. "Don't say that," I tell her. "You want to talk about why you were crying?"

She gives me a small smile, shaking her head a little. "I don't."

Sitting back, I skim my tongue over my teeth, taking a deep breath. "If it's Jay, we could get out of here? Do something together that makes you forget whatever is bugging you," I say, staring at my inked hands.

"I wish," she rasps, laying her head on her knees. "I can't seem to figure you out." Those chocolate colored eyes find mine, waiting for a response.

I stare blankly at her for a moment. "Goes both ways, and remember I'm a roller coaster, babe. If you want, you can ride it."

She flashes me a beautiful smile. "Screw you," she says, locking eyes with me again.

"Is that a promise?"

She tries to stand, but I grab her hand, she fucking lets me, and after a deep sigh lays her head against my shoulder.

Stretching my legs out in front of me, I expel a long breath. Without really thinking it through I grab the back of her head pulling her face toward me, touching her heated cheek with the tips of my fingers. "Tell me what I can do to make it better?" I ask, wiping the moist from under her eyes. She's an inch away from my parted lips. I smile and a tremor runs through her. I love the fact I get to her.

"You're doing it."

"I'm sorry for telling you to basically fuck off when you first got here."

"I know why you did it," she says.

"Why?"

"For Jay," she smiles.

"I know you're leaving in a couple weeks, Shorty," I say. *Fuck,* why is my mind going here? Why do I want her, when everything tells me to back the fuck off, before I ruin everything I built? Even Jay warned me not to get involved with her. "Why not have a good time together, just friends?" my voice hopeful, as I slide the pad of my thumb over the curve of her bottom lip.

"I…I," she whispers. With her flushed cheeks and wide-eyed stare, a low growl escapes from my lips, I can't fucking help it. I let my gaze drift down to her nipples; they are poking against the tight fabric of her dress. I flash her a pained smile.

She places her hand on my thigh, her nails disappear into my leg, and I get hard instantly. I need to bite back a groan. *Fuck,* my dick hurts from pressing against the zipper of my jeans.

"Hunter," she whispers, never taking her eyes away from mine.

"It would be fun, you and I," I say in her ear. I don't know who I'm trying to convince here.

"I don't doubt it." She stiffens but relaxes as I start to move my fingers through her thick hair, touching the back of her neck. She closes her eyes as I move my lips over her cheekbone to the corner of her upturned mouth.

"But I don't know if I can." She clutches my thigh with her hand, and I swear to God, I get hard to the point of combusting. I need to stay away from her; my relationships never last longer than a couple hours between the sheets. She's not the kind of girl you spend only one night with. Something tells me once you do, you want to wake up every morning with her sleeping next to you.

Leaning forward, I rest my forehead against hers, still holding her firmly in place. I feel my dick throbbing. I thought this only happened in sappy romance novels and shit, not in fucking real life. I rub my nose against hers ever so slowly, scenting her. Her warm breath on my lips shoots ripples of pleasure through me.

She opens her eyes, and I can only stare as she places her hand on my chest and my heart rate kicks up like I've run forty miles straight. Her touch is a bolt of electricity coursing through my body, lighting everything in its path, even my fucking cold heart.

"Hunter," she breathes. Her eyes burn through me and it's too much. She opens and closes her fingers, taking a deep, shuddering breath. "You don't want me," she whispers.

I pull away, letting her go, knowing where a kiss with her could lead. She drops her hand from my chest and keeps staring at me.

"Sometimes a mistake is the best thing that can happen to you," I tell her, my voice challenging.

"And sometimes it can destroy you," she counters.

"You promise, Shorty?"

She purses her lips together. "You're nothing like I expected."

Gazing out to the ocean, I ask, "What did you expect?"

"I might have checked you out online," tiny crinkles appear at the corners of her eyes. Like she knows how much I crave the attention, the validation.

"You did?" I ask, trying not to sound too smug.

A slow smile spreads across her face. "Lose your cocky smirk, Hunt. I shouldn't have said anything to blow up that already inflated ego of yours."

I dig my fingers in the sand as I lean forward, and a couple strands of hair fall in front of my eyes. "And did you like what you saw, or is the real version even better?"

She shakes her head. "You really don't have an off switch, do you?"

"You're the first chick," I say.

She gives me a look.

"The first *woman* I've met who can throw a punch, and take it as well," I state, staring at the waves crashing on the beach. Licking my bottom lip I turn my attention back to her. Sky's eyes go big, and I burst out laughing. "Fuck, I didn't mean it literally, babe."

She hesitates a moment, "I get what you mean, but I'm not as strong as you think I am," she says, her voice cracking. Her eyes roam across my body. "Under all your ink, you really have a big heart, don't you?"

Growling, I run my tongue over my teeth. "Depends on who you're talking to."

She holds my stare, but is the first one to turn away.

I glance around the beach. We are all alone. The sun is finally setting. With shaking hands, she pulls her black sweater over her head. I can't help but stare at her breasts while she does it. They're fucking perfect, damn what I would give to feel them pressing against the palm of my hand. Her hard nipple teasing my rough skin. My dick twitches and I have to adjust myself. I'm such a pervert, stealing glances at her body. The girl is breathtaking and she doesn't even know it.

"Are you cold?" I ask, draping my leather jacket over her shoulders.

"A little," she says putting it on. A piece of paper falls between us in the sand, I pick it up and read it. It's a prescription for legal marijuana. Why the fuck is she smoking?

"Long day?" I ask, nodding to her shaking hands.

I hand it back to her and she folds it, pushing the paper into the pocket of her dress. "Something like that."

"What is going on?"

"Nothing concerning you," she says averting my gaze.

"I get it's none of my business, but..."

"No, it isn't. Can we talk about something else, have you been riding today?" she asks, changing the subject, guilt sliding across her face.

"Yeah, working on the bikes and driving around." Our eyes meet and I can't help but smile. "I thought you didn't care what the fuck I did all day. Most girls don't anyway."

"I'm not most girls, and you forget I grew up around this life." Her eyes roam to my mouth then up to my cheekbone and the cut there. "What happened to your face?" She reaches out but quickly pulls her hand back.

I crack my neck. "I'm not made of sugar, I can take a beating. Been doing this all my life."

From the corner of her eye, she watches me, like she doesn't believe what I'm telling her. "What happened?"

"I was doing this thing where you angle the bike so you get more grip when you're going around the bend," I say, explaining it to her by using my hands.

She turns to me, a big question mark reflected on her face.

"You don't want to hear about this," I say, looking away.

She lays a hand on my arm, and the warmth of her touch goes right through my shirt. We stare at each other. "Tell me," she says, her voice soft.

"I fucked up and I crashed. Happy now?" I grunt. She laughs.

"Shut up," I say, the corners of my lips hiking up.

"When is your next race?" Her eyes are tender like her voice.

"In a couple weeks."

The wind picks up, and I close my eyes for a second. "I need to be at my best. It's the last race of this season before we have eight weeks off, and it really starts to count."

"Jay must be pushing you hard?"

"Yeah. If I want to keep being number one, he needs to." I flick open my lighter and grab a cigarette and talk around it, before I inhale deep. She eyes it.

"I shouldn't," I say, blowing out through my nose, "but sometimes you have to die a little before you can live, if you know what I mean."

The blood drains from her face, and the way she closes her eyes like she's in pain leaves me feeling guilty, like I made a stupid mistake.

"I need to go," she mumbles, her legs wobble the moment she stands.

I rise as well. "Sure, let me help you."

"No, I'm fine," she says, walking to the car. Swaying a little, she almost falls.

I throw my cigarette on the ground and hold her up. "Man, how much did you have to smoke?"

"Smoke?" she asks, her voice shaking like her body.

"The marijuana, Shorty?"

"Nothing," she whispers.

"Yeah, don't bullshit a bullshitter."

"Let me go, Hunter," she says, throwing my jacket in my face and putting on her sunglasses. I take the car keys from her hands.

"Give them back." There's a threat in her voice.

"Done a lot of fucked up things in my life, but I'm not going to let you drive home still high as a kite."

She crosses her arms in front of her, holding out her hand, standing her ground.

"Get in," I order, motioning to the truck. "I'll put my bike in the back."

She hesitates and after another few seconds of our staring contest, she slowly hauls herself into the passenger seat, muttering under her breath.

I take the ramp out of the pickup and get my bike into the truck bed, fastening the straps around the wheels so it doesn't slide. I hop in the truck as darkness sets. *Fuck*, how could we go from hot to ice cold in a matter of minutes?

"I promised Jay to keep my distance, but I'm taking you home, babe," I mumble, putting the car in reverse.

"When you talk to Jay again, you can tell him to go fuck himself," she snarls, getting all red in the face.

"That's cute, Shorty," I drawl, accelerating out of the parking lot and onto the highway, heading home.

"Fuck you, Hunter."

"Man, you're a roller coaster indeed," I tell her, focusing on the cars in front of us. "So how many joints did you have?"

She throws her sunglasses on the dashboard, and there are tears in her eyes. I put my hand on her shoulder, lingering for a moment. Letting her go, my hand is on fire. I try to pay attention to the road again. "Believe me. I know how you feel," I tell her, changing lanes.

"You have no idea," she whispers, staring out the window. "No idea."

CHAPTER 8

Sky

"Then tell me what's going on, Sky," he growls out, turning onto the quiet road leading up to the house.

"I can't, not yet." I want to take a sledgehammer to the overpriced Ram monstrosity. I want to scream, I want to cry, I want to feel something other than pain. I turn on the surround sound and a guitar solo blares through the speakers.

"No?" he growls, killing the music. I don't know why his voice makes my heart race, and my panties damp.

Nausea takes hold of me. Because I know what I want. I want to do something crazy. I want him. I want Hunter to make me forget, even if it means nothing to him.

"Stop this damn truck right now," I scream, gasping for air, the panic attack engulfing me, and I punch against his seat.

He points a finger in my face. "Shorty, talk to me..." He snaps his mouth closed, clenching his jaw.

"I don't want to talk," I spit out, hitting him in the shoulder. Taking him and myself by surprise.

He shakes his head. His eyes lock on mine for a second, and my mouth dries. Hunter's eyes are cold and hard like him.

I slam my hands on the dashboard. "Stop, stop this motherfucking truck!" I demand, angry tears blurring my vision. *I need to breathe, I need to get out of this car, and away from him.*

He turns onto an abandoned road and hits the brakes. We skid to a halt. Slamming his hands on the steering wheel, he curses under his breath.

I try the handle but it's still locked. "Open the door." My voice is icy and calm.

"You don't want to tell me what is going on? Then fucking go," he says, hurt underlining his words, and unlocks the car. I open the door, but before my feet hit the pavement I slam it shut again. I'm done running away from him, from myself, from what I want.

"I don't know what to do!" I yell, fear taking hold of me.

"Talk to me, whatever it is, you can tell me," he drawls. He clicks his seat belt open, and I slump back against the leather, my tears spilling over while I scream.

"Sky, babe. Stop it," he says gently, taking my hands in his. "I didn't mean to scare or hurt you. Please stop. Talk to me. Fucking let me in." His deep voice breaks. He pulls me into his chest.

I turn, pushing him away, and before I know it, my palm lands hard across his cheek. My hand stings and the expression in his eyes changes from shock to pure anger. I lean against the door, not knowing how he'll react.

Biting his lip, he licks the blood from the corner of his mouth. He traces his bottom lip with his thumb, a wild look in his eyes. A cocky grin spreads across his face, scaring me and making me pant with want. Before I can blink, he boxes me in, one hand on the door, the other behind my head.

"What are you doing?" my voice trembles.

"Tell me what is going on with you, why did you come here?"

I shake my head. "I can't." Tears run down my cheeks. I lean forward and rest my face against his chest. He gasps and slowly buries his hands in my hair holding me close.

"I thought I could stay away, but I can't. I need someone like you," I whisper, as his hands travel to my shoulders, and down my arms. I lean my head against the crook of his neck, and inhale his scent.

He freezes and then starts moving his fingers over my waist. "Hey, whatever it is, it doesn't matter." His voice breaks. "I can take it. Tell me what you want and I'll do it."

I scream into his shirt, grabbing the fabric between my fingers. "I'm so angry," I say through my sobs.

He clutches my hands and holds them against his warm body. His heartbeat pounds against my palm. Hunter is trembling with anger, or is it fear? Leaning forward, he grabs the back of my head, pulling me into him.

"Don't, I'm not good for you," I say, heat pooling between my legs. Our mouths are inches from each other.

"You said you needed someone like me," he whispers the words, wetting his lips.

"Maybe I do," I say, wanting to kiss him, to get lost in his strength.

The temperature in the car turns from icy cold to scorching hot. His lips touch my cheeks kissing away the tears on my face, breathing in deeply.

"No, this is wrong." He tries to push me away, but I move on top of him. Straddling his hips, I shift my weight over his hard thighs. Grunting he pins my hands behind my back, holding me prisoner, showing me who has all the control here.

"I'm not going to do this with you still high," he groans. My dress hikes up, his jeans and my lace panties are the only things separating me from his erection. The denim straining against his hard-on presses almost painfully against my throbbing center.

"I'm not high," I tell him, and he twitches against my drenched underwear. I bite on the inside of my cheek, but I can't help it when a moan escapes between my lips. The friction is heaven and hell. I need him, want him more than he can imagine. But this is wrong, what I'm doing to him is wrong.

He keeps pleading with his eyes for me to make him stop. I don't want him to. I want to fuck him, make love to him. I want to hurt him so bad he has to let me go, even if I don't want him to. He drops his hands, and I fist his long hair, wanting him to kiss me. He strokes his fingers upwards along my naked legs. My hips have a mind of their own as I tilt up. He grabs my ass hard, his fingers digging into each cheek as he yanks me down and over his erection. His lips turn up slightly, as he watches me.

"Fuck, do whatever you want, Shorty." The heat reflected in his eyes dries my mouth. His jeans stretch across his hard cock.

I keep the pressure against my panties constant as I slowly move back and forth. I kiss his temple, he sighs and closes his eyes. His hands slide up my sides stopping just below the contours of my bra. My chest rises and falls, as he strokes his thumb over the lace fabric. I fall forward against his chest, and he holds me in his arms, slowly rocking me from left to right.

"Damn babe," he murmurs, and starts to nibble my ear. He parts my thighs and presses his hand against my butt crack, his middle finger stroking my drenched pussy through my dress.

I whimper, and when he says, "I can feel how fucking wet you are," desire laces his hoarse voice. We are both panting hard, gasping for air, for each other. I don't know if it's because I barely know him or the fact we are alone in a car parked on an abandoned road. He growls and pushes me against the steering wheel, without warning he grasps both my breasts in his big hands. "Have been thinking about this every damn night," he tells me. He holds my stare and parts his mouth as he takes one of my nipples between his fingers through the fabric, and rolls it over his thumb, and my butt shoots off his lap.

His right hand moves down, over my stomach to my knee. His eyes lock in on mine as I drape my arms around his neck and nod. He trails his fingers up and under the flimsy dress. I can smell my arousal filling the truck.

He brings his fingers to his mouth and wets two, my eyes roll into the back of my head as he pushes my underwear to the side and slips them into me. I groan loudly, and he swears when he makes contact with the line of curls above my pussy and my engorged clit. I've never heard the sound that leaves my mouth before. A satisfied smirk curls his lips, "You okay? Fuck, Shorty, you're soaking wet."

"Yes, oh god, Hunter," trying to ignore the throbbing. I can't come like this, from his touch alone, can I? "You're an asshole," I grit out, pushing myself against him, swirling my hips and wanting to come so badly I could scream.

Grabbing the back of my neck with his other hand he holds me in place as he slowly strokes my inner folds. He speeds up his fingers, fucking me with them. Pleasure takes over and I'm dripping over his hand. The way his fingers open me up, stroking my pussy lips leaves me breathless as I focus on the sensation.

He husks out, "I can say the same about you." He inhales deeply, and roughly kisses me. I can still taste the blood from his bottom lip on my tongue, from when I slapped him.

"Shorty," he huffs, thrusting his palm against me. He's still swirling his fingers deep inside, raising my hips I ride his hand. I couldn't escape this man even if I wanted to. And I don't want to leave. I want him, all of him.

"Tell me not to fuck the living shit out of you. I've been fantasizing about this moment since you told me to fuck off," he growls, his nose skimming along mine, and my clit pulses from his words. His fingers stretch me as he rubs my nub. Without warning he pulls his fingers out of me, and licks them clean as I watch.

He smiles and stares into my eyes.

I lean in and brush my lips over his. He kisses me again, first hard, then, when his tongue invades my mouth, he becomes softer. I can taste myself, a satisfied smirk curls his glistening lips, as I crash my mouth against his again. The way his piercing rolls against my tongue makes me moan. He nibbles on my bottom lip. Keeping his kisses soft, he teases me with his stubble, trailing his lip piercing over my mouth.

Opening his eyes, he gives me a lazy smile. Hunter knows he's in charge; he has the power to make me do anything, to make me come, and judging by the look in his eyes, he wants it that way.

I love the taste of him on my tongue. I move against his erection, and heat builds between my legs.

"Shorty," he groans through our kiss. I break away from him and try to catch my breath, my eyes flying to the massive bulge pressing against his zipper. He pushes me off him and I yelp. The dress hugs my hips, and he tugs at my panties. "Get those off," he murmurs darkly, his voice rough and thick.

Yanking the front of my dress open, he pushes my hands high above my head so I have to strain my back. I can't move my wrists; I'm at his mercy. Leaning his forehead against mine, he kisses my temple. I angle my head and find his lips, the heat of his body covering mine.

Letting go of my hands he licks the shell of my ear. Goose bumps break out all over my skin. Pulling down my bra cup he watches me carefully, his eyes shining before he moves down and encircles my nipple with his lips. The metal of his piercing scrapes over my sensitive flesh and I gasp.

"Fuck," I whimper. My clit is throbbing from the sensation. *I want to feel his tongue disappear between my pussy.* He nuzzles the place between my breasts before he finds my nipple again and sucks hard as I scream his name, and he chuckles, letting the hard peak go with a pop. I get comfortable against the leather seat and he moves over me, hungry eyes roaming up and down my body.

Rough fingers caress my cheekbones, my chin. His eyes burn through me as he traces the line of my neck to my stomach, stopping before he reaches the place where I want him most. He places open-mouthed kisses between my breasts, slowly moving up to the corner of my mouth, my temple, his hands tunneling in my long hair. All the while, he pins me with his full weight.

"Oh God," I say. I want Hunter. I want this.

He grinds his pelvic bone against me, and I gasp. The heat between his legs pushes against my entrance, making me wetter with each stroke. I shiver as he presses his arousal hard against me.

He reaches down and I watch him open his zipper, his erection clearly outlined against the cotton fabric of his boxers.

I caress his face, tracing the line of his eyebrows. Leaning into my touch, he kisses my forehead. Our warm breath mixes.

There is a question in his eyes. "Make me stop?" he whispers the words, pleading with himself.

"Don't stop. Touch me, Hunter," I beg, pushing against his hard-on, letting him know I want him, I want this. He could never hurt me like I'm hurting him.

He kisses me harder, demanding, and I want to get lost in his touch. I reach out and rub my palm over his dick. He moans and I bite on his earlobe. He grabs my hand. "Fuck, babe," he rasps, his breathing erratic.

He nuzzles my neck, and a tear spills over my cheek. His large hand caresses my left breast, thumb stroking back and forth over my nipple making it so sensitive I'm lost in the sensation. My back arches and his mouth encloses over the tip. I slide my fingers into his hair, pull him closer, and he groans. He sucks hard. A low scream leaves my lips. His hair slips through my fingers. Lifting up, I bury my nose in his hair, inhaling his scent, loving the smell of his musky sweat coating his neck. My hands disappear under his shirt, and spread across his muscular shoulders, tracing each hard line, every dent and rise, all of him.

Wetness seeps through my silk panties. His fingers dive under my dress, rubbing the fabric over my pussy.

He tries to yank off my panties but he hits his elbow against the dashboard. "Motherf…"

I smash my mouth to his, playing and teasing him with my tongue. I'm breathless when he pulls back.

"Even for a big truck, this shit is too small," he says in my ear, clutching his bruised ribs.

"Is that a euphemism for something else?" I joke, catching my breath. His big, hard dick presses against my thigh. My lips fight his, hard and wanting, tasting and teasing.

He pushes himself up and watches me. "Damn, I like your smart mouth," he murmurs, his eyes filled with mischief. Pressing me against the seat, he growls.

He grinds his pelvis into mine, the friction of it is just right, making me throb and pant with want.

Swearing, I plead, "Shut up and fuck me," tugging his belt and zipper fully open. He chuckles as he finally manages to tear off my panties, the pressure from his body pushes me further into the warm leather of the seat. Fingers glide over my chest, between my breasts, to my stomach. He cups my sex with the palm of his hand, grinding against my clit while two fingers disappear expertly inside. The feeling of him filling me is overwhelming, just like the soft strokes that set my nerves on fire. I open my legs even wider giving him full access. He glides out then back in, deeper this time, finding my sweet spot. I cry out from the wonderful intrusion.

"So fucking wet and warm," he purrs in my ear, and rubs his thumb softly over the place below my jaw where my heart hammers in my throat. He seals our mouths together, plunging his tongue in deep, letting my pussy go; I protest and he growls.

A sensation runs through me. I want him to fill me so much I can't think straight. He lowers himself over me. I need to feel his weight on top of me. I stretch my legs as far as I can in the tight space.

I run my fingertips over his face. The right side is red from my slap. He opens the glove compartment and digs out a condom.

I slide my hand down into his boxers, tracing the velvet skin of his hard dick. My stiff nipples press painfully against his muscular chest. I shiver in anticipation. Feeling brave, I slide my thumb over his shaft. He is wet with precum, and a desperate sound escapes me.

I glance down and my mouth dries. My fingers finding a metal bar piercing.

"You feel it?" he groans, as I squeeze him.

"What the hell is that?" I ask, stroking him softly.

"I have my glans pierced, feel those two metal balls on the end?" he drawls, giving me a maverick smile.

"Yes," I swallow a couple times, as he pushes his jeans down over his hips, followed by his boxers.

He rests his forehead on mine, pushing against my hand with his hips. "When I fuck you, you'll come even harder."

"Promise?" I ask breathlessly, kissing the side of his upturned mouth. I release the grip on his shaft and he hisses.

"Fuck yeah." He tears the condom packet with his teeth, and rolls it down over his length. He instantly positions the head of his cock at my opening and with one swift movement he is in me, filling me to the hilt. It hurts, but I love the way it stretches me and makes me burn. He thrusts into me, my inner walls hugging his erection like a glove. I'm so slick, slowly he rocks himself back and forth in my tight entrance. Rotating his hips, I whimper as pain mixes with pleasure.

Lowering his face to mine, I dig my fingernails into his biceps. He swears under his breath; good to know he loves a bit of pain. I drape my legs around his waist and pull him against me. I crave the way the metal ball in the middle of his tongue rolls across mine. We kiss more eagerly, hard and demanding, his tongue sliding in and out of my mouth. The rumbling sound deep in his throat makes my clit throb.

He pushes hard into me, I thrash my head back never breaking eye contact. It isn't pretty. I'm so close. He grips my hair, and I cry out as he hits that place deep inside with the metal ball. We are angrily fucking each other, and I love it. Ripples of desire shoot through every nerve ending of my body.

After thrusting in deep, making my body arch off the seat, he pulls all the way out incredibly slowly. Stroking my slit with the head of his cock, the little metal ball of his piercing connecting with my clit with each upward pass, he hovers over me before driving in deep again. I cry out his name while he pounds into me. I buck my hips to meet his thrusts. My orgasm builds, little currents of electricity pulsing through my clit. And he's right, the way those metal balls hit my G-spot every damn time make my head spin.

His body trembles as he grinds into me, building and building me to the point of ecstasy. My inner muscles stretch around him, his relentless and unforgiving rhythm making me scream as I dig my fingernails in his back. *Fuck, it hurts, but in such a good way.*

"Please, Hunter," I beg. He shakes his head, slowly pulling out again. His tongue slides along his lower lip, his piercing peeking out. We kiss in a heated frenzy, the metal ball dancing over my tongue. I slide my fingers over the grooves of his defined *V*, and he trembles as my nails brush the top of his dick. I flick my clit with my trembling finger, wanting to reach my release.

"No," he growls, kissing me again. He scrapes his teeth over my sore, puffy lips.

"We do it the way I like it. Do you have a problem with that?" he asks. A threat is in his voice, but there's softness in his eyes as he kisses the tip of my nose.

We stare at each other. I slowly shake my head.

He pushes into me again, and I like how he takes command. I groan at the feeling of being filled again. My head rolls to the side. The tingling sensation starts in my stomach while he fucks me deep with powerful thrusts, slow and hard at the same time. The muscles in his jaw clench. I know he's holding back.

I whimper when he hits my sweet spot, almost pushing me over the edge. His nose flares as he takes a deep breath. After pulling the front of my dress open farther, he takes my nipple between his teeth. He sucks, licks and bites, his metal ball rolling across my hard nipple. He places his hand on my ass, pulling me against him. I gasp when he goes in deeper with every stroke.

Rising on his knees, he almost hits his head against the ceiling of the truck. I plead, "No, Hunter," as he pulls out, leaving me empty, and I close my eyes in protest.

"Fuck, Shorty, hold up," he murmurs in my ear as he pinches my clit, and my eyes shoot open.

"Oh God, please don't stop."

"Slow or hard?" he asks, voice hoarse, his knees dig into the leather as he slides his hand up and down over his hard shaft.

"Hard, Hunter, harder. Do what you want with me. I can take it."

Staring at me, he leans in and kisses me passionately. I grab his dark hair and tuck the strands behind his ears. He takes my hand in his and kisses my palm. Sinking himself inside me, he grunts through clenched teeth, as my pussy swallows his dick. There is heat in his eyes, as he bites his bottom lip.

"Let go, Hunter. Fuck me like you want," I tell him. His hair slips through my restless hands.

He shoves his right hand under my ass, tilting my pelvis to grant him the best access. He plunges himself into me, pushing in hard, over and over. Pounding and ramming his dick inside me and it's exactly what I need. I can feel how wet I am, as he pulls out. I shudder when he grabs his shaft and runs the pierced tip over my sensitive clit before sliding easily into me again. I let him take control, fucking me harder and harder. I love the way it burns and aches at the same time; I can't get enough of him.

I kiss his throat, trailing my tongue over his stubble, my lips tracing his jawline. I suck and tease his earlobe while he disappears into me.

Grabbing my wrists, he pushes them above my head. Our eyes lock and there is a wildness in his expression, hunger and anger all swirling around in his ice-blue depths. Grinding his hips, he forces me down. "Fuck," he huffs into my hair. It comes out like a promise. "I'm close." His voice is muffled against my neck.

"I want this, I want you," I plead, while his weight pins me to the seat. He lets go of my hands and I let them move over his tattoos, kneading his ass.

He slams into me, and kisses me hard. Crying out his name, spasms rock my body and light explodes in my vision as my orgasm rips through me, taking me by surprise. I scream as I explode, my walls clenching around his big cock. Hunter stays seated inside my tight wet throbbing pussy, and I think my body can't handle it as I feel him driving me to the edge for a second time, stretching me wide open. My release is building again, or maybe it never stopped. He orders me to kiss him. The orgasm tears through me, ripping a scream from my throat as I thrash under him.

He roars with his own release. It's rough and hard, pain and pleasure mixed together. I scream his name, still riding out my release. He collapses on top of me and knocks the wind right out of my chest.

The smell of our lovemaking fills the truck—sex, anger and hurt. I want to keep him buried deep inside me, I want to keep feeling his strength. I'm panting and shaking. Holding his face between my hands our eyes clash, I kiss his cheek, his temple, the side of his upturned mouth. I kiss up to his forehead, tasting the salt of his sweat on my lips.

I move my mouth to his nose, his cheekbones, and when I finally plant my parted lips on his, he lets me take control, and I plunge my tongue inside. It isn't pretty or soft. Our kisses are hard, demanding and rough. His stubble scrapes my neck and he moves to my breasts and he kisses them both.

Hunter looks up and his lips find mine, he's still slightly hard inside of me. I feel whole and strong with his big body on top of me. My thumb feathers across his parted lips.

"What the hell just happened?" he whispers, caressing my face.

"I don't know." I kiss him again.

After a while, he lets me go and moves off me. I push my dress down. Hunter picks up my torn panties from the floor, handing them back to me with a sly smile on his face. He grabs a tissue softly stroking my pussy with it, before he disposes the condom in a plastic bag. Pulling up his pants, he fastens his belt.

We both smile. I reach out and run my fingers over his sweat-soaked hair covering his left eye, he takes my hand in his, and plants his lips against my skin. After kissing the back of my hand and then my fingers, he holds my palm against his cheek. The red from where I slapped him is almost gone. Letting my hand drop on his knee, he starts the car and pulls out onto the road without saying a word.

We are quiet the whole way home. He merges, when he shifts gears and our eyes lock they're wild and cold at the same time. His face darkens, like his thoughts are taking him someplace else. I sense he's pulling away from me and I have no idea how to talk to him. He parks the car in front of the garage and keeps holding onto the steering wheel. "I'm sorry, Shorty," he mumbles. "We shouldn't have done that."

He can't even meet my eyes.

Sniffling, I fight against the urge to bury my face in his chest and let him hold me forever. "No, we shouldn't have," I say, my heart breaking.

Piercing me with his intense stare, he sighs. "Sky?"

It's a question when he says my name. But I can't stay here in this truck with him, because if I do, I'll never want to leave.

I open the car door but he reaches out and covers my hand with his, and says, "Please stay, Shorty. Don't go."

CHAPTER 9

Hunter

I glance at her before I turn my attention to the main house. What the fuck just happened? She closes the passenger side door and looks at me.

I tap my fingers on the steering wheel. "If you want, contrary to what some people believe, I'm a good listener." I refuse to let her go without her telling me what the hell is going on. I'm not going to back off, no matter how hard she tries to push me away.

She flashes me a small smile. "I don't know where to begin to tell you the truth."

"We all need a friend you know. I thought I didn't need anyone for a very long time, and that worked out great until I changed, or started to change," I answer. All the lights are on in the house, if Jay finds out what we did he'd probably grab his shotgun. Then I spot Drew, Mac and the man in question sitting on the porch, talking and laughing.

Jay turns his head and stands, looking in the direction of the truck. She shrinks back in her seat. The car windows are slightly tinted and still a little fogged up so he can't see us—I hope.

His smile turns into a grimace. I swear under my breath, because I forgot my dirt bike is in the truck bed.

"Want something to eat?" I ask, at the same time that Jay shakes his head and turns around. Better if he doesn't see her like this, like she just got her brains fucked out.

"You're always feeding me," she says, smiling.

"Babe, one gust of wind and you'll be flying to the track," I joke.

She grins, shaking her head. "Okay. With Jay probably wanting to kill us both," she says, motioning to her father, "what did you have in mind?"

"I know a great place not far from here." My hands grip the steering wheel tighter. I hope she'll say yes. "Least I can do for being my asshole self for the last couple of days. And damn, babe, I'm starved after what we just did."

She is quiet for a moment, biting her lip, probably weighing her options. "And maybe we can talk about what just happened," she says after a couple seconds. "You're not an asshole, Hunter. Maybe a pain in the ass, as Jay would say."

"I'll take it, babe," I answer, barking out a laugh.

It doesn't take me long to get to the diner and park in the rear, luckily she looks a little better. "I'll just send Jay a quick text," she mumbles, typing on her phone.

"That we're having dinner?"

She locks eyes with me. "Should I?"

"Shorty, you can do whatever the fuck you want," I say, stepping out.

Following me outside she asks, "This is it?" a soft smile playing on her lips.

"Yep, this is it," I say, spreading out my arms.

She stares up at the old nineteen-fifties style eatery, the side of her mouth twitching.

"Hasn't changed one bit since nineteen-fifty-eight," I explain to her.

She nods, not saying anything, following me toward the door. Once inside, the bell dings, and some Elvis tune is playing in the background. The restaurant is packed.

"Well, by God," May, the seventy-year-old owner drawls. "Clay!" she yells, calling her husband. "It's Hunter, with a cut under his eye."

"A black eye?" Clayton yells from the kitchen. He pauses. "Again?"

I roll my eyes at Sky, and she laughs.

May gives me a hug, and a kiss on my cheek. Clay comes out and slaps me on the back. "Boy, I haven't seen you in here for a long time," he says.

"I know," I tell them, focusing on the tiles on the floor. "Been doing competitions."

May pinches my cheek. "Have you been walking the line, honey?"

"I try." I smile. Man, why am I fucking nervous?

May gives me a knowing wink looking at Sky. Sky's shy smile darts between the three of us.

"May, Clay, this is Sky Alexander, Jay's daughter."

May's eyes light up. And I feel nervous all of a sudden. These are my people, what if they don't like her?

"Welcome, dear," she says, taking Sky's hands in hers.

"Your diner is awesome," she tells May, checking out the place. The old jukebox in the corner is playing Elvis Presley tunes on repeat. Everywhere you look there is chrome, and neon art hangs on the wall. May guides us to the only empty booth.

"I'll be right back with your regular. You want a vanilla shake, Sky?" Clay asks.

She nods. "Sure."

"Coming right up," Clay says, shuffling to the counter and giving the order to one of the girls there. The whole diner is filled with locals, people I recognize. Meeting their gaze, I smile, and some nod.

May beams at me and then at Sky. "You two make a handsome couple."

Sky is the first one to talk. "We are not a..."

"Shush, dear. Let me enjoy the fantasy. This boy needs a good girl to keep him out of trouble. The black ink and funny hair doesn't appeal to everyone you know." She winks at me. I know Clay was in the Navy during World War II and has enough tats to prove it. I can't believe the guy is still working at ninety-four.

Sky grins at May, her dark eyes meet mine, and my mind immediately goes back to the truck, the way she kissed me, held me, damn it. "Thank you, May." I swallow. "For that."

May leans against the red leather booth. Grinning, she turns to Sky. "You know he used to come in here with a bloody nose, oh, and a black eye, almost every week. Eating pancakes like his life depended on it." She shakes her head, pinning her locks of grey hair in a bun. "I called Jay once; he said the boy was always on the track riding his bike, and crashing it more times than he could count on his two hands. What a long way you've come."

I nod, silently praying she isn't going to tell some awkward story from my teenage years.

"I also remember you carrying ..." She pauses, tapping her chin, as if searching for the memory. "What was it...oh, gosh, a little teddy bear! You carried it in your backpack everywhere you went."

My cheeks heat with embarrassment. "Thanks, May."

Sky laughs. I fucking love that sound.

"Well, enough of this," May says, brushing her hands on her apron as Clay brings us two vanilla shakes. "I'll leave you kids alone. I'll come by in a couple minutes, give you enough time to look over the menu."

She shoos Clay away as well, who takes her hand and kisses it.

Sky chuckles, and I'm praying the ground will open up and swallow me hole.

"A teddy bear, when you were a hellraising teenager?"

I drop my forehead on the table, brushing my hands through my hair. "Ahh come on, your dad gave it to me," I say, watching her take a sip from the shake. "I'd never gotten a fucking toy in my life, and the little guy is still our mascot. Last year Drew gave him a little shirt with my sponsors on it to wear, and I'm not making it better, am I?"

"Hunter, don't you dare lie to your sweet girl," May yells from behind the counter.

Sky laughs again.

"I shouldn't have brought you here," I murmur, but I'm not getting off the hook so easy. She takes my hand in hers and squeezes, and I let her.

"Thank you," she whispers, "for taking me here, and taking my mind off things."

We keep staring at each other until she lets go of my hand. *Why would she want to take her mind off things?*

"I didn't picture you as a vanilla man though," she says, before sucking on the straw.

"I'm not, don't you agree?" I deadpan, and she almost chokes on her drink. "Are you okay?" I laugh. "I mean with what happened between us in the truck?"

She nods, her eyes sparkling, wiping the vanilla from her chin with her thumb. What I would give to lick it off her.

Fuck, don't go there! I scream in my head. "I know that was a one-time thing, wasn't it?"

"No, yes. I don't know. I didn't come here to cause a rift between you and Jay," she says, and sucks on her finger. My dick pulses and throbs against my zipper in response. I brush my sweaty palms on my jeans, hoping to calm my racing heart.

"Why did you come here then?"

She ignores my question and says, "Tell me more about you, Hunter," taking me by surprise.

I pause. "You don't want to know about my boring story." Getting uncomfortable, I focus on the menu. Neither of us says anything for a moment, but she keeps staring at me.

I sigh, laying the menu down. "It's not the greatest story in the world," I grumble, my voice grim.

"It doesn't matter. Whatever you want to tell me, I'll listen."

Groaning, I know I can't ignore her. "Okay. I'll admit, I did carry the damn bear around."

"Thought so." She takes another sip before she asks, "What was my dad like before?"

"Before what?"

She smiles. "Tell me about your life with him, Hunter."

We order dinner and I tell her about Jay and the competitions we went to. About how he always carried a picture of her wherever we went, and the stories he told about her from when she was younger. It isn't weird like I thought it was going to be, having fucked and all. Sometimes I catch her smiling like she can read my mind. After all, it was the hottest sex I've ever had in my life.

I ask her about herself, and I listen to every word she says. I can't stop laughing when she tells me anecdotes about her running around New York at barely sixteen, and getting into clubs she legally shouldn't have. About living in the city and her summers in the Hamptons. She doesn't elaborate about a boyfriend or anything but I figure she must have had one back East at some point. It makes me jealous, even though I don't have any claim to her, not yet anyway.

The conversation flows easily. She teases me, and doesn't mind if I do the same.

She reaches out and points to the dog tags I always wear around my neck. "Are those your father's?"

I nod, taking a sip from my drink. "His name is Oliver," I murmur, reading the name on the tags: *Oliver Cole*. Shaking my head, I say, "He goes by Zombie now."

"Zombie?" she rasps.

"Yeah, the name he got when he joined his brothers," I tell her, raking both my hands through my hair.

"What do you mean?"

"His motorcycle gang of degenerates."

She takes another bite from her hamburger. "Like *Sons Of Anarchy* or *Mayans*?"

I roll my eyes, snorting. "They're actually called Devil's Sons."

"Devil's Sons," she whispers. "Sounds ominous."

"Yeah, fucking Devil's Sons. He's the president of the club now. I never talk about my father, not even with Drew and Jay."

"Dads aren't easy to get along with," she mutters.

I chuckle sarcastically. "My *dad*. He doesn't even know what the word means."

"What happened between you two?"

"How long have you got?" I ask, and she grins. "Fuck, I don't know. Ever seen a war movie where a soldier can't handle being back in the real world?"

She nods.

"How they couldn't stand being home?"

"Yes," she says.

"His body came back but he left his mind somewhere in the desert," I tell her. "He drowned himself in alcohol, cocaine, heroin, like he did between tours to fight his demons. When he was home, he only wanted to be with his buddies to feel normal again. My mother tried everything, but when she stopped trying he closed himself off even more. He joined the club, and mom hoped it would do him good. It did in the beginning, but after a while, he changed." I sigh. "When my mom died from an overdose of his drugs, he lost it and got locked up. He left me with his brother, before I took to the streets, but you know that."

"I'm sorry, Hunt," she whispers.

I grimace, staring at the dog tags I'm clutching in my hand. I swallow hard before I go on. "Jay, Mac and Drew saved me in so many ways."

"I'm so sorry," she says.

Scratching my stubble, I continue. "I almost went into the system if Jay hadn't taken custody of me. I made the same mistakes my father did, only I was twenty years younger."

"Do you ever visit your dad?" she asks, reaching for my hand.

I shake my head, brushing my thumb over her knuckles. "Oliver called me in the beginning. I never responded. I blamed him for everything; on some level, I still do. I know I used him as an excuse for all the things that went wrong in my life. Easier, I guess, to blame someone else for your mistakes."

"I guess so," she answers, getting a faraway look in her eyes. "Do you want to see him?"

I give her an uninterested shrug. "He got out the day I turned eighteen, but I didn't want to go to him or his club. Don't know, don't care."

She pushes me in the shoulder. "You do care."

I scrub my face with both hands. "Zombie wouldn't care. I wouldn't recognize him anyway."

"Why don't you find out for yourself?"

"What about you? How are you and Jay getting along?" I ask, raising my brows.

"Now I know why you don't want to talk about it," she answers, smiling.

We keep the conversation light after that.

After we finish eating, we say goodbye to May and Clay.

"Bring Sky by again, Hunter," May whispers in my ear, pushing some leftover pie in my hands.

"I promise, May," I tell her, giving her a hug.

"Stay out of trouble, son," Clay says, slapping his hand on my shoulder, and winking at Sky.

Sky nods, not saying anything. She is quiet the entire way home, slowly pulling away from me. I don't know what I did wrong. But I make myself a promise to find out even if she doesn't want me to. I never fucking back off from a challenge, and I think she is going to be my greatest one yet.

CHAPTER 10

Sky

During the drive, I try to focus on the road ahead, but instead I keep staring at him. My mind wandering back to our moment in the truck. I lost my mind, but damn it was the best sex I ever had in my life. I stare at his hard thighs, the way the muscles in his arms flex, and how the long strands of his hair fall in front of his eyes. I know he keeps a lot of stories close to his chest, but who am I to judge when I'm the one who's not only been lying to myself, but to everyone around me as well?

Hunter keeps stealing glances at me probably thinking I'm not paying attention. I watch him, memorizing the way his tattooed hand shifts gears. My cheeks flare, imagining what more those hands could do to me. What's wrong with having a little fun?

I love the way he talks about his life with Jay. I know he'll walk away in the end. I shouldn't let him in, not now. What is the point anyway? We had fun, but that's it. We could never become something more.

I scoot to the side of the seat and stare out the window, not saying anything as I focus on the changing scenery.

Hunter parks the car in front of the garage. Tapping his fingers on the steering wheel, he says, "We're back."

My heart rate picks up, and my palms start to sweat. But I don't want to think about it, about us. Because I'm afraid where giving him my heart could lead. "Thank you for a lovely dinner," I tell him, handing him May's pie before opening the car door.

"Sky? Are we good with what happened before?"

I nod, and he follows me to the front of the house.

"It was fucking amazing." His deep voice low. Putting his left hand in his pocket, he shyly says, "and I like talking to you." He is quiet for a moment, staring at the box containing the pie. "When you're ready, you can tell me about the drugs."

He hands me back the plastic box.

Wow. I didn't see that one coming. I'm not going to go there with him. I want to enjoy what we have a little longer before it gets complicated.

I take a step back, opening the front door. "See you later, Hunter," turning my back I take a step inside the house, leaving him standing on the porch. I lean against the doorjamb and watch him walk away, pulling his hoodie over his head. Glancing over his shoulder, he stops to light a cigarette.

I slowly head for the stairs holding onto the wall for dear life, my muscles cramping with each step I take.

Jay peeks out from the kitchen. "Did you have a good time with Hunter, Skylar?"

I cringe, leaning against the wall. Trying to focus on my breathing, I hope the dizziness will subside.

"Yes," I say slowly. "Goodnight, Jay."

"Sleep tight, baby. Wait, hold up. I got you something," he says, opening a drawer from the closet in the hallway. He hands me a couple of envelopes and pieces of paper. "I thought maybe you would like to write some things down," he says, sounding insecure. "I have trouble finding the right words to say sometimes, and I thought you might have the same problem."

I put my arms around his waist, taking myself by surprise. "Thanks, Dad."

He kisses my hair and hugs me tight to his chest, before letting go.

"Want to hang out with me before you crash? I can make hot cocoa," he says, his voice hopeful.

"Only if we share the last of this pie?" I ask, holding the box in the air.

"Hell yeah, make yourself comfortable, I'll be right back with the drinks."

I walk over to his extensive record collection that fills the better part of the wall next to the fireplace.

"Want to put on a record?" he asks, setting two cups on the coffee table.

"I like that you have this one," I say, pulling a Frank Ocean record out. He takes it from me and cleans it before putting it on. The first chords echo throughout the living room, as I take my seat next to him on the comfy rug.

"Where did you two go tonight?" he asks, trying very hard to hide the curiosity in his voice.

"We went to a diner," I tell him taking a small sip, I grab a fork and dig into the pie.

"May and Clay's place?" he asks, after he takes a bite himself.

"Yeah, how did you know?"

He grins, and in that moment he looks like the twenty-year-old surfer dude my mom fell in love with. "Best pies in Chula Vista."

"You still surf?" I ask, changing the subject, motioning to the picture of him catching a big monster wave.

He follows my gaze, "Yeah, that one was in Hawaii about ten years ago," running a hand through his long hair, he puts his cap on backwards again. We spend the better part of the evening talking about his early surfing days, and the moment he got hooked on BMX. I tell him about mom and my life in New York. I love our time together, it isn't forced or awkward, we're getting comfortable with each other again. And maybe one day I can tell him everything.

I wake in the middle of the night, I'm drenched in sweat and gasping for air. My legs are cramping and I need to throw up. My tongue feels like sandpaper. I try to move my fingers but I can't. I'm starting to get scared.

My breathing intensifies with every gulp of air I try to fill my lungs with. *No, stop it! I need to breathe. Breathe, Sky, breathe!* I order myself.

Then Hunter's smiling face flashes through my mind. The way his eyes light up when he's talking about something he loves. The way his lips curl into a bad-boy grin.

I wiggle my fingers and then my toes. Taking a deep breath I get myself under control. Pulling myself up and out of bed, trying to feel my way in the darkness, I stumble into the bathroom. I turn on the lights and grab the sink for support.

I want to disappear. I want to hide myself away in New York. I can't deal with the pain, love, rejection. Kneeling to the floor, I bury my head in my hands.

I cry until the morning light shines through the window.

Holding onto the banister with two hands I make my way downstairs, looking at the clock, it isn't even six.

I open the door and Jay is sitting on the porch wearing last night's clothes.

"Hey, Jay," I say taking a seat next to him.

Jay quickly runs his hands under both his eyes like he's trying to hide his tears. Hanging his head, he buries his face in his hands. "Hey, baby."

"Have you been sitting here the whole night?" I don't know what to do. I've never seen him like this before. He always carries himself with this happy go lucky surfers' attitude, like everything will work itself out. This time it won't.

"Yeah," he mumbles. "Damn it, Sky, you're as stubborn as I am. I thought last night you'd open up to me. And I told that boy to stay the fuck away from you."

I lean against the cushions. "Why are you mad? Because we didn't follow your rules? Why did you warn him about me?"

"You know why," he mumbles, locking eyes.

"No, I don't, *Dad*. Because he fucks around—is that it? Or you think I'm not good enough for your precious broken prodigy?" I ask, stumbling over my words, while I fight against my own tears. I know I should stay far away from Hunter. I don't want to hurt him.

"You're so far from the truth, kiddo, it's not even funny," Jay drawls, putting his baseball cap on backwards.

"Well, I was having fun with him. You should try it sometimes," I counter.

"You were having fun," he grumbles. "Does he know what's going on with you?"

I snort. "No. Do you?"

"I do, kid," he says, matter-of-fact.

"W... What do you mean?" my breath catches, my heart hammering in my ears.

"Your mom called me, sweetheart, after the last race. She told me everything."

"She *what*? That's why you said you weren't expecting me 'so soon' the first day I got here?"

"We still talk sometimes, Sky."

"Why?"

"Because we share a daughter, for heaven's sake," he seethes. "Fuck, kid, I'm going at this all wrong. What I mean to say is..."

"A daughter," I repeat, sarcasm ringing through my voice.

"Damn it, I'm your father and you should talk to me. You

can talk to me; that hasn't changed." He stands and leans against the railing staring at the track.

"I can talk to you?" I bite out. "I'm losing myself, Jay. How's that for conversation?" My voice breaks at the end.

"Sky, baby." His eyes mist over.

"Don't, Jay. It's the reason I wanted to come here, to mend things with you, but also to forget what my future is going to be like. Now I want to have a little fun along the way, and you want to take that from me," I say, knowing I'm acting like a spoiled little brat but I don't care. "You used to be so carefree; you didn't care about what other people did, and now I see you've become the father I never had for *them*, and it hurts."

"You know what hurts? You not letting me into your heart. Not visiting here for five fucking years. Why didn't you come? I was waiting for you."

"You want to know why I didn't come?"

"Tell me, I want to know." He kneels in front of me, taking both my hands in his.

"Because I didn't want to see how happy you were without me and mom," I whisper, unwanted tears filling my eyes.

"Sky, baby," he says.

"Why did you go? Why did you let us leave? W-hy didn't you c-come g-get me?" I stutter, tears streaming down my cheeks. "Why didn't you love me enough to stay?"

"Kiddo," he breathes, his face wet from his tears. "Because I loved you. I needed to let you two go, although it broke my heart," he says, dropping my hands and taking a seat next to me. "I was messed up back then. I was always drinking, partying and doing drugs. I wasn't the father you needed. I wasn't the husband your mother deserved." He takes a deep, shuddering breath before he continues. "I was living for myself and nobody else. I didn't care what happened as long as I won the gold. I stayed on top for years but it came with a price."

"What?"

"I lost you two. The day you turned six, I was too drunk to stand on my own two feet. Your mom went out to get your cake, but I forgot you were there with me in the trailer." He clears his throat a couple times before he speaks. "I was doing cocaine, and you somehow got your little hands on some leftover coke while I was passed out on the couch," he says, pinching his eyes shut for a brief moment. "When your mom came home, you were unconscious, and they had to rush you to the hospital where you stayed for a very long time. Child protective services almost took you away, and your mom never forgave me. And I never forgave myself."

"Jay, I didn't know," I tell him. Why didn't mom ever tell me? Why did she protect him all these years?

He shakes his head, holding my hand for a second. "Took a lot of convincing your mom to let you visit me during the summers. When you stopped coming at fifteen, I didn't blame you. I was still figuring out the man I was supposed to be. It took those boys and Mac to get my life in order. The company gave me purpose, and I was ashamed."

"Why?"

"You and your mom should have been my purpose. But Hunter became the son I never had, and I let you go again. And I'll hate myself for every minute of the time we have left, knowing the years we could have spent together."

I stop fighting against my tears because I know mom never stopped loving him, and I didn't either. Maybe being angry with Jay was easier; I could pretend I didn't need him. Like I convinced myself nothing was wrong with me for a very long time. I'm done pretending, I want to leave it all behind.

"What is going to happen, baby?"

"I don't know," I tell him.

He reaches out and holds my hand for a while. "I'm glad you came home. I'm so proud to be your father, you know that?"

I smile through my tears. He grabs the back of my neck

and rests his forehead against mine. "You are a fighter, like your mom," he says.

"When did you become so good with words, Jay?" I ask, flashing him a small smile while I wipe the moisture from my eyes.

"Are you gonna stay?" He sounds scared.

"I don't know," not knowing what to tell him.

"I'm not leaving you again. You can stay here forever," he whispers, kissing my forehead. "When you're ready to talk some more, I'll be here."

"What about Hunter?"

"What about him?" Jay asks, the muscle in his jaw twitching.

"We're friends, Dad, and I like spending time with him."

He snorts. "Be careful there, kiddo. He has a past."

"I will, Dad, and I know. He told me about his father, and being in NA."

He furrows his brows, like he's surprised. I stand and hug him. We hold each other for a while.

"I'm scared, baby girl," he confesses, tears pooling in his eyes.

I caress his cheek. "Me too, but I've felt more alive in the time I've been here than I have in years. I don't know how much time we're given, but I'm glad I'm spending it with you."

I let him go, he adjusts his cap and I smile; sometimes he looks so young.

"Hunter is fun," I tell him, biting on my lip. "Don't be hard on him."

"I know," he says. "Be careful, honey, with your heart."

I pick up on the pain in his voice. He closes his eyes, knuckles turning white while he grabs the railing. "We'll get through it. You're so god damn strong."

Tears sting my eyes, because I don't know if I am.

CHAPTER 11

Sky

"No, Hunt, that's not the fucking way to balance yourself," Jay yells up the starting hill. I've been sitting in the stands for the last hour, watching Jay and Hunter go at it during training. Drew hands me a coffee, and takes his seat next to me on the bleachers.

"Thanks, Drew," I say, focusing my attention on the men who are one swear-word each away from compiling their own dictionaries.

"Anytime," he answers, watching Hunter make his way down the hill.

Hunter comes to a screeching halt inches away from my father. "No, do it again," Jay bellows.

Hunter says something to Jay I can't make out. They look ready to punch each other in the face.

"That's trouble right there," Drew mutters under his breath, checking the messages on his phone, before taking a sip from his coffee.

"Is it always like this?" I ask.

He shakes his head. "Sometimes it is. They take it easier if Hunt's injured. He's lucky he only bruised two ribs, could have been worse. I'm glad we still have a couple weeks off though."

Hunter raises his shirt, and tightens the white rib wrap around his chest. He motions with his hands to the track. Jay shakes his head, and shows him something on his iPad. Hunter nods, running a hand through his long hair before wiping the sweat from his forehead.

"Are you liking it here, Sky?" Drew asks, while we watch them adjust something on Hunt's bike.

"I am," I tell him. "It's beautiful, and I like hanging out with you guys."

"Me too," he says, smiling. "Have you talked to Jay about what's going on with you?"

"What makes you say that?" I mumble.

"I've had my fair share of hurt, Sky. I know when someone is going through the same thing," he says, laying his hand on my shoulder.

"I'm fine."

"But are you okay?" he asks softly.

"Why?"

"The way you talk is different."

"What do you mean?" I ask, shifting uncomfortably on the bench.

"It's much slower than it was last week. Don't get me wrong, a man like me can appreciate a slow, husky voice, but ..." he says, clearly waiting for my response.

This is it. I brush my hair out of my face. "I don't know what to tell you, Drew."

"Is it bad?" he whispers.

I nod, not saying anything for a while as I watch Hunter laugh about something with my father.

"I know we don't really know each other, but I like you," Drew tells me, laying his hand on mine. "Hell, it's like I've known you for the better part of my life, with Jay telling me all these stories about you."

"I like you too." I chuckle. "And don't believe everything you hear."

"Hey, dipshit," Hunter yells. "Are you going to sit there all day?"

Drew flips him off and Hunter does the same in return, then sticks his tongue out at him and winks at me.

"I love that boy out there, and he likes you more than he wants to admit. I've never seen him look at a girl this way," Drew says, locking eyes with me.

"I like him too," it comes out like a sigh.

He nods, not saying anything for a while as we watch Hunter make his way down the starting hill and the track while Jay screams pointers at him.

"Hunter looks great out there."

"He does, doesn't he?" he answers. "He's beautiful."

I give him a look, and can't help but grin.

He nudges me in the shoulder. "Not like that. Don't get me wrong, I have thought about it, the boy's hot as hell. Everyone should get a man like Hunter once in their lives, but I guess you already did?"

"You mean with tats and all?" I say, my cheeks heating.

"That too." He smiles. "Someone who will love you no matter what. Be careful with him, Sky. He might act tough but his heart isn't."

Hunter makes his way over the hills. He turns a corner, and stops in front of Jay again. They both crouch next to the bike.

"What do you mean?" I ask, my voice low.

"I think you know. He doesn't often take a girl to the beach, and buy her dinner, or take her to his favorite diner. Let alone have an actual conversation with her. I've lived with the guy for almost ten years; he doesn't let people in easily. I don't know what happened with you two last night, but be careful."

My cheeks heat even more thinking about the way he kissed me, made me come.

"He likes you, Sky, even if you don't like him that way," he states, as I bring my wandering thoughts back to the present.

"I like Hunter, but I can't get involved with him." My voice is barely a whisper.

"Friends can have fun together," he tells me, winking. He drapes his arm over my shoulder, and hugs me tight to his chest. "Jay told me he's happy you're here."

I snort. "I hope so. We talked yesterday, but we still have so many things left to say."

"Give him time. He's a grumpy old bastard, but he loves you and has missed you these last couple of years."

"I missed him too," I confess, looking at my father. "I want him to know that."

Nausea hits, and I put my hand to my stomach, breathing out hard through my nose.

Drew lets me go. "You okay?"

"I don't know."

"You look kind of pale. Do you want some water?"

I grab the iron bench for support, closing my eyes for a couple of seconds, hoping the urge to vomit will subside.

"I'm going to be sick," I whisper. Scrambling to get up, Drew follows me to the side of the bleachers. He lays his hand on my shoulder, holding my hair back while I brace myself over the garbage can and vomit, my body heaving every couple of seconds. After what seems like forever, I wipe my mouth with the back of my hand.

"Here you go," Drew says, handing me his bottle of water.

"Thanks," I rasp, and take a small sip. The wind picks up, and a shiver runs through me. I'm sweating like crazy.

"What's going on?" Hunter asks, walking up to us.

"I'm okay," I reply, rinsing my mouth with water.

He locks eyes with me. "You don't look okay," he says, the crease between his eyebrows deepening.

"I'll be fine," I tell Hunter, my voice still hoarse.

Jay is right on his tail. "You okay, baby girl?" he asks concerned.

"Yeah, I'm fine," I hope the smile I give him is a little braver than I feel.

"Are we expecting company?" Hunter asks, motioning to the black matte Tesla making its way up the drive.

Drew shakes his head. "No," he murmurs, taking out his phone and scrolling through his messages. "No, nothing today."

The car stops next to the house and Tim steps out. I can't believe he's really here.

"Tim," I yell, closing the distance between us with a couple unsteady steps.

Spotting me, a look of concern crosses his face before his smile turns electric, and he heads in our direction.

"Honey." He kisses my cheek, and takes me into his arms, spinning me around. I close my eyes for a second, nausea hitting me like a tidal wave. Letting me go, he wipes my hair out of my face. "How are you feeling?" he asks.

"I missed you," I whisper, not wanting to answer his question.

"Me too," he says. Still holding his hand, I turn around. "This is Tim," I tell Drew, who followed me to greet my best friend. Drew keeps staring at him with his mouth slightly open.

"Hi man," Tim says, holding out his hand for Drew to shake. Drew's momentarily speechless.

"Drew," he finally answers, swallowing hard.

"I know," Tim replies, giving him a devastatingly handsome smile, and Drew actually blushes.

"This must be Hunter," Tim says, turning to him. "Nice to meet you, dude."

"Likewise." Hunter's deep voice rolls over me. Although his jaw twitches, and the look in his eyes hardens, sizing up Tim.

"Hey, Hunt," my father says, walking up to us, "we ain't done yet." Jay's eyes light up as if he recognizes Tim.

"Jay, this is Tim, my best friend from New York."

Both men shake hands. "Glad to finally meet you in person."

Tim nudges me in the shoulder. "Don't look so surprised, honey. I talked to Jay last night. Had to make sure you were doing okay."

A soft chuckle comes out of Jay. I narrow my eyes at him, then at my traitor of a best friend, and get two winks from both in return.

"It's only been a couple days, Timothy," I huff.

"I couldn't stay away," he says, kissing my temple.

"Do you have a place to crash?" I ask, looking up into his grey eyes.

"Yeah, I'm renting a house not far from here at the beach," he says, locking eyes with Drew, whose cheeks turn an even deeper shade of red.

"That's awesome," Drew responds.

"If you like, you can come check it out. Sky told me you guys all love to surf."

"I'd love to," Drew almost yells. Hunter and I chuckle. It's like looking at a cartoon while hearts float above their heads.

"We'll be done with training in an hour. Do you want to stay for dinner, Tim?" Jay asks.

"Thanks, Jay, I'd love that."

"D-oo you w-want a tour of the p-lace?" Drew asks, stumbling over his words.

"Sure," Tim answers. He squeezes my hand, leaving me alone with Hunter while he and Drew head back to the track with my father.

"He seems like a nice guy." Hunter grunts.

"He is," I answer, watching Tim talk to Drew.

"I especially like the way he kissed you."

"Jealous?" I ask, before I can swallow back my words.

"They seem to have hit it off." He motions with his chin toward our friends. They couldn't be more different, Drew wearing a Hawaiian shirt with shorts and flip-flops, his blond long hair finishing the whole "surfer dude" picture, and Tim, the outlaw businessman in his pristine suit and buzz cut.

"I hope they will," I reply, and he nods.

"I saw you throwing up. You feel better?" he asks, frowning.

"I'm fine, Hunt."

He keeps staring at me, raising one brow.

"But..."

"You looked good out there," I say, changing the subject.

The line between his brows deepens. "Thanks," he replies, running his knuckles over his stubble jaw, giving me a questioning look. "I'm trying. The ribs are healing. Drew and I even went surfing again early this morning." He laughs, pushing his hands down in his pockets. "More like Drew went surfing, and I hung out in the water, watching him catch wave after wave. I think our moment in the truck took a toll on me," he drawls.

I turn my face away trying to hide my glowing cheeks, but he reaches out and caresses the back of my head. He lifts my chin up, and we lock eyes. "Whatever it is, you can tell me, babe."

"Hunt," Jay yells, motioning for him to get a move on.

"That's my cue. Sure you're okay, Shorty?"

"I'm sure," I tell him, loving the way he calls me that.

"See you at dinner," he promises, turning around.

He walks away, rolling his broad shoulders.

"What's wrong with having a little harmless fun?" I try to convince myself.

Drew and Tim hit it off during dinner, and somehow he talks Hunter and I into going out with them to a bar. Mac and Jay will stay home and clean up.

I change into my favorite blue dress and head downstairs. I close the front door, and find Tim leaning against the porch railing.

"I've missed you, honey," he tells me, draping his arm over my shoulders as we walk to the garages.

"I missed you too, Timmy," I tell him, tightening my grip around his waist.

"Peter was asking about you. He said you're thinking about not taking your medication?"

"I stopped last night. I've been on them for months now, and I've got all the side effects in the books."

"Are you sure? Since you're having trouble with your voice? And you barely touched your dinner. Are your hands hurting?" he asks, pausing in front of the garage.

"I don't want to talk about it right now, Tim," I huff.

"We need to talk about it," he says, grabbing my arm.

"No." I shrug his hand off. "I want to have one carefree evening."

"Damn it, Sky."

"You think I didn't run every scenario through my mind?" I whisper. Drew and Hunter exit the garage and stop by the truck a good thirty feet away from us.

"It's your choice." He kisses my forehead. "Damn, girl. The pictures on their website weren't lying," Tim says, changing the subject, looking at the guys. I grin up at my best friend. "When was the last time you had sex?" he asks.

"I'm working on it," I blurt out.

He raises an eyebrow as a dare. "You slept with him already, didn't you?"

"Yesterday in his fucking truck, okay?" I mutter, smiling broadly.

"I'm so damn proud of you. Nothing wrong with having a one night stand. The way the guy kept his eyes on you the whole evening tells me he wouldn't mind you fucking him some more. I'm planning on getting mine tonight," he tells me, his Cheshire cat grin a mile wide looking at Drew. "What was he like, does he have more piercings than the ones in his face?" He asks, waggling his brows.

Hunter says something to Drew, and Drew rolls his eyes.

"We settled on being friends, Tim. And yeah he has more, nosy asshole."

"Damn, I always wondered what it feels like. And friends can still fuck, babe," he drawls.

"You guys coming?" Hunter asks.

Tim and I both look at each other, and I feel my cheeks overheat.

"What?" Hunter asks, frowning at us.

"Nothing," we both say at the same time.

"Get in the car," he orders, a crooked smile tugging on his lips.

We stop at a local bar not far from the house. There are a lot of bikes and trucks parked out front.

"What kind of bar is this?" I ask, following the boys out of the car.

Drew smirks. "A bar where they don't ask questions," he answers, as we follow him in.

The place is packed. Bikers, jocks, and surf dudes fill every inch of the floorspace.

They are all men. *Oh.* Is this what I think it is?

Hunter guides me to the bar while Drew and Tim hit the dance floor.

"What is this place?" I smile, looking around and loving the decorations that are sort of Playboy mansion meets biker bar.

Hunter orders two drinks, and a couple of guys stop by to say hello.

"It's a gay bar," he yells in my ear, trying to get his voice over Cher's as she sings about love. "When we're home, we usually stop by. May and Clay's son owns the place." He motions with his chin toward a big, burly guy slinging drinks behind the bar.

"Here you go, Hunt. Two Shirley Temples," the bartender says, giving me a wink.

"August, this is Sky, Jay's daughter," he introduces me.

"Nice to meet you," August says, shaking my hand. "Have a great time, and if this asshole gives you any trouble, I'll be happy to throw him out for you."

"Ha! Real funny. That was one time."

"Uh-huh. I got my eyes on you, pretty boy," August counters.

Hunter pouts like someone stole his favorite toy, and I laugh.

"Everyone seems to like you," I say, looking around.

"Yeah, too bad I play for the other team." He snorts.

I grin, taking a sip from my drink. "I didn't picture you as a Shirley Temple guy."

He rolls his eyes. "There's a lot you don't know about me, Shorty."

"I'm starting to figure that out."

He stares out to the dance floor and I study him from the corners of my eyes. "Did a lot of fucked up things in my life I'm not proud of, but living with Drew and Jay isn't one of them. I owe them more than my life." Tim spins Drew around on the elevated dancefloor, and Hunter laughs.

"We all deserve a second chance. Jay got one with you guys," I tell him.

Hunter nods. "Jay keeps lecturing me about second chances. But living with your mistakes, without letting them consume you, is something entirely different."

"I know," I say, taking a sip from my drink. "When are you going back on tour?" I ask, trying to push the conversation in a lighter direction.

Hunter tells me about the upcoming tour, clinics and sponsor events planned. I love listening to the way he talks. And for the first time in weeks, I'm starting to feel better. The numbness in my hands seems to subside, and I'm not so dizzy anymore.

"Look at them," he says, dipping his chin in the direction of Drew and Timothy, still dancing. Tim has lost his jacket, his white dress shirt straining across his muscled arms and chest.

Drew's hair is tousled and a satisfied smile lights up his face. I grin. The culprit seems to be Tim's hands. They disappear into Drew's long locks, and the boys kiss.

"That's nauseatingly sweet," Hunter mutters. "You wanna dance? And show those assholes how it's done?"

"Let's go." I smile. He takes my hand and spins me around until we're on the dancefloor.

I lose my footing.

"Whoa, you okay?" he asks, holding me close to his chest.

"Lost my balance there for a second."

He pushes my hair behind my ear, the pad of his thumb moving over my cheekbone.

"Hunter," I whisper, staring into his eyes. "I don't want to hurt you."

"Then don't," he counters, running his knuckles over my jaw. I tremble in his arms, and his eyes go big.

"I want to have some fun," I confess.

"I know. You've told me that a couple of times," he says, chuckling, still caressing my cheek. "We could take it to the bedroom next time?" he asks, resting his forehead against mine. "Let me kiss you again, babe."

I swallow hard. "I might let you."

His cocky grin is gone before I can blink, his lips meet mine and I have trouble standing on my own two feet again. First, he kisses the left corner of my mouth, then the right. His tongue dips in the middle, and his piercing pushes against my bottom lip. The way the metal teases me is intoxicating. Kissing me deeply he takes my breath away. My chest is rising and falling. My nipples stiffen from the sensation. His pupils are wide with lust as his ocean eyes track down my face and back to my lips again. He clutches my hand and closes the small distance between us, until we are stomach to stomach, his erection presses against my belly almost painfully, and I shiver in anticipation.

He tilts my chin up, leaning down his breath feels cool on

my wet lips, before he smashes them to mine. I melt into his chest. He tastes like cherries, and I groan, as our tongues tangle.

"Fuck, Sky," he murmurs against my lips. I moan into his mouth and he deepens the kiss like he feels it too. It's all consuming, and scary at the same time because I know I never want to kiss anyone else for the rest of my time.

Pulling back, a slow, roguish smile spreads across his lips.

"That was …" I whisper.

"Fun?" he finishes for me.

I'm speechless. I'm in big trouble. Our kiss wasn't fun; it was life-changing.

CHAPTER 12

Hunter

Straddling my bike, I slide my helmet on. Revving the engine, I ride off, leaving my sponsor's place in my rearview mirror. Why do I keep thinking about *her* face? The way her brown eyes would light up as we were talking about second chances, or how she melted in my arms when I kissed her? The time we fucked in the truck was mind blowing, but kissing her, really holding her and tasting her was like I took the first step to something new, something real.

Bill, my NA sponsor, knew something was up. I've never smiled so much in my whole damn life as I have since last night. For the first time, I told Bill I was sober—no drugs and no drinking. Damn, but I keep imagining her full lips kissing mine, even though I know having real fucking feelings for her could ruin everything between me and Jay by being with her. She can't be my new drug.

The light turns red and I come to a full stop, thinking about the way Sky looks at me with distrust, with curiosity, the way she furrowed her brow when she took her first sip from the drink I bought her. The way she sucked on the straw went straight to my dick.

I can't believe I kissed her like that. How she pressed her breasts against my chest was sexy as hell. I'd never gotten that hard before from a kiss alone. Bucking under me, and rocking her hips as I made her come in the confinement of the truck is one sweet memory. I'd never lost myself like that.

But the conversation I had with Jay about staying away from her keeps occupying my mind. And the way Timothy winked at me when he caught me kissing her forehead after our fucking epic kiss? What was that all about? Like the fucker knows something I don't.

She should stay far away from me—I've slept with too many chicks. BMX takes me on the road for the better part of the year. Maybe they're right. I'm an asshole. What will keep me from tossing her aside like I do with all the other women in my life? Chasing that gold has always been more important than building a life with someone.

She will. It echoes through my head. Something about Sky is different. It's like I care, like I'm slowly falling for her.

What the actual fuck?

A car honks behind me. "Move your bike!" A guy yells.

I look up at the green light. Shit.

Flipping him off, I speed away. Maybe some perspective will do me good.

I turn onto the road leading to the house, and she's sitting on the porch steps, reading a book. My hands start to sweat, and my heartbeat hammers in my ears. Maybe she is sitting there waiting for me. We didn't talk more about that night in the truck, and I don't blame her. It was just sex. But could that kiss lead to something?

Yeah, not in a million years.

But when I turn off the engine and swing my leg over the bike, she's watching me. And I have to turn my head away before she catches me swooning like a school girl. *Actually swooning damn it.*

Drew is already taking out the bikes for the kids. I love training the little hellraisers as part of the program we started a year ago. Most come from broken homes and don't have enough money to take the bus out here, or pay for a bike and gear of their own. I fund everything through my winner earnings; that's why it's important to keep fucking winning. For myself and those kids. I can't afford any distractions.

"Hey, man," Drew says, pulling me from my thoughts.

I salute him. "Need help?"

"No, think I've got everything ready. Get your ass over here," he jokes, slapping my butt.

"You know, pinching this ass is going to cost you cleaning duty." I laugh, shaking my butt in his direction.

"Will you ever stop making those lame jokes?"

"No," I state, trying to kiss his cheek, but he shoves me playfully away. "I think that's gonna be Timothy's job from now on, isn't it? Judging by the way you fucked him with your eyes."

"Jackass." Drew laughs.

I spend the rest of the day teaching the kids new tricks, and how to balance their bikes against the starting gate. Some get it on the first try; others need a little more work. But, all in all, it's a good day.

I say goodbye to the munchkins and head inside the garage, leaving Drew with some of the parents asking him questions about next year at the track. I'm going to buy new bikes for them—call it an early Christmas present.

As I brush the sweat from my forehead, Sky strides up to me. Faded, torn skinny jeans hug her curves, and her white shirt leaves little to the imagination. She twirls a stray lock of hair around her finger like she always does when she's nervous. *Why do I even know that shit?*

"Hey, you sleep okay?" I ask, sounding like a moron. Fuck, can she see from the look on my face I jerked off to the memory of her lips and the way her breasts pressed against my chest last night?

Throwing the soaked through towel on the workbench in the garage, I sigh. I need to figure my shit out when it comes to her.

She eyes me warily and nods. "Yes, I did. I had fun last night. But I thought about what happened in the truck—don't you think it was—"

"A mistake," I finish for her, judging by the look on her face.

"I'm not looking for anything serious right now," she tells me, her voice a little shaky.

"Me neither," I counter, not meaning either word.

"Okay good, friends then," she says, holding out her hand for me to shake. When our palms touch, I have to run my tongue over my lip-piercing, flicking it back and forth so my dick doesn't burst out of my pants.

"What did you want my help with?" I ask, trying to wipe the sweat from my fingers on the front of my jeans.

"Well, with Jay holed up inside with the accountant going over his books, and Drew busy with the kids, and Tim coming over later, I hoped you could maybe take me to the mall," she says, running her tongue over her lip and I have to stifle a groan.

"What do you need there?" I bark out.

She cocks her head, and those big brown eyes find mine. I need to take a deep breath to get myself together.

"None of your business," Sky says, her lips twitching a little, scanning the garage, while she pushes her hands in the pockets of her jeans. "You got some new bikes?"

"Some are, others Mac and I built from spare parts," I say, grinding my teeth together. Her fingers skim the workbenches and then over my dirt bike. I need to get out of here. The way her hand glides over the frame of my bike twists me in knots. Like her fingers are actually trailing a path over my dick.

"So, can you take me or what?" She smiles up at me.

"Why?" I really should swallow my tongue. Her voice brings me back to the present.

"Because I hate to drive a big truck right now." She flexes her fingers again.

"If you have trouble shifting or something you can take your dad's car," I grumble.

She bites her lip again, hesitating a second before answering, "I don't trust myself when I'm this tired."

I don't think this is such a good idea, after last night and the way her mouth tasted. Locking eyes, I say, "Sure, whatever. Will it take long?" I avert my intense stare, and focus all my attention on my boots.

"No, probably not," she murmurs. "I have to go to the pharmacy."

"Okay, but I'll have to be home around eight because I have something to do."

"Shouldn't take more than an hour." A beautiful, bright smile warms her face. "Let me get my bag and then I'll be right back. Thanks, Hunter, for doing this."

She turns around and walks into the house and I can't take my eyes off her perky ass. I shift from one foot to the other, adjusting my jeans. Sky gets to me; I like talking to her, and damn she's beautiful. Fuck, Jay is getting into my head, but what is wrong with doing a friend a favor?

She regrets our kiss, and the sex didn't mean anything.

End of story.

I run my tongue over my lip piercing before I scrub both hands over my face. I really need to wake up. Maybe it would be better to treat her like the asshole I am. I can't put my relationship with Jay on the line, or my training.

I groan, thinking about the way she tasted, how she cried my name as she came, and her little intake of breath when my lips touched hers.

Fuck, this friends thing is going to be harder than I thought.

Sky

Straightening my shoulders, I fix my beach hair and walk up to him, head held high. What's wrong with being friends with the guy? He's a great listener, and most importantly he gets my state of mind without even knowing he's doing it, with or without his dick.

Grinning I say, "Looking good." Checking out his firm ass straining against his black jeans, then up at his dirt bike.

He drops the wrench on his foot. "Motherf…"

Trying not to laugh, I ask, "Are you okay?"

"I'm fine," he bites out as he grimaces, his face turning red. Throwing the wrench in a toolbox, he shakes his head and narrows his eyes at me. Immediately, dark locks of hair fall in front of his eyes. We stare at each other, and smile at the same time.

"Did you want to take the motorcycle?" he asks, eyeing the dirt bike.

"Euhh, yes?" I don't sound too convincing judging by his grin.

Both of us stay put.

"Probably should take the car, right?" he asks, rubbing at the back of his neck.

"I'm not getting on your death trap," I tell him.

"Death trap?" he asks, the corner of his mouth hiking up.

"Your bike is daunting." I grin. I want to add *like you,* but I don't.

"Scared, Shorty?" A lopsided grin warms his face.

"That would be a yes," I mutter, not knowing if I'm talking about the bike, or him.

He runs a tattooed hand through his hair, his biceps flexing. "Too bad. It's like an explosion between your legs," he says, with a cocky grin.

A giggle escapes my lips, and I try to keep a straight face. Damn he's funny without even trying. My eyes travel to his crotch. I quickly glance up when he chuckles.

"Don't blame me, someone said it on TV. Couldn't resist repeating it in real life."

I shake my head. "Explosion or not, let's take the car."

"I promise you, one day you'll want to ride it again," he drawls.

"What?" My cheeks are probably the shade of a tomato.

He laughs. "The dirt bike. You did ride one when you were a kid, right?" He taps the seat with the palm of his hand.

"I did once or twice." Heat pools between my legs as his lazy hooded eyes lock on mine, and I take a deep, shuddering breath when he scratches his stubble. What would his two-day growth feel like on my skin if he went down on me?

I sigh. I should quit daydreaming about his eyes, and his abs, definitely his mouth.

He cocks his head to the side, his eyes boring right through mine, like he knows what I'm thinking. It scares the shit out of me. His tongue slides out over his lower lip, stopping before his piercing. I can feel my nipples peak in response. *Sneaky bastards.*

"Come on," he commands, his voice dark and hoarser than normal.

I nod. It's the only thing I can apparently do. Letting him lead the way, taking in his broad shoulders, the way his muscles flex as he walks to the car, makes me want to touch him.

And I don't know if this friends' thing is ever going to work.

Hunter

"You good?"

She bites on her bottom lip, straightening her spine, red creeping up her neck. I quickly focus on my Vans when she notices me checking her out. *Shit.*

"I am."

"Umm, I-let me open the truck," I stutter, opening the door for her and slamming it right into my knee. "Damn it fu…"

She turns her head away but I hear her chuckle anyway.

"You okay?" she asks, and I can still pick up on the smile in her voice.

"Yep." I stumble to the driver's side.

"Thank you," she says, I get behind the wheel and she gives me curious eyes.

"D…don't m…mention it," I stammer, and I put the car in drive. I hope the hard-on I'm sporting doesn't light up her radar. She doesn't need to know what our little pissing contest does to me.

Luckily, she is staring out the window when I take a right.

"So, we have some time to kill before we get there, what do you wanna listen to?" I ask, shifting gears and flexing my fingers.

"Anything eighties rock," she says, that smile of hers is a mile wide.

"Good choice," I say, changing the station to some Pearl Jam tune.

"Do you know where the mall is?" she asks, grabbing her phone from her bag.

"Yeah, been there once or twice. You know, babe, I have a life outside of riding my bike up and down the track." I wink at her.

"I never said you didn't."

Tapping my fingers on the steering wheel, I listen to Skid Row singing about remembering some long lost love. Damn, my mind immediately wanders to the days I spent strung out looking to score on that same street.

"You like it here?" I ask, taking a deep breath and trying to focus on the road, not the way her shirt hugs her curves perfectly.

"I do, more than I thought I would," she says.

"I'm glad you decided to come, even if we didn't get off to a great start at first. I guess we made up in spades," I mutter, checking my rearview mirror.

She holds my stare for a second before I focus on the road again.

"When I so eloquently ordered you to not stir shit up," I say, trying to clarify and digging my grave at the same time.

She licks her lip and says huskily, "You don't have to keep apologizing for that. It takes two to tango after all, and I guess we did stir shit up, didn't we?"

I bite hard on my bottom lip until I taste blood—anything to keep the bulge straining against the zipper of my jeans in check. *Stay focused. Don't smile. Whatever you do, don't smile.* When her lips hike up, I'm already meeting her halfway. I check the rearview mirror passing a car and spot the stupid grin on my face. *Fuck.*

"I'm going to be in so much trouble if you keep looking at me like that." I grunt, not meeting her eyes. The sooner I get this over with, the quicker I can go to an NA meeting before I want to kill someone. Clutching the steering wheel hard until my knuckles turn white, I hold back a growl. When I turn to her, a sly smile has formed on her lips.

"So, where are we going besides the pharmacy? Are we gonna rob the place? My balaclava hasn't gotten much action in a while," I tell her, winking.

Her big innocent eyes roam over my body, and her cheeks flush. "No, just the pharmacy, and the natural remedy store." She pauses, stretching her back, and of course she catches me staring at her cleavage.

"Great, I was hoping for something more exciting like the Bass Pro Shop," I joke, rolling my eyes.

She gives me a sideways glance. "You never know what I might find once we're there." She stops talking and stares out the window, still smiling.

After about five miles of silence, and listening to the radio, I take the exit leading to the mall. "No hunting and fishing gear then?"

"Maybe underwear, since you destroyed my favorite pair." Her voice is small and filled with mischief.

I slam on the brakes before the stop sign. The picture of her wearing those skimpy black panties I ripped off her flashes before my eyes. She has to brace herself to stay in her seat, as I hit the gas pedal.

"Fuck my life," I mumble. The grin on her face is pure evil.

"You don't have to come with me if you don't want to, you can stay in the car," she purrs.

Parking the truck near the entrance, I ask, "And do what? Twiddle my thumbs?" I turn toward her. The thought of her in some white lace outfit makes me want to slam my head against the steering wheel. *Count to ten and think about something non-sexual. Changing the tires on the truck. Checking the oil, mowing the lawn. So...not...working.* She hasn't stopped staring at me, and judging by the look on her face, she is totally messing with me.

"You're pulling my chain, aren't you?"

She giggles. "You're such an easy target, but now I think about it, I do need a new pair of pajamas."

"Lord have mercy," I mutter under my breath.

"You could stay here and do nothing or you could come with me." She lifts a brow like a dare. "But if you're too chicken, then stay in the car." I follow her out of the truck.

"No one calls me chicken shit," I yell, slamming my door shut, and catch up to her.

"Didn't think Mister Tough Guy had it in him." She grins.

"Yeah, well, whatever," I mumble, gazing at my shoes as I walk to avoid ogling her again.

She gives me a sideways glance I try to ignore, but my lips hike up anyway.

I hold the door open for her to enter. The air-conditioning inside the mall cools me instantly.

"Please let this nightmare end," I joke as we walk inside.

"Oh, lighten up," she teases, linking our arms together.

"Wait here while I pop into the pharmacy," she tells me, guiding me to a lounge area where a couple other guys are waiting. She pushes me down and I take a seat. "I'll be right back."

She leaves me alone and enters the store.

"Girlfriends, man. They like to shop," one of the other guys says, staring at a game he's playing on his phone.

"Yeah," I return. I slump down further into the seat and close my eyes hoping to get myself under control.

Someone grabs my shoulder and instinctively I hold the fucker's wrist ready to strike.

"You okay?" she asks, clutching a paper bag in her arms.

"I'm sorry, I was just resting my eyes for a bit," I mutter, letting her go. Standing, I yawn.

She grins up at me and I return her smile.

"Come on. I checked out the map, and I know where to go." She beams, tugging on the sleeve of my shirt.

I follow her through the mall. A couple of young girls pass us and giggle. They give Sky jealous looks, and I don't know why it makes me smile even wider.

"Oh my God, do girls always stare at you like that?"

"Like what?"

"Like they want to have you for dinner?"

I chuckle. "Probably dessert, don't you think. Or the appetizer in your case, babe."

She snorts and studies me from under those thick black lashes. "If you say whipped cream, so help me." She swallows, staring at my pierced lip. "There's the store," she says, pointing, and her cheeks flame red.

"Really? I thought you meant a Walmart or something." I've never been in a shop like this before, all pink and shit, and full of scraps of lace that pass for lingerie. Man, this is not a good idea, imagining her in those little, teeny, tiny... *fuck*.

"Are you coming, or are you scared?"

I didn't know I'd stopped walking. I flash her my best devilish grin. "No." I don't sound even remotely like myself.

"Well, let's go then."

Swearing under my breath a couple of times, I follow her in like a damn puppy.

All the girls in the store gape at me when we enter.

"What do you think?" Sky holds up a white sexy ensemble from a rack.

I swallow. "Is it hot in here?"

She gives me a sideways glance, taking a basket from one of the sales girls. "Don't think so," she answers, still grinning.

I follow her around the store like a dumb-ass. She grabs some black and red lace panties and bras. I have to bite the inside of my cheek so I don't explode from the sexual tension coursing through my body.

"If this is your version of foreplay, I'm in," I murmur, my eyes zeroing in on a tiny red whatever-it-is, letting it slide through my fingers.

She turns around and I immediately let go of it, like I've been burned. My gaze zeroes in on a display with sparkly SpongeBob SquarePants underwear. I grab one that looks like a boxer short, and drop it into her shopping bag to piss her off.

"Do you need help?" a girl asks.

"No, I'm good. Thanks though," I answer. Taking a step, I almost bump into a display. I catch the mannequin midair before a boob slams into my head.

Sky snorts while I stumble, trying to put the display back into its designated place.

"I'm going to try these on," she briskly says, and I want to strangle myself with a purple thong in the middle of the pink store. "Are you coming?"

"I wish," I mumble, adjusting the front of my jeans and nod to a couple salesgirls when they smile at me.

I knock on her door.

The store girl gives me a warning look. I wink at her. She blushes, and luckily, leaves the dressing area.

I knock again. "Is this some form of torture?" I ask.

"Torture?" Her voice is all innocent.

"Are you doing this to piss off Jay, or me?" I ask, and I hear a chuckle from behind the door. "Sky," I roar, slamming my palm flat against the frame. "Did Jay tell you what we talked about?" I ask.

She is quiet for a while. "What about Jay?"

"I made him a promise," I confess.

"You did what?" she asks, and I pick up on the anger in her voice.

"Can we talk about this later," I mutter, "when we're alone?"

"No. What did he say? I want to know," she grits out.

"He asked me to leave you alone..." I begin.

"He did *what?*"

Sky opens her dressing room, and she almost gives me a heart attack. She is wearing the all-white ensemble. I grab hold of the doorknob before my legs give out. Her scowl and the way the little lines around her eyes crinkle tell me she is pissed and amused as hell, and I like it, means she cares enough to hate me. *Yeah, she got me good.* I let my eyes roam over her from top to bottom, from bottom to top. *Do not stare at her boobs, for God's sake, do not stare at her boobs!* They're perfect, the way I fucking like them. I got a small taste in the car, but now I want to suck on them the whole damn night. Maybe I can make her come just by doing that?

Before I know what I'm doing, I let my gaze travel south. *I'm screaming in my head to get a fucking grip.* I can't turn my eyes away.

"Come on, babe, close the door. Friends should never see friends wearing that shit," I mutter, trying to keep my voice steady.

"You already did, and yeah, friends kiss each other and have mind blowing sex, and don't really talk about it again," she counters, sarcasm ringing through her voice. She taps a finger on her mouth, those red lips fixed in a naughty smile.

"Mind blowing? I—you and I ..." I stutter, not knowing what to say or do, other than drool, apparently. She's a centerfold. All legs, toned tummy, and fuck me, her tits are barely staying in the lace bra thing she's got on. I can see the outline of her pussy through the silk panties. A dark line presses against the flimsy fabric. I love it when chicks forgo the wax, pretty old-school but it turns me on. I rake my fingers through my hair, trying to get my body and mind under control.

"What did you and Jay agree on before you made me come?" she asks through clenched teeth. "I'm not a fucking toy you play with," she huffs, slamming the door in my face.

A couple of girls exit their dressing rooms. One of them murmurs "jerk"; the other says "asshole."

"Ladies," I say, tipping my imaginary hat.

Turning around, I slam my fist on the closed door again. "Let me in," I rasp.

She snorts.

"Come on. Hell, I don't know, let me explain. The fucking part was awesome, you know, Shorty, it was so much more. And our kiss was nothing like I expected. If you wanna have another night of fun wearing that shit, I'm down..."

She opens the pink door, wearing an all-black lace thing that makes me choke on my tongue, and almost makes me come in my pants. Before I can apologize, she grabs me by the shirt and drags me into the dressing room, closing the door behind us. She shoves me against the mirror.

"I don't think this is store policy..." I begin.

She cuts me off by pressing her finger in my chest. I pinch my eyes shut for a moment before I blow my load.

"Listen here, buddy." She taps her finger on my pecs, pulling me out of my dirty thoughts. "I'm not a kid anymore. Jay doesn't get to decide what I do, and neither should you, Hunter. I thought you were the wild one here, or some shit, who doesn't care about what others say," she shrugs. "But I guess not."

I growl, torn between kissing her and walking away, but something makes me stay. "You want me to betray a promise I made to your father?"

"Technically, you already did. I thought you wouldn't have a problem with taking your pants off for me a second time, but then you said us kissing was a mistake, and now you're telling me it was *awesome*. But the way you keep looking at me tells me something else," she grounds out.

I'm stunned. She's asking me to fucking sleep with her again? "So you're saying it wasn't a mistake?"

"No, not for me." The anger no longer evident in her voice. "Use me like one of your French girls, Hunter," she says, a soft smile playing on her lips.

"Leo didn't say that shit, Shorty," I tell her, already grinning from ear to ear.

"You were the one who said I needed to have a little fun," she winks.

"I did, didn't I?" I mumble under my breath. "Think good and hard about what you're giving me. I take what I want, and I'm fucking demanding when it comes to shit like this."

She pushes me again. My spine presses against the cold mirror.

She grins. "Why don't you kiss me and find out for yourself?"

"I don't know how to say no to you," I whisper. The corners of my lips hike up when she tries to get in my face. She has to stand on her tiptoes to reach my chin.

"Then don't," she purrs, caressing my cheek. Her fingers

skim over the line of my jaw, leaving little currents of electricity where she touches me. Resting my hands on her waist, I love the feel of the tiny lace straps digging into her hips as they slide against my fingers. I pull her toward me and she doesn't resist. Her body trembles, heat radiating from her. Her scent is intoxicating, vanilla and wildflowers.

Swallowing, I hang my head when she closes her eyes. She is offering herself to me, for fucking real. I rub my thumb over her bottom lip; her breath catches. I want to lean forward and—

Someone knocks angrily on the door. We both break free from each other. "No more than one person in the room at a time," a stern female voice warns, "or I'll have to call security."

"Sorry," Sky says, laughing, focusing on the bulge clearly present in my jeans.

"Give us a minute," I grunt, adjusting my belt.

"A minute," the voice on the other end reminds us.

"Actually, I think I need more than a minute," I huskily say, turning around and leaning my forehead against the mirror.

Sky licks her lips. Our eyes meet in the reflection. That sexy grin of hers makes me want to sink to my knees, rip the panties off her, and sink my tongue between her tight little pussy. I want nothing more than to drape her creamy thigh over my shoulder and bury my nose between her legs, smelling her arousal before I lick up and down her slit. Over and over, until she's slick and wet, sucking on her clit while she's begging me to make her come. I place my palm on my crotch, the way my dick is straining against the zipper is almost enough to push me over the edge like some pimple face teenager.

"I think I have to buy these now." She grins, holding up the lace panties.

"I guess you probably should."

We leave the store after Sky pays for the pieces. The woman ringing up the tab even says, "Enjoy," directed at me. I am this close to answering, "I fucking will."

Without speaking, Sky and I head out to the car. It's already dark. She takes her seat next to me. I don't know what I should say, so I keep my mouth shut.

I start the truck to fill the silence with something other than my beating heart.

"That was fun." She giggles, her smile naughty.

"Sky, you mess with my head," I say, heading to the highway, while she turns on the radio and Post Malone blasts through the speakers.

"Think about it," she tells me, getting comfortable in her seat, grinning from ear to ear.

I try to hide the smile on my face with my left hand, checking her out. My dick twitches again. Jay is going to fucking kill me when I give in to her again.

CHAPTER 13

Sky

When we get home, Hunter helps me with my bags. "Here you go. If you want me for anything else let me know," he rasps. "I'm leaving tomorrow evening after the kids' lessons for the race on Saturday. You're meeting us later, right?"

"Yeah, I am, and thanks, I will definitely let you know," I tease him, swinging the shopping bag back and forth in front of him. I like the crinkle that appears between his brows every time I tease him. His cheeks redden. I love that I can make the bad boy of BMX blush like this. "Good luck with the race."

"Don't need luck," he promises, running a hand through his hair. "Check you later, Shorty." He heads to his front door, a roguish smile tugging on his lips.

"Bye, Hunt," I whisper, and head to the back porch, willing my legs to move.

The next morning I'm waiting at the track when Jay walks up to me. "You sleep okay, kiddo?"

"I got your message late last night. Why did you want me to meet you here, Jay?" He's probably going to give me hell for going out with Hunter again.

"Look," he says, pointing to the kids pedaling their little bikes down the track. Hunter and Drew are standing to the side, watching them. "That out there is all I have. This house, the track—those boys are my life."

"Great. Thanks for the info, Dad," I say, sarcasm ringing through my voice.

"They give color to each day. But you are the reason for my life. I know we haven't really talked to each other in years, but know this," he says turning to me. Reaching out, he brushes a stray lock behind my ear. "I love you, and whatever is going to happen, know I will never leave you again. I wanted to tell you, I should have told you this the moment you got here."

"I should have come sooner, Dad," I can't help it when my tears start to fall. "I'm angry," I whisper, wiping at my eyes. "I'm scared because I keep thinking about the things I should have said, and the things I didn't do when I had the chance. And now it's too late."

"It's never too late, kid. I should know."

"Isn't it? We've lost so much time. Those moments are gone, and we're never getting them back."

"I know, honey." He takes me into his arms. "You're still a long way from the finish line. You're stronger than you think."

I smile through my tears, leaning my head against his chest. "Thanks, Jay." He kisses my forehead.

"I would take your pain away if I could," he rasps. "I know he would too, if you'd ask him to," he tells me, and I hear the reluctance in his voice. "I'm still your father, but I'll take a step back when it comes to Hunt."

"Thank you," I whisper, hugging him tight.

"You deserve some light in your life," he tells me, brushing his lips over my forehead again.

Hunter

The next day

It's practice day when Neil, Ryan's trainer and manager, walks up to me.

"Have time to talk?" he asks, taking a seat outside the trailer.

"What do you want?" jumping out, I try to wipe the grease from my hands.

A couple of girls walk by, waving at me. I nod to one I used to hang out with between the sheets.

"Ladies," Neil says, watching them walk away, pulling his gold-rimmed sunglasses from his nose.

"Spill, Neil. What do you want?" I ask, getting impatient with the guy.

He runs his fingers over his goatee. "You're doing good, Cole."

"No insults? No 'I'm gonna report your ass?'" I mimic his voice and shake my head. "Man, you're slacking."

He doesn't laugh, only eyes me. "I'm here to make you an offer," he drawls.

"One I can't refuse?" I finish for him, snorting.

He shakes his head, probably not understanding the reference. *What an asshole.*

"One that will get you more chicks." His voice is slick.

"Tell me something I don't know, and I'm good man," I mumble, waiting for him to stop talking.

"Have you ever thought about branching out?" he asks, pulling up his sleeve and showing off his gold Rolex.

"Branching out?" What the hell does he want from me?

"Yes, more sponsor deals, a modeling contract, the works," he says, sounding excited.

"A modeling contract? Man, come on." I push my hair back. The dude is full of shit.

Neil takes out his wallet, eyeing the stack of one-hundred-dollar bills in there, then he hands me his card. "Here, I got a new number. Since our deal hasn't started yet, I don't see why I can't earn some money from you now. Start recouping on my investment."

"I don't have time for that shit. I'm still with Jay."

Neil holds up his hands. "For now," he says, walking away.

I keep staring at the card and his name in gold letters on it. "Neil!"

He turns around.

"You know what my deal is with Jay, don't you?"

He flashes me his too-white smile. "Jay isn't here right now, is he? And I haven't forgotten *our* deal. Have you?" He spreads out his arms.

Watching him walk away a second time, I mutter, "No."

I stare at my reflection in the window of the bus. Okay, maybe I could make some money on the side. Girls like the bad-boy BMX package. Fucking depressing to think about it. But whatever, my dick doesn't complain so I shouldn't start. At least, I didn't, before those brown eyes began haunting my dreams.

Shaking my head, I kick my boots against the bus. Whatever. Screw Neil. I'm not going to become a centerfold. *Fuck that shit.*

I hop onto the bus. Mac is reading a magazine, and Drew is busy working on his laptop.

"What was that about?" Drew asks.

"Nothing concerning you," I tell him, parking my ass on the leather couch, twirling the card in my hand.

"Hunt?" he asks.

"What?" I grunt, searching for a pack of Lucky Strikes.

"You wouldn't really be thinking about leaving Jay?" he sounds concerned.

I throw Neil's card on the table toward him. "Fuck no," I state, shaking my head.

I'm not going to tell Drew about the deal I made with Neil when Jay was burning money faster than it was coming in, and how I used the advance to sponsor the kids. I'm in deep, and even with my winner's earnings, I'm never going to be able to pay Neil off. "You know he offered me a modeling deal."

Drew snickers. "With your ugly mug?"

"Yeah, I know." I grin, staring out the window and lighting one up. "Shit is fucked." But I don't know what or whom I'm referring to.

I spend the whole night awake in my bunk, thinking about her. Jay and Sky meet up with us the next day, a couple of hours before the race is planned to start. I try to focus on the task at hand, but I can't seem to find my center.

"You okay, man? You checked your bike ten times already," Drew says, while he goes over the videos of my races from this morning on his iPad.

"Five minutes!" Jay yells into the trailer. I give Drew a look.

"We're almost ready," Drew answers for me, pleading with his eyes. "Chill the fuck out."

I grab my gloves, check my helmet, and suddenly Sky and I having sex in the truck flashes before my eyes. I should have never fucked her, and made things more complicated with that kiss than they already are. What the hell am I doing with her?

"Screw this," I huff, scratching the side of my shaved head.

"What?" Drew asks.

"Nothing," I mumble. "All fucking A-OK." I flash him a mocking smile and pull out my piercings.

I crack my neck, following Drew out to the tracks. I need

to get my head straight. I keep thinking about Sky, fucking her, and the way she tasted on my lips. What the hell is she doing to me? It's the last race of the season before we have eight weeks off, I have to make up a couple of cancelled runs that were supposed to happen before we went on tour in Australia and New Zealand. I can't wait and dread it at the same time. Time off always makes me nervous, makes me think too much, leading me to go off the tracks—literally.

I walk to the starting gate, bike in hand. I check if my shoes will click in the pedals the way they should. I spot Ryan on my far left. He flips me off, and takes his position next to me. Fucker is not worth it. Flashing him my pearly whites, I notice Jay and Sky in the crowd watching me.

The two commentators start introducing us. I raise my hand when my name gets called. Luckily, Jay got me out of the charges that were pending after the fight at the last race, but he made a deal with Neil. If I ever punch Ryan's lights out again, I will be in serious trouble. Jay doesn't know about the deal I made with Neil on the side, and I need to keep it that way.

"Nice side piece you have," Ryan says, without looking at me.

"What the fuck are you talking about?" I grit out.

"The hot beach babe. If you're not screwing her, I will."

I almost fly off my bike to punch him in his smug face, but a referee holds me back.

"Watch your goddamn mouth, Ryan."

"She smiled at me earlier. I'm gonna tap that ass."

"You're dead," I bite out. I slap my hands on my knees trying to let the memory of her moaning my name fade away. I'll be damned if I let a fucker like Ryan have his way with her. I stretch my neck trying to focus. I'm on the road to pure gold. I've won the previous two races today. I've checked on the other riders from the sidelines and made mental notes while I watched them moving over the track. Some of the younger guys have real grit.

I focus when the referee says, "Riders, ready! Watch the gate!"

Taking my position, I stand and click my feet on the pedals. When the beeping ends, I'm off. I take every turn, and angle my bike in the air to gain speed, and there is the finish line. I can taste victory.

Ryan is making headway; we're now shoulder to shoulder with one hill in front of us. The crowd is screaming and the commentators are yelling, and then he angles his bike into me. I need to redirect my line immediately, losing traction on the turn. I have enough speed to recover, but not enough to bridge the gap between me and him.

My bruised ribs ache. I bite my lip until I taste blood. "Motherfucker," I huff under my breath, and I know he's winning. The audience roars and his bike finishes first, and I'm a split second behind him.

I slam both my hands on the handlebar of my bike, take off my helmet, and brush the sweat from my brows.

Jay walks up to me. "You almost had him, if you kept your focus," he says, disappointment ringing through his deep voice.

I shake my head and kick my BMX to the ground. "Fuck!" I yell before I pick the bike up, and make my way to the trailer.

Sky congratulates me but I ignore her. I'm not used to losing. Throwing my gloves on the workbench, I growl out, "Shit!" I'm so incredibly mad at myself for screwing with my number one position.

"What happened there?" Drew asks, hopping into the trailer.

I shake my head. "Nothing, man. I wasn't fast enough," I swear, slamming my hand against the wall. I fucked it up gloriously. The adrenaline still courses through my veins, and I spit on the ground.

"Probably not a good idea to go looking for trouble, dude. I recognize the murderous glint in your eyes," Drew mumbles.

Grabbing the side of my body, I know he's telling the truth.

"Can't argue there. I didn't sleep last night, and maybe I overdid it when lifting weights because my ribs hurt like a motherfucker," I grunt, laying my hand on his shoulder to steady myself and scan the backstage area for Ryan.

Fucker is standing against his truck, talking to Sky. The son of a bitch is leaning into her like he's ready to kiss her. *That little piece of shit is probably doing it to get back at me.*

I ball my fists and jump out of the trailer. Drew yells at me to stop.

"Fuck you, Drew," I shout, making my way to Sky. *Not fucking now.* Gritting my teeth, I'm ready to pop a vein in my neck.

Sky

I watch the heat from beginning to end. Jay kept explaining the intricate details of the race and the backstory of the riders, their stats, and how Hunter should be riding. I listen to everything he has to tell me. Hunter looks amazing, waiting up there with his fellow seven competitors. He raises his hand when the commentator introduces him as one of the best in the world.

As the race progresses, Jay and Drew exchange worried looks with every hill Hunter takes.

"He's taking too long," Jay yells in Drew's ear. Drew nods, crossing his arms.

"Too long for what?" I don't know what they're talking about.

"He needs to pedal harder." Jay points to Hunter. "He's losing. Shit!" Jay slams his hands on the railing.

Shielding my eyes against the sun, I follow Hunter making his way down the track. "But, Jay, he's in front."

Jay shakes his head. "There," he tells me, pointing to another rider in blue behind Hunter. "He has more speed."

And sure enough, the guy passes Hunter with two-tenths

of a second to spare. Hunter slams his hands on the handlebar when he comes in second.

"I can't believe it," Drew mumbles.

Jay rakes his hands through his hair. "This is going to cost us big time." He spits out the word, "Fuck!"

I follow them backstage. Drew walks up to Hunter and they start arguing about something.

The race is still flashing before my eyes when the winner walks up to me.

"Hey." He shakes my hand, introducing himself as Ryan. "You new here?"

I nod. "I'm Jay's daughter."

"Oh, Jay's daughter," he drawls with a smile too bright for my taste. But then he seems to register my body language.

"And you're with Hunter?" he asks, a curious undertone in his voice like he can't believe it.

I shake my head. "No, we're friends."

"Yeah, I also look at my friends the way he checked you out before the race. Dude never looked at me like that when we were friends." His smile is kind, like he's remembering something from his past.

"You were friends?" I ask.

He tousles his blond hair. "We were, before the gold became too important for both of us."

"What happened?" I ask.

He grimaces and places his hand on my shoulder. "Frankly, I don't know. He..."

Someone pushes me out of the way.

"Get your hands off her," Hunter bellows.

Before I know it, Ryan punches Hunter in his chest. "Fuck you," Ryan shouts.

"Right back at ya," Hunter roars. In the blink of an eye, they start wrestling and rolling around in the sand.

"Fucking teenagers," I yell, trying to get their attention, but of course, beating the living shit out of each other is much more interesting than listening to me.

"Dad!" I scream, looking around for help.

Jay and another man come running, and after several tries, and dodging a couple blows, they get the boys off each other.

"Don't fuck with him, Cole," the other man roars.

"Stay out of this, Neil," Ryan yells at the guy.

Both Ryan and Hunter are bleeding when they are finally separated. I follow Hunter to his trailer, leaving Jay behind to smooth things over with Neil.

"Hunter, what was that all about?" I ask, laying my hand on his shoulder. My heart is racing in my chest, and I am having trouble filling my lungs with air. He shrugs my hand off, wiping the blood from his nose with his sleeve.

"Hunter?" I plead, trying to catch my breath with my hands on my knees.

People are staring at us; some riders shake their heads. Hunter stops, straightening his shoulders and balls his fists. Turning, he stomps toward me, stopping inches away from my face. I stand my ground as he stares into my eyes, swallowing hard when he opens and closes his fists, towering over me.

"Don't, Sky. Not now," he warns with a growl in his voice, those ocean eyes holding me captive.

I hold up my hands. "Don't what?"

He takes another step, and I don't move an inch. "You... don't...know—shit!" He bellows, his nostrils flaring.

"Don't know what?" I ask, my voice small.

He drops his chin, the warmth of his shallow breath tickling my parted lips. But his eyes are still hard. Slowly, his gaze moves to my mouth, his tongue darting out and touching his lip piercing. I anticipate the touch of his lips on my own. My stomach does a little back flip.

"Don't look at me like this. I don't fucking deserve it," he warns, turning around.

I let the breath I was holding escape and watch him walk away from me as I whisper, "What look?"

During the drive home, Jay and Hunter don't talk to each other while I sit in the back seat. Jay parks the truck behind the bus, Drew and Mac are already waiting for us. Without saying anything, Hunter jumps out.

"Hunter!" Jay orders.

Hunter shakes his head and heads into his apartment, slamming the door shut. Dad watches him go with a disappointed look on his face. He grabs the steering wheel hard until his knuckles turn white. "Damn that boy."

"Do you want me to talk to him?" I ask, leaning forward in my seat.

He shakes his head. "Better if you didn't," he says, a warning in his voice.

"Come on," I say, getting out of the truck. I don't want to tell Jay that I might be a part of the problem.

He nods, throwing his baseball cap on the passenger seat. "Okay, but be careful. The kid has a freaking temper."

"And you don't, Dad?"

Passing Drew and Mac, I smile. They give me reassuring nods while they open the back of the trailer.

I knock on Hunter's door. He doesn't answer. After a couple of seconds, I knock again.

"Go the fuck away!" he yells. Something smashes against the wall. Taking a step back, I open and close my mouth, debating what to do. I have no idea how to calm him down. Should I leave him be or not?

"Come on," Drew says, putting his hand on my shoulder, leading me away from the door. "He needs some alone time."

CHAPTER 14

Sky

Hunter never showed up for dinner, and after the guys go to bed, I make my way toward his room. Guitar music is traveling through the closed door. I recognize the haunting melody from Outlaw, one of my favorite bands. I knock on Hunter's door, and he stops playing.

"Go away. I told you to fucking leave me al…" He opens the door, clutching the electric guitar in his hand.

I tear my eyes away from the instrument, and my breath catches in my throat. He's bare-chested, hair still wet from a shower, his tattoos and piercings on full display. He takes a step forward, and I back away from him.

"Sorry, thought you were Drew busting my balls yet again," he drawls, running his fingers over the strings before setting the guitar in its holder. He turns off his amplifier.

Putting my hands in my jeans pockets, I look around his room. "Drew is out with Timothy."

"Great, that's fucking awesome, another poor asshole that's gonna get his heart broken," he says, sarcasm underlying every word.

"Tim's not like that."

He scoffs and searches the coffee table that's littered with junk for something. After rearranging the mess, he finds what he was looking for—a pack of cigarettes.

He lights one up. I have no idea what I should do... walk away or go into his room.

"Want something to drink?" he asks, the cigarette dangling from his mouth as I lean against the door I just closed. This bad boy picture is too much, and I can't suppress a grin, which he returns.

"Sure." I nod, walking around his place, taking it all in. The black and white pictures on the wall of him surfing or riding his bike. The books lying around. I scan the titles—Oscar Wilde, Jane Austen, Kevin Powers, and a book of poems by Mark Strand I recognize.

I tug at the collar of my shirt. A clammy film coats my skin.

"God, is it hot in here?" I ask.

"Yeah it is. I need to fix the air-conditioning. Haven't gotten around to it."

I let out a shaky breath. He holds up his hands. "Before you tell me it has been over a hundred and twenty degrees for a week now ..." He locks eyes with me. "Drew already beat you to it." He winks and I can't help but smile.

He takes two glasses from his little kitchen and pours some pink lemonade in them. "Drew made it."

I glance around his room, focusing on anything but him. He has a small living room, an open kitchen, and a screen obscuring the rest of his place, probably hiding his bedroom.

I don't know what to do. I lean awkwardly against the armchair of the couch, trying not to focus on his nipple piercings. I'm failing, of course; the guy is half-naked and when he turns away from me, I can't help but stare at the big tattoo of a skull and some writing on his lower back. In the truck he kept his shirt on, I only felt his nipple piercings then. They're even hotter up close. I bite my lip, peeking up at the ceiling. That's the safest option.

"Want to sit?" He nods toward the couch, handing me the drink.

"Sure," I say, smiling, taking my seat next to him.

He stretches out his legs, smoking the last of his cigarette before grinding it in an ashtray. He looks like Ryan Gosling in *The Place Beyond The Pines*.

He waggles his eyebrows and smiles. "See something you like?" he asks, tapping his fingers impatiently on the glass.

Shaking my head, I set my cup on the table and stand. "I now know you aren't still beating your head against the door, so I should probably go."

He's on his feet in a second, blocking my only exit. "Shit, Shorty," he mutters, his eyes darting around the room, almost as if he's uncomfortable. Goose bumps break out on my arms. "Sometimes my mouth has a mind of its own. And I say stupid shit."

"Say or do?" I taunt, giggling.

He winks at me. "Both." His voice low and smoky.

I'm so irritated with myself, I should stay away from him. I'm playing with fire, thinking about the way his lips pressed against mine, or the way he moaned my name. I hope he's going to kiss me again, but he turns his head away, breaking the spell.

My eyes travel south, zeroing in on his nipple piercing, making me think of all the other places he has a piercing. Running my tongue along my bottom lip, I quickly divert my gaze before my cheeks turn any redder than they probably already are.

"What is Timothy's deal?" he asks. Dipping his chin toward the house, he crosses his arms. "Did he give you drugs before leaving with Drew?" he growls, leaning against the wall, his angry voice going right to the spot between my legs. I squeeze my thighs together. What the hell is wrong with me that him going all drag-you-by-the-hair-to-my-cave makes my heart race?

"That's none of your business."

His laugh is mocking. He brushes both his hands through his disheveled hair. The muscles in his ripped arms flex in all the right places. My eyes go big, and I place a hand on my stomach, silently cursing the butterflies in there. I shouldn't be having these feelings. Not now, not when it will lead to nowhere. My eyes skim over his dark jeans, ripped at the knees. I spot the tattoos on his ribcage, and his neck. I furrow my brows. There's a razor blade tattooed in black below his jaw. I never really noticed it before.

"Why did you get that?" I ask, pointing to his neck, squinting.

He flashes me a sly grin. "Got it on the road."

"Does it have any meaning?" I ask, meeting his eyes.

"The past." He turns his head away, like he's embarrassed.

"Really?"

He adjusts the front of his pants, his hand lingering on his waistband. "Yeah, really."

"You're not going to tell me more, are you?" I ask.

He matches my smile. "You may think I'm…" He snaps his mouth closed.

"What?"

"It's to remind me the cut you inflict on yourself is always the deepest. The rest, what others do to you, is only superficial."

I'm speechless.

"Fuck," he says, his bright blue eyes darting to my mouth. He wets his lips. "Hadn't told anybody that."

"I'm glad you told me."

His gaze darts over my face. "Want to sit outside so we can talk? We could go to the track. It's clear out—probably can catch a couple stars if you're into that kind of shit." He pulls on a black shirt, combing both his hands through his unkempt hair. "Man I sound like a fucking…shit." He grins, putting on his Vans. "I promised Drew I wouldn't swear so much around people."

I stifle a giggle. "And how's it working out for you?"

He rolls his eyes. A lopsided grin warms his face. "Fuck if I know. You win some, you lose some." He winks at me. "So, outside—better than sitting in this pigsty?" he asks, straightening his shoulders.

I take a deep breath, trying not to pay any attention to the butterflies fluttering around in my stomach. "Sure," I say, following him.

In silence, we walk to the track. He helps me get onto the hill. "Watch out. It's pretty steep here," offering me his hand.

"Th…thank you," I stutter, grabbing hold of him. He stares at our linked hands. When I smile, he lets go like I've burned him.

Plopping down next to him, I shiver when the cold sand hits my butt. Hunter's right. It's a clear night, and there are so many stars illuminating the black sky.

"Right there is Orion," Hunter says, pointing to a cluster of stars.

I lie back, taking in the vastness. "Where do you think we all go?" I mutter under my breath.

He shrugs. "Into the great unknown."

"I'm being serious," I say, playfully slapping his shoulder.

He turns his head toward mine, his breath ghosting over my lips. "My father always said a place where you're free, like in that song," he says, staring at the sky.

"'Free Bird', you mean?"

"Yeah. How did you know?" he asks, matching my smile.

"Jay loved to listen to Lynyrd Skynyrd when I was a kid. He gave me this necklace." I show him the silver bird. "Jay wanted to be free. I guess he found freedom out here with you guys," I whisper, swallowing back the lump in my throat.

"I guess he did," Hunter says, staring at me. When we lock eyes, he whispers, "I'm glad you're here, Shorty."

"Me too," I confess.

"I like it, and it pisses me off at the same time. I can't seem to figure you out."

"Keep telling me about the stars, Mister Lightyear," I joke.

He chuckles. "Right there is the Big Dipper." He points upward.

"I like it when you call me Shorty," I say. My skin heats when he skims his fingers over mine.

He shakes his head, a soft smile playing on his lips before he goes on. "You should blame your dad if I don't get the constellations right. He's the one who took me and Drew out here almost every night to gaze at the stars." He stretches his big body out next to me.

"What happened today?" I ask, turning on my side.

He stares at his inked hands before closing his eyes for a moment. When he opens them, a cloud rolls across his face. "Nothing, really. I malfunctioned. And then Ryan was messing with my head, talking trash how he was gonna fuck you, and that took me on a trip down memory lane right back into your arms."

"I'm sorry, Hunter," I whisper.

"Don't be," he mutters, placing both hands behind his head, focusing on the sky again. "But, babe, having a preview like that, fucked me up a little. I know our screwing was a one-time thing, but that damn kiss in the bar made it seem like there could be something more. I don't know. I'm not good at this shit."

I smile, glancing up. After a while, I get the courage to ask him, "Why did you fight him?"

He snorts, "We go way back, Shorty, and frankly when it comes to you, I get fucking possessive."

The way his deep husky voice rolls over me has me biting back a moan.

"Me and Ryan have a couple of unresolved issues, besides you." He shifts uncomfortably. "And I didn't like the way he was leaning into you."

"Nothing was happening, or going to happen."

"No?" he asks, sarcastically.

"No, nothing," I say, my hands shaking a little.

He glances at my fingers when I ball my fists. "You okay?"

"I'm fine. I should probably call it a night. It's getting late."

He sits, and reaches for my hand, but pulls back at the last moment. "Please don't go."

I sigh. "Why, Hunter?"

"You know why," he husks out, holding me captive with his intense stare. His eyes travel to my mouth. He smiles, dimples popping. "Give me a chance, Shorty, let me in," he says, taking my hands and placing them on his chest.

Closing my eyes, I feel his heartbeat slamming against my fingers, and whisper, "I don't know if I can."

CHAPTER 15

Sky

He holds my gaze and I actually miss the piercings in his eyebrow and ears. Luckily, the ones in his lip and nose are still there.

"Why not?" He sounds angry, hurt by my dismissal. "I know, because of Jay." He pauses. "But Jay, he…"

"It's not because of Jay," I say. He takes my hand in his, slowly tangling our fingers together. It scares me, what I'm starting to feel for him. "It has nothing to do with Jay," I repeat.

"Was it the fucking sex? I know I was a little too *Fifty Shades*," he says.

"You weren't, and I loved it."

His thumb strokes my skin and I almost come apart right there on the track. Bringing my hand to his mouth, he skims my fingers along his cheek to his parted lips. I close my eyes, wanting to remember this moment. He shifts against me, the warmth of his breath tickles my cheek. Our gazes lock as the sweet scent of him engulfs me. I lick my lips, and a satisfied smirk lights up his face. He leans in and brushes his piercing across my parted lips. "Shorty," he breathes.

"Hunter," his name comes out like a plea. I try to ignore my throbbing pussy, I'm already so wet.

He pulls away from me with a sigh. I take my bottom lip between my teeth, and he kisses every part of my mouth again. It turns from playful to demanding. His tongue plunges in, exploring me. I want him, groaning I let go of my control. We are a tangled mess, and I whimper from the way his tongue piercing pushes against me. A shudder runs through my body. My fingers disappear into his hair, tugging on the strands, pulling him closer. He slowly moves his body on top of me, his erection digging into my thigh. His dark, hungry gaze devouring me. He grunts in my ear, and I arch my back, wanting to feel the connection.

"Sky, is this okay?" he asks a little breathless, his lips skimming my ear.

"Yes," I whisper, my heart pounding.

"Fuck." He bites my lip, pulling a little then tracing it with his tongue.

"Take me back."

His gaze searches mine. He pushes himself off me, putting all the weight on his arms. "You want to head to your room?" he asks, his deep voice vibrating through me.

I brush my hands through his hair to the back of his neck. "No, take me back to your place," I whisper, pulling him up by his hands.

"Fuck, babe, you mess with my head." He smiles, reaching out to grab my chin. He makes a sound deep and low in his broad chest before pressing his lips to mine. We leave the track and stumble into his room, almost falling over his skateboard.

"Would have cleaned up if I'd known this would be going down," he rasps.

"Yeah, keep spinning that line," I say, smiling against his

mouth. I help him out of his shirt, my fingers dancing over his arms loving how he feels under my fingers. I trace the details of his tattoos.

"They're beautiful," I whisper.

He grunts, not believing a single word I'm saying judging by his smile and eye roll.

"They are," I repeat, meeting his stare, and I swallow hard, anticipating what he's going to do.

Slowly, his hands skim over the sensitive skin under my bellybutton, then up to my ribs as he pulls my shirt over my head, his fingers dancing over my waist as he does it. Gliding his calloused hands from my neck to my bra he traces the contours of my breasts. My heartbeat is pounding in my chest.

Touching my nipples through the lacy white fabric, he bites his lip. "You have no idea what you're doing to me, do you?"

I shake my head and my nipples immediately stand to attention and I crave more. I run my hands slowly up and down the hard ridges of his tattooed arms. Our eyes lock, he leans forward and runs his parted lips over my collarbone. He nibbles my neck with his teeth and I shudder as he presses a kiss on my shoulder. My hands tighten in his hair. Reaching out he holds the necklace I'm wearing in the palm of his hand, asking, "What about Jay?"

"Let's not talk about my dad."

He grins. "Sorry." He shakes his head, and a lopsided smile warms his handsome face. He stares at me, and I begin to squirm as his eyes rake up and down my body. Reaching out for me, I smile when I notice his hands are shaking a little.

"Fuck, Sky, I can't get enough of you," he murmurs against my neck. He runs his tongue over the skin below my ear, and I tremble with desire.

My head falls to the side, "Don't stop, Hunter."

Groaning, he scrapes his stubble over my jaw, "Not planning on it, Shorty."

He guides me through his apartment, and we stumble to

his bedroom, our hands exploring each other. When my legs hit the bed, he slowly pushes me onto the sheets. Like a predator, he moves on top of me. I love the way his mouth tickles over my naked flesh. I bring my hands to his ass and knead it, pressing my hips into his growing erection.

My panties are drenched with need, my clit pulses, wanting to feel his touch.

"Hunter, please," I gasp, panting.

Tracing my breasts, his fingers move over the indents of my ribs to the button of my skinny jeans. He teasingly brushes his fingers over my zipper, applying pressure but not enough. I want him deep inside me and he knows it.

I arch my back leaning into his touch. Still kissing me, he moves his lips to my stomach, rubbing his stubble on the sensitive skin there. Tracing my bellybutton with the tip of his tongue, I lift my back, loving the way he runs the metal ball over my burning skin. Tugging on my jeans, he stops and takes my All Stars off, along with my socks. He moves back up my body and his lips find mine, kissing me hard. He growls, running his teeth along my shoulder, as his fingers trail to my neck and he buries his face in my hair. He inhales deep. Using his lips and his tongue, he draws a line down my throat. On instinct, my head tips back and my chest pushes forward, opening myself up and giving him full access to my body. Heat flares along my skin everywhere he touches.

"Oh fuck," it comes out as a sigh, as his soft mouth closes over my nipple and he sucks hard. It's a direct line to my clit and I grab his shoulders, holding on to keep from flying off the bed. His hand comes up and squeezes my other breast as his tongue continues to torture my nipple. Flicking back and forth I feel the peak harden. He makes a noise in the back of his throat grunting his approval. "So pink and hard," the vibration from his voice shoots through me and my fingers grip his hair, I'm not sure if it's to hold him back or pull him closer. He draws my attention by stopping what he is doing and peeks up from my breasts. They feel so heavy and my nipples are tight little buds, poking into the air almost begging him not to stop.

His hand glides over my skin until it reaches the button on my jeans, scanning my face the whole time. His fingers work fast and the button pops free of its hole.

"Shit," I place my hands over his, stopping him before he can pull down my jeans.

I don't know what he reads in my eyes but he pauses.

"What?" A slow grin spreads across his face.

"I didn't have anything to wear except this." I laugh

He frowns, and continues tugging my jeans over my knees. He throws them in the corner, and when he spots my underwear, he chuckles.

My hands fly in front of my eyes to mask my embarrassment.

"Hey." He pulls my fingers away, kissing each palm. He locks eyes with me again, and covers his mouth with his hand, hiding his grin. I'm wearing a high-waisted white boxer-short covered in sparkly SpongeBob Square Pants characters. He looks more closely, his maverick smile making me giggle. "Is that Mr. Krabs? I tossed them in your bag for fun when you were torturing me in the store."

"You're crazy," I moan.

"Shorty, look at me," he drawls.

I can't meet his eyes; I'm too embarrassed.

"Sky," he orders.

Reluctantly, I meet his gaze, rubbing my sweaty palms on the sheets.

"I love them." He traces the top of my panties with his calloused thumbs. "Wait till you see me in my Supernatural boxers—then we can form a little team. The Gives No Shit What We Wear club." He flashes me a cocky half-smile.

I reach out and pull him on top of me. He slips a hand

around the hollow of my neck and stares deep into my eyes before kissing me gently, sucking on my bottom lip, his long hair tickling my collarbone.

He moves one hand down between my legs, and runs his fingers over the drenched fabric of my panties. Pushing it to the side he dips his finger inside my wetness. He uses his thumb to make slow circles over my swollen clit. I press into his hand, never breaking eye contact until sparks start to fly.

"Sky," he orders, and my eyes shoot to his. His are shining with lust, and hunger is reflected in those ocean eyes.

A proud smirk curls his lips as he pinches my throbbing nub. "Come against my hand baby." The orgasm rips through me out of nowhere as I thrash and roll my hips upwards never wanting it to end, "Oh fuck, Hunter, fuck," I chant, the sensation making my toes curl.

"That's the plan, babe," he drawls, licking my release from his inked fingers, a look of awe and tenderness on his face.

I pull him toward me by the dog tags he wears around his neck, and trace the inside of his throat with my parted lips. He swallows heavily as I kiss his jaw. I let my tongue glide along the shell of his ear, and he shivers. Encouraged by his reaction I bite down lightly on his earlobe. He groans and pushes his crotch into mine, our eyes meet again.

"You sure?" he asks, cupping my cheek. The slow, burning sensation of having him here with me hits me more than the heat and wetness building between my legs.

"I am," I tell him, as he stands, watching my reaction while he drags his jeans to the floor, leaving his boxers on. The outline of his hard dick makes my mouth water. Sitting up I let my fingers move over his tattooed stomach, tracing the lines of his six-pack, he trembles and looks at me with his lust-filled eyes. The pad of his thumb moves over the inside of my arms, he covers the healed puncture marks from all the IVs and the blood tests with his palm. For a moment I freeze.

He frowns. "You okay?" he asks, searching my eyes for answers, but I can't give them.

"I am now," I whisper, I run my hand back up his chest and wrap it around the dog tags pulling him into me.

Moving on top of me, Hunter supports his weight on his arms and grinds his hips against mine. His breath hitches, and his lips part slightly as I smooth the hair from his forehead. My eyes dart from the bulge straining against the fabric of his boxers to his eyes. Rolling his arousal against my thigh, he slips his hand through my hair, pulling my head back.

"Take off your bra," he commands, his voice rough and thick, letting me go.

I arch my spine and honor his request. He follows my every move, staring at my exposed breasts, he grins. "Tell me what you want," he says, his eyes searing me.

"I want your mouth, your dick, everything," I confess, fighting against my embarrassment.

His answering smile is sexy as sin. My fingers clutch on the strands of his hair, drawing him into me. He leans his forehead against mine, making me meet his eyes as he presses his pelvic bone hard against my clit.

Wanting more, I rock against him, moaning his name. He grinds his erection into me making sure I know who has the upper hand. My wetness builds and soaks through my panties. I close my eyes as a tingling sensation starts up in my stomach.

"Fuck, babe, you smell sweet," he grunts, grabbing my chin. Taking my lips between his, Hunter sucks gently, then harder as I breathe into his mouth. I move my tongue over his piercing and he growls, his dick pulsing against my thigh. With his left hand, he trails a path over my waist before linking our fingers together, holding my hand prisoner above my head. I stare up into his eyes. His eyelids are heavy when his finger teases my exposed left breast. He blows cool air on the tip as I push up, and takes my nipple between his lips and bites, sucking me into his hot wet mouth again. We both groan, and my pussy is screaming to be filled.

"The way you're rocking yourself against me isn't going to make me put my dick into you faster, Shorty," he teases, leaning up on his elbows so he isn't crushing me with his full weight. "This is called foreplay, babe, ever heard about it?" His eyes fill with mischief as he moves south to my stomach and dips his tongue into my bellybutton, and I'm shivering under him.

He chuckles when I narrow my eyes at him, trying to catch my breath.

"Hunter," I plead, as his finger traces the line of my panties, his hair brushing across my skin.

"Yes?" he purrs, his hands sliding between my legs and pushing them apart. He kisses the inside of my thighs. His lips linger on my skin, prolonging the sensation.

"I'm ..." I bite my lip when his finger slides into my underwear and across my center, pushing in. He pulls my underwear to my knees so I can't move my legs, the slight tremor that runs through my body makes him chuckle.

"You're dripping wet." He growls staring at my pussy in awe, his pupils blown wide with lust. His pierced mouth is inches away from my pubic bone, and I want nothing more than to press myself against his mouth. Instead he holds me down with both hands, and leans forward and parts my lips, blowing cool air against my engorged clit. Tracing his tongue down my center, he dips inside licking and lapping at my cream. My toes curl, and I pant as he presses the metal ball against my pulsating nub. I grab his long hair between my fingers, pushing and grinding against his face.

His eyes roll up to meet mine, and holy fuck it's hot as hell.

"Fuck, Shorty," he growls, lapping lazily at my clit. "I can't get enough of your taste," his voice is hoarse as he moves up my body, his smile holding me captive. Cradling my face, he kisses the tip of my nose. He draws in a ragged breath when our eyes lock.

I stifle a groan, swirling my hips, wanting more. I beg him to bury his big cock deep inside me, to stretch me, to fill me. He places his thumb on my clit and starts to move both fingers inside, like a scissor, rubbing my inner walls and getting me even wetter.

My legs buck off the bed, "Fuck, Hunter," I grumble, wanting to chase my building orgasm. I squeeze my eyes shut for a moment and I almost reach the edge. He stops abruptly. I open my eyes as he pushes both fingers into his mouth and sucks.

"P-lease H-unter." I press my legs together, wanting to speed up my release. He pulls his fingers out of his mouth.

Parting my legs with his knee, he shakes his head. His eyes are darker than normal. I lean back, watching him as his hands move over my body. Reaching out I let my fingers glide through his hair, holding onto the long strands.

"You're so beautiful," I whisper. His cheeks flame a bright shade of red. He shakes his head a little, like he's embarrassed.

"Glad you like what you see." His voice is thick with emotion. Running my nose over his jaw, I inhale his scent, and then kiss his cheekbone. I caress him through his boxers and his cock twitches as he pushes against my fingers. He moans into my mouth as he lets me explore him.

I dig my nails into his broad muscular shoulders. He growls, piercing me with his intense stare. After tracing the line of his spine to his lower back, I take both ass cheeks between my hands and pinch a little while he grinds his pelvic bone against mine again.

A broad smile spreads across his face. "I want to take it slow," he says, his tongue between his teeth.

"Don't," I tell him. I want more, I want him, everything that he can give me.

"I like it when you talk dirty," Hunter's muscles flex as he leans over me, opening his drawer. His pierced nipples are inches away from my mouth. I can't resist a taste. I take one between my lips, and suck while I twirl my tongue around the metal. A hiss escapes him when I bite the piercing with my teeth and suck on it.

"Fuck me." He growls, pushing his hard-on against me again. I whimper as his heat slides over my sensitive, swollen flesh. He knows what he's doing, judging by the wild look in his eyes. Then I notice the string of ten condoms he obviously pulled from his bedside table, and I start to laugh.

"Thought you might get lucky?" I clasp my arms and thighs tighter around his waist.

He smiles at me, his hair falling in front of his eyes. "Come on." He laughs. Slowly, he tears one condom off with his teeth, his eyes heating with want.

"I never thought I would get this lucky again," he whispers, waggling his eyebrows.

I close my eyes when his nose skims my neck and he inhales, branding me with his stubble, scraping my soft flesh.

"You're beautiful, Shorty." He grunts. "Fuck me. You're everything."

I open my eyes, and his gaze roams across my face. I swallow hard before I lose my nerve. "Make love to me, Hunter," I husk out.

His eyes go big. He is the first to smile, and I melt when he presses his mouth to mine. Soft then harder as he traces the swell of my breasts. His lips follow a path to my nipples. Taking one hard peak in his mouth, he licks it slowly before sucking it between his teeth and biting. My butt lifts off the mattress as the tingling sensation hits my toes. His scent surrounds me, and I'm intoxicated by his blue eyes and the maverick smile playing on his lips.

My hands pull at his boxers, trying to get them off, needing to hold him in my hands, all of him. To feel him bare against me and, judging by the moist ring clearly present against the cotton of his underwear, he wants me just as much. I swallow hard when I see his piercing outlined against the fabric.

"In a rush, are we?" He bites his lip, a brightness in the blue depths of his eyes.

"Lose those." It comes out like a plea.

"My pleasure." He grins, taking off his boxers. His dick springs free. My mouth dries staring at the big purple head of his hard cock as he rolls the condom over it. That night in the truck, everything happened so fast. Now I want to savor each moment, and I'm going to take my time. Fuck, he's beautiful, hard and ready. I want to ride that edge with him.

He pries my panties off, murmuring sweet words the whole time he's doing it, his eyes lingering on my pussy, as his hands leave dents in my hips.

He licks a path down my jaw, his mouth and tongue exploring every part of me. I part my legs even more, giving him better access. Arching my back I push myself into his waiting wet mouth. Hunter thrusts his tongue deep inside me, licking and rubbing his stubble against my quivering thighs while I grind myself against him. I moan into the pillow when the metal ball presses against my clit.

"Fuck, I can't get enough of your sweet pussy," he says, his voice husky against my throbbing mound.

"Hunt," I gasp, fisting the sheet.

He moves up and kisses me again. Licking his lips, Hunter rolls the condom further over his erection. God, he is so beautiful and strong—pure muscle. He nudges my entrance. I part my legs and hug them around his waist, locking my ankles together.

My heartbeat thunders throughout my head, and my body shudders as he enters me slowly. Inch by inch he fills me to the hilt. My inner muscles stretch around him.

His breath tickles my neck, and pain mixes with pleasure while I squirm under him. I grab his muscular shoulders, running my nails to the swell of his ass as he settles himself between my thighs, catching his breath.

Dropping his forehead against mine, he looks down at our

entwined bodies. I love he's shaking just as much as I am. Tilting my chin up he looks at me, while he throbs deep inside. I watch him, taking in every emotion reflected in his eyes, the sounds he makes, and each stroke of his hand through my hair.

He slowly starts to move. A look of raw pleasure flashing across his face. He hits that one spot deep inside with his piercing, and I cry out in pain.

He stiffens and stops.

"You okay?" he whispers, pulling out a little. His breath coming out in sharp pants.

"Yeah, I'm good. Fuck, you're so big," I groan, when he pushes in again. His lips curl into a full blown cocky smile.

"Does it hurt more than before?" he asks, keeping most of his weight on the front of his arms. A hum rumbles from his throat. His scent, a mixture of cigarettes, motor oil, and sweat, leaves me breathless for a moment.

"Yes, but it's so good," I whimper into his mouth, locking his lips to mine. It hurts and aches at the same time, like this is the first time we've made love.

I tilt my hips up and he disappears inside me again and I swear under my breath, I'm so full, too full, but it's so perfect. Wanting him to take me over the edge with him, I thread our fingers together. His eyes flare for a brief second as my slick pussy walls hug his shaft. Breathing hard through his nose, he stretches out on top of me as far as he can, crushing me with his weight, and I love it.

He moves again, pushing up my leg, going even deeper, still kissing me until I'm seeing stars. We hold each other's gaze and it is the most intimate thing I have ever experienced—him watching me, me watching him as he picks up his pace and takes it slow again. I shiver when his cock jerks deep inside me. My orgasm is starting to build, and he knows it too. His breathing becomes shallow and his thrusts jerk.

I close my eyes, rocking harder against him.

"Open your eyes, Shorty," he commands through clenched teeth. Gripping my left knee as he slams into me. My eyes fly open, and his nostrils flare. I love the way his sweat drips between our stomachs; and I taste the salt on his lips.

"Hunter," I whisper, cupping his jaw, as his hair clings to his forehead.

He's still for a moment. "Yes?" His breath comes out labored against my parted lips. He isn't giving me everything he wants, judging by how his body and arms tremble.

I want to tell him what is happening to me. "I…"

He pushes into me again, much harder this time, chasing his own release.

"Make me come, Hunter, please." I close my eyes.

"Look at me." His voice is soft, and I do. He's still seated deep inside me, filling me, stretching me to the point of pure ecstasy. "You're so fucking tight." He grunts, biting my lip and holding it between his teeth. He lets go, and grinds himself in deep, his fingers digging into my flesh.

"Can you feel it, babe? Let go. Let go," he says, kissing me hard, his pelvic bone making contact with my clit.

It's so tight, so dirty the way that piercing glides against my walls. My inner muscles stretch around him, milking, chasing my orgasm. He pushes into me, over and over until my eyes roll into the back of my head. I hold my breath as the burning sensation washes over me, and I come, screaming his name.

He thrusts again, swearing until he finds his own release, and in that moment, I know I'm falling for every broken part of him. Shouting my name, he collapses on top of me.

I push his drenched dark hair out of his eyes. He kisses my shoulder and pulls out. I turn and caress his cheek, tucking a stray lock of hair behind his ear. His eyelids seem heavy as he tries to catch his breath, his chest heaving. Leaning into my touch, he smiles when I lay my hand on his chest.

"I'll be right back," his voice low and husky. Kissing my

forehead he sits up and takes off the condom, ties it, and walks gloriously naked to the bathroom.

After he flushes the toilet, he comes back and lies next to me. Craving his strong body I turn to him, and drape my leg over his stomach, resting my breasts against his tattooed chest.

He kisses my forehead, and I can't help it when tears start to fall from under my closed lids, because I'm falling for him harder than I ever thought I could.

"Hey?" His eyes roam over my face and body. "Did I hurt you, was I too rough?"

I shake my head, staring into his ice blue eyes. His calloused thumb wipes away the moisture.

"No. You made me feel, Hunter," I whisper.

"Feel?" he asks, an adorable crease appearing between his brows.

"Something I never experienced before." I kiss him and he leans into me.

When we come up for air, he frowns. "Are you okay, Shorty?"

"I am now," I tell him, laying my head in the crook of his neck, licking the place where I feel his pulse.

He shivers, and presses his lips to my temple.

"How did I get so fucking lucky," he asks, searching my eyes for something I'm afraid to give him. Because once I do there is no going back, for either of us.

"How about a round two to make you feel really lucky?" I ask, feeling bold. His body shudders and he laughs before he disappears under the sheet, grinning mischievously.

Hunter

Watching her sleep, I trace my fingers over her breasts, her face, her spine, every soft curve.

My dick twitches from the connection. I imagine her bucking under me while I pound into her from behind, screaming my name in pleasure as I ram into her tight pussy. Christ, all the things I'd like to do to her flash before my eyes like a porn movie. I want to lick her until my face is wet with her juices. I want my fingers to plunge into her one by one, to rub her clit with my thumb until she shatters. *Fuck,* I even imagine my dick disappearing into her tight asshole, owning her, fucking her raw until she's begging me to let her come.

Christ, what the hell are we doing? I sit back against the headboard. I don't know where this is going, but I do know I want this girl for all she is, hoping she takes all I have to give her. Even if it's fucking little.

Sky's eyes flutter open. Her hair is all tangled, and looks well fucked. She makes my dick hard just from looking at her.

"Want something to drink?" I ask, leaning over to kiss her forehead. My lips linger while I breathe in her scent. I can smell myself on her and I love it.

"Yes, please," she whispers, turning onto her stomach, the sheets covering her naked body.

I grab a glass of water from the kitchen. She takes it from me and starts to drink. Her eyes never leave mine. She sets the cup on my nightstand and I jump back into bed, pulling her against me. She lays her head on my chest and I grab her hand and kiss her palm, tracing the lines. Fuck, she's so small and almost fragile.

There are bruises on the inside of her arms. I frown, staring at them.

"Why are you looking at me like that?" she asks.

I trace the purple marks on her body. "What happened there?"

"Nothing," she answers, her fingers trailing over the tattoos on my chest, and the red angry scar on my lower abdomen. I know she is keeping secrets from me. Most of the time, it's the other way around with the chicks I fuck. But with them, I'm already out the door before they ask me to stay.

My fingers skim her bruises, and I don't care how long it will take for her to let me in. I'll wait, because for the first time in my life, I want to stay.

"Want to listen to some music?" I ask. I hate the quiet, even with her here. There's too much to think about.

"Yes." She nods, resting her hand on my chest again.

"You pick," I tell her.

Taking the phone from me, she scrolls through my Spotify list. She presses play, and I smile as the first chords of one of my all-time favorite songs fills the room. "Free Bird" by Lynyrd Skynyrd.

Her lips press against my pecs and my dick twitches.

"I do have happier songs on there." I laugh.

"No," she says, closing her eyes, snuggling against me. "This is perfect."

Her mouth moves as she whispers the lyrics.

"I love this song," she tells me, resting her hand on mine. She holds my stare humming along with the tune.

She closes her eyes. Tears escape from under her lids, and she quickly tries to wipe them away. I want to ask her what is going on, but something makes me hesitate. Sky falls asleep with her head on top of my chest. Turning the surround sound off, I trace my fingers across her ribs and sing the words to the song in my head. She is everything, I think as I close my eyes. Shorty is going to be my last race.

The next morning, I wake with a start. Stretching, I try to take Sky into my arms but my hands grab nothing but air. Sitting up, it hits me. I'm alone in my bed, the tangled sheets and her lingering scent the only testimony to what we did last night.

I brush my hair out of my eyes and groan, hating my empty

room. After stumbling out of bed, I take a shower and throw on a shirt and shorts. I swear under my breath. Why did she leave before I woke up? Glancing at the clock, I sigh. It's almost nine in the morning. Time to teach.

Drew is already waiting at the track when I head outside. "Everything okay?" he asks, lifting an eyebrow.

I nod. "Yeah, fucking fantastic."

"Who bit you in the ass?" he asks.

I shake my head, giving him a knowing smile. I take the clipboard from him, and ten little kids walk up to us with their parents in pursuit.

"Hunt?" Drew asks. "What's up?"

"Nothing. Let's get on with it." I grunt and say hello to the rascals. Drew rolls his eyes, and leaves it alone for the rest of the morning.

The lesson goes by in a blur. While me and Drew explain a couple of new techniques for the whole damn hour and a half, I think about Sky. Even when I'm saying goodbye to the munchkins, my mind is somewhere else.

"Hunter?" one of my best pupils asks.

"Yeah, Cody? What's up?" The kid follows me around while I make sure each piece of equipment is accounted for.

"Can you help me on Friday with the new jump we tried out?" he asks, lowering his voice, probably trying to sound older than his nine-year-old self.

This kid is focused on the track. Off the track, his mother has a difficult time keeping him in check. I'm probably the only male figure who he actually listens to.

"Sure, man, we can go over it again," I tell him. He's young but already a promising rider, and most of the time, also a pain in the ass who beats me when I'm not paying enough attention. I saw Cody ride in Huntington Beach a year and a half ago and was blown away by his flawless style. He has all the chops I didn't even have at his age to make it.

"Come on, Cody," his mom calls from the stands. She's a beautiful redhead who worked three jobs so Cody could ride with me. After I found out, I let the kid ride for free so she could spend more time with Cody, she is the reason why I started to do this pro bono work for all the little shits we've got under our wings.

"How are you doing, Quinn?" I ask, shaking her hand. Quinn is only a couple of years older than me. Pushing her Wayfarers up into her hair, she flashes me a wide smile. "I'm doing okay. Thanks, Hunter, for everything. Cody loves riding with you." She beams at her son.

"Mom," he says. His cheeks flush, like he's embarrassed she's telling me this.

I hold out my fist for him. He bumps it. "Always a pleasure, man. Gnarly stuff out there." I tip my chin to the track.

"Really?" He sounds proud, his long reddish-brown hair blowing in the wind.

Quinn and I lock eyes, and she gives me a wink.

He smiles up at me. "Thanks, Hunter."

"Anytime, bro," I say goodbye to them and walk to house. I need to talk with Jay about our plans for the upcoming season.

I hop onto the porch. Jay and Sky are yelling at each other. I watch them going at it through the window.

"Sky, don't you want to go home? It's easier to get to a hospital in New York. You need to do what's best for you," Jay pleads.

"I'm doing what's best for me," she sobs, shaking her head. "I don't want to go back, I want to stay here with you," she says, her voice breaking.

"I want that too, fuck I want you to stay. But we're so off the grid here, I don't want you getting hurt." He sounds desperate.

She shakes her head, slamming her fist on the table. "Stop it, Jay. Just let us enjoy our time together."

He holds onto the kitchen counter, hanging his head. "And what about Hunt?"

She stands, walking to the sink, grabbing a glass of water, and turning her back to him.

"What about Hunter?" Sky asks, no emotion in her voice.

"Don't be so goddamned selfish. You can't do this to him, you need to tell him what's going on," he snaps.

"Jay, there is nothing going on. You, of all people, are actually lecturing me on selfishness?" She slams the glass in the sink and it breaks.

I take a step away from the window. What the fuck? What are they talking about?

"I heard you coming in early this morning, so don't start with me," Jay tells her.

"It means nothing," she murmurs.

"Means nothing? What the fuck?" I mutter, turning around and storming off the porch. I need to get out of here. I head to the garage, start my bike, and get as far away from her as I possibly can.

Fuck her.

CHAPTER 16

Sky

The roar of his motorcycle echoes through my chest when he drives off, the sound softly fading in the distance.

"Why do you think I came here, Jay? Because you made it perfectly clear I needed to make the first step. Why didn't you have the guts to come to New York and see me?"

"You want to know, kid?" he asks.

"Yes, I do," I state.

"Fuck," he swears, running a hand though his long hair, putting his baseball cap on backwards. "My life was this uphill battle I needed to climb. I needed to lose myself to find myself. I know how corny it sounds but it's the truth. After your mom left, I went on living my life like I used to. Drinking, doing drugs, doing women. I never knew what shit I was going to pull next or where I might end up."

He clears his throat, and runs a hand over his beard. "I won the championship in California that same year. I was celebrating, and I drove home drunk from the bar and crashed my truck into a damn tree. My legs were pinned; I was there for hours. It wasn't until early morning an off-duty firefighter spotted the car on the side of the road, and I was unconscious when he pulled me out. My knee and ankle were shot. To make this even more of a cliché, I got addicted to painkillers. I could never ride again. I thought my life was over, but it was only beginning."

"I'm sorry, Dad. I didn't know."

"It was actually a damn blessing in disguise. You were too young to notice, and it took everything in my power to convince your mom to let you stay during the summers. With everything I had already put you both through, with the drugs, I didn't blame her for not trusting me. I promised Chelsea I wasn't using hard drugs anymore, and would never put you at risk. Never again. You remember how I was living back then in those two trailers, before I built the house?"

"I always thought something was wrong but I was afraid to ask," I tell him.

"I tried to beat it but every time you left I relapsed."

"So it was my fault?" I ask, raising my voice. Fuck him for blaming me for his own shit.

"No, it wasn't your fault. I took you leaving as a reason to start using again. When Mac contacted me and moved onto the property, he took me to meetings. He was volunteering at the prison not far from here, and asked me to come along. That's where I met Hunter's dad, who was still doing time back then. We'd gone to high school together, and he told me about Hunter's problems and asked me to take custody of him. I signed the papers the year you stopped coming around. He was a screwed up, angry kid, but I knew he used to ride BMX. I'd seen him riding, and he blew me away. He didn't want anything to do with me back then because he thought I was some kind of asshole who wanted him or the drugs he was slinging. The streets, his father and uncle not looking out for him, screwed with his head; he thought everyone had an angle or was out to take advantage of him. I wanted him to follow the dreams I couldn't finish. My dreams became his in the end, and my demons became his as well. Fuck, the irony," he mutters.

"He told me he's been going to NA," I say, staring at my hands. "He didn't tell me much about his father, only that he never sees him."

"He must really trust you, baby—he never talks about himself, he learned that from my sorry ass. When the judge granted me custody I helped Hunter stay on the straight and narrow, and he did because he found his outlet in riding and competing. I guess that's why he never visits Oliver—because his father reminds him of a time in his life he wants to forget. I guess the reason why I didn't come to New York, or what I tried to convince myself, is because I was ashamed, but also because I didn't want to leave Hunt and Drew when they needed me. I knew you had a good life with your mom in the city, I didn't want to mess up your life…not again."

I glance up at my father, he looks so heartbroken.

"I needed you too, Jay, and I'm sorry I never came around the last five years," my voice cracking.

"Kid, come here, I'm so sorry, for everything," he says, giving me a hug and letting go after a minute. "Sometimes the ones you care about are also the people you hurt the most."

"I don't want Hunter to care about me," I whisper.

He caresses my cheek. "Why, honey?"

When I lock eyes with him, he's crying. He holds my stare, brushing his hands over his face.

"I don't want to break his heart, like mine was broken before I came back here." I let out a slow breath.

"I'm so sorry," he says after a while, resting his hands on his knees.

"Jay …" I shake my head. "You don't need to say anything."

"But I want to." His voice is strained as he kneels before me, clutching my wrists. "I'm so, so sorry," he sobs.

"Jay, it's okay," I promise, laying both my hands on his shoulders.

"It's not, but I'm glad you're here," he tells me, his face wet from his tears. "I'm grateful," he chokes out.

I take his hands in mine. "Me too." My voice is barely a whisper.

Brushing the tears from his eyes, he says, "I...I didn't know how to talk to you."

"Dad, it's okay, I didn't either," I tell him, trying to be strong.

Taking me into his arms, he crushes me against his big body. "I love you, kiddo," he repeats, while I bury my head in his chest.

He kisses my forehead, a sob escapes him, and I tell him, "It will be all right, Jay."

"You need to be honest with Hunter. This is not some Nicholas Sparks movie." Jay sounds exhausted.

I smile. "You know who Nicholas Sparks is?"

He blushes. "I read every once in a while," he says. "Please. Me and Drew are going to San Diego to meet a couple sponsors. Take the time to talk to Hunter." Tears shine in his eyes when he stops talking. Grabbing the chair for support, he shakes his head.

"It will all work itself out," I say.

He shakes his head, adjusting his black cap. "Don't make the same mistakes I made. I love you," he whispers, kissing my hair.

I close my eyes and hug him, "I love you too, Dad," I tell him, and for the first time since I came back, I'm truly home.

An hour later, I watch him and Drew get the truck ready. Leaning against the porch railing, I wave at them as the car drives away.

Timothy picks me up later that evening, and I spend the night with him, watching movies and eating junk food. I know I need to talk with Hunter when I get back. I need to tell him the truth. I need to give him the chance to walk away.

And I'm so angry, angry knowing what's to come. I'm angry I have another reason for wanting to stay, and I blame Hunter for it, for everything.

CHAPTER 17

Hunter

I spent the night talking to August and crashing at his bar, we had breakfast together and I drove around for a couple of hours to clear my head. I don't want to be her friend anymore, or her occasional hookup; I want all of her. So fuck her and her perspective. I'm done playing games. My whole life is a game and I've had enough, reached my damn limit.

But why can't I stop loving the way she whimpered when I held her in my arms? Why can't I stop thinking about her laugh? Why can't I turn the fuck around?

I skid to a halt in front of the porch where she's sitting, and hop off my bike.

"Fuck this." I grunt, getting angrier with each step I take toward her. Storming up the steps, I slam my helmet on the table in front of her. "What the hell do you think you're doing?"

She peeks up at me through those thick black lashes of hers, resting her book in her lap, eyes all innocent. But she has another thing coming if she thinks she's fooling me even one small bit.

I take a seat in the chair next to hers. "Don't fucking play me." I point my finger in her face, the same finger that disappeared inside her not so long ago. Stretching out my legs, I try to shift, not wanting to stare into her innocent doll-like eyes. I need to control myself. I'm fucking mad as hell. I am a total shit if that deer-in-the-headlights look of hers actually makes me want to smash my fists into a wall. "Did you spend the night at Timothy's?" I drawl. "Didn't take him long to change teams." I motion to Drew's place where Tim disappears inside.

"Fuck you, Hunter. I crashed at his place. I didn't sleep with him," she tells me, walking to the door. When she tries to open it, I'm right behind her, pinning her body with my own, making it impossible for her to move.

"Why did you sleep with me and walk away like nothing had happened?" I ask, and she shivers.

"Because," she whispers, leaning into me.

"What?" I ask, turning her around, resting my palm flat against the door.

"Leave me alone, Hunter," she grits out, pushing my arm away.

"No, I want you to tell me the truth," I bellow, pressing her against the wood. Her body burning me. "I think it's fucking obvious I want to be more than friends, Shorty. Even after Jay warned me to stay away, I couldn't. This is the first time something has felt real in my life."

"What do you want me to say?" she mutters, pushing me away from her.

"Tell me the goddamn truth, Sky. Do you feel the same about me?" I roar, drawing my brows together

"I-I-I don't know." She can't even look me in the eyes.

"You don't know?" I ask, exasperated.

"I can't, Hunter. Just go," she pleads, walking a couple steps, she grabs the railing and turns her back to me.

"Why not? I need to know the truth, and I'm not walking, so tell me." I try to keep my voice level, but it's hard with my heartbeat hammering in my ears.

"You want the truth?" she almost yells.

"Yeah, babe. Give it to me straight."

"Damn you, it was fun. I wanted something to get my mind off what is happening to me, something meaningless, something quick and painless, but then you say shit like this to me," she says, tearing my heart out.

"It was fucking fun, but it became so much more for me. I thought we were friends?" I ask, and I hate that my voice sounds hoarse.

"Then be my friend and leave me alone. I'm no good for you, Hunter."

"You weren't giving me the friend vibe when you were moaning my name, Shorty."

She shakes her head. "You never quit do you?" she whispers, her voice a slow drawl.

Now, I only begin to register how her voice has changed over the last couple of weeks. It's much slower, and hoarser than it was when she first got here. Why do I get the feeling she is still hiding something from me? I stare at her face, her pupils aren't dilated like she's been smoking pot the whole day. Maybe she's just tired?

"I'm no quitter, babe."

Sky

"Forget it, BMX guy," I say, taking a deep breath. My throat hurts from talking.

"No. Damn it. I'm not used to…"

"Talking," I continue for him.

"Fuck. Is there something going on? You know you can talk to me, right?" he pleads, sounding sincere.

"Not about this. I can't."

"Why not?"

"Because we were supposed to be just fun, you asshole, but then I really got to know you and it wasn't fun anymore."

"It wasn't," he purrs, that smug, cocky grin of his creeping onto his beautiful face.

"No, damn you. It became real."

"You make my blood boil," he murmurs, reaching out to caress my face with his big hand.

I push him away. "I don't need a friend, and I definitely don't want to fall for the son my father never had."

"You're scared," he says, crossing his arms. "You're scared to love someone who doesn't fit in the Park Avenue picture you've concocted in your head."

"What the hell do you mean?"

"Oh, give me a break. I saw the way you looked at me whenever I talked about my fucking addiction. You've been searching for an excuse to bail."

"I was scared, of you, my feelings, being back here," I growl, and I want to slap that maverick smile from his face.

He rubs his calloused thumb across his lower lip. "Why did you ask me to sleep with you then?"

"I wanted to feel something. I wanted y..." I stop mid-sentence. I can't tell Hunter I'm falling for him.

Hunter

She watches me, the fear reflected in her eyes. I want to take her to my room and fuck the truth right out of her.

"I'm not the one fooling around." My voice is determined.

I shake my head, and pull back from her, lighting a cigarette. "Damn you."

"I'm not playing games with you either," she murmurs. "Enjoy the cigarette, by the way."

I notice a couple pill bottles sticking out of her bag on the floor. "What are you hiding?" I nod to the pills.

"Nothing." She shakes her head. She hasn't even got the guts to meet my stare.

"Fuck, this is not nothing," I roar.

She shivers, and briefly closes her eyes taking her seat. I'm scaring her but I don't give a flying fuck.

"And what's with the joints?"

"What do you want from me?" she asks, staring out in the direction of the track.

I grab her chair and slide it toward me, so she has to look me in the eyes. "You tell me. You wanted me to fuck you and I did, didn't I?" I yell, slamming my fist on the table.

She hesitates. "Don't you yell at me," she whispers, tears pooling her eyes.

I get right in her face. She leans back. "Don't tell me I know nothing about drugs. Pills, joints—I did it all."

Her bottom lip quivers. "I'm not taking drugs, not anymore." Her eyes fill with tears.

"No? You sure?" I ask, sarcasm ringing through my voice. I snatch the bottles out of her bag. "What's this? Riluzole? Antidepressant meds and Tramadol, and a couple others I can't even fucking pronounce? Don't tell me this is nothing."

She grabs her purse and pushes the pill bottles back in before she stands, slapping my arms away. "Do not tell me you know! Because you don't. You don't know shit!" She screams the words right in my face. But she doesn't sound angry; she sounds scared.

After flicking my cigarette away, I grab her arms and pull her against my chest. She tries to push me away but I'm too strong. I stand and shove her against me so she knows what she does to me. Her eyes go big when I press my hard-on against her stomach.

"Hunter, don't make me," she pleads, focusing on the ground. "I can't tell you, it would ..." She shakes her head. I sigh, and before I know it my nose is in her hair, inhaling the sweet vanilla scent of her shampoo.

"If you're not going to let me in," I whisper in her ear. "Then let me kiss you," I say pushing her against the railing of the porch.

Her head falls to the side when I kiss her throat, and she groans, her hands disappearing into my hair.

"Take me to your room," I order. I need her. I need to feel something other than anger, other than rage. I pick her up, and she drapes her arms around my shoulders and her legs around my waist, and I smash my mouth against hers before I carry her upstairs.

Sky

My emotions are all over the place as he places me gently on my bed. Tension still radiates from his body. I don't know why it even turns me on—it shouldn't, but I know he would never hurt me. Not like I'm hurting him right now.

I follow the line of a big scar on his rib cage below his abs. Hunter pulls away from me when I let my fingers skim over the red line. "What happened there?"

"Nothing," he grunts.

I shake my head. "My shirt isn't coming off till you tell me."

He cracks his knuckles, and his eyes narrow on me. "Is that so?" he asks, with humor in his voice.

I nod, smiling, and I relax instantly. "Well?"

"I ran into a knife on the streets," he drawls, running his fingers over the scar.

I can't breathe. "A knife?"

He focuses on his tattooed hands. "You should see the other guy." He grins, tracing my chin with his thumb.

"This is not a joke, Hunter," I warn him. "A knife?"

He shakes his head. "No shit," he mutters, the muscles in his jaw twitching like he's debating whether to tell me more or not. Stalling, he scratches the side of his shaved head. "I'm not getting any before I tell you, am I?"

I nod. "No way."

The bulge in his jeans seems to grow. Smiling a little, and focusing on his lips, I suppress a groan.

"Damn, okay. Scoot over." His voice is hoarse as he adjusts himself.

I sit against the pillows. He lies beside me, putting his hand under his head.

"What do you want to know?" he asks, brushing his long hair behind his ear.

"Everything," I tell him. "How did you get stabbed?"

He shrugs like it was nothing. "I was high as a kite, and me and some guys were hanging at Venice Beach. I got into a stupid argument with some asshole who usually dealt there. There was this huge fight and when I tried to protect one of my friends from the fucker's switchblade, I woke up in the hospital the next day tied to a fucking bed because I was coming down from all the drugs I had in my system."

"That's not all, is it?"

He gives me a sad smile, and says, "You don't want to know everything. Hell, even I don't want to remember."

"Come on, Hunter."

He sighs, putting both his hands behind his head again. "I bounced around between my uncle and the streets until I came to live full-time here with Jay. Damn he's a good guy, took a lot of my fucking shit back then."

"Did he tell you about his own addictions?"

He flashes me a grin. "Yeah he did, probably the reason why he feels more like a father to me than my real one," he says, matter-of-fact, no emotion in his voice. "I got into fights on a daily basis on and off the track. Went to parties and couldn't quit that fucking white powder." He stops talking, not finishing his sentence.

He swallows. We're both quiet for a while. I don't know what to say, so I wait until he's ready to continue.

"My anger issues became too much. I stole and got into fights, and got my ass arrested numerous times." He pauses, pulling me into his chest. "I was a screwed up punk. I made Jay's life a living hell. He didn't know how to take care of me, but he made it his mission to save me from myself. Be there when nobody else had been," he says, his deep voice soft. He turns on his side. "Not like my junkie mother or my father."

"Where is he now?" I ask, caressing his cheek.

He sighs, picking at an imaginary thread on his black shorts. "He lives with his motorcycle buddies not so far from here, in the desert. These," he says, tugging on the dog tags around his neck, "are a reminder to never walk down my father's path."

"Are those his?" I ask, staring at them.

Nodding, he lets the tags go as if his hands are on fire. "Yeah, he wore them during Operation Desert Storm, and gave them to me before he went to prison."

Hunter

"What was he in for again?" she asks.

I swallow, trying to hold back the lump in my throat. Why I still care for my father is beyond me. "For possession, selling dope and guns for the motorcycle gang he's still part of. For being a shit excuse for a father."

She lays her hand on my shoulder, warming my skin. "I'm so sorry."

I shrug. "Doesn't matter, he wasn't there for me. Jay was there. Even when I was a screwed up teenager." I grind my teeth together.

She rests her head against my chest. "What was he like?"

"My dad? Don't know, don't care." I grunt.

"And Jay?" she asks, her voice soft.

I smile, shaking my head. "The greatest. He took care of me. Bought me my first real BMX bike." I inhale sharply. "At first, I didn't want to ride for a living but one day I rode down the hill, and I got hooked. I found what I was meant to do."

She touches the silver bird she always wears around her neck.

"I'm glad you're wearing his necklace. I know it means a lot to Jay." I say.

"This was the only thing I wanted from him for a very long time." Her eyes find mine, a look of embarrassment crossing her face. "I used to be so angry with him. With Drew, even you."

"With me?" I ask, raising my eyebrows.

"Yes." She nods. After biting her lip, she says, "I'm not angry anymore."

I tap my fingers on my leg. "What changed?"

She diverts her eyes from my stare. "Life," she whispers, giving me a sad smile.

I put my arms around her and pull her into my chest. We are both quiet for a while.

"What happened?" I'm dreading the answer but I need to know.

She peeks up, kissing the tattoo above my nipple, and my dick twitches against my shorts. "I can't," is the only thing she says after a couple of seconds. "Why did you have to become real?"

"I'm real, Shorty. Is that why you were pushing me away so hard?" I ask, brushing my lips across her forehead.

"I never asked you to go after me. I never asked you to be my friend." She pauses and takes a deep breath. "I never asked for anything other than…"

"Than what, babe? You sure as fuck never asked me to fall for you, and I fell hard. What do I need to do to convince you?" I rasp, running my hand through her long hair.

She locks eyes with me. "Time, Hunt. I need time." Her voice is barely a whisper.

I hold her in my arms. "I tell you I want you, and you want more time?" I chuckle, trying to make light of the situation and hide the hurt in my voice.

She coughs. It's like she has trouble speaking.

"Did you smoke too much again?"

She shakes her head. "I …" she begins, taking a deep breath. "Not smoking," she whispers like it takes everything she has to say those words. She feels so brittle in my arms. Her ribs poke out. Fuck, she needs to eat more.

"I'm falling for you, Shorty," I repeat, my lips inches away from hers. I love the way she melts into me.

"I'm falling too," she whispers. "But I'm so tired."

I kiss the top of her head, and she hugs me.

"Why did this have to become real? Once you know the truth, you'll hate me. Just let me hold you like this a little longer."

I don't know what she means, but her words hit me right in the heart. I hold her in my arms, promising myself I'm never going to let her go.

"What are you doing to me, Sky?"

She kisses the tip of my nose and I grin. "I love your freckles," she says, sitting up. "I need to brush my teeth." She leaves me alone on the bed. I watch her slowly move around the room. She tiptoes on unsteady feet, sometimes using the wall for support.

"You okay?" I ask. She is staring in the mirror in the bathroom. She turns to me, and her eyes are weary, "I'm okay, Hunter."

After brushing her teeth, she turns off the light, gets into bed and lies next to me.

I pull her into me. "I hope you don't …"

She places her hand on my cheek, running her fingers over my stubble. "Don't what?"

"Judge me, because now you know everything about me, even my fucked up past."

"Your past is your past." She touches the line of my bottom lip with her thumb.

I roll my eyes. "That's what Drew always tells me."

"Clever guy." A soft smile plays on her lips.

"Yeah, he is. He's my brother."

She closes her eyes, shifting, and drapes a leg over mine. I kiss her forehead. "I like this."

"I like this too." She sighs, tracing my jaw with her cold fingers. "You make me happy."

I kiss her forehead and seconds turn into minutes. She gasps and wheezes for air.

"Fuck, Shorty," I say grabbing her arms.

"I'm okay. Just tired," she croaks, breathing in deep.

I stare at her face, cast in shadow thanks to the darkness of the room. "You sure?" I ask, and kiss her knuckles.

She nods, and I close my eyes, slowly drifting off to sleep.

I wake in the middle of the night with a start. Her body is shaking hard, like she's having a seizure. Her muscles spasm, her legs, her arms. *What the fuck is happening?* I flick on the lamp.

"Sky!" I try to wake her, and she shouts my name without opening her eyes.

After the worst ten seconds of my life, she opens them. "Babe, are you okay? You were dreaming and calling out and shaking. I-I-I d-d-didn't know what to do," I stutter, brushing her damp hair out of her face. She is drenched in sweat.

With big eyes, she scans the room. "What?" she slurs a little.

Grabbing my shirt, she buries her face in my chest and I let her. I love how she holds on. Like she needs me. *Me*.

"Honey, you fucking scared me. Should I call a doctor or Jay?"

Shaking her head, she gulps for air, her tiny frame moving up and down. "No." She squeezes her eyes shut for a moment. "I'm a bit thirsty."

I hop out of bed and get her a glass of water, and wet a washcloth.

She is sitting against the headboard when I hand her the drink.

"Thanks." She takes it from me, her hands still shaking. I put the cold washcloth against her forehead, and she locks eyes with me.

"This feels nice," she whispers.

Tilting her head up, I kiss her lips. "Should I stay or go, or…"

She takes my hand in hers. "Please stay." She winces. "I like you sleeping next to me. It calms me."

"You were shaking and calling out in pain," I tell her.

"I was?" she asks, startled. She shakes her head, laying the washcloth on her nightstand. "Probably a bad dream. Will you stay with me throughout the night?"

I want to answer, *I wanna stay with you forever,* but instead I say, "Yeah I'll stay with you." I watch her fall asleep, something isn't right. I don't know what the hell is going on. Usually I see through everything, but with her, it's like I'm staring into the void. Maybe I don't want to figure it out, because once I do, I'm scared she will take more with her when she goes than I can spare, like my fucking heart.

I don't know when I fall asleep again but when I wake, it's still dark outside. Sky is staring at me. I turn on my side and brush her hair behind her ear. "Want anything, Shorty?"

"Only you."

"How long was I out?" I ask, brushing the sleep from my eyes.

"A couple hours. Please kiss me, Hunt," she says, never breaking eye contact.

I kiss her lips and her hands travel along my spine, pulling me against her. I shift and guide her on top of me.

"Are you sure?" I rasp, doing everything in my power not to devour her.

"Yes, I want you. Every part of you. But ..."

"What? You can tell me."

"I don't want you to hold back," she whispers, smiling against my parted lips.

"Shorty, I love it when you talk dirty to me," I tell her as I lean forward and bury my nose between her cleavage. She giggles when I bite one nipple through the fabric of her tank top. I push it down exposing her creamy skin, and she arches her spine, moaning as my teeth skim her soft flesh.

I pull her shirt up over her head, I want to feel her skin to skin. I love how silky she feels under my calloused hands. Fuck, she has the most beautiful tits; they fit perfectly in my hands, like they were made especially for me. I turn her on her back, and she yelps in surprise, the sight of her beautiful plump lips curling at the sides. Burying my nose in her neck, she squirms and tries to push me away while I tickle her with my stubble. My tongue glides down to her stomach, tasting the salty sweet essence of her body. She opens her thighs, her tiny panties rising up. Her pussy lips are outlined against the red cotton, and the damp spot in the middle has me biting back a growl. My dick twitches because I'm doing this to her. I'm getting her this wet. I roll my tongue above the waistband of her panties, from left to right, the dark spot growing bigger.

"Hunter," she pants. My name escapes her mouth like a plea. "I don't ... I ..."

I smile up at her, my hair falling in front of my eyes. "Lie back, babe, and let me do this for you."

She nods and her head falls into her pillow. The moon shines through the open balcony doors, illuminating her body, and she's so beautiful, and all mine.

I slowly pry her panties off, and damn her cream seeps from her tight pink pussy. Before I bury my tongue deep inside her, I part her lips. She grabs the sheets between her trembling hands and I grin. Her tiny clit is glistening and engorged, and begging to be sucked.

"Shorty, I'm going to fuck this tight pussy with my tongue," my voice sounds hoarse to my own ears.

"God yes," she whispers, arching her back when I blow on her clit. I grab her thighs and lie on my stomach, aligning my mouth with her sweet smelling cunt. Digging my fingers in her flesh, she parts her legs even more, giving me fantastic access. I'd die a happy man if this is the last image on my retina.

She gasps when I lick her folds, damn I love her taste. I dip my tongue in deep, stabbing and prodding. She mewls and I grin, licking my wet lips. Moving up I focus on her clit, pressing hard against it with the metal ball in my tongue on her nub. I lap at her sweet spot. *Fuck, she tastes good.* She clenches her ass cheeks, but not before I see that puckered rim gasping for my finger. I run my index finger over that tight hole, and fuck me she opens herself even more so I can push the tip of my finger in. She swallows my digit, and I bury my face in her pussy lapping at her juices and fucking her with my finger.

Her hips jerk, and I come up for air, not wanting her to come just yet. I want to savor this moment. "Now I know why you have your tongue piercing," she purrs.

"You're on to me." I smile, only pausing for a moment before I'm pushing against her again and again with my tongue, teasing her drenched pussy. Her hips buck and I know she's close. I like how she's not entirely bare, and the way my tongue trails across her wet lips.

I've never tasted anything this sweet. Her musky scent makes my dick even harder, pushing against the top of my Motocross pants. I'm glad I'm not wearing jeans; my cock wouldn't survive. I growl against her mound, the vibration making her wetter.

Her hand travels into my hair, holding on, and I like how she pulls on the strands. She gives me the right amount of pleasure and pain. I swirl my tongue over that engorged bundle of nerves, and I swear I feel her heartbeat against my tongue. I know she needs more, her pleading has my dick twitching and throbbing in my pants, as precum seeps out. I lick my middle and index finger, getting them nice and wet. Not that she needs it because, fuck, her cream is dripping down her leg. Pushing in two fingers I make a little hook with my index finger, going deep.

Coming up for air I stare at her, she is watching me through hooded eyes. Her chest heaving, the redness on her cheeks only adding to the thrill. With my fingers still scissoring her inside I crawl up her body, and she licks her bottom lip while she closes her eyes.

"Shorty," I tell her, "open your eyes."

She does, holding my stare. There is something in her gaze I've longed for and in this moment, I know I love this girl. I want to protect her and be a better man. Give my life for her.

Resting my forehead against hers I kiss her temple and move down until I reach her mouth. She plants hers hard against mine, searing me with those strawberry colored lips. I push in my tongue at the same rhythm with my fingers, gliding along her slick inner walls. Her breath turns shallow, as if she's reaching the edge.

I pinch her clit, and she starts to beg me to make her come. Her sweet pleas making me harder than I already am.

With my mouth still on hers I dig my fingers out of her little cunt, and she swears. I grin watching her never take her eyes from me as I push my pants down and my dick springs free, begging for release. I leave a trail of precum on her thigh, but I don't care, I want to mark her with my fucking seed.

Starting up the assault with my thumb on her clit I swirl it around, applying only light pressure in circular motions until she starts to breathe heavy, closing her eyes. Watching her face, bliss written all over it, I push three fingers into her. Her gasp is so fucking sexy. I start moving my fingers and thumb faster, fucking, and grinding against her until she is a withering mess. I place my thumb and one finger on each side of her clit and pinch hard, leaving my middle finger deep inside her and she comes, screaming my name and collapses into the pillows. I pull my finger out of her and bring it to my mouth, licking the fluid off. I'm looking at her knowing there's a big cocky smile on my face.

Placing my hand on her cheek I whisper, "Hey." I trail my knuckles over her cheekbone. "Don't."

Opening her eyes, she husks out, "Don't what?"

"Don't be embarrassed," I tell her.

"It's not. This is way..."

I smile. "You like it, don't you?"

She nods, all sense of embarrassment gone. I kiss her gently and she pushes her naked body against my hard-on, and I groan into her mouth. "I love every part of you," I say against her wet lips, cradling her pussy with the palm of my hand, "and I love going down on you."

"I like it too," she says shyly.

I run my pierced lip over her mouth, and Sky shudders.

"I plan on going down on you many times." I grin.

She nods and before I know it, she is on top of me, holding my hands above my head. I like the way she takes control. She doesn't exactly know what to do, judging by the look in her eyes, and her inexperience makes me harder than I was before. Fuck, this girl is going to be the death of me.

Sky

I hold his hands above his head. He smiles up at me with a devilish grin, a hint of mischief in his eyes. I lean down and kiss him, holding his bottom lip between my teeth. I can taste myself on his lips, and it's hot as hell. Letting him go, he sits up and pushes himself against me, his hard dick twitching against my stomach. He grabs his hard shaft, and starts pumping up and falls back against the sheets. I can't tear my eyes from him. I lean up on my knees and he angles his dick right below my wet pussy. Begging to be filled with his big cock, I open my drawer and pull out a condom. He reaches out and runs a finger through my pussy lips, my inner muscles throbbing in response.

"What do you have in mind?" he asks, licking his finger.

I sit back on his thighs, trying to open the package with shaking hands.

He lets go of his dick, and digs his fingers into my legs.

Sitting up on his elbows, he stares at my pussy. "I'm falling hard for you, Shorty." Our eyes clash, we look at each other and I can't help it when a lump forms in my throat. Taking my mouth hostage, he pushes me against his hard chest. The precum already wetting my stomach.

"In a hurry, babe?" I ask, and grin, placing the condom next to his head.

Winking at me, he says, "You have no idea."

Pushing him down onto the sheets, I smash my lips against his, moaning into his mouth. Then I kiss his freckled nose and he chuckles, eyeing the condom I'm clutching in my hand.

"This, Shorty," he says, kissing the side of my upturned lip, "is all I ever want."

Our kiss turns slow and passionate. I softly stroke my tongue against his piercing. He growls when I pull back again.

Giggling, I hold onto his hands locking our fingers together in a tight grip. I start to move my wet center against his abs, scooting over his dick and kissing down his chest. I take his nipple piercing between my lips. My breasts are so sensitive it's almost painful, he wiggles his ass against the mattress, unties one hand from my grip and pinches and rolls my right nipple between his fingers until I'm seeing stars.

Raising one brow I let go of his other hand, lean forward and suck on the metal. "Fuck, it hurts," he hisses, closing his eyes.

I sit up. "I'm sorry," wiping the saliva from my lips.

Opening his eyes, he drawls, "Hurts in a good way. I like you teasing me with your mouth."

I grin and take the other nipple between my teeth, I let my tongue dart out to lick the tip, and he groans as I dig my nails into his chest.

Pinching my waist, he says, "You're evil."

"I know." I smile, kissing the corner of his mouth.

He leans in, but I pull away and grab the silver foil, opening the condom with my teeth.

"And what now?" he asks, his hair a halo around his head, crossing his arm over his inked stomach. "Never done this part before?" he rasps as I nod. "Slowly put the top…"

"On top." I laugh.

He grins too. "Yeah, on top, and roll it out."

I bite my lip, stealing a glance at him. I want him so much it hurts, because every day I know I'm letting go of more parts of myself and giving them to him.

"Hey?" he says, pulling my chin to him.

Pushing the thought from my mind, I kiss him again, tracing the tip of his throbbing cock with my thumb. I put my wet fingers in my mouth, tasting him, and he grunts.

"Fuck." He smiles, helping me roll the condom over his hard erection. *Damn, the man is big.* Using my knees as leverage, I keep staring at him, slowly sliding myself on top. I gasp as I feel his dick spreading me wide open.

He licks his lips, his attention on his length disappearing

inside me. A deep hum rumbles from his throat when he bottoms out, the metal of his piercing teasing along my inner walls. It is one of the most intimate things I have ever done in my life.

"That's it." His voice is thick and even hoarser than usual. His heavy breathing turns into grunts. I grab hold of his hands, lacing our fingers together, and slowly start to move.

"Ride me, Shorty," he says gritting his teeth, his eyes fluttering open and closed. I push against him; it's much deeper this way. I repeat his name as I slide myself back and forth. My pussy lips spreading wide, exposing my clit.

Without warning he wraps his arms around my body and sits up. I gasp as his hardness pulses inside of me, the metal ball at the end adding to my pleasure. It's so tight and wet the way my pussy fits him like a glove. Draping my arms over his shoulders, I sink my teeth into his neck to try to hold in my screams as he pushes up against me. My oversensitive clit throbbing, and begging to be rubbed, pinched, slapped, anything to make me come.

I start to tremble.

"You want me to rub that tight little nub, don't you babe?" he asks, his breath hot against my ear.

I rock up and down his shaft, every time his pubic hair makes contact with my clit I whimper. "Yes please, Hunter, I need to come."

He smiles against my neck, and licks below my ear before his stubble scrapes the spot below my jawline, and I shiver. I trace the shell of his ear with my teeth, and he groans. My hands travel over his tattoos, as he fucks me with deep powerful thrusts.

I kiss his chest and I lick his nipple ring again, biting a little and watching his head fall to the side. With heavy eyelids, his hands travel over my spine to my bottom, grabbing me hard and pulling me forward on him in a sharp motion, causing his cock to hit me in the most amazing places. Our sweat soaked stomachs press against each other. Tracing the lines of the muscles in his arm up to his jaw, he kisses me again.

I shift my weight and I'm building, my pussy clenching around him. I moan and shudder as we move against each other, face to face, stomach to stomach.

He takes both my ass cheeks between his hands, spreading me open, cold air hitting the tight throbbing rim. I need him to push his finger inside, to fill me in both holes, and I cry into his mouth from the thought. "God, Hunter."

"You want my finger inside you? Filling you both ways, my cock milking that tight pussy, while my fingers spread you open from behind?" He rumbles, his voice low and sexy.

"Yes, god, yes I can't..."

Grinning he pushes his finger slowly into my ass, and I stiffen from the sudden intrusion, "It's so full." He starts fucking me from behind, and I scream his name as he pushes in another finger.

"Trust me," he whispers, and after the notion of being too full subsides, it is so dirty and hot as hell. His cock is still pumping inside me. His fingers stretching me open from behind is too much, and I scream when the first spasms of my orgasm tear through me, and I come, pulsing around him. I smash my mouth against his, every muscle in my body starting to ache, and I sob, my release taking me by surprise.

On a growl, he thrusts hard and fast a few more times and then he releases himself inside me. "Fuck," he swears, panting hard.

Leaning his forehead against mine, he catches his breath. We are both drenched in sweat. He shattered me, my pussy still throbbing, as I come down from my orgasm. He collapses onto the mattress, taking me with him. Slowly opening his eyes, he flashes me a lazy smile.

He pulls out, leaving me feeling empty. I kiss his chest as he closes his eyes again for a second. He hums softly when I lick the place below his jaw. He grabs a tissue from my nightstand, takes the condom off, and drops it on the floor. His semi-hard cock twitches against my hand.

I wrap my hand around him, tracing the tip with my finger.

"Are you trying to kill me, babe?" he asks, laughing into my hair.

I smile against his mouth and I kiss him. Shaking my head, I lay my chin on his chest.

After a while, he says, "Look at me, Sky."

I put my hand under my head, turning to him. He suddenly looks shy. "What?"

I hold my breath, and tears pool in my eyes, no one has ever looked at me like this before. He traces the line of my mouth with his thumb. Kissing me lightly on the lips, goose bumps break out all over my body.

His voice is a hoarse whisper when he says, "Let me be the one for you, Shorty."

He stares deep into my eyes. I know he means it.

Hunter is still staring at me, waiting for my response. I move up his body a little more, wetting my lips. My hands tighten in his sweat-soaked hair before I trace the metal in his ear, and kiss him hard. His hand comes up to grab the back of my head and words filled with promises leave his mouth, before his tongue plunges in deep.

I come up for air, and I know what I need to tell him.

"I think I…"

But the words get stuck in my throat, as I lay my head on his chest listening to his heartbeat while he falls asleep.

CHAPTER 18

Hunter

I wake and leave her alone in bed. Sometime during the early morning, Jay's truck moved up the drive. I debated going downstairs and taking the easy way out, but I couldn't tear myself away from her. Like a teenager, I take another small step, and the wood of the stairs creaks under my foot.

"Want a coffee, Hunt?" Jay asks.

"Motherfucking shit," I mutter under my breath. I brush a hand through my hair and enter the kitchen. Straightening my clothes, I roll my eyes, who the fuck am I kidding.

I catch my reflection in the window. *He's gonna punch my lights out.*

Jay gives me a once-over as I lean against the island counter. Who would buy the idea that I came in through the front door wearing yesterday's clothes? I mean, why would I even be here at seven—*no, fuck*—six-thirty? I'm never up this early on a Sunday and he knows it.

"Coffee?" he asks again.

"Thanks, Jay," I murmur, taking a seat at the kitchen table.

I need to explain to the man who has been like a father to me the last ten years that I'm screwing his daughter, and with my track record, things aren't looking great for the both of us. "Jay," I begin.

He holds up his hands. "Save it, Hunt," he says, leaning against the kitchen counter. "I want her to be happy, even if it's with an asshole like you." He snorts.

I take the coffee from him. I can't give Jay the finger and bullshit him; he would smell it from a mile away. "I'm falling in love with her," I tell him, looking straight into his eyes.

He quickly averts his gaze, and stares into his coffee cup like he wants to break it in two or smash it against my forehead. He takes a deep breath before focusing his attention on me again. "Take care of yourself," he murmurs, the muscles in his jaw twitching.

I frown. I didn't expect that from him. "What do you mean?" What's the old man talking about? Me taking care of myself? What the hell is going on?

He sighs. "I mean..."

"Good morning, Dad," Sky says. She's fucking radiant in her jeans and white shirt.

"Sky," Jay nods, giving her a long look she ignores.

I turn from Jay to Sky, then look at the clock. I slide my chair in reverse. These standoff situations are not my cup of coffee so I do what I do best—get the hell out of Dodge.

"I'm going to get ready for practice. Drew is probably wondering where I am," I tell them, passing Sky. I let my hand skim hers. She gives me a wink, and I close the door behind me.

I grab the porch railing when I'm outside. What the hell just happened? I'd anticipated Jay punching my lights out. I thought he'd beat me up for sleeping with his daughter, or for checking her out the way I've been doing.

"Sky," Jay says, sounding sad and angry at the same time.

"Leave it," she bites back.

He slams his fists on the table. What the f...? I want to open the door and march back in but something makes me wait.

"It isn't fair to..."

"Jay." Her voice is calm, much calmer than his.

"Don't 'Jay' me. Don't act like you're the only one hurting here, Sky. You can't use him like this."

"Dad, please. I'm a grown woman; he's a grown man." She pauses. "What do you want me to do? Stop seeing him? Stop being with him, loving him?"

She loves me? Really loves me? No, I probably didn't catch that part right.

I take a step to the door. Both are quiet.

"I don't know anymore," Jay says, his voice cracking.

My hand hovers above the doorknob. It would be so easy to step inside. But I turn around and head to my own place.

After taking a hot shower, I walk to the garage to lift some weights, passing the Tesla parked in front of Drew's front door. All the while, I'm thinking about what Jay and Sky were talking about. *You can't hurt him like this.* Did he mean she is going back to New York, back to NYU? *Fuck, I have no idea.*

"Hunter!" Drew calls out to me.

"What, man?"

"I've been calling your name for, like, five minutes. Where you at?"

I shake my head, dropping the weights. "Getting fucked," I tell him gruffly as I pass him.

"Did you spend the night with her?" he asks.

I give him a sly smile while I crouch and lace up my shoes, then grab a towel to brush the sweat from my arms. "How did your date go, by the way?" I pause. "Timothy still here?"

His face turns a bright shade of red. "None of your damn business."

I shake my head. "It is my business when the guy is a certified dealer. I'm not stupid. I know a major player when I meet one. We have a business to run and with the kids here..."

"Don't you think I don't know?" he asks.

"I do. Do you?" I turn the tables on him.

He grabs me by the arm, dragging me back into the garage.

"Don't fuck with me, Drew!" I roar.

"Why not? When fucking shit up is your favorite pastime?" Drew gets right in my face. "Just because you screwed up doesn't mean the rest of us will be traveling down your road any time soon."

"And here were go again."

He shakes his head. "No, I just don't want to see you getting hurt, or hurt someone else."

I start to laugh. "Good one, jackass. No need to confront me with my failures. I've not forgotten them."

He nods. "What is going on, man? Are you...?" he says, and his face screws up.

"Using, no I'm clean, Drew," I say, but he has a point.

"Are you really? You know you can't ride with that shit in your blood."

"Fuck no. I'm...I don't know," I reply, staring at the bikes we've been working on for the last couple weeks with Mac. "I don't want to blow it this time with her, like I always do." I wince, scraping my tongue piercing across my teeth.

"I get it dude."

I punch him playfully in the shoulder. "So, you and Timothy?" I ask, changing the subject.

"I know what you're trying to do, motherfucker." Drew grins.

I give him a pat on his stomach. "Warn me next time when you take him back here. Don't want to walk in on your skinny ass again."

He slams me in the arm with his fist. "Shut up." He pauses.

"We're heading to a party at the beach tonight. Wanna come? You look like you could blow off some steam."

I glance back up to the house. "Nah."

The only steam I wanna blow off is with the woman hiding inside those walls.

I wink at Drew when he looks at me, and we both walk to the track, ready to start with the kids' class.

I didn't talk to Sky after I overheard her conversation with Jay. During dinner, she acts like nothing has happened between us. I am this close to popping a vein in my neck.

"Would you like to come to a party?" Drew asks Sky.

"What party?" she says, while taking a couple of glasses to the kitchen.

"Down at the beach," Drew replies with a smile.

It's like she forgot the way we made love. The way I held her during the night. What we talked about. I can't understand what I've done to make her pull away from me like she has. Then again, I can't really blame her. I told her all those things about me. My past is playing catch up, and I hate myself because of it. I hate that I told her about my demons when I knew it would only push her away in the end. I shouldn't let anyone get this close again.

Jay and Mac help her clean the table. I'm still grabbing the armrests on the armchair, almost breaking it in two with sheer willpower, hoping there isn't any smoke coming out of my ears.

"You kids go." Jay smiles.

"We'll get our hands dirty." Mac nods. "Let the old guys worry about the dishes."

Sky's eyes narrow on me. I shift in the chair, and my dick twitches. Those fucking doll eyes somehow always get me hard. I give her a cold stare in response.

"Yes, I'll go," she says. "Give me a couple minutes to get ready."

She disappears up the stairs.

When Drew and I are the only ones sitting outside, I officially lose it. "Damn, dude!"

"What?" Drew asks innocently. The fucker is up to something.

"What are you doing?"

A smug smile shifts his lips. The bastard planned this. "Oh, this morning you told me you weren't going." He feigns innocence.

"I wasn't, but now I definitely am." I growl, standing abruptly, the chair falling backwards.

"Who is going?" Sky asks, while I grab the chair and put it upright. My mouth dries. She's wearing a tight-fitting black dress, the same she wore that night in the truck when we fucked. Her cleavage is on mouthwatering display. Our eyes meet, and she immediately looks away.

Drew whistles. "Girl, you're hot. Sorry I don't swing your way or I would totally go for you."

I punch his shoulder with my fist.

"Aw, what was that for?" he asks, cradling the injured spot.

"For being a dick," I grumble, storming to my truck. Looks like I'm going to the fucking party now.

On the drive over, I do everything in my power not to stare at her naked legs. *Fuck,* that dress. I need to bite the inside of my cheek so I don't let out a groan. I'm constantly shifting in my seat.

Sky wets her lips. She can't *not* notice the bulge in my black jeans. *Shit.*

She ties her long hair back when I stop the car next to the water's edge, spotting Timothy walking up to our truck. *Fucking fantastic.*

Drew jumps out. "Later, guys!"

The bastard even has an escape plan—to ditch me with

Sky while he's going off doing God knows what with his new boyfriend.

Timothy hugs Sky when she exits the car. I walk over to them and shake his hand.

"Hi, man. You good?" he says calmly, while we break knuckles. Dude is a freaking terminator with his shaved head and defiant blank stare.

I grin at him, giving him a chin-tip and wanting to punch him in his smug face at the same time. "Yeah, are you?" I drawl.

"Come on," Drew says, taking Timothy's hand, and pulling him toward the bonfire glowing in the distance on the beach. Timothy grins at me. The guy is not fazed at all, and I like him even more because of it.

"Play nice, children." Tim waves, draping an arm over Drew's shoulder. He whispers something in my best friend's ear, making him laugh.

I put my hands in the pockets of my pants. "So, want to check out the party?"

Sky nods. "That would be nice."

"Nice," I mutter. When did we become so polite with each other? I fucking hate this.

Following her onto the beach, I say hello to people I know. Everyone here is either a surfer or a BMX rider. There is a huge bonfire in the middle of the sand, warming my skin. The smell of burning embers fills the cool night air.

"Want a beer?" I ask her, pointing to the keg.

She nods, staring out to the ocean.

"Wait here. I'll be right back," I say, turning around, and I pick up a cup for her and a soda for me.

Before I know it, one of the brunettes I've slept with is standing next to me.

"Hi, Hunter."

"Hey, Lydia." Fuck, I actually know her name. I shake my head. "How are you?"

Her eyes widen in surprise. "Good." She smiles up at me. "I see you brought a date." She nods at Sky, who's talking to Ryan.

Motherfucker. Sky is laughing and he's smiling too. She motions with her hands, the wind blowing her hair back, and I'm this close to picking her up and taking her home to my place to have her all for myself.

"You're different," Lydia says, her voice kind.

"How so?" My eyes are still angrily following Sky and Ryan. The cups shake in my hands.

"I don't know. It's like you found *the one*," Lydia says, kissing my cheek, taking me by surprise as I watch her head over to Ryan and Sky. Sky introduces herself and my former friend puts his arm over Lydia's shoulder.

Before I make it back to Sky, I'm stopped by a couple of riders from the circuit. Sky walks by me and I pass her a cup.

I don't talk to her the whole evening, but keep following her with my eyes, drinking one soda after the other. She is avoiding me, talking to people she doesn't know when she could be spending time with my grumpy ass. I'm getting angrier as the night progresses, the bonfire becomes larger, and the voices louder.

Drew slams me on my shoulder. "Hey man." He takes the cup I'm crunching out of my hand. "I think you've had enough to drink."

Timothy is talking to Sky. They are both laughing and he's explaining something, his hands moving over his buzz cut. She smirks, her head falling back.

"What the fuck is going on, man?" I ask, not looking at Drew.

Drew focuses all his attention on the fire. "I..."

"If you know something, now is the time to tell me. I've given her space when I thought it was what she needed. What do I get in return?"

Drew takes a sip from his beer. "She needs to tell you."

"What the fuck does that mean?" I growl out.

"Like I said." He pauses. "She needs to tell you."

"You can't even look me in the eyes. We've always been honest with each other, don't you forget it," I warn him.

She says goodbye to Timothy, and turns around, walking to the water's edge. "Screw this," I say. I make my way to the surf, not stopping when Drew calls after me.

I flip him off, turning my attention back to Sky. She stops and takes off her shoes, then dips her toes in the water. I grab a Coke from the cooler and keep on walking. She takes a sip from her beer, a soft smile playing on her lips.

"Will you tell me what the fuck is going on?" My voice sounds angry, and I down half the can.

"Nothing is going on," she murmurs, averting my eyes.

"Horseshit," I yell, throwing my drink in the sand. She takes a step away from me. Her eyes dart to the party, wide, alarmed. The music is blaring through the speakers and I spot Drew and Timothy talking angrily with each other, not noticing our little screaming match.

"I … I …" she stammers, turning away from me.

"What? I gave you space. I guessed that was what you wanted, but time's up. I'm done playing Mister Roll-Over Lay-Down," I roar, grabbing her by the arm. "Tell me what the fuck is going on. Let me in there!" My voice cracks as I point to her heart.

"Let go of my arm," she bites out. Shaking off my hand, she walks away, dumping her cup next to the keg.

"Don't walk away from me. Fucking fire away. Hit me with your best shot, Sky. I can take it. Why? Can't you? Huh?" I yell. People are watching us as I run after her. Stumbling through the sand, she falls face forward onto her hands.

"Oh no, Sky," I say, already hot on her heels, *I hope she hasn't hurt herself.*

She brushes the sand from her palms. "What do you want from me?" she screams, still sitting on the ground like she's a lost little girl.

"What do *I* want from you?" I yell back. "I want you. Damn it, Sky, I want you."

"You don't want me," she murmurs, her face wet from her tears.

"Is everything all right?" Ryan asks from behind us.

"Yes, thank you, Ryan," she mutters, wiping the sand from her dress, ignoring my outstretched hand.

I spin around. "This doesn't fucking concern you, so get lost."

Ryan helps Sky up.

"Get your hands off her." I grunt, balling my fists, ready to strike.

"Hunter," Sky pleads, locking eyes with me.

"What is your problem, man?" Ryan gets right in my face.

I hit him in his chest with my flat palms. "Don't even try me, *man*," I roar.

Ryan pushes me in my stomach. I've had enough of this shit. I need to end this or end him once and for all. "Do you want to have a go?" I ask, cracking my knuckles, shoving him away from me again.

"Yeah, let's settle this," he taunts, rolling his shoulders.

Before I can throw the first punch, Drew grabs both my arms. Timothy takes Ryan in a choke hold.

"Let it go," Drew commands, his voice serious. I grit my teeth and shrug his hands off me.

"Don't ever touch her again," I tell Ryan, pointing a finger in his face.

Lydia stands back, taking Ryan's hand in hers with tears in her eyes. *Shit, what have I done? What the fuck are we doing?*

I grab Sky's arm and pull her with me to the truck.

"Let me go." She doesn't scream but her body trembles. I'm done waiting for her to explain to me why she's avoiding me. She plants her feet in the sand, trying to get me to stop but I'm a man on a mission. I open the passenger side of the truck and throw her in, then slam the door shut.

She kicks the side and grabs the handle, trying to open the door, but I've already locked it from the outside.

I get into the driver's seat and Drew runs up to the car. "Hunt, don't drive. You drank too much," he pleads.

I turn the key, the engine roaring to life. Opening the window, I bite out, "It was fucking soda, asshole." I flip him off.

Timothy grabs hold of Drew's hand. "Let them go," he says, but he slides his finger across his neck, like he's going to kill me if I hurt her. I salute him, and the asshole laughs, doing the same.

I put the car in first gear and speed away. I'm barely out of the parking lot when she starts to scream at me to stop. I shake my head and hit the gas pedal, flying across the road.

CHAPTER 19

Hunter

"Talk to me, Shorty, what the fuck is going on?"

"Nothing," she murmurs, breathing hard through her nose.

Turning onto a back road leading to the house, I skid to a halt, and turn the ignition off. "Why do I always feel like I have to pull the truth out of you?" I ask locking eyes with her, and drape my arm behind her head.

"Or fuck the truth out of me?" she says, and it hurts hearing her say those words.

I lick my lips, and let my eyes travel to her naked legs, and before I get a chance to say something she jumps on me. Pinning me in my seat, with her knees on either side of my body. Leaning back against the steering wheel she pushes the front of her dress down to reveal her red lace bra.

My body responds instantly and she flashes me a coy smile, starting to open the buttons of my shirt.

"Sky, we need to talk," I plead, placing my hands on her small waist. She wiggles back and forth over my growing erection and I catch a glimpse of her red underwear. My dick twitches against her core as she whispers dirty things in my ear and kisses me. Getting lost in our kiss, I pull her against my chest and ravage her mouth.

Her hands pry at my clothes, she opens my belt, eases my zipper down slipping her hand in, and grabs my hard cock.

"No talking," she purrs, brushing her thumb over my dick piercing, and my head falls back.

"Stop it, Sky," I get out, before she starts kissing my neck, leaving a wet trail where her tongue traces my Adam's apple. Damn, she needs to stop, I'm angry and turned on. And the only thing I want to do right now is flip her on her stomach, push her underwear to the side, and pound into her from behind. I want her to hurt, like she's hurting me.

"Fuck me like you did before, Hunter," she says pushing my underwear down, my dick springs free leaving a wet trail against my six-pack.

"No, stop it," I growl, dropping my hands.

"Your dick is saying something else," she says against my parted lips. Leaning forward on her knees she grinds her drenched panties against my erection.

"No!" I tell her, but she keeps kissing me. Swearing under my breath I grab her by the waist and push her back to her seat.

"What the fuck?" she asks, fixing her undone dress.

"I told you to stop!" I growl out, hiking up my pants and underwear. I turn the ignition and drive up to the house.

"Screw you, Hunter. You were the big tough guy who dragged me from the party and now you can't even fuck me," she says, pushing me back in my seat before jumping out of the car.

"You can't use sex to avoid talking to me!" I yell. I slam my fist against the steering wheel and watch her go.

"Fuck you," she roars. She can't get away from me fast enough.

I slam the car door, and fix my belt as I walk over to Drew and Timothy waiting for us. Didn't take them long to get back here. Scratching the side of my shaved head, I'm trying to figure out what to tell them. I need to go to a meeting first thing in the morning. I can't lose myself like this ever again. Like I'm losing myself in her.

Sky walks past Drew and Timothy not even stopping for them. Tim tries to grab her arm but she shakes her head.

"What the hell?" Drew asks.

Timothy stands next to him. "Drew, let him explain," he says, crossing his arms, giving me a chin-tip. Drew turns around. "Don't, Tim. This is between me and dipshit over there." Threat and despair ring in his voice.

Shaking my head, I fight against the urge to slam my fists against the wall until they're covered in blood, anything to get what happened between us out of my mind. I can still smell her on me. I swear under my breath, remembering how she bucked on top of me, the way she ached for my touch, but I can't give it to her until she tells me what is going on.

"Forget it, Drew," I mumble.

"I was scared you were going to crash the truck." He follows me into my apartment. "Are you okay?" he asks, his voice shaking.

He eyes me as I walk around the room. I'm starting to pace, never a good sign. Slowly, I breathe in and out, trying to focus on my heartbeat, and flexing my fingers. I haven't felt like this in a fucking long time. Slowly, the anger takes over like it used to do, and back then I'd turned to drugs, taking the easy way out.

"Hunter?" he pleads.

"Yeah?" I ask, picking up the damn skateboard and throwing it on the couch in the living room. *I don't know if I hurt her. Shit, did I hurt her?*

"Hunter," he warns again, "look at me."

I shake my head, the thought of losing her is ripping my heart out.

He grabs my face, holding me captive between his hands. "Breathe, man," he orders.

I try and push him away but he keeps holding on.

"Hey, look in my eyes."

I nod, trying to focus on his voice, a couple seconds pass before I can speak. "I'm okay."

He gives me a hug. "Really?"

I step away. "I don't know. She's messing with my head, dude." I take my seat on the couch, pushing the skateboard on the floor.

"Don't get hurt," he whispers.

"What is it with everyone telling me not to get hurt when I'm the one hurting her?"

He gives me a sad smile when I stand, watching me stomp around the room, pulling at my hair. "I know she is going back to New York, to NYU. I fucking know, okay? I'm someone to mark the days on a calendar with. Something in between until she gets married to a doctor or something."

"Hunt," Drew begs, tears pooling his eyes.

"What?" I stop pacing.

He keeps quiet.

"What?" I ask again, getting in his face. "What?"

He shakes his head, taking a deep, shuddering breath. "I'm going to bed."

"Sure, whatever. Fuck you." I turn around, head to the bathroom and slam the door shut behind me. After taking off my shirt, I hold it to my face. It still smells like her.

There is a knock on the door. "I love you, man, and I'm here. I'll always be here."

I hang my head, and place my hands flat on the wood.

"Tim is here as well whenever you need," Drew says.

I nod, leaning my forehead against the door. Drew sighs and after a while he leaves but I still whisper, "I love you too."

I look in the dirty mirror at the man staring back at me. The tattoos on my body and my neck, the piercings, my hair falling in front of my eyes ... *is this what she sees? The part of me everyone notices, not the man I am underneath, the man underneath this black ink?*

I've shown her, haven't I? Fuck, I don't even know anymore. I should talk to her about what happened in the truck. It felt like she wanted to prove something to me, or to herself, I don't know.

I spit out every swear word I can think of until I run out of steam. My knuckles turn white as I grab the cold surface of the sink. My pupils are dilated. And the only one I see staring back at me is my father.

"Motherfucker," I growl, punching the mirror. It shatters into a million little pieces, and my hand turns red from blood. But I don't give a damn. I only care about the fact she has woken a part of me I thought I buried a long time ago. Still, she is going to leave me one way or the other, and I'm not sure if my heart will be able to take it when she does.

CHAPTER 20

Sky

Early the next morning, I get a coffee and settle myself on one of the porch chairs watching the sun come up. I pull the sleeves of my shirt down, hiding the bruises he gave me. I shouldn't have jumped on him like that. What was I thinking, using sex to distract him from the real reason I didn't want to talk? I can't break his heart.

I walk to the track and lean against the fence, watching Hunter practice for half an hour. He is a force of nature, the way he defies gravity by jumping high and never losing his balance, pedaling the bike like it's easy. His head moves up when he notices me. He skids to a halt as I approach him, and takes off his helmet and gloves. Stopping right in front of him, I get a whiff of his sweat, and I bite my lip when his dark eyes meet mine.

Brushing my sweaty palms on my shorts, I tell him. "I'm sorry."

Hunter

Those big brown eyes make me swallow a couple times before I find my voice. "For what?" Shit, I sound angry as hell.

She flinches but stands her ground. "I'm sorry for last night, Hunter. I should have never thrown myself on you like that. I know I owe you an explanation," she says, her voice trembling as she turns the rings she wears on her fingers.

"What about?" I ask.

"Us," she whispers.

I swear under my breath. "Is there really an us?" My voice sounds husky to my own ears.

"I know I haven't been honest," she tells me.

"Forget it, Shorty." I grimace, pushing my gloves into the back of my shorts, and placing the helmet on the bike.

"No, I won't." She focuses on the ground. Her voice is small as she asks, "Give me a shot, please?"

"You need to give me time to figure some shit out," I tell her and kiss her forehead before walking to the garage. I'm falling for her, for the first time in my fucked up life, I'm imagining a future with her by my side. She doesn't follow me. Probably for the best. She isn't ready for what I have to tell her, and a part of me believes she never will be.

Sky

I take the back porch steps one at a time, and Jay looks up from the letter he's been staring at.

"What is going on there, kiddo?" he asks, motioning to Hunter, who storms into the garage.

"Do you really want to know?" I mumble, taking my seat next to him.

"No, I don't." He leans forward, and flashes me a small smile. "What's going on with you, Jay?"

He lets out a deep breath. "Hunter signed with someone else. Kid's in deep."

"How did you find out?" I mutter, staring at my hands.

"Drew thought something was up, so he called Ryan, one of Neil's riders, last night. He's a good kid, and he confirmed it. Fuck, I can't believe Hunter did that to save my ass," he says, heaving a sigh.

"What do you mean?"

"I've had some money problems the last couple of years, and he probably figured this would help us all in the long run. Damn, I don't know what I should do. Maybe Hunt's father can help us," he drawls, tipping the brim of his baseball cap up. "To tell you the truth, I don't know what to do anymore."

"What's in the letter, Jay?" I ask, trying to change the subject.

"Something I didn't have the guts to say to your face," he confesses, leaning back in his seat.

"I'm sorry I never talked to you," I rasp.

"Same here, baby girl, that's why I've been carrying this damn letter around, trying to find a good time to show it to you. I guess I didn't want to upset you. I wanted to keep you safe. I didn't want him to break your heart."

"I think I'm breaking his."

"No, darling, you healed it. Because of you he's never felt more alive. I see it in his eyes, the way he smiles, the way he is on and off the track. Hunter is still a combustible asshole but he's trying to be a better man," he says, sounding proud.

He stands and kisses my forehead. "But I want you to read something I wrote to you a long time ago," handing me the envelope.

"We'll be gone early tomorrow for the races in New Mexico

and Colorado, but we will be back by the end of next week, take these days to figure out want you want. You can stay here as long as you like."

"Thanks, Dad, I will," I say. He flashes me a sad smile before leaning against the windowsill. With trembling fingers, I open the letter and start to read.

Dear Sky,

I'm writing to let you know I miss you. I've missed you ever since you and your mom left California.

I'm sorry I haven't been the dad you needed these last few years. I talked to your mother and she told me you are going out a lot in the city. She also told me about you spending time with Timothy. I hope you are happy, baby girl.

Do you still wear the necklace I gave you? Every night, before I go to sleep, I put on the song I used to sing to you—"Free Bird," you remember? I hope you hear it all the way out there on the East Coast.

I need to tell you something. I took in a kid; his name is Hunter. He is a couple years older than you are. He reminds me of myself when I was a hell raising teenager, always getting into trouble.

His past still haunts him, and I try my best to stop him from fucking up. He makes me smile and makes me want to kill him on a daily basis. You two would probably get along.

I hope one day you'd like to come and visit. I am here.

We still need to talk about all the things we didn't say. And I'm sorry I never visit you. I blame it on the traveling and training, but I'm scared. Scared of the young woman I'll meet. I wish you were here, kiddo. I'm still trying to find the man I never got to be.

I know I'm selfish but I hope someday you will forgive me and maybe then I will start to forgive myself for leaving you the way I did.

Your Dad

With tears streaming down my cheeks I clutch the letter to my chest.

Jay hugs me from behind. "I'm sorry for everything."

"I'm sorry too. I love you," I tell him, meaning every word.

His body shudders, "You have no idea how much that means to me. Having you here is a dream come true. Stay a little longer, baby girl," he pleads.

"I will, Dad," I promise him. "I'll keep holding on."

Jay, Mac and the boys leave for Phoenix early the next day.

"Sure you're going to be all right?" Dad asks, giving me a hug.

"It's only two weeks, go win some titles," I tell him, leaning against the porch railing as I watch Drew and Mac put the last of the suitcases in the van. I wave at them and they do the same.

Hunter hops up the porch, and stops a couple of steps down from me, so we're on eye level.

Dad hugs me again, and gives him a pat on the shoulder before he heads to the car.

"You gonna be okay alone?" Hunter asks, pushing his hands in his back pockets.

"I will be, Jay stocked up on food, and I've got enough books to read and records to listen to."

"I know I told you I need time," he murmurs, looking anywhere but at me. "But if you get bored," he says, locking eyes, "you got my number, Shorty," he winks, and kisses my cheek.

"Hunt!" Dad growls, "get down here."

"Duty calls. Hey, if you're lonely at night hit me with a *u up*," he grins, flicking his tongue over his lip piercing.

"My fingers had enough practice being alone these last years," I tell him, and his eyes flick to the tiny shorts I'm wearing. I like teasing him, and judging by his smile he loves every minute of it too. "Maybe I'll FaceTime you, and let you watch," I joke, but mean every word.

He stumbles down the steps and I giggle, "Fuck, Shorty, don't tease a man," he sighs dramatically, and gives me a two finger wave before he gets in the truck, and I watch them drive away.

I open the door and my phone dings with an incoming text, *please let me watch?;)*

Go win some medals BMX guy, and maybe you'll get lucky:) I answer and catch myself smiling the whole time I'm making coffee.

During breakfast I can't shake the feeling I need to find out more about Hunter's past. I do some research and discover a lot about his father and the Devil's Sons MC. Some things I find are good—a lot are very bad. But then again, you can't believe everything you read online. I call Timothy and ask him to take a little trip with me.

I smile, looking at Tim sitting behind the wheel of his car. I get in the passenger seat and he asks, "Ready, honey?" as he puts the car in Drive.

"Ready as I'll ever be," I tell him, looking out the window.

I found out the MC has a clubhouse an hour or so from Chula Vista, somewhere in No Man's Land, an old military building. It's built like a fort apparently, four stories high with concrete walls and bars in front of the windows like a prison. There are no other houses in the vicinity. Great. They'll see us coming from miles away.

Tim stops outside the metal gate. My hands start to sweat. There are about twenty motorcycles parked in front of the building in a neat line. A couple of guys with leather vests are standing around the bikes, probably guarding them or something. I squint and take a closer look at them. The word *prospect* is stitched in white letters on their leather cuts.

"Shit," I mutter. I read Hunter Thompson's book about the Hell's Angels a long time ago. I wonder if this club is anything like them. Apparently, the Devil's Sons are one of the biggest clubs in the country.

Tim kills the ignition. "You sure about this?"

"I need to do this for Hunter." My voice trembles a little.

"I'll be here if you need me. Sure you don't want me to come in with you?"

I shake my head. "I'm okay. I'll send you a text in case something happens."

"Good luck," he tells me, hopping out and opening my door for me.

Slowly, I get out of the car and walk to the main door. I pass the gate and stop near the bikes. The four guys turn around and look me over from top to bottom. I'm not wearing anything special—just black skinny jeans, boots and a black leather jacket.

"What do you want?" one of the older guys asks. His tats don't scare me; they make me think of Hunter, and I smile when his tough demeanor should probably make me want to run for the hills.

"I'm here to meet Oliver Cole," I say, keeping my voice steady.

"Oliver Cole?" the guy asks, a threat in his voice and a blank look on his face.

I sigh when another guy about my age walks over, eyeing the car and Tim, who is smoking a cigarette beside it, with suspicion.

"Zombie?" I ask, my voice small.

"What do you want to see the Prez for?" he asks, seeming uninterested.

"My business." I keep my voice composed and matter-of-fact. Shit, I hope they let me in, and I don't have to give them a secret handshake or tell them some password.

The man nods in the direction of Tim. "Who's the dude by the car?"

"My Uber," I state.

"Sure, whatever, girlie." He walks to the door and slams his fist on it.

It opens and I take a step back when a big, burly guy stomps outside and gets in my face. "What do you want?"

He closes the main door behind him. I look at his vest. It has a Sgt. at Arms patch and above it, the word *Animal*. Great. His name isn't giving me much hope for a positive outcome.

"I want to talk to Oliver Cole. I'm his ..." Yeah, what am I to him really? "His daughter-in-law," I reply, straightening my shoulders.

Animal raises his brows, like he doesn't believe a word I'm saying. After a beat, he nods. "I'll take it from here," he says, addressing the other guys. "Come with me."

"Thank you." My voice sounds strong, and I follow him into the clubhouse.

I don't know what I expect to find. I read enough to imagine it being some kind of fight-meets-strip club, and some illegal underground facility where they plot to overtake the government. Inside, it is nothing like I thought it would be, but even bigger than I imagined. A bar sits immediately on the left. Pool tables and old couches are on either side of the room with chairs and tables scattered around, and two jukeboxes are in the far right corner because apparently one isn't enough.

There are a couple of women behind the bar, cleaning and tidying up or handing out drinks. They don't look so scary. More like they belong, wearing the same vests as some of the guys walking around. Others are sitting, talking to each other while Led Zeppelin plays in the background.

No one really notices me. Some nod, but most continue shooting pool or carrying on with their conversations. It's so not like the gatherings I've read about. Sure, it's a Monday evening, but still.

I get more anxious as the seconds tick by. I follow Animal across the room to a long hallway.

The guy stops in front of a nondescript door and knocks. "Zombie?"

"What?" the voice on the other side asks. Do I recognize that tone?

"You busy?" Animal says, and opens the door, motioning with his chin to let me know it's okay for me to enter. I do, and he slams it shut behind me.

The big handsome man sitting behind an old wooden desk glances up from the files he's reading.

He pushes his chair back, brushing one hand through his short dark hair, taking his glasses off, and smiling like he recognizes me. I squeeze my eyes shut for a moment, relaxing when clear blue eyes stare back at me, the same shade as the eyes on the man I'm falling in love with.

He points to a chair across from his desk and chuckles. "Take a seat, kid."

Damn it. *What have I gotten myself into?*

CHAPTER 21

Hunter

Two weeks later

I've been on the road for two weeks, and I'm still no closer to the number one spot. Sky talks to Jay every other day on the phone. I text her every night; we talk about everything, and I get to know her even more. One night she even let me watch as she got herself off, and I was right behind her. My dick twitches in my pants at the thought, fuck that was hot. I can't wait to go home and spend more time with her, maybe I can convince her to stay in California, with Jay and me. The BMX season is almost over. I won most of the previous cancelled runs, but lost in Colorado. I'm behind Ryan in the stats but I still have a couple of races left to ride in Chula Vista. I missed her, for the first time in my life I want *my* girl to watch me from the sidelines. *My girl,* has a nice ring to it, I think, going through my sponsor boxes.

"Have you forgotten our deal?" Neil asks when he catches me alone in the BMX trailer.

"Fuck you, Neil," I tell him, tossing a sponsor shirt on the workbench. "I'm not gonna race for you. I don't care what I have to do to get out of our deal, I'm done."

"You are making a big mistake, boy. You know how much money you can earn riding for me."

I shake my head, grabbing the edge of the table for support.

"You promised you would ride for me when you got what you wanted from Jay. We signed a contract. If you forfeit, you have to pay up even more than you already owe me."

I jump out of the trailer and Neil follows me. "It was a mistake to sign that deal with you. I'm going to tell Jay everything. I'm not going to leave him, we'll figure it out on our own."

Neil shakes his head. "You better pay me back," scraping knuckles, which are decked out with gold rings, over his jaw. "You are just like Jay."

"You bet your ass I am," I sneer.

He glances at his gold Rolex watch. "No eyes for the stars. You two deserve each other."

"Fuck you, Neil," I spit out.

"Just give me my damn money, boy."

I watch him leave, not knowing what to say. "Fuck," I yell, throwing a bike wheel against the ground. How the hell could I've been so stupid?

Sky

The next day

It's late in the afternoon and I'm starting to get hungry. I put the leftover pizza in the oven from yesterday evening, when the guys came back from Colorado. I smile thinking about the talk I had with Hunter's father. He was a kind man, not scary, like the picture I concocted in my head. I told him about Hunter's and Jay's money problems and he promised to help where he could. He walked me back to Timothy who was laughing and talking to a couple vest wearing guys. No matter where Tim goes he always makes friends. I didn't tell any of the guys I visited the clubhouse. I did get a text this morning from Oliver saying he was going to take care of everything. I didn't want to ask what he meant by that.

Jay and Drew left early in the morning for another meeting with Mac in San Diego. After their meeting they would cross the border for Tijuana to meet up with a friend of theirs who works on BMX bikes in his spare time. I didn't talk to Hunter last night, or when he came over for breakfast; I pretended I was sleeping. He did send me a couple of texts saying he was going on a drive up the coast to clear his head, and when he came back we needed to talk about us. I didn't respond, because I have no idea what I should tell him, because when I do there isn't going to be an *us*.

I almost lose my balance and grab the kitchen table for support. I run my hands through my hair and cringe as the greasy strands slide through my fingers. Maybe a shower will do me good.

Slowly, I head up the stairs. I click on Spotify and Oasis fills the room. I strip and turn on the warm shower, letting the water soothe my skin. Dizziness takes me hostage, and I lean against the wall.

I push my wet hair out of my face with trembling hands, trying to shift from one foot to the other. After a while, my legs start to shake and I clutch the shower curtain for support before my knees give out and I slump down the cold tiled wall onto the floor. I try to stand but my legs won't move.

"No, please no," I whisper. I hug my knees to my chest, shaking as the water slams against me. After a while, I close my eyes and let my tears run free. I can't fight it anymore. I don't want to.

And then it hits me how much I've missed Hunter these last two weeks. I love him, and I hate myself for loving him when I know I will only break his heart like it has been broken before. I need to let him go; I will destroy him if I don't. But I need him, and I fucking hate and love him for giving me another reason to stay.

Hunter

I rev my bike as I motor up the driveway. I reach the house; there's smoke coming out of the kitchen window.

"What in the ..." I mutter, placing my helmet on the bike and running to the house. When I open the back door, the kitchen is filled with smoke.

"What the fuck?" I choke. There's something burning in the oven. The smoke begins to disappear after I open another window. Still, I almost stumble a couple of times because I can't see shit.

Angrily, I grab a towel and place the black mess in the sink. Damn. The smoke alarm starts ringing. "Christ," I grumble, grabbing a chair and turning the alarm off. "Shit, Shorty. What were you thinking?" I drawl, coughing my lungs out.

The shower is running upstairs. I grit my teeth. Screw her, I think, as I stomp up the stairs, taking them two steps at a time. It doesn't matter if there is a fucking big chance she pushes me away. I'm going to talk to her right now.

After knocking, I wait for a couple of seconds.

There's no answer. The shower is still running and I don't care; I'm done with her ignoring me. Opening the door, I walk to her bathroom, slamming my fist on the wooden door.

"Sky," I yell, waiting for her to say something. "You know you almost burned the damned house to the ground."

I punch my fist against the frame again, making it rattle. Still, she says nothing. I'm getting angrier by the second.

"You know what could have happened?"

"Go away, Hunter." She sounds different, like she's been crying.

"Sky, what the hell is going on?" I roar.

She sniffles. "Go away," she cries.

I try the door handle. "Open up," I order, raising my voice.

"No, leave me alone."

"Open the damn door or I'm coming in," I bellow, waiting for her response, my heart breaking from her sobbing. "That's it."

I put my full weight against the door, and force it open. The bathroom is filled with steam. "How long have you been in here?" I raise my voice and open a window. "Sky, what are you doing?"

"Go away, Hunter," she sobs.

I try not to look, but when I do, she is sitting in the corner of the shower, her hair plastered in wet streaks against her face. She holds her legs against her stomach. Her eyes are bloodshot red.

"Get up," I order her with menace in my voice.

"No." She shakes her head, not letting go of her legs.

"We need to talk about what happened. We can't keep doing this. Fuck, I can't keep doing this. I'm not letting you go. You are not going to push me away. I won't let you," I tell her.

"Will you just go, Hunter. Leave me alone." Her voice is weak.

"No," I bark, slamming my hand against the wall. "You are going to tell me what the fuck is going on." I grab a towel. "Get out of the shower," I tell her, holding it in front of me.

"No, I can't." Her voice breaks.

"What do you mean 'I can't'? Come on, get up," I say, losing steam.

Her body shakes, and her teeth are clattering.

"I can't."

"What do you mean?" My voice loses all its anger and I kneel so we're at eye level. I don't gape at her naked body; I hold her stare and seeing her like this pains me to the core.

"I can't, okay? I cannot move my legs." The panic in her voice tears me in two.

"What?" I don't understand.

"I can't move my legs," she screams, her eyes wide. "Hunter, my legs," she sobs, pain underlying each word. "I can't move them. I can't." She hiccups and starts to hyperventilate.

Without thinking, I take off my dirt-bike boots and step into the shower with my clothes still on. I crouch beside her, tucking the wet strands of hair behind her ears. "Breathe, honey. Look at me," I say. She relaxes slowly as my hands travel over her arms while the warm water cascades over our bodies.

"Sky, come on, get up. I won't be angry if you smoked too much," I say, my voice soft. "I shouldn't be a hard-ass about that shit. Hell, a joint was my best friend not so long ago."

Her legs are shaking. What is happening to her? I never experienced anything like this when I used. She gazes up at me with vacant big eyes. It fucking scares me.

"You're all wet," she says. Her voice sounds different, far away.

I stare at my clothes and start to laugh. "Yes, I guess I am." I pull my shirt over my head.

Her shaking hand skims my naked chest. I take my pants off and sit next to her, letting the warm water cover us like a blanket. She lays her head on my shoulder and tries to take my hand in hers, but she can't open her fist. I kiss her knuckles. We sit there not saying anything. I hold her close until my fingers start to prune.

"Are you getting warmer?" I ask, my voice a little unsteady.

"Yes." She nods, quiet tears running down her face. "I am. Thank you."

"You almost burned the house to a crisp," I say, kissing her forehead, and she winces when I do. My lips brush her temple, and she closes her eyes.

"I'm sorry," she whispers. "I'm sorry for not letting you in, for not telling you the truth from the beginning."

"I'm sorry for yelling at you. I love you, Shorty, and I don't care if you don't feel the same."

She closes her eyes in pain. "We shouldn't… I'm only going to hurt you."

"No, you gave me purpose. You make me feel wanted." I tell her, and she buries her face in my shoulder.

Turning her cheek, I kiss her lips, and she lets me.

She pulls me into her. "I'm so sorry." Her eyes are big. She grimaces as she slowly moves her legs.

"Are you okay?" I ask, concerned.

Shaking her head, she replies, "I don't know how to answer that question anymore." She bites on her lip like she's in pain.

"Can you get me off the floor?" she asks after a while.

"Sure," I answer, taking her into my arms, her naked wet body against mine. She lays her head on my shoulder as I turn the shower faucet off. I carry her in my arms and set her on the bed. I grab a towel and put it over her shoulders.

"Let's get you dry," I husk out through the lump in my throat, and my eyes start to sting. She nods and lets me dry her off. It is the most intimate thing I've ever done in my life. And she lets me.

She closes her eyes when my hands skim over her naked flesh. Goose bumps cover her body. It's not sexual; it's something else, like she trusts me unconditionally.

I drape a towel around my waist. I catch her watching me, and she smiles. "Don't peek," I say, winking.

"Nothing I haven't seen before." She tries to smile but her eyes are sad.

I kneel in front of her, pulling a tank top over her head. After going through her drawer, I grab the white lace panties she bought all those weeks ago. I help her stand and slowly trace the lines of her long legs while I pull her underwear up. My mouth is face-to-face with the place I want to bury my tongue in, but I don't.

I lick my lips as I stand, towering over her. She's so helpless, so small, swaying a little when she places both her hands on my chest, steadying herself.

"Do you have trouble standing sometimes?" Fuck, what the hell is happening to her? When we texted last week nothing seemed wrong, but what about the way her voice sounds almost hoarse, like she has trouble speaking every now and then? And the fact she can barely lift her arms, or use her legs? This isn't from smoking too much marijuana. My stomach actually turns and I feel bile rising in the back of my throat, is she sick?

"Yes, I do, it's gotten worse so fast." Her hands are cold. For a brief moment I close my eyes, having missed her touch. I crave it more than I want to admit.

Gotten worse so fast? What the hell is she talking about? I hold her for the longest time, rocking her from side to side, her feet not even touching the ground. I kiss her lips over and over.

"You want to lie down?" I choke on my own voice, and the lump in my throat. She nods, and I help her get under the covers.

I lie down beside her. She lays her head on my chest, and I kiss her damp hair.

"What's going on, Sky?" I ask, the uneasy feeling never leaving me.

She swallows and gazes up into my eyes. "I'm sick, Hunter."

"You need me to get you some aspirin?" I ask, scanning the room, placing my hand on her forehead. She doesn't feel warm.

She grabs my hand. "Not that kind of sick," she answers, her voice breaking.

"What?" *What is she telling me?*

"I've been sick for a long time now," she whispers.

"What the fuck are you telling me?" I demand, frowning

at her. I get out of the bed, and big fat teardrops run down her pretty face. She closes her eyes, "Please, Hunter, don't go, let me explain," she whispers, and winces like it takes her a lot of strength to reach out to me. Dread fills me, and *I can't lose her* flashes through my mind. I try to push the thought away.

"How long have you been sick?" I hate that my voice trembles.

She flinches. "Sit, Hunter. Please let me explain. I..."

"Tell me what the hell is going on," I yell, anger takes hold of me. I've seen the signs, haven't I? Why didn't I ask her about them, why didn't I? *Because I don't want to fucking lose her* echoes through my head, over and over like some goddamn broken record.

She closes her eyes, and when she opens them, she tells me. "Hunter, I'm dying."

CHAPTER 22

Sky

I can't breathe. Hunter's brows descend, and I turn my head away. Clenching his jaw, he grinds his teeth together.

He takes a step away from me. "No, you can't be. I mean, you're twenty-one; you can't die," he pleads, scared, hurt. "If this is a fucking joke, so help me."

"No." I shake my head, trying to stand but I immediately sit, reaching for his hand. He balls his fists, holding them against his body, shaking his head over and over. "What are you telling me?"

"I have Motor Neuron disease." Even saying it out loud makes me want to scream.

"What?" he asks incredulously.

"ALS or Lou Gehrig's disease is what it's called," I tell him.

"What the hell? Is it like cancer?"

I shake my head. "No, but it's very rare. Only one percent of people get it under the age of twenty-five. Basically, my muscles will slowly weaken, every single part of my body will shut down. I will lose the ability to speak, to swallow, and one day when my body can't take it anymore, I will stop breathing," I state, like I'm reading the weather report out loud. I hate that there is no emotion in my voice, but I can't break in front of him.

He swallows hard. "I thought only older people got things like that." He closes his eyes. "I didn't mean … I can't …" He shakes his head. "What?" He's lost and scared at the same time.

I try to keep my voice strong. "It's very rare but younger people can get it too. And the last couple of weeks I've gotten a lot worse."

He paces the room. "How long have you known?"

I can't stand to tell him. The answer will tear him apart like it is slowly destroying me. "For a while now, that's why I came back here."

He stops walking. "What?" he yells. "And Jay? Does Jay know?"

I nod. "Yes, my mom told him."

"When?" Hunt asks, with anger in his voice.

"The day before I got here."

He takes a step toward me. "Does Drew suspect? Does he know, Sky? And Timothy?" He is too calm; he's starting to scare me.

I bite my lip and nod. "Yes."

He punches the wall, leaving a dent. "And you figured, 'Let's not tell Hunter to play some twisted game,'" he bellows. "Make me fall in love with you while you knew this whole time." He sits on his haunches, brushing both his hands through his hair. "You all fucking knew."

I reach out for his hand but he stands, backing away from me. "I didn't want to let my fucking disease destroy us like it is slowly destroying me. I didn't want you to know, okay?" I have trouble speaking the words. My eyes tear up. "I didn't want you to look at me like you're doing now," I whisper. Fury blazes in his eyes, and a shiver runs through my body.

He runs both hands across his face. His muscles flex, like he's going to punch the wall again. I lean against the headboard, scared of what he might do.

"I didn't want to talk about it every damn day we spent together," I say, not meeting his stare.

His voice cuts through me like a knife. "You made me want to build a life with you, and you knew all along, and were using me. For what?"

I open my mouth, he gets right in my face, and I can't form the words.

"You played some twisted fucking game, got me to love you, then planned on leaving me, like everyone has done all my life." His voice is hoarse. "I love you, Shorty. You are not leaving me, get that? I won't let you."

I try to hold onto his arm but he shrugs my hand off him. I caress his cheek. "Please, Hunter. Don't." A sob escapes my body. I can't breathe; knowing I'm breaking his heart hurts too much.

He closes his eyes, leaning into my touch. When he opens them, I know I'm losing him like I am slowly losing myself.

"Don't what, love you?" His voice is stern. He's staring straight at me.

"Please, Hunter. You need to understand I never wanted to fall in love with you. I didn't need this." I raise my voice, tears falling on the white sheets. "I love you and I hate myself for being so selfish ..." I pause. "... but I love you. I love you so much. It hurts more than knowing I have to leave you one day."

"You don't need to love me," he yells. "You didn't need to fucking use me, or try to be my friend. I ..."

He stumbles backwards, like it hits him just now that I'm going to die. He takes another step away from me while I try to move my hand to grab his, but I can't. His body shakes with anger. There is pain in his eyes. Our gazes meet, and I want to forget the last weeks ever happened.

"Please," I beg. "I love you."

"Don't you fucking say that," he growls.

"Please, Hunter. Please listen to me. I love you."

"No," he says, storming to the door. Looking over his

shoulder he says, "Leave me alone," his voice cold and full of hate.

"Hunter, don't." My hands are shaking. I cover my mouth. "I love you. I'm so sorry," I sob.

He shakes his head. "Don't," he whispers, leaving me alone in my room, slamming the door shut behind him. I need to go after him. I grab hold of the chair. My legs start to wobble and I fall, hitting my head, and everything fades away.

Hunter

I storm out of the house, slamming the front door behind me.

I run down the steps. "FUCKKKK!" I yell, pacing in front of the house. My knuckles are raw and covered in blood. I smear the red on my wet shirt. Falling to my knees, I scream.

"Fuck, no!" She can't die; she can't leave me. I place my hand over my chest, the place she tore my heart from.

Slowly, I stand and walk to my apartment, stopping every time I take a step. "Keep walking. Keep walking," I tell myself until I stop. I can't leave her alone; I love her. I fucking love her more than she knows. Running back into the house, I take the stairs two at a time.

"Shorty?" I search the room. She's not in her bed. I open the bathroom. *Where the fuck is she?*

"Sky, where …" Spotting her lifeless legs I run to the other side of the bed.

"Babe?" I plead, turning her over. *Why isn't she waking up?* Bile rises in my throat. I shake her hard. She isn't breathing. "No, God, please," I beg.

I check her neck for a pulse. It's faint. I grab her phone from the nightstand and hit the emergency button.

"Nine-one-one, what is your emergency?" the dispatcher asks.

"It's my girl. She isn't breathing," I sob. I don't know what to do.

"Slow down, sir. Explain to me what happened," she says.

"She's dying. We need an ambulance," I shout, giving the dispatcher the address, and drop the phone. "Don't leave me," I yell, shaking Sky. She slowly opens her eyes. "Honey," I cry, kissing her lips. Her hand on my cheek is so cold.

"You came back," she breathes.

"Baby, hold on." I pick her up, and carry her downstairs. She closes her eyes again. "No," I whisper, walking outside with her to the porch. It's like time stops until the sirens reach the house.

"Shorty," I plead, swaying her in my arms. Tires screech, followed by the EMTs running up the porch steps.

"What happened?" One of them asks as they take her from me and check her vitals. "I don't know." I stammer, "She—I—had trouble breathing, she fell and lost consciousness."

"Are you her husband?" one asks. I nod.

They examine her briefly, checking all her vitals, and her airways. One paramedic rushes over and brings a gurney. They lift her on it.

"I need to intubate her," the older guy says. Once she's intubated, and her chest expands from the new air that enters her lungs, the color slowly returns to her cheeks.

"We need to go now," the paramedic says.

"I'm not leaving her," I tell them, my voice cracking.

They share a look and the female paramedic nods. "Get into the back," she tells me.

I follow them out and step into the waiting ambulance. I take Sky's hand in mine and we speed away.

I kiss her knuckles. "Don't leave me," I sob. "Don't you fucking leave me," I splutter, tears blurring my vision of her beautiful face.

CHAPTER 23

Sky

Present day

I wake, slowly opening my eyes and scanning the room. I don't recognize anything. I don't know where I am.

Then I hear the buzzing noises all around me, footsteps of people walking in the hallway. Slowly, I try to flex my fingers, focusing on the beeping of the machines hooked up to me.

I'm in a hospital bed. Hunter is holding my hand and sleeping next to me, his head on my shoulder. Brushing my hand through his dark hair, I watch him. Judging by his stubble, he hasn't shaved in days. The piercings are all gone.

Drew and Dad are dozing on a couch under the window. I smile. I'm not alone; they didn't leave me. The tiny oxygen tube in my nose tickles, making it easier for me to breathe.

"Hey," I whisper, my voice hitching in my throat as Hunter opens his eyes. He has dark circles under them, like he hasn't slept

"Babe?" he chokes. He kisses my forehead. "We thought we lost you."

"I'm still here," I tell him. My voice sounds funny.

Dad rushes to my side, and Drew gives me a sad smile. "I'll let the nurse know she's awake," he says, and leaves us alone. I grab my throat, looking between Hunt and my dad.

"They had you sleeping for days, does it hurt?" Dad asks.

"Yeah," I whisper.

"They needed to put a tube in your throat to help you breathe," he croaks.

I nod, focusing on Hunter, whose eyes are as red as my dad's.

"What happened?" My voice is brittle.

Jay takes my other hand. "You…"

The door opens and a doctor walks in with Drew.

"Hi, Sky, I'm Doctor Harper. I need a couple minutes alone with you to do some tests." The doctor's voice is soft.

Dad gives me a reassuring nod.

"I'm not leaving her," Hunter says, matter-of-fact.

"It's okay, Hunter," I rasp, trying to plead with my eyes.

He focuses his steely gaze on the doctor then kisses my cheek. His warm breath against my cold skin feels like heaven. "I'll be outside." He clears his throat. "I love you. Don't you forget," he whispers in my ear, his face wet from his tears.

"I love you too."

Hunter

I walk out of the room and hold onto the wall for support.

"Shall I get you a coffee?" Jay asks.

I nod. "Thanks. I'm going out for a smoke. Catch you in a couple," I grumble.

Drew takes my hand. "Need anything else?"

"Some air," I tell him. He flashes me a soft smile and follows Jay.

I watch them walk down the hall. Timothy pushes off the wall and joins them, draping his arm around Drew's neck.

I try to slowly breathe in and out but I can't. The blood drains from my face. I'm about to throw up. Frantically, I scan the corridor, looking for an emergency exit. Anything to get me away from her room, this floor, this hospital. Spotting an exit sign, I make a run for it. I slam the door open and grab the railing of the stairs leading to the parking lot.

A warm breeze heats my cold arms. Slumping against the fence, I start to hyperventilate, and bury my face in my hands. My head starts to spin; I don't know what to do. Leaning forward, I put my head between my knees, swallowing back the bile rising in the back of my throat.

Pinching my eyes shut, I try to forget what happened. *Why did I leave her alone in her room? Why did I yell at her? Why? Why?* I slam my hand into the iron bar. It hurts like hell.

"Fuck," I huff, flexing my fingers. I let the tears spill over. I don't care. My inked hands shake. Everything hurts. *I am going to lose her*. The thought echoes through my head. *I am going to lose her*. I lean my temple against the balustrade, staring out over the packed parking lot.

A couple of nurses pass me; I don't say hello. I want to be alone. Remembering what my sponsor said, I try to calm myself. *Never let anger be the solution when love is the answer.* I hate my NA sponsor's hippie Yoda quotes.

The door opens again.

"There you are," Jay murmurs, carrying two cups of coffee.

I turn my gaze, pulling my hoodie over my head. I don't want him to see my tears. "Here I fucking am."

"Scoot over, will ya?" he asks, taking his seat next to me. He hands me a coffee. "What a fucked up week, kid." He clears his throat.

"I was so scared," I confess. I'm nauseous as hell. I haven't slept much these last days. I feel like roadkill and probably look even worse.

He nods. Jay's eyes are as red as mine.

He sips from the coffee not saying anything for a while.

"Can I bum a smoke?" he asks, breaking the silence.

"Sure." I pull out my Lucky Strikes from my back pocket and hand him the pack.

Jay takes the Zippo lighter from me and lights one up. He inhales deep, and blows out through his nose. "Man, I haven't had one of these in years."

"Makes one of us." My fingers are shaking like hell as I light my cigarette.

"How are you holding up, son?"

"What kind of question is that?" I ask. "It is what it is." I'm still holding the cigarette between my teeth. "Why does it hurt like this?" I ask, mostly to myself.

"Because we both love her."

"Jay—"

"No, son. It's okay." His voice is strained and sad. "Sounds sappy as fuck." The side of his mouth twitches, but he doesn't smile, instead he puts the cigarette between his lips with trembling fingers. "The doctor told me they're afraid of her getting pneumonia, she can't really breathe, or swallow like she used to. She should stay in the hospital so they can monitor her, and put her on antibiotics."

I look at him, and the tears barreling down his cheeks. "She's not going to do that, is she?"

He shakes his head, "No."

I grunt, shaking my head, *fuck Shorty*. "I should have noticed something was wrong with her. The way she slurred her words, the way her voice changed. Damn, and all the times I caught her when she almost fell."

"She didn't want you to know," Jay says.

"It wouldn't have changed anything between us," I mutter. I flick my Zippo open and light another cigarette, then drag a restless hand over my stubble. "I can't feel anything."

Jay puts his arm around my shoulder.

"Why did it happen to her? I fucked up so bad. Why can't it be me?" I ask.

He stares out to the parking lot. "I don't know the answer. Sometimes things don't make sense. You can't blame yourself for something you have no part in." He shakes his head, letting his arm drop from my shoulder. "But I've been asking myself the same question." His brows descend, and he looks ten years older. "Why couldn't it be me?" Jay says slowly. "God knows, I deserved it. But you need to have faith."

"Faith," I say angrily, blowing out the smoke through my nose. "Fuck faith."

Jay shrugs. "Some of us have faith; others have regrets."

"What if you have neither?" I ask, looking at him sideways.

"I guess you have to figure that one out for yourself," he admits.

We watch a couple of ambulances drive up. We're quiet, taking a sip from our coffees.

"I never want to let her go," I say, pulling my hoodie back.

"Then don't," he tells me, smoking his cigarette.

I stand, the bile rising in my throat again. I can't show weakness; I need to be strong for her, for them. I can't break. She needs me to hold it together. The 'fuck everyone and everything' attitude takes hold of me. I need a fix, need a hit.

"What kind of answer is that?" I yell. "I'm so fucking mad I could kill someone. You know what it feels like? You know what I could do?"

He nods, watching me pace the small area. I lean against the cold railing. "For once in my life something made sense and now …" I stumble over my words and my shoulders shake. I throw the coffee on the ground, hiding my face in my hands. Jay's arms come around my body, holding me. I bury my head in his chest and cry like I've never cried before.

"Talk to her. Don't shut her out. She needs to know your fears. She needs to know your pain," he says, his voice breaking.

"I don't know if I can," I answer, taking a deep breath and wiping away my tears.

"You need to, or else you've already lost her." He taps my chest with his finger. "I'm going to check on her."

"Thanks, Jay," I rasp.

"For what?"

"For letting me love her."

He kisses the top of my head and walks back into the hospital.

"Fuck!" I yell, slumping against the railing and crying my heart out, while the last couple of weeks I spent with her flash through my mind.

CHAPTER 24

Hunter

I grab the marble of the sink until my knuckles turn white. Turning on the faucet I splash some cold water on my face. Staring into my bloodshot eyes in the hospital bathroom mirror I swear under my breath. She is still sleeping, like she has done the whole damn day. I skim the pill bottles on the sink with shaking fingers. I grab one and scan the label, before opening it. Everything I once wanted is right here in these bottles: Percocet, OxyContin, the works. I fucking hate hospitals.

"What are you doing?" she asks.

I twist the top back on and place the container back.

"Nothing," I murmur, kneeling beside her bed. "Are you okay? Need anything?"

"You," she whispers, and I get under the covers and pull her against me. "Only you." I bury her face in my chest.

"I'm tired," she whispers.

We both know she's not talking about needing a good night's sleep.

"I know," I husk out, kissing her temple and holding her in my arms. She is so brittle and small. "How are you feeling, Shorty?"

"I'm glad we're going home tomorrow." Tears pool in her eyes.

She looks away. Reaching out I cup her cheek, before taking her hand and kissing each finger.

"Stay with me," she whispers, our noses almost touching. I close my eyes for a brief second before a tear rolls over my cheek.

Her gaze meets mine, and she tells me, "I'm sorry."

"For what?"

"For pushing you away when it became real, when *we* became real. I love you, Hunter," she says.

I cover her hand with my own. "I love you too, Shorty. I know you were only pushing me away because you were sick and you didn't want me to see you like this. Is that it?"

She nods.

"But Drew, Tim and Jay—they all knew. Why didn't you trust me enough? You didn't even give me a chance. What did you think? That I would walk away once I discovered what was happening to you?"

She nods.

"That isn't what love is supposed to be, babe."

She doesn't say anything but keeps staring at me, tears running down her face.

"I didn't know what to do. It was just easier," she begins.

"Easier how?"

"If you didn't know, then I could pretend it wasn't happening to me. But I'm dying, Hunter. My body is giving up. I'm so tired I can't hold on anymore. Some days I have trouble speaking; other days I can't get out of bed, and it was easier to keep my heart closed than to hurt you."

"It fucking broke me, Sky," I confess.

"Not as much as it would have destroyed me to see that look in your eyes every day you had to take care of me."

"And what if I wanted to take care of you, Shorty?"

"Stop talking about what *you* want. I love you, and I didn't want you to love me out of guilt or because you felt sorry for me," she says, her voice insecure.

"That's what you're afraid of? That I wasn't going to love you for the right reasons?"

"How can you love me?" she whispers, casting her eyes down.

I lift up her chin to make her look me in the eyes. "Don't you get it by now? I thought I didn't need anyone. I closed my heart for years. I barely let Drew, Jay and Mac in. You tore down my goddamn walls with a bulldozer. You remember the flat tire?"

She nods in response.

"The way you took my hand when I caressed your cheek? That was it for me, babe. I tried to believe in the friend angle for you, but I couldn't stay away and when you wanted to hang out, and I got to know the person you are, the bricks came tumbling down. When we fucked in the truck and kissed at the bar my previous life disappeared and I saw a future I thought I never could have had," I tell her, my voice a little unsteady.

"I won't be there with you," she rasps.

"Shorty, you'll be with me wherever I go. You changed me. You made me see what I was missing."

"What?" she asks. The small hospital bed creaks as I lean forward and kiss the side of her mouth. I drape my arm over her tiny waist and pull her into my chest, my breath mingles with hers and she smiles.

"A love that's layered, babe. Violent and dirty," I tell her, running my thumb over her bottom lip. "A love that makes you feel alive. I'm alive because of you. I know how much you're hurting. I know you're tired, and it's okay. I'm right here." I whisper with dread in my voice.

"I'm sorry." Tears stream over her cheeks onto the pillow.

"For what?" I ask, softly stroking her forehead with my thumb.

"For letting you go," she breathes.

"Babe, you didn't. I don't remember the man I wanted to be before you came into my life. I love you, Shorty. Promise me you'll hold on a little while longer," I husk out, kissing her cheek.

"I love you," she whispers, not saying anything more. We keep looking into each other's eyes, and I hold her while she sobs into my chest.

Sky

The next day, I go to Jay's house, my new home. After some debating, Jay is okay with me staying in Hunter's apartment.

Mom visits with Conrad for the first week. We talk for hours. I love and cherish every minute of it.

Someone knocks on my door. I open my eyes and Hunter is standing in the doorway next to Stevie. "Do you have time for one more visitor?"

"Always," I tell him, holding out my hands for my little brother to come to me. "Wanna get into the bed?" I ask, raising the covers. He jumps in next to me while Hunter puts on another record—Pink Floyd this time. Our eyes meet. "I'll come by later to get him, all right?"

"Okay," I whisper.

Hunt taps his fingers on the doorway. We are quiet for a while, a promise of love in his gaze as we keep our eyes locked on each other.

"Are you sick, Sky?" Stevie asks, his tiny hand caressing my forehead. His eyes are so big and scared.

I put my arm around his small shoulders. I nod. "Yes, I am."

He is quiet for a moment. His mouth trembles. "Are you going to die?"

I close my eyes, and when I open them Hunter is still staring at me. He looks broken.

"Are you, Sky?" Stevie clutches my hands in his.

I kiss his forehead. "I am, buddy."

Hunter hangs his head and leaves me alone with Stevie.

"That sucks," Stevie says after a while. I start to laugh, and he grins. I kiss his forehead. He puts his little arms around me and hugs me tight.

"It really does," I whisper.

For the next hour, we talk about the extra science classes he's taking after school. He shows me a book about space and explains why he wants to become an astronaut. Stevie falls asleep in my arms. Mom walks into the room after a while and gives me a reassuring smile.

"Was he good?" she asks, trying to sound strong but her voice trembles when she takes my hand. "I missed you, baby."

"I missed you too."

She is quiet for a while, staring at Stevie. "We are going to take him to the hotel."

"Mom, he needs his school, his friends," I tell her.

She sits on the bed. "I don't want to leave you."

I take her hand in mine. "I'm not going anywhere, not yet. He needs a normal life. I'll know when it is time, before..." I bite my lip when she closes her eyes and winces.

She kisses my forehead. "You are so much stronger than I am. I love you so much, Sky. You make my life so beautiful. I'm so proud to be your mother."

"I can't come home, Mom," I tell her.

"I know."

"You do?"

"Yes, because you have been my home all these years, baby. I want you to stay here. Jay and Hunter need you."

"I love you, Mom."

"I love you too," she says, caressing my cheek. She takes my hand in hers, and together we sit there for a while, holding each other.

Mom, Conrad and Stevie leave the following day, when Hunter, Drew and Mac come back from San Diego after giving a clinic sponsored by Red Bull.

"Hey, kiddo," Dad says, walking into Hunter's apartment. "The boys are unpacking the truck."

"Hi, Dad," I say, getting comfortable on the couch.

"I just said goodbye to your mom; she looks happy with Conrad," he says, flashing me a warm smile. "Want something to drink and listen to a record?"

I nod and he turns on a Lynyrd Skynyrd LP. He puts on a kettle before he takes his seat, reaching out, he brushes his hand through my hair. "Each night before I would go to sleep I'd put on the song I used to sing for you."

"Free Bird," I say, smiling.

He nods, taking the necklace I wear in his hand. "And I would sing along with the lyrics and know I'd failed as your father." He hangs his head.

"Dad." I put my arms around him, and bury my face in his neck. His body shudders. "I'm thankful for our time together."

He kisses the top of my head. "I finally feel I have a chance, have you back in my life." He chokes on his own words. "And this time, you are leaving me."

"Jay." I take his cheeks between my hands. The same brown eyes as my own, roam my face. "I'm not leaving any time soon, Dad, and it's okay, because you are with me. We are in this together."

He kisses my temple. "God, I'm gonna miss you."

"Me too, Daddy," I whisper against his heaving chest. "Me too."

CHAPTER 25

Hunter

"Hunter?" she asks, knocking on the garage door. "Can we talk?"

"Why aren't you in bed?" I ask, gazing up from the bikes me and Mac are putting together from the scrap I've accumulated from all the riders during the last season.

"I didn't feel like it," she says, closing the garage door, before leaning against the workbench.

"Didn't the doctor say you needed to take it easy?" I place my hands on the wood. Guns N' Roses echoes through the garage.

She rolls her eyes, walking over to me. I turn my back to her. "I want you," she says, hugging me from behind.

"Sky, please," I sigh, while her hands move from my chest to my belt. She slowly traces the line of my zipper with her fingers, and I'm getting hard already. Her lips ghost over the side of my neck, and she bites my earlobe. "Man," I growl.

She chuckles, still standing behind me, teasing me and

opening the zipper of my black jeans. I push against her hand. "Fuck."

"That's the plan." She giggles. Grinning, I turn around, and in one swift movement I box her between the workbench and my body. With my legs on either side of her slim frame, I hold her captive. When I lift her up by her legs and step between them, Sky's sweet little intake of breath goes right through me. Right to my heart.

Sky

I push my stomach forward, and his erection presses against my belly button. He takes my cheeks between his rough hands and kisses me, first on the corners of my mouth. He traces the line of my lips with his finger, opening my mouth farther until he slides his thumb in. Closing his eyes as I suck on him. I moan, and his hard shaft skims my thigh. His eyes fly open, and they travel to my exposed stomach.

I let his thumb go and he curls his hand around the side of my throat. "Damn it, Shorty." His fingers slowly trail along the line of my jaw. A lopsided smile is still plastered on his face. His gaze locks on me, and I tilt my head to the side, wetting my lips.

"Why are you taking it slow?" I ask, moving against him, wanting to experience the friction.

"I need to savor this moment," he says against my open mouth, before reaching out and locking the garage door. Getting on his knees in front of me, he lets his fingers move up my bare legs under my skirt, tracing the inside of my thighs, not going near the place I want him to.

My hands glide through his hair. "Can you move your hands farther toward the middle?" I rasp as he traces the line of my damp panties with his calloused fingers.

"No." He laughs, his eyes rolling up to meet mine.

"Please," I groan, swirling my hips at the same moment as he presses his nose against my underwear. His tongue darts out, pushing against the wet lace, and I shiver.

Letting out a low growl, he sits back on his heels, eyeing me. "Not yet, although I do like the way you're already wet for me," he purrs, waggling his eyebrows.

I tug on his hair harder than I intended, which brings a big smile to his face. Staring at my mouth, he stands, and towers over me. He pushes me against the counter with his body. Leaning his head against mine, he picks me up and places me on the steel workbench, the cold surface under my butt making me gasp. Expert hands move under my skirt, caressing the top of my ass.

"You are a tease, Mister Cole," I joke, trying to fill my lungs with air although they burn.

He chuckles in response, his lips skimming over my neck and down to my breasts, his stubble leaving a tickling sensation of want where his mouth used to be. I lie back on the bench, opening my legs for him. He skims his nose over my drenched panties again and I tremble, my clit already throbbing. He lifts up my skirt and tugs my panties down to my knees. Pressing the metal ball against the place where I ache for his tongue, I whimper, and my head falls back. He laps at my folds in circular motions, rubbing my oversensitive clit while my fingers clutch the long strands of his hair. I scoot forward and grind myself against his mouth. His stubble burns my thighs and only adds to the overwhelming sensation. "I can't get enough of your taste," he drawls. "Fuck, I love your pussy."

"Hunter," I plead, I need to come. I'm already out of breath and squirm as he starts running his piercing over my clit, over and over until I'm a withering mess. The orgasm tears through me, and I moan, and thrash against his face loving the way his stubble scrapes my inner thighs. He grins, kissing his way back up my body.

"Hunt," I whisper, nibbling below his jaw, following the lines of his neck tattoos with my fingers. Grabbing my face between his big hands, he kisses me hard. His mouth slams into mine, our tangled tongues moving together as we kiss and tease. He tastes so sweet on my lips, his stubble leaving my skin sore and hot at the same time. Cupping my breasts, he plays with my nipples, rolling the hard peeks between his fingers. Wrapping my legs more firmly around his ass, I tug him into me. I tremble as he pulls my arms around his neck and my legs more firmly around his hips.

We are at eye level now, and the cocky lopsided grin I love has my heart rate picking up. Gently, he pulls me closer, his right hand moving under my skirt as his other slips behind my head, holding me in place. I try to move but he shakes his head. Then his fingers trace the top of my pussy. I squirm, pushing myself against his palm.

Moving his fingers to the middle, he groans as he makes contact with my clit. Locking his heat filled eyes on me only builds my tension. Slowly he moves his thumb up, and I beg and plead. He's teasing me, not sliding in deep like I want. When I try to sink myself against his finger, he smiles.

"You're evil," I shudder, as he traces the line of my slit again.

"Am I now?" He grunts in my ear. I want him so bad my pussy is begging to be filled, and he kisses my temple in response. "I love how wet I can make you. Means I'm doing something right."

His hand tightens around my neck. Pressing my thighs against each other, I hold his hand hostage between my legs. Smiling against my mouth, he plunges two fingers in. I gasp, my back arching, my stomach making contact with his. "Fuck," I mewl.

"I think you need to lose those sweet panties of yours," he says, ripping the fabric from my legs. He reaches behind me and in one swift movement, sweeps all the stuff on the ground. Bolts and nuts fly everywhere. Slowly he pulls my shirt up, over my head and locks my wrists behind my back. He turns the fabric of my shirt so my hands are bound, and I can't move.

Using his free hand he unclasps the front of my bra, exposing my breasts. The tips instantly harden and judging by his growl, he notices it too. His fingers tickle across my collarbone, and then his wet mouth encircles my left nipple, sucking hard, and I almost come right then and there.

I'm so close, I want to rub my thighs together to find my release but he's still standing between my legs. Chuckling, he suckles on my nipple and I cry out his name. "Please, Hunter," I groan.

He opens his belt and then his zipper. Tugging down his pants to his feet, followed by his boxers. I stare at his straight cock and my mouth starts to water. He's already fully erect, and the glistening tip is inches away from my entrance. He pushes up my skirt, I part my legs even further, and my ass moves up when he kisses the inside of my thighs.

"I can smell you. Now I want to taste that sweet pussy and trace your clit with my tongue piercing. Do you want my mouth on you again, or my cock inside you?" he asks, the vibration of his voice against my pussy lips making me beg for him to fill me to the hilt.

I nod breathlessly.

"Spreading you, getting you right to the point of release till you are begging me to bury all of my hard cock inside your tight little cunt?"

"Oh God, yes. Yes," I repeat, while he rises.

"Gets you every time, doesn't it? Me talking dirty." His breath is warm against my neck. "Maybe I should eat you out more often. I do love the way you taste," he husks out, his mouth inches away from my earlobe.

I try to lift my hands but can't raise my arms. I cringe.

"Shorty, what happened?" he asks, his voice hoarse.

"I'm sorry," I rasp, avoiding his eyes.

"Don't be, babe. You don't have to do anything."

"But I know how much you like it when I pull your hair hard to help you get there."

His mouth is inches away from mine. I blink furiously, those blue depths holding me captive. Why is he smiling?

"I don't care about any of that," he says, freeing my arms from my shirt and massaging my wrists, kissing the inside of each palm. "I care about you, and what we have right here, right now. As long as we're together, and I get you there, I'm happy. Close your eyes. Don't think too much." His voice is deep.

I hesitate but when he raises his eyebrows I do as he commands. I moan as his tongue moves over the inside of my thighs, pressing his nose against my mound he inhales. Then his piercing starts teasing my slit from left to right until he stops and presses the metal ball hard against my clit. Pleasure takes over and I hiss, repeating his name like a mantra, my hands traveling into his hair. He chuckles and I get even wetter. His piercing still teases the spot where everything aches and hurts in all the right ways.

"Yes, right there," I say as his tongue flicks up and down, the metal ball punishing my clit with little stabs and I buck, my butt coming off the table. His head comes up and his strong hands lift me and I gasp. He helps me wrap my legs around his naked ass. Placing my arms on his shoulders, I draw him in closer to me, kissing him.

His cock presses and twitches against my entrance. "Fuck, Sky," he whispers. His breathing comes out labored and hard. Nudging and teasing my clit with his slick cock, I whimper. Gliding my hands over his strong back muscles, has him tensing beneath my touch. I love the way I can still make him hard, but why is he holding back?

Maybe because I have trouble using my hands. Is it because some days I need help going to the bathroom, need help to shower? How can he love me like this?

Hunter

I hold her against me, kissing her hair. She is so fucking beautiful. She flushes, her cheeks rosy. The scent of sex lingers in the air around us. My sweat is mixed with her perfume, and I choke up knowing we aren't going to have years of this. We are not going to grow old together. Have kids, share a life. Yell at each other because I forget to do the dishes or take out the trash.

"Babe, where did you go?" she asks, nudging against my hard-on. Her heat against my own brings me back to the present. I hate myself for being so weak, for spoiling this moment between us.

"I love you," I whisper while she runs her knuckles through my hair. Fuck. I almost come apart.

"I love you too."

I line up my dick with her entrance, then thrust. Moving inside her till I'm fully seated in her tight pussy. She lets her head fall to the side, and I growl because I'm doing this to her. I'm the one making her this turned on. Leaning forward, I capture her mouth with my own, and slowly start to move.

With every plunge of my hard dick, she repeats my name like a plea, like a promise, never breaking eye contact. I ram my cock in and out of her; damn it's a snug fit, and sexy as hell. My dick glides against her pussy walls, and I swear under my breath, because I don't want to blow within seconds. I fuck her slowly and pick up the pace when she needs it. I'm steadily building my tempo. Hell, I fucking need it. I need *her*. I grind my hips and thrust in. Holding her up, I bite back my tears. She weighs fucking nothing.

I force my hard dick into her deeper with every stroke. Each time brings me closer to the edge as her tight pussy milks my shaft. I hold my breath as I screw her into the table, my hand moving under her ass, tugging her against me. I stab inside of her, over and over. Sky shudders in my arms. Fuck, I'm close. My dick throbs in her tight passage, and I swear under my breath.

"That's it, baby. Please make me come," I beg, smashing my lips against hers again. She clasps her pussy around my dick while I move in and out of her. It's hot as hell, and she knows it judging by the way her mouth hikes up in a full-blown smile.

"Where did you learn that trick?" I ask, my voice shaking.

"A girl has to have her secrets." She grins, her hand caressing my jaw.

She does it again and I almost blow right then and there. My skin prickles and heats. I stagger a little, blinking a couple of times. She laughs, a beautiful full chuckle as her head falls against my chest. I pull out excruciatingly slowly and ram inside of her again.

She sucks in a breath and I know she's almost there.

"Give it up for me," I order her.

I pound into her again and she finds her release, and screams my name. I'm this close to reaching my own bliss while she rides out her orgasm, milking my cock. I come too, taking her with me again for the second time.

Closing my eyes, I grunt her name and pull out, shooting my cum onto her thigh. I grab her knees to steady myself. My eyes traveling into the back of my head. I love the flutter in my chest. Resting my forehead against hers, I'm dizzy from inhaling her scent. This was perfect, and fuck, I hope I wasn't too rough with her.

Sky

He pulls his shirt over his head and dabs my thigh with it, and I slowly slide out from the barrier of his arms. After fastening my bra, I pick up my shirt from the floor and put it on. My legs are like jelly, and I grab the workbench for support.

"Sky, babe, let me help you," he says, his voice soft. He cups my cheeks, "Shorty, you're burning up. You need to rest."

"No, I don't," I spit back. He can't see me like this. I try to make it to the door, but my legs give out and I fall face-forward.

But, as always, he's right behind me and holds me up. "Give me a sec. Did you take your wheelchair over here or your walking stick?" he asks as he places me on the workbench.

"I don't need your help," I grit out, crossing my arms in front of me.

Circling my knees with affection, he rasps, "Don't be like this."

"Like what?" I gulp, raising my brow, hoping that if I pick a fight he'll let me go. My legs start to spasm, and I bite hard on my lip, praying he won't notice. His eyes widen when he places his palms on my shaking legs and I break.

"This was a mistake," I mumble, diverting my eyes from his intense stare.

"What?"

"A mistake." It takes everything I have to hold his broken stare as I tell him this without any emotion in my voice.

There is so much hurt and anger in his eyes. He opens and closes his mouth, a pained look crossing his face. He blocks my escape, his body boxing me in. Hanging his head, he softly says, "You mean the having sex part or us in general?"

"Both," I whisper, trying to keep my voice hard, although I don't mean it.

He shakes his head and pushes off the workbench. He paces the room, anger radiating from his body.

"Everything is a mistake. I'm never going to be enough for you." I need to hurt him; I need him to leave me. Although it breaks my heart, he doesn't deserve to be part of what is going to happen. It will destroy him.

I shove him hard, and he stumbles back a couple of steps. I grab my chest, my lungs hurt like I'm being stabbed. I cough, trying to fill them with air.

Then he's right in my face, holding me up. "Is this really what you think? I don't believe you, Sky." He lets out an anger-filled roar. He growls. His nostrils flare as he closes the space between us.

I'm so tired, I have barely eaten these last couple of days, knowing what I have to say to get him to leave I bite out. "I thought I could love you but I can't. It hurts t…"

"You don't love me?" he snaps. "Don't fucking say that, Shorty. I know you do." He caresses my cheeks between his shaking hands. "You fucking love me," he pleads, his voice breaking.

I shake my head, trying to pull his hands away.

"Don't you fucking do this," he whispers. Kissing me, he parts my lips with his tongue, and I melt, disappearing into him with all I have. I love him so much it hurts—it hurts too much. I grab his waist, bumping him in his chest with my fist, not wanting to look in Hunter's eyes which are red from unshed tears.

"Stop looking at me like that," I scream at him.

He holds his hands up in defeat. "Baby, please, it's okay."

"Stop saying it's okay when it's not," I yell, throwing the stuff he has lying around on the workbench on the floor. And he lets me do it, making me more angry in the process. "I'm dying. Why, Hunter?" I sob.

"I don't know," he whispers.

"And you are still here. Why are you still here? Do you get off on this? Having me helpless and defenseless? Is this what makes you tick?"

He shakes his head, not saying anything.

"Go away, Hunter. Just go." I keep screaming, keep breaking.

Grabbing my arms, he says softly, "Shorty, it's okay. I'm here."

"Stop saying that. Stop telling me I'm strong. I'm not. I am scared. Scared of what will happen. Scared for you. I know by the look in your eyes you are dying too. I can't. I won't be responsible for this. Leave me alone," I sob, tears streaming down my face.

"Sky, please, it's okay. I'm here. I'm not going anywhere."

"Stop it. Stop saying it's okay," I scream. "Why? Why did you talk to me? Why did you kiss me? Why did I ever come here? I hate you. I hate you!" I yell, slapping him, my fists against his chest, his arms—anywhere I can hurt him.

Holding out his hands, he cries, "Please don't say it."

Turning away from him, I mutter, "Why did you make me fall in love with you?"

"Don't do this." His voice is laced with love and hurt.

I stand on unsteady legs and push him some more. "Why do you say you love me? Why do you have to love me?" I shove him with all my might. He staggers back. I keep going at him while he tries to grab my hands but I slap them away. "No, you can't help me. No one can."

"Honey," he begs.

I hit him hard in his chest, over and over until his spine slams into the wall.

"I love you," he keeps repeating while I'm hitting him.

"Stop," I sob. "Just stop." I hit him again. My palm print is red on his cheek. I hug him, holding onto him, and I scream until my voice is hoarse.

"Tell me. Tell me everything. I can take it."

"I don't want to leave you," I cry. "I hate that I'm going to leave you. Why am I going to leave you?"

Grabbing the back of my head, he pulls me into his chest, holding me against his body. He kisses me over and over, from my nose to my eyes, until he takes possession of my mouth.

Hunter

"I love you," I tell her, pressing my forehead to hers. I kiss her again, giving her everything, my heart, my fucking life.

Sky's frail body shudders against my chest. She lets out a sharp cry, breaking my heart. I need to stay strong for her, but my tears are spilling over. I want to fix everything, still I feel defeated, because this is something I cannot fix. My chest hurts from all her hitting, but not as much as my heart. She is going to leave me behind and I can't imagine living my life without her.

"You are an asshole," she says, her voice muffled, a soft smile forming on her lips. "Why do you let me do this to you? Let me scream, swear, hit you?"

"Because I love you, and I'm the asshole here," I grumble. Chuckling, I trace her temples with my inked fingers.

"I'm scared you'll forget about me," she confesses, laying her cheek against my shoulder.

"Babe." I tilt her head up. "Look at me." She shakes her head, biting her lip, but I grab her chin. When we lock eyes, the beauty of her soul knocks the wind out of me. "I will carry what we have, what we are, with me for the rest of my life."

She smiles, shaking her head, her face wet from all her tears. "Hunter," she whispers.

Tugging her head against my neck, I inhale her scent and pull her body closer to my own. Everything hurts—my skin, the hair on my arms. My heart. I'm about to throw up, knowing there will come a day when the memories of her will be all I have left of her, of us.

CHAPTER 26

Sky

"Are you ready?" he asks.

"I am," I say, my smile splitting my face in two.

"Okay, hold on. Let me put you down." He holds me upright, his strong hands clutching my hips. He can easily wrap both his hands around my waist; I've lost so much weight.

A wave hits my bare legs, and I stumble backwards a little. The water feels fantastic, like heaven against my skin as my toes disappear in the sand. Hunter holds me, hugging me from behind.

My hands travel back into his hair. He kisses below my ear. Goose bumps break out over my arms. "Thank you for bringing me here. This is one of my favorite spots," I tell him.

"Why?" he asks, with a question in his eyes.

Turning around, I clutch him to me. "You remember the time we spent together on the beach, and we made love in your truck?"

"Yeah, I remember." He snorts. "You couldn't get away from me fast enough."

I place my palm on his cheek, his stubble pricking my hand. "You know why?"

He shakes his head.

"Because that's when I knew I would hurt you by loving you. And I couldn't do it." I bite my lip. "I hated myself for feeling that way about you."

"You loved me then?" he asks, his eyes misty.

"I loved you then and I love you now. Now until forever." I promise him, standing on my tiptoes to kiss him.

"Tell me you're mine," he rasps, his hot breath warming my chilled lips.

"I'm yours and always will be. You are my once-in-a-lifetime." I kiss his forehead, his temple, his upturned mouth. "Remember this when I'm not here to tell you." I smile and then say, "I love you."

His ice-blue eyes make my heart skip a beat. We keep staring at each other; we don't have to say anything anymore. Our love is enough to fill all the silences still to come.

When we are back at his apartment, he carries me inside and helps me get undressed.

"You want to take a shower to wash the beach off of you?" he asks, his voice shaking a little.

"Would you?"

He kneels in front of me. "Yes."

He takes off his shirt, revealing his perfect body. He stands, pulling his black shorts and then his black boxers down, before helping me out of my clothes. He winks when he picks me up and walks into the shower.

He holds me in his arms as the water cascades down on us both. My feet barely touch the ground. And I love him for all that he is. He's shown me what it is like to love without fear, without regret. A love that isn't clean and straightforward, but messy, dirty with peaks and valleys, like the races he rides.

He frowns, and worry haunts his eyes. I reach out and catch his chin, turning his face to mine. He blinks a couple of times, droplets of water running down his face, and into his eyelashes.

"Damn, Shorty," he says slowly. I clutch him to my naked body and stare up at him. He's holding me because I can't stand anymore.

"Thank you for loving me," he whispers, running his stubble over my cheek. "Thank you for making me the man I have become," he drawls, kissing my lips.

Sky

I turn my head to find him sleeping next to me in his bed, his face inches from mine. His facial features are so soft when he's asleep; he looks so young. I let my gaze run over his face to the line of his neck, his throat to his tattoo-covered shoulders to the swell of his bare ass hiding under the white sheet.

Hunter grins when he opens his eyes. He reaches out to trace the lines of my face, and I love the connection. He hasn't left my side in the last week.

He takes my hand in his and lays it on his cheek. The little bristles of his two-day beard scrape across my palm and my fingers tremble.

"Hey, Shorty," he says, a slow smile tugging on his lips, those brilliant blue eyes flashing.

"Hi," I whisper when he takes off my oxygen mask. We keep staring at each other, not saying anything. After a while, he leans in and kisses me, a soft kiss that fills my heart.

"What time is it?" My voice is raspy.

He lifts up on his arms and checks the time on his phone. "Around five in the afternoon. You have been sleeping for eighteen hours straight, babe."

We keep staring at each other. He caresses my cheek, his calloused thumb moving over my forehead. Those ice-blue eyes still make my heart skip a beat.

"I thought I'd have so many things to say." He lets out a strangled cry. A single tear escapes from under his closed lids.

"I know," I tell him, taking shallow breaths.

"But when I look at you, I know you know every answer to my questions, don't you?"

I can only smile. "Yes."

He takes my hand in his, locking our fingers together. "I love you," I tell him.

He closes his eyes. Tears start to flow, and sobs escape him when I hold him tight.

"Let go, Hunter." I trace the line of his jaw with my nose. My knuckles move over his parted lips, the warmth of his breath tickling my skin, and he opens his eyes. "You have to promise to let me go. You will always have my heart, as I have yours."

"You are my once-in-a-lifetime," he says and kisses me. His tears fall on my cheeks, mixing with mine. "Cross my heart," he whispers. And I hold him while he cries, until he falls asleep, and I know it is almost time.

"Catch you in my dreams," he drawls, his voice hoarse, and I open and close my eyes, promising him I will.

Hunter

I hand Drew a new wheel for a bike we picked up in San Diego. "Here you go."

He takes it from me. "Thanks, man."

I slam my fist against the frame. "Fuck," I growl, holding onto the bench until my fingers start cramping up. "I want to ..."

Drew stops working on the bike. "You can tell me, Hunt."

"I want to take a whole bottle and swallow all the pills. I want to crash my bike if it could mean she would stay here. I want to fucking murder someone."

Drew tries to take my hand, but I slap his fingers away.

"I don't understand how this could have happened? I know she's been sick for years, but fuck I only just found her. Why is she deteriorating so fast? It's like she's been holding on for so long, like her heart can't take it anymore," I say, pacing back and forth.

His eyes are sad as he watches me fall apart.

"I don't know what to do." I kick my Vans against my dirt bike. The lump in my throat gets bigger until I topple over with my hands on my knees. "I need her, Drew." I grab his hand, and he pulls me into his chest, and I let myself go. Burying my face in his shoulder, I sob. "Why is she leaving me? Why is she leaving?"

"I don't know," he answers, kissing the top of my head.

My legs give out and I fall onto the floor, taking him with me. Drew still has his arms around me. "I-I-I h-hate her for leaving me," I stutter, letting the tears flow. I lean my butt against the workbench, focusing on his calm eyes.

"I know, man. I know," he whispers, his voice breaking. He looks to the ground probably trying to hide his tear stained face. Leaning my head against the metal leg of the bench, I scrub my knuckles over my stubble. "I hate that I can't save her," I husk out.

"I know, Hunt."

"I'm so angry, so fucking angry," I repeat staring into his red rimmed eyes.

Drew lets me vent and holds me for what feels like hours, thank god for my brother, my best friend.

Later in the evening, I take a cold shower and try to get myself together. I give Sky and Jay some time alone, and go for a drive. After an hour, I park the bike in the garage and hang my helmet on the handlebar, then make my way to the house. Jay is sitting in the living room, watching TV, when I enter.

"Hey, are you okay?" he asks, raising his brow.

"Can I talk to you?" I ask, leaning my butt against the couch.

"Sure. Want to sit outside? Sky's not here," he says, walking toward the kitchen.

"Where is she?" I ask, following him.

"Tim took her to his house. Want something to drink?" he asks, opening a cabinet and taking out two glasses.

"I'll take whatever you got," I tell him and he smiles.

We step out onto the patio and I take my seat in the chair next to him. Staring up at the stars and the lit track in front of us, I tap my fingers on the cold glass filled with iced tea.

Jay throws his baseball cap on the table. "Timothy got some new weed. Said it could help her," he says, wiping at his eyes. "I know her lungs are shot, but maybe it will help, I don't fucking know."

I nod, taking a long sip from the drink. I bite hard on my lip until I can taste the blood. "Jay, I can't ride anymore," I tell him, motioning to the track.

"I know." He nods.

"I need to stay here with her. Even if it means I can't be the world's number-one rider. It doesn't mean shit to me now."

Jay taps his fingers on his glass. "She wouldn't want you to give up on your dreams."

"Like you gave up on her?" I regret saying it the moment the words leave my mouth.

Jay gives me a look that could cut through glass. "Because you love her I will forgive you."

We are both quiet for a couple of minutes. "What will you do, Jay?"

He shrugs.

"Come on. We need the money if we ever want to extend the track and train more kids pro bono. And I didn't tell you but I'm paying for a couple after-school classes for some new riders."

He smiles, shaking his head. "Hunt, you amaze me and piss me off at the same time. But we don't have to worry anymore."

"What?" I drawl.

"Sky put her trust fund in my name after she talked to her mom and Conrad. We are set for the rest of our lives."

I shake my head. "She shouldn't have done that," I say, leaning forward and scratch the shaved side of my head, the long strands falling in front of my eyes.

"She told me it felt right."

I chuckle. "She keeps surprising me, she is your daughter after all." I take another sip, debating if I should also tell him about my fuck up with Neil.

"Yeah," Jay answers, staring out to the track.

A car stops. Tim gets out and helps Sky into her wheelchair. "She's back," Jay mumbles, laying his hand on my shoulder. "I'm going to hit the hay. You stay here and wait for her. She needs you more than you will ever know. She loves you, son. Take care of her."

A single tear barrels down his face, and I hold his hand. "I will, Jay," I promise.

We both watch her slowly being wheeled by Timothy to the porch. He helps her out of the chair and up the steps, before she sits next to me.

"Hey, guys. Didn't think you would still be sitting outside." Her voice is soft; she's beautiful but so tired. I recognize it in the way she talks.

Tim places the wheelchair next to the door, saying goodbye to all of us, kissing Sky on the cheek and shaking my hand.

"Bye, Tim," I say, nodding. He winks at me, making his way to Drew's. I stretch my legs, smiling at her, and she blushes.

Jay kisses her forehead. "Catch you tomorrow, baby."

"See you tomorrow, Dad," she says, watching him go.

She picks up my glass with both hands and takes a shuddering sip. When I reach out to help her hold the glass, she shakes her head. I love this about her; she's not afraid to do what she wants. She closes her eyes for a moment, and when they lock on mine, she's smiling at me.

"Why are you looking at me like that?" I ask her.

"Nothing. I'm happy," she muses.

"Happy?" I murmur, taking the drink from her and downing it. Looking at the wheelchair, my stomach turns. After a while I tell her, "I'm not going to race anymore."

"What?" She sits back with an angry scowl on her face. Her pupils are dilated. She is high as a kite.

"I'm not racing again," I tell her, more calmly this time.

She shakes her head angrily. "And why the fuck not?"

"Don't swear." I stand, placing my glass on the table. "I don't want to."

She pushes my drink over the edge in one swift movement, and it shatters into a million little pieces on the floor.

"Horseshit." She points her finger in my face. "You live for the ride. It doesn't say *live to ride, ride to live* on your back for nothing."

"I don't want to ride anymore. I want to stay here with you," I grunt.

She shakes her head. "Do not put this on me. Don't use me for some fucked up excuse. You wanted to be number one. Don't you dare use me like this."

I pull her chair toward me, and get right in her face.

"Oh no? Tell me what I should do then. Leave you, like Jay did years ago?" I yell.

She slaps me hard across the face. It stings like a motherfucker but I guess I deserved it. "Don't ever talk that way to me again," she says, biting her lip. Her body shakes with anger.

I blow out through my nose, calming myself. She shoves me out of the way and tries to stand. I pick her up in my arms like I've been doing ever since she came home from the hospital and walk her inside my apartment. She doesn't meet my eyes, and I don't blame her when I set her down on my bed.

I strip and slide in next to her. I kiss her shoulder and I turn her face toward me. She's crying, but she lets me hold her. "I love you, Shorty. I'm sorry for being such an asshole sometimes."

Sky

"I love you too," I whisper, not breaking eye contact. I kiss him, my hands clutching at his hair, pulling and tugging the way he likes it. I kiss his jaw up to his ear, and he doesn't hold anything back. He takes me into his arms and holds me like he never wants to let go. "Don't give up your dream for me," I say.

"You are my dream, Shorty," he hesitates but after a while he says, "but I promise I won't."

We kiss for a long time and I memorize every smile, every whisper, every moment.

He falls asleep in my arms and I stay up until the morning light shines through the window. I watch him sleep, his chest peacefully moving. I'm starting to let him go, one day at a time.

I grab a blank piece of paper from the nightstand and start to write. Loving him is the best thing I ever did. I know he's a broken man, and I know I've hurt him but I wouldn't want to change a thing. Because all the mistakes I ever made led me to him.

I write down each memory, every smile, my pain, and my love. Lately it has gotten harder to put the words to paper, and I know there will come a day when even picking up the pen will hurt too much.

I turn the pages and read what I have written.

To the love of my life.

I wipe away my tears, and let my trembling fingers skim over the words.

"I love and hate you for giving me forever," I whisper in

Hunter's ear, leaning against the pillows I trail my fingers over the tattoos on his back.

Watching him sleep I hold the letter against my heart, and smile, kissing the place between his shoulder blades before I let the shaking pen touch the paper again.

There are so many things in life I took for granted. Every hour, every minute, every damn second. I barely made it through the day without feeling like shit. I was scared to fail, scared of success. Love and happiness were some distant dream I couldn't remember when I woke.

You changed everything. You remind me every day to live life in the moment. You make me remember; you give me strength I didn't even know I possessed.

Babe, you inspire me, and you see everything every color, every light, and every shade. The best and the worst. You see all the pieces of myself I lost along the way, the pieces you helped me put back together.

He rolls over onto his side, resting his head on his tattooed bicep. Clutching the pen more firmly between my aching fingers, I adjust the notepad and push through the pain in my chest before I can't write anymore.

I'd never met anyone who lived his life exactly how he wanted, screw the consequences, until you. You don't care about other people's opinions, or what they say or think about you. You face life head on with a big "fuck you" smirk on your face. You live life with no regrets, taking credit for every success and every failure that's led you here. How many people can say that? Truly say they did it all? You can, and you will.

You once told me you were a mistake. Babe, you are the best mistake I've ever made.

You are my home, my life.

My love. My once-in-a-lifetime.

You made me lose myself and helped me find what was missing.

I love you from now until forever,

Cross my heart

I put the letter in an envelope and slowly place it on the nightstand. Turning around, I tell him, "I love you," and softly brush his hair out of his eyes before I kiss his forehead.

I press my lips against his, and the corner of his mouth hikes up.

"No one told me holding on would hurt more than letting go," I say, the tip of my nose touching his.

"Don't let me go, babe." His voice is a hoarse whisper as he rolls over, holding himself up on his elbows.

Tracing the line of his jaw with my shaking fingers, I smile through my tears.

"Love can make you believe anything—even in a fucking forever," he rasps, his voice groggy as he scratches his unshaven cheek before he locks eyes with me. His sad smile tears me apart.

"I guess it does," I tell him, slowly moving my fingers through his long hair to the stubble on the side. He closes his eyes, the side of his mouth curling up the tiniest bit.

I've been watching him sleep for hours, his strong body moving with every breath he takes. It's like I'm seeing him more clearly with each passing day. He closes his eyes again, pushing both inked arms under his pillow, and turns his face to me. I skim my fingers over the ink on his broad muscular back, to his sleeve, and try to smile through the tears moving over my cheeks.

I kiss the skull tattoo, then kiss every line of the letters on his shoulder blades and lower back, all the way around to his rib cage. He shivers under my touch, and butterflies take flight in my stomach. Hunter slowly opens his sapphire eyes, taking my breath away. An ocean of tears is reflected in those bright blue depths. There's love, anger, hate and everything in between. They're eyes to get lost in forever.

"What are you thinking about?" he asks, turning on his side.

"About our forever." I smile, dabbing away my tears with the sleeve of his black shirt I'm wearing that swamps my small frame.

"Fuck forever," he whispers pulling me into his arms and kissing the top of my head. His lips linger on my skin. I love how he tries to hold on, making a memory out of every touch, each moment. Burying his nose in my hair, he links our fingers together. Tears blur my vision as I stare at the new *free* tattoo on his knuckles.

"Promise me you'll stay." His voice breaks.

I kiss his temple, laying my hand on his heart, trailing a path over his chest with every shuddering breath he takes.

"I'll never leave you," I tell him, skimming my fingers over the stubble on his jaw. Leaning forward, he kisses me softly, his calloused thumb caressing my cheekbone.

"I don't know what to do," he whispers, voice strained.

"You will, babe," I tell him, staring into his eyes. "You will."

"I don't know how to live without you," he rasps, his hurt underlined in every syllable. "Fuck I love you," he says, closing his eyes. "So fucking much," a sob escapes him.

"Cross your heart?" I ask, caressing his cheek. Blue eyes find mine. He shakes his head and grins as I brush away his tears. With trembling fingers I trace his lips, eyes, his freckled nose. Memorizing every line, every laugh wrinkle. Every beautiful part of him.

"Cross my fucking heart," he whispers, pulling me into him.

When his lips touch my own I know what it means to love without fear. True love isn't pretty; it is messy, layered and sometimes plain dirty. It hurts, makes you feel alive, and destroys you in the best possible ways. And, for the first time in my life, I'm not afraid to lose this race I'm in anymore.

I know I've already won.

CHAPTER 27

Hunter

Two weeks later

I'm angry as hell. Doesn't help I started drinking tequila when the sun rose. I strut up the porch steps, trying to walk in a straight line. Jay and Marian, the nurse her stepfather Conrad hired a week ago to take care of Sky, smile while they drink their coffees. Jay looks different with his trimmed beard and his long hair brushed behind his ears. He has been taking care of himself since Marian came along.

"Jay, can I talk to you?" I ask, trying to keep my voice steady.

"Sure, son. Take a seat," he replies, giving me curious eyes. Dude can probably smell the fucking booze on me. Marian stands, placing her hand on his shoulder. Jay covers it with his own, and squeezes affectionately. "I have some dishes to do."

"No," I reply, shaking my head and swaying a little before I grab the table for support. "This concerns you as well."

"Okay," she says hesitantly, sitting again.

"I need …" I begin, the lump in my throat slowly choking me. Grinding my teeth together, I focus. I need to say this. "I want to take care of her," I plead with both of them.

Jay's jaw twitches. "She needs real medical attention, Hunt. Not some drunken asshole."

"I need to be the one to take care of her," I tell him again.

"Son, what you are doing is more than enough," Jay says. "You have so much on your plate."

"What is that supposed to mean?" I frown.

Jay brushes both his hands across his beard while he leans against the wooden railing. His eyes are sad. "First, we need to talk. I knew something was going on when Drew told me about your run-in with Neil, and I put two and two together. I know you owe him money. I've even talked to Oliver about it."

"What?"

"You think I don't know what goes on under my roof?" he says. "I'm not stupid."

I cringe, crossing my arms. "It's none of your damn business, and what about Oliver?" I ask him angrily. "What has this got to do with me wanting to take care of Sky?"

Jay stares out to the track. "You have always run away when things have gotten hard or ugly. You need to face your past before you can focus on your future."

"I know what we, what I'm facing," I slur. I can barely look at him.

"Oh yeah? You do?" he asks, his voice hard.

"Yes. She is going to die and she's going to leave me alone. Leave me alone, like I always have been left in my life."

Jay grabs my arms, shaking me. "Yes, she is going to die, and yes, she is going to leave you, but I need you to be strong, kid."

"No." I shake my head from left to right. He lets go of my arms. "Don't talk about what is going to happen or my father. What do you know about him?"

"More than you know," he grumbles, his eyes glazing over.

I brush both my hands across my face, fighting against my tears.

"Oliver knows everything, Hunter."

"What?" I growl through clenched teeth, sobering up a little. "Come again?"

"I've been keeping your father in the loop," he says.

Tears blur my vision. I cover my ears with my trembling hands. Promising myself not to cry. "I don't believe you."

"You need to reach out, son." His voice is soft.

"I can't," I return.

"You need to, don't keep your pain locked in there," he says, tapping my chest before he sits, burying his face in his hands.

"Fuck you, Jay. You have no right, no right. All those years, you and him were keeping in touch behind my back?" I roar, balling my fists.

Jay nods. "I love you, kid, but damn, you can hold a fucking grudge."

I look at Marian, not knowing what to say. "I need to be there for her, not rekindle something which never was and is never going to be with my father."

Marian's eyes are kind when she stands, laying a hand on my shoulder. "I know you want to but she is really weak. These last weeks she has gotten so much worse. I think she is much sicker than she leads on, Hunt, and with her condition she needs so much care."

I shrug her hand off me, and get right in her face and she swallows hard. Jay is on his feet and pulling me back before I know it.

"Don't, Jay," Marian pleads.

"I … I need …" I start to pace. "I need this."

"Sky needs more," Jay yells, while Marian tries to grab his hand. I'm sick to my stomach.

"Give me a chance," I plead.

Jay shakes his head with disdain. "No. You can't even take care of yourself. Your NA sponsor called me. You haven't been to a meeting in two weeks, Hunter."

"I couldn't," I mutter, stumbling forward.

He points his finger in my face. "I love you, and I'm not going to lose you too," he says, with a threat in his voice.

I shove him in his chest. "What are you going to do? Keep her away from me?" I bellow. I punch him in his shoulder, and send him flying off the steps of the porch.

Marian tries to grab my arm. I shrug her off and she falls to the floor.

"Motherfucker," Jay roars, launching at me. He punches me hard in the stomach and I topple over.

"Fuck." I cough out a breath, bile rising in the back of my throat. I raise my arms and plow into him, taking him by surprise, knocking Jay to the ground.

He throws a couple of good punches, and takes another swing at me. Before I know it, we are a mess of tangled limbs rolling on the grass. The asshole busts my lip; I can taste the blood on my tongue. I give him a sucker punch right in the jaw. Before I can blink, Timothy takes me in a chokehold, trying to get me off Jay. Drew grabs Jay by the arms, and pulls him against his chest. When they break us apart, we are both bloody messes.

"Don't keep her away from me," I choke out.

Jay spits on the ground, blood dripping from his chin.

"Stop it, Hunter," Timothy warns, holding me tight against his body.

"You are all keeping her from me," I yell. Angry tears blur my vision. I slump to the ground, and Drew lets go of Jay's hands.

"I think you should go," Jay says, eyeing me as he drags both hands over his face.

I frown, brows drawn together. I'm paralyzed. "No. I'm not leaving her alone for a minute."

"You already left," he says, matter-of-fact, wiping the blood from his cheek. "You're a fucking mess. You started drinking again, doing God knows what, going out to August's place, and getting in late." He swallows hard, his Adam's apple bobbing, and there is desperation in his eyes mixed with disappointment. "After everything we went through, you are not going to make her an excuse to fuck up the things we worked so hard for. Get it into your thick skull that this is not about you for a fucking change."

I glance up at him, and I know he's right, and I hate myself for it.

"Don't throw away everything, you ungrateful son of a bitch," Jay sneers. He looks at me with a disgusted scowl.

I sway a little. The old man got in some good punches. I think I bruised another rib. But I still can't leave. I won't. She needs me.

"Fuck you, Jay. Only she can tell me to leave," I whisper, wiping the blood from my mouth.

"Walk it off, Hunter," Sky says, her voice trembling.

We all turn around. She stands in the doorway, leaning against the frame for support.

"Walk it off?" I ask.

She nods. "Go."

The hurt in her eyes tears me in two, and I leave like the coward I am. I'm so fucking angry, so I head to the only place I feel safe: the track.

"Fuck," I mutter to no one in particular, and I sit. I messed up. I shouldn't have pushed Jay, and certainly not Marian, who has nothing to do with my own personal shit.

I lie back against one of the hills. It is a warm, soft evening. Tears pool in my eyes as I stare up at the sky, but I can't cry. I need to stay angry. I need to fight. I need to be strong for her.

I spend the whole night on the track thinking about my past, my father, and the mistakes I made. I think about the drugs I took, the anger that consumed me, and I close my eyes.

The sun comes up, painting the sky like a Bob Ross artwork, and I know what I should have done a long time ago.

I get on my bike and drive away. I'm doing ninety on the freeway and I skid to a halt at Neil's beachside condo. Stalking up the steps to his house, I knock on the wooden door.

"Neil, open up," I yell, trying to peer inside. A freaking party is going on.

I jerk the door open. The noises from the music and people talking give me an instant headache. Strutting through the house, I spot girls in bikinis. There are more fake breasts here than there should ever be in one room. Ryan and Lydia are talking in a corner. She's flapping her arms around, angry as hell. Ryan dips his chin at me in greeting; I do the same in return. Then I see Neil talking to a couple of guys who look just like him, each with a trophy wife on their arm.

"Neil," I yell, trying to be heard over the music.

He stops talking. His eyes bulge like he's scared of me being here in his house. Spinning on his heels, he heads down the hall.

"Neil," I roar again, sprinting after him. "What the hell, man?"

He tries to open a door but it's locked. Turning around, he holds his arms in front of his chest to keep me at a distance, but I push them away.

"What are you doing here, Hunter?" He sounds off, not like his normal fucker self.

"I know I owe you fifty-five grand. I'll find a job, because I won't fucking race for you after this season is over."

He shakes his head. "It's done, Hunter."

"What do you mean 'it's done'?" I frown.

His hands are shaking. What the hell did I miss?

"It has been paid," he states.

"You're not making any sense, Neil."

"It's taken care of, okay?" he says, holding up his hands. "Please go now."

"Who paid it?" I grit out, getting in his face.

He raises his hands like I'm about to go all *Rocky* on him. "He made me promise not to tell anyone. Especially you."

"Neil, who?" I ask, dreading the answer.

"A couple guys on motorcycles came by the house," he says, his voice shaking. "One big angry guy paid your debt in cash, and threatened to break every bone in my body if I tried to sign you again."

"What were they wearing?" I mumble.

He shrugs. "I don't know. Leather vests."

"What was the name on the vests?" The dude is off his rocker. His eyes are wide. Sweat glistens on his forehead. It's probably from all the cocaine he snorts.

"Devil's Sons," Ryan says.

I turn around to see him right in front of me. How long has he been standing there?

I clear my throat. "Damn," I swear, brushing both my hands through my hair. Zombie paid Neil off—my fucking father. How did he know? *Fucking Jay.* I shake my head.

"Is that why the younger guys are always looking for a way out, Neil?" Ryan asks.

Neil gazes from me to Ryan, his eyes narrowing.

"Have you made them sign the same fucked up contracts as me? Making them dependent on you, although they wanted to leave and race for Jay?" Ryan shouts.

I turn to Ryan, wiping the sweat from my brow.

"Neil told me you were the one who fucked with my bike when I crashed it in Florida all those years ago. Or was that also a lie, Neil?" Ryan says.

"I did *what?*" I roar.

Neil raises his arms in front of him as I take an angry step toward him. "Fuck you, Neil. I would never put another rider in danger," I tell Ryan.

He looks at Neil, his eyes full of hate.

"Come on, guys. It's all good. You're one of the best; I made you." Neil's voice rises an octave higher.

Ryan shakes his head. "You didn't make me, and how much have you been skimming from me? From the other guys?"

"I-I-I h-haven't," Neil stammers.

Grabbing him by his shirt, I raise him up against the wall. "How much?"

"Something here and there," he says, his voice a high pitch.

I let him go and he falls against the door. Turning around, I shake my head. My fingers itch to take a swing at him.

"Guys," Neil pleads.

"This is it, Neil. I'm out. Once the others hear about this you will have no one left to race for you," Ryan seethes.

"Come on, Ryan. He's not worth it."

He nods, walking away with me.

"If it wasn't for me, neither of you would have raced as well as you did," Neil shouts desperately.

"Fuck you," Ryan spits out. Lydia is already waiting for him by the door.

"We have a contract," Neil yells, coming after us.

"Not anymore. Not when I tell my lawyer everything. Don't think you're the only one with dirt up his sleeve," Ryan says, smiling at me. "Ready to leave?" he asks Lydia.

"Ready when you are, honey," she says, kissing his cheek.

When we are outside, I get on my bike. Before I put my helmet on, Ryan walks up to me. Lydia smiles. I nod and she gets into Ryan's car.

"Hunt," he says, focusing on the ground, then on me. "I need to apologize about ratting you out to Drew and Jay. And I'm so sorry about what is happening to Sky."

I shake my head. "I don't blame you for telling him. I'm glad you did and this blew up in my face. I should have never signed with a piece of shit like Neil. And I'm sorry for never taking the time to talk it out with you," I say, shaking his hand.

"You think Jay would be open to taking on another asshole?" Ryan asks.

"Don't know why he wouldn't be." I wink.

"You have no problem with me beating you even if we're on the same team?" He grins, putting his hands in his back pockets.

"Don't push your luck, I still have the last race of the season to kick your ass," I drawl. "After that I'm done. We had a good run."

"I know we did, but are you sure?"

I nod, and he smiles like some sort of understanding passes between us. He turns and walks to his car, taps his fist on the hood and says, "Later, Hunt."

"Later, Ryan." I nod, putting my helmet on and driving away. I need to make one more stop before I find my way back home, back to her.

CHAPTER 28

Hunter

It's late in the afternoon when I park my dirt bike next to a couple dozen Harleys standing in front of the concrete building I vowed to never set foot in ever again. Music travels through the air, and I smell burning wood; they probably built a bonfire in the yard behind the property. The four prospects standing around and guarding the bikes eye me suspiciously. One, who's about eighteen, walks up to me, checking out my bike like he wants to take a sledgehammer to it for insulting the customized choppers and Harleys parked around. I recognize an older guy with long black hair who stops him, dismissing him with a stroke of his hand.

"Took you long enough, dipshit," Animal says, holding out his hand for me to shake.

"Is he here?" I ask, clasping his hand.

He nods. The prospects keep their mouths shut but study me with renewed interest.

Animal motions to the clubhouse. "Yeah, he's been waiting for you."

I follow him in. The place is packed with men and women of various ages all wearing their own leather jackets that bind them to an old man, the same as my mother used to wear. Being here sure as shit brings back memories.

There are also girls with barely any clothes on strutting their stuff. Shit. I run a hand through my hair. It's too familiar, being here, too fucking familiar.

"He's in his office," Animal says, checking out the girls putting their hands all over him.

I follow him through a narrow corridor. A couple of guys pass us in the hallway. They do a double take like they recognize me. I guess the color of my eyes gives me away. "How've you been, Jake?"

Animal grins when I use his real name. "Can't complain. Could use some of that sweet ass in my life like you have."

"What?" I ask, stopping. Animal shakes his head, smiling before knocking on a nondescript door. Fuck. Does he mean Sky came here to talk to my father instead of Jay?

"Prez?" he booms.

"Come in," a familiar voice says.

"Good luck, kid," Animal mumbles, holding the door open for me.

When I enter the room, my father is leaning against his desk. He's older, but he hasn't really changed. He's built as if he were still in his twenties. His hair is short, and his stubble has a hint of gray in it. He's unmistakably my old man, and still a good-looking son of a bitch. Both his arms are filled with ink and when our eyes lock, I don't know what to say. It's like staring into a mirror.

"Zombie," I state, nodding.

"Hunter," he returns.

Examining his office, I spot cutouts from local newspapers

and pictures of me and my sponsorships decorating the walls. *Damn, I didn't expect him to have those hanging around, like he's proud of what I do.*

"You want to take a seat?" my father murmurs, motioning to a chair.

I shake my head. "No, this isn't going to take long," I tell him, putting both my hands in my pockets. He does the same while we both stare at the floor. After a couple seconds of awkward silence hanging between us, he sighs.

"You didn't need to spend your money. I was handling it."

He stares at the pictures hanging on the walls. Exasperated, he says, "You were handling it? You were handling shit, boy." He laughs.

"Don't you *boy* me. I've been on my own long enough to take care of my own fucking mess. I don't need your help, or your blood money. I haven't heard from you in years. Let's keep it that way," I seethe.

He shakes his head. "And whose fault is that?"

"Fuck you." I ball my fists.

"Right back at you."

"Goddam it, Dad."

"I'm glad you've come, son." His voice is rough.

I clear my throat. "Well, I'm not, so cut the fucking crap. Why did you pay the debt?"

"Hunter, aren't you tired?" he asks, rubbing his knuckles over his chin.

I lean against the wall, staring at my shoes, my hair falling in front of my eyes.

"Tired from all the shit that went down between us. I know I can never bring your mother back," he says. "And I should have tried to build a relationship with you when I got out."

"Yeah you should have," I grumble.

"In the end, Jay was the father you deserved. I was still dealing with my own shit."

"So there wasn't room for me in your life? Is that what you're saying?"

He taps a cigarette pack on his wooden desk, and says, "I thought I was doing you a favor by giving you space. But, son, I needed you as much as you needed me. Your mother died, and instead of banding together, we fell apart."

"Save the speech. And leave Mom out of it," I rasp.

"We need to talk about her, because she is the goddamned reason you started popping pills," he bellows.

Shrugging, I drawl, "Guess I learned from the best, huh, Dad?"

"Christ, son. I can't change the fact I got put behind bars, and couldn't keep you in check. But we're both different people now," he says.

"Really? This is your version of an apology? Fuck you," I growl, balling my fists. "Guess who was dealing the pills for this piece-of-shit club in the first place? *Dad?*"

His voice is ice cold when he says, "Leave the club out of this. You know better than to piss me off. I know what I did. I owned up to it. You need to do the same. We need to put this shit behind us. If time has taught us anything it should be this."

I bite on the inside of my cheek, exhaling hard through my nose. I can't start hyperventilating. Not here, not with him. I can't have a fucking temper tantrum.

"Hunter?" He steps toward me, holding up his hands, trying to calm me.

I start to sweat, and it drips down my spine. "Stay the fuck away from me. And m-my l-l-life," I stutter, frantically scanning the room for a way to escape him, my past, the present, my future. I want to disappear like he did, like she's going to do.

"Why did you take care of it?" I grit out.

He holds my gaze. "Because you are still part of me, and where I come from we take care of each other, blood or no blood."

A mocking laugh escapes me. "Rich, hearing you say that," I answer, pacing the room.

He slams his fist on his desk. "The greatest mistake I ever made was leaving you. But I did and I…"

"Your greatest mistake?" I say. "Give me a break. It was the easiest thing you ever did."

He bites his lip, getting that thousand-yard stare in his eyes. "I can't turn back the clock. No matter how hard I try, or try to make amends, it's never going to be enough, is it?"

When his eyes focus on me again, I shake my head. I'm not prepared for him, for this.

"I'm sorry, son. I know whatever I say or do will not make up for the fact I was never there. I know you needed me, and I couldn't be what you wanted me to be. 'Messed up' doesn't cover the person I was, or what you became because of me."

"I became fucked up?" Sarcasm underlies my words.

"Yes, dammit, you fucked up, but you are the strongest son of a bitch I've ever met, and I'm proud of the man you've become. I'm proud of you, Hunter."

I can't look at him. My eyes will probably give me away. I can't admit how much him saying that means to me.

"I'm glad Jay took you in when you needed a home," he says, lighting a cigarette.

"Jay said you were the one who told him about me," I mumble.

He slowly nods. "Yeah. We went to high school together." He blows out the smoke through his nose. "When I was in prison for a couple of years we got back in touch, and I asked him to take custody of you."

"Why?"

"Because he could give you something I never could."

"What?"

"A home, son. A future."

Sighing, I stare at the man I hated for so long. The man who

I'm reminded of every day when I look in the mirror. A man I fucking hate and love at the same time.

"I blamed you for so long," I tell him.

"I know," he says, stamping out his cigarette.

"Do you, Dad? Do you really?" I ask, punching my fist against the door.

"Son, it's okay." He grabs my arms, turning me around.

The dog tags, *his* dog tags, I've been wearing my whole life suddenly feel heavy around my neck. When I meet his eyes, my father is staring at them. I didn't realize I was clutching the tags so tight. My fingers are digging into my flesh. I shake my head from left to right, hitting my skull against the wall over and over again.

"It's not your fault," he says.

I drop the dog tags, pushing him away from me. "Fuck you!" I yell.

There is a knock on the door and Animal asks, "Prez, you okay in there?"

"Yeah, give us a sec," my father orders.

"Yes, sir." Animal knocks his knuckles on the wood in confirmation.

"Hunter, look at me," my father demands.

I shake my head.

"Hunt," he orders, grabbing my face.

I ease back and lock eyes with him.

"It wasn't your fault. Your mother dying, me going to prison," he says, grabbing my shoulders, trying to hold me still.

"Don't you goddamn tell me this," I grit out, pushing him away. He lets me. The son of a bitch isn't even putting up a fight.

"Son, it's not your fault," he repeats softly, and squeezes his eyes shut for a moment.

A sob escapes me, and I can't hold myself together any longer. My knees give out but my father holds me and takes me into his arms. I punch my fists into his chest, and he lets me, not saying a word. Before I know it, I bury my face in his shoulder as he holds me until I can't cry anymore.

When he lets me go, some kind of understanding has passed between us. The anger and the hate slowly slip away. The son of a bitch is right.

"Want to sit?" He motions to a chair, the right side of his mouth twitching like he's fighting against his emotions.

"Sure," I mumble, embarrassed by my outburst, my fucking weakness. I have been running against the wind for so long, and I'm tired, so damn tired.

We talk until I lose track of time. My father tells me he went to every race in California he could go to. He even shows me a picture of his new wife, a lawyer he met four years ago when she got him out from under some charges.

He tells me about her son, Danny.

"You have a son?" I ask, staring into his eyes.

"Yeah, I adopted him when I married Debra. A great kid—has been a light in the darkness for a long time," he says, his voice soft.

I look at my inked hands. "How old is he?"

Smiling, he tells me, "He's twenty but has the mind of a four-year-old."

"What?" I ask.

"He is disabled and has severe autism," he explains, "He's a great kid." He shows me a picture from his wallet.

"Does he live with you?" I ask, handing him back the picture.

He shakes his head, puts his feet up on his desk, and takes out a pack of Lucky Strikes. "What's that smile for, kid?"

"I smoke the same ones," I tell him.

The side of his mouth hikes up when he taps the carton on his leg and offers me a cigarette. He lights mine before the flame dances in front of his own.

"Nah, he lives in a great home. He needs twenty-four-hour care. Debra used to take care of him when he was younger; she couldn't after a while. But he's happy there. You should meet him."

"I'd like that," I say, looking at the dog tags hanging around my neck.

We are both quiet for a while, smoking our cigarettes, listening to the muffled sounds of the party still going on outside.

"Did Jay come here to talk to you?"

He smiles. "Jay's daughter actually, a couple weeks ago. She made me promise not to tell you. The girl loves you. She knew you wouldn't let her pay the money you owed, so she asked me. Kid's got balls coming here, I'll tell you that much."

I'm momentarily speechless. "Can't believe she did that," I say, inhaling deep and blowing out the smoke through my nose, the cigarette shaking between my fingers. "You know what is happening to her?"

He leans forward, putting his hands on his knees. "She told me. There's one thing I know." His eyes are kind. "You got a good one there."

I bite my lip. "I'm scared, Dad," I say.

He places his hand on my shoulder, pinching a little. "I know, son. I know."

"I'm not ready to let go yet."

He smiles at me. "Then don't."

He's right.

We talk throughout the night, and well into the early morning. There are still a lot of things left unsaid but I know we've passed some sort of imaginary line. We talk about memories shared, and dreams we have but have never reached. And I listen until I find what I'm looking for. I want to understand, to get to know the man who left me, the man whose dreams didn't include me.

He talks about Jay as an old friend. When he points to the wall of my clippings, of articles and pictures, I spot the pride in his eyes.

"You gave me everything to succeed, Dad. Without the pain, without the hate, the hurt, I could never have ridden the way I did." I swallow hard. "I never needed anyone."

"And now?" he asks, with red-rimmed eyes.

"I guess you know the answer to your question."

He smiles. "I guess we do."

We both stand and I hold out my hand. He takes me into his arms, slapping my back twice. When he looks into my eyes, I can't help but smile.

"I'm going to pay you back," I say, promising him right then and there.

"You don't have to." He shakes his head, smiling. "It is what *I* wanted to do."

"Either way, I am going to do it."

"You know how long that is going to take you?" he asks.

I smile, tipping my chin to him. "If I take it slow, probably the rest of my life."

He pulls me into his chest. After a while, he grunts and pushes me away from him.

"Get the fuck out of here," he says, wiping both hands across his face.

"Catch you later, Dad." I smile, walking to the door.

"Looking forward to it, son," he says, his voice breaking as he takes his seat behind his desk.

I leave the door open, a promise I will return.

Sky

There's a knock on my door.

"It's open," I say.

"Hey, munchkin. Jay said you wanted to talk to me?" Tim asks, closing the door behind him.

I slowly take his hand in mine. "Thank you for coming."

"Sure. Why wouldn't I?" he asks, sitting back.

I trace my bottom lip with the tip of my tongue, suddenly nervous as hell.

"Honey, what's up? What do you want? You know I'll do anything for you," Tim says.

Tears fill my eyes. "I need you to get me something to kill myself," I whisper.

He's speechless for a moment.

"What? Come again?" His voice skips a beat.

"I need you to get … something to kill myself."

"I know what you said," he replies, swallowing hard.

"I can't anymore. It hurts too much." My voice is hoarse. "Please, you said you'd do anything for me."

"Sky?" He stands and walks to the window. "Do you even know what you're asking me?" He has trouble keeping his voice level.

"I know what I want," I say calmly. "I have been thinking about it for a long time. I'm not going to Switzerland like in some novel. I want to stay here with the people I love."

Staring out of my window, he kicks his foot against the wall. "What you plan to do…I can't." His voice trembles. He rubs at the back of his head. Sweat forms on his forehead. "Do you know what? I …" he begins, leaning against the windowsill. After a while he gets up and kneels next to me. "You … no. I can't, Sky," he says, and hugs me tight.

"Timothy," I say, taking his hand in mine. I hate myself for even asking this from him. "I know what I'm asking of you is wrong on so many levels."

"Illegal is what it is. Morally wrong, fucking wrong, Sky. What would God think?"

I smirk at him. "You don't believe in God."

He clears his throat. "Well, maybe I don't, but what would the big boss upstairs say if he or she could talk?"

I burst out laughing.

"Stop it," he says angrily.

"Please," I whisper.

"Does Hunter know?" he grounds out.

"Hunter doesn't know. No one knows. It would destroy him. He's already losing it over the painkillers I'm taking, the weed, everything. I can't do that to him."

"But to me you can. I'm not going to be the one to help you knock on heaven's door. Fuck, babe," he swears under his breath.

Shaking my head, I say, "Don't."

"Don't do what?" He raises his voice.

"Don't make me ask again."

He blinks furiously, as if trying to keep his tears from spilling over.

"You're a drug dealer, Tim, and I know you still have contacts everywhere. Don't act like you don't."

"But what you're asking me. That we ... we, I ..." his voice falters.

"Please, Tim. I can't go on like this," I tell him, sounding braver than I feel.

He brushes both his hands across his face. "I can't, honey."

"Think about it," I plead.

He takes me into his arms, burying his face in my hair. He kisses my forehead then the corner of my lips. "Don't make me do this."

"Please," I beg, my cheeks wet with tears. "I wouldn't ask you if I wasn't one hundred percent sure. I can't live like this anymore. The doctors can't tell me why I'm getting worse so quick. It's like I've been holding on so tight these last couple of years, that my body is finally letting go. Please, Tim," I beg. "Promise me you'll take care of it. I can't hold a cup of coffee in my hands. I can barely walk anymore. I'll lose my speech. I already lost my left arm. I will lose everything."

He shakes his head violently. "Fucking hell."

"Promise me."

"I promise."

"Thank you, Timmy," I say, brushing my wet nose with my sleeve. He hugs me tight to his chest, holding me while we both cry.

Hunter

I park the bike in front of the garage and place my helmet on the seat. It's almost nine in the morning. I need to talk to Sky later and apologize, and thank her for reaching out to my father. After taking a quick shower, I crash on my couch and wake after a couple hours. I pour myself a cup of coffee when there's a knock on my door.

"It's open," I yell, walking out of my kitchen, cup still in hand.

"Hey, Hunter, got time for a talk?" Timothy says, tapping his hand on the frame.

"Sure, man," I say reluctantly, pulling a sweater over my head. "Want a coffee?"

"Yeah," he says, taking his seat on the couch. He brushes his palms on his jeans. After placing his coffee on the table, I take my seat in the chair opposite him. Spreading his legs, Tim crosses his arms in front of him like he owns the place.

"So," he begins, leaning forward, "can I bum a smoke?"

I nod. "You can have the pack."

After he lights the cigarette and blows out the smoke, he takes a small sip of his coffee with shaking hands. "I know we haven't exactly been friends since I came here."

I snort.

"We both have wanted to protect the people we love, each probably in our own fucked up, flawed way," Timothy says, his voice rough.

He eyes me and I don't blink. "If Drew made you talk to me, you can take your story and sell it somewhere else, like your fucking dope," I tell him, motioning to the door.

"Do you have a problem with my chosen profession, or is it me in general," he jokes, spreading out his arms.

I flip him off. "Eat shit and die, fuckwad." I manage to growl, but I smile anyway.

"Right back at you," he grins.

"I recognize the look in your eyes, Hunter. I see it each day when I stare at my reflection in the mirror." Timothy blows out the smoke in tiny rings. He sits forward, resting his elbows on his knees. The hardness returns to his features. "I ..."

Immediately, I sit up straight. "Man, is Drew okay?"

He chuckles when I mention Drew's name, shaking his head repeatedly. "I know what you've done for Drew over the years," he answers with love in his voice.

"Yeah, well, he's my best friend."

"I know everything, and I owe you for taking care of him. For protecting him when scumbags tried to beat him up." His strong voice skips a beat.

I scratch my stubble. "You would have done the same."

He nods. "I probably would have ended them."

"I don't question that you would."

A slight smirk seems to tug on his lips. "You are not the man I thought you were."

"Hell, most of the time I don't know who the fuck I am, so get in line." I grin. "Want something real to drink?" I ask, standing.

He eyes his coffee. "Sure, what do you have?"

I open a couple of kitchen cabinets, scanning the shelves for a bottle. "Jack?"

"Sure, Hunter."

I hand him a glass. He drowns one quarter of it before he looks at me again. "I didn't come here to talk about Drew."

"Oh no?" I ask, finishing my coffee.

"Sky asked me for something." He downs his drink and pours himself another, finishing it too.

My eyebrows immediately shoot up.

"If you're going to punch me, I have to tell you Drew likes this face."

I grunt, rolling my eyes. "What did she ask you?"

"You are acquainted with my former line of business, aren't you?"

"Former?" I ask, sarcasm ringing through my voice.

"Well, I have turned over all my contacts to new distributors, so yeah, I'd say I'm retired. Been starting up a legitimate business with the help of a guy from Nashville."

"You know, John Wick said the same thing," I joke.

He chuckles, but his smile falls. "She asked me if I could help her kill herself."

"She fucking did what?" I growl, flinging the table between us through the air before I grab the motherfucker by the throat and push him up against the wall, ready to kill the son of a bitch. "And what did you tell her?" I belt out.

Drew busts through the door. "Hunter, let him go," he roars, stepping over the broken glass.

I push Tim higher up against the wall and he lets me. The jackass could probably put up a serious fight, which pisses me off even more.

"Hunter," Drew orders again, taking a step closer to me.

Timothy grunts at him. "Drew, stay the fuck out of this. This is between me and Hunter."

"Tim," Drew pleads. But Timothy shakes his head while I let him go and box him in.

"I don't want to but she is in so much pain."

"Don't you think I don't know?" I scream in his face, my hold on him faltering. "Don't you think her not being able to walk, to eat, to go to the toilet alone or take a fucking shower doesn't tear my soul in two?" I seethe, blind with rage.

He jerks me into his body. "I know," he whispers, shaking me, making me look at him. "I fucking know, and I hate myself for not being able to give her what she wants."

"Do you?" I push him against the wall again.

"Let her hate me," he mumbles, his voice breaking. "Not you."

I swallow back the bile in my throat. All the adrenaline leaves my body. Tim pulls me against his chest and holds me in his arms, and I close my eyes. He lets me go and our faces are wet with tears.

"Damn," I huff, brushing my hands across my face. "Why the fuck do I keep hugging people and breaking down whenever the moment strikes?"

Drew sets the table back, he passes me and takes my face between his hands, kissing my cheek.

"What was that for?" I ask, staring at the tattoos that decorate my hands.

"For not killing him." Drew grins, as he takes a seat next to Tim, and hands him the pack of cigarettes from the floor, their fingers skimming each other.

"What should I do, Tim?" I ask desperately.

"Go to her and tell her I'm sorry I can't fucking do it," he murmurs.

I grab his shoulder. "Thank you for telling me."

After I close the door behind me and look through the window, Drew takes Tim in his arms as he breaks, clutching Drew's shirt between his fists, his body shaking.

I walk up to the house.

Before I can knock on the front door, Jay opens it. "Hunt, I'm sorry," is the first thing he says to me.

I shake my head. "No, I'm the one who's sorry," I apologize, following him in. Marian is stirring a steaming pot on the stove as the scent of garlic and tomato fills the air. She gives me a smile when she notices me. "Staying for dinner, Hunter?" I nod, swallowing back the lump in my throat.

"Come here, you son of a bitch." Jay's voice breaks as he takes me into his arms.

"I'm sorry, Jay." I bury my face in his chest.

He sighs, still embracing me. "Right back at ya, kid. Right back at ya."

CHAPTER 29

Hunter

I knock on her bedroom door. She doesn't answer at first. When I tap again, she says Tim's name. Fuck, her voice sounds broken.

I push through the door. She's lying in her bed, music softly playing in the background. "Yeah, you probably thought it was Tim, didn't you?" I mutter, slamming the door behind me.

She eyes me suspiciously. "Why?" she asks, damn she sounds and looks so fragile.

"Oh, I don't know," I grumble. "Because you fucking asked him for something to kill yourself with." I choke on my own words, slamming my palm on her bed.

She crosses her arms in front of her and looks at me with a defiant stare in her eyes. "So what?"

I almost pull my hair out of my skull, dragging an angry hand across my nose and lip piercing. I started wearing them again because Sky told me she likes them. "So what? So what, are you fucking crazy?"

"No, I'm not crazy," she says, her voice eerily calm. "I asked him to help me end it." *Like it was nothing, like what we have between each other is nothing.*

"But what if I don't want it to end?" I growl at her. "Fuck."

"Guess what, Hunter? It's not up to you," she says and coughs, turning her head away from my stare.

"I know what you're doing. Don't you do this to me," I beg.

"Do what?" she says, challenging.

"My whole damn existence, I've been waiting for the day when everything would make sense," I sob, catching my breath. "When someone would be there for me as I would be for them. Someone who was going to love me all the fucking way. I never believed what we have would be in the cards for me, with a past like the one I keep dragging along behind me. Do you, Sky? Do you love me?"

"Please don't." Her voice is small.

"I know what you did with my father, and although I'm angry, I owe you everything."

"You owe me nothing," she whispers, her face wet with tears.

"Fuck this shit, and fuck you." I point a finger in her face. "Fuck you for not giving me a chance."

"This isn't about Tim, is it?"

"Oh, it is about so many things, Sky," I say, pacing at the end of her bed. "Why did you go behind my back to Tim, to my father? What the hell were you thinking heading over there with all those fucking bastards?"

"I did it for you. When I'm gone, you are going to need all the love you can get, even from your dad."

"Why did you ask Tim?" I huff out.

"I can make my own decisions." Her eyes are full of fire.

"Not about this. Not when you ask him to end your life," I rasp, hanging my head, gripping my knees. I bite back my tears but they fall onto the wooden floor. "Fuck that, Sky. Before you, there was nothing. I got up in the morning, collected those medals, the applause, the money. The fame, whatever that meant. But it was nothing compared to what it's like waking up next to you, being with you. Figuring out life together. You love me all the way—don't pretend I only get half of your heart, because that's bullshit. You have my heart. All of it."

She blushes and averts my gaze.

"And you know it, Sky." My voice trembles.

"Why do you love me when you know this," she says, motioning between us, "is not going to last?"

"Don't you get it? There isn't a timespan on loving someone. You know some people spend their whole lives looking for something like what we have. We have it. I don't care if this story only lasts five minutes, fifty years or fucking five seconds. This, what we have here, right *damn* here, Shorty, is what's going to help me live the rest of my days. This is what will help me get up in the morning. It's what will help me breathe and feel the sun on my skin. This love." I grab her face. "This love, this fucking love, baby."

She smiles through her tears.

"This love will last forever. You have my heart. Shorty, you saved me," I say, letting her go.

"Hunt," she whispers.

I turn around, and sit next to her on the bed, and bury my face in my palms trying to hide my tears.

"Okay," she whispers. She lays her head against my shoulder and kisses my neck.

Sky

His whole body is shaking. I run my knuckles over his cheekbone with my trembling fist. "I'm sorry," I tell him. His hands caress my face, and he rests his forehead against mine.

Closing his eyes, he says, "I'm so sorry," his hot breath mingling with mine when he kisses the corner of my mouth.

I have trouble sitting but I bite through the pain, through the exhaustion I'm already experiencing. I lose my balance and he catches me.

I wanted him to leave so he wouldn't be with me as I fell apart. I didn't want the last memories of him and me to be like this. For him to not see me as the person I was when I met him. The person he deserves. But now I know he takes me as I am. Broken, but so incredibly loved.

"You thought you could push me away but here I am. And I'm not fucking leaving you again," he declares, a slow grin stealing across his face.

"Why?"

"No, babe, let me say this before I lose it. Does my love have to make sense for it to be real? You may not know this but when you love someone, truly love someone, you let them in on the good, the bad and the ugly." I smile but he's serious. "I love you now until forever, cross my fucking heart."

"You do?" I ask, my voice hoarse.

"Because you are still you. Don't you know I would give my life for you? I fell in love with your soul, not your body. Nothing lasts forever but give me this—our perfect fucking forever."

I shake my head, wanting to believe him. "Fuck forever," I whisper.

"The feeling of never being good enough—you changed that. You changed me. You love me for who I am. You know me. Every light, every shade, and still you want..."

I close my eyes. "Look at me," he orders. I shake my head. "Babe, please?"

He drops his face so we are at eye level. I gaze into his eyes, and they are blazing. "This is it, honey. Okay?" he asks, his deep voice cracking.

"Okay," I tell him, nodding. "But there will come a time when..."

"I know," he says, strained, and takes me into his arms. "I will be right there beside you when it happens."

"This isn't a mistake, is it?" I whisper, my mouth moving across his parted lips.

He smiles. "Babe, every mistake I ever made led me to you." Gently, he lays me down, getting in right beside me.

Licking my lips, I tell him, "You know it hurts to even speak." I clear my throat. "Sometimes when I open my mouth I can't."

"Jay told me," he says, wiping away my tears with his thumb.

"That is why I asked Tim—because I couldn't see the track anymore. I wanted to reach the finish line," I state.

"You will when you're ready," he says, kissing my temple. I snuggle into him, resting my head against his chest.

"You know I came here looking for my past." I smile, tracing his jawline, his lips, his earth-shattering smile.

"Have you found what you were looking for?"

Pressing my lips to his, I whisper, "I found something better. I found you."

CHAPTER 30

Sky

"Are you ready?" Drew yells up the stairs. Timothy and Jay are already waiting for us in the living room.

"Yeah, we are," Hunter shouts back. It's taken him about an hour to get me dressed.

"You're sure you want to go to the beach?" he asks, holding the back of my head.

I nod. Even talking has become too much for me.

He puts my left arm in a black sling while I sit on the edge of the bed. The muscles in my other hand have started to atrophy as well. I hate this fucking disease. My brain still works, my thoughts are the same, but my body is dying.

Talking takes up too much energy. My days are spent sleeping, going to the bathroom and eating a little through a damn tube.

"Are you okay?" he asks, sitting back on his heels, his calloused hand stroking my cheek.

I try to smile.

"Your eyes always give you away."

"I love you," I tell him.

"I love you too," he says before he takes my cheeks between his big hands and softly kisses my lips, then my temples, my jaw and both corners of my mouth. Loving every single broken part of me.

Hunter

"Come on. I'll carry you," I whisper, kissing her forehead, adjusting the oxygen tube in her nose, I drape the straps of her tank over my head, the metal pressing against my side. Holding her in my arms, I slowly take each step one at a time, descending the stairs. Her arms feel brittle around my neck. She nuzzles my earlobe and rests her cheek on my shoulder.

"Babe, stop it." I grin when my dick twitches. Fuck, I can't be sporting a hard-on right now, holding her tight as I walk outside.

Jay keeps the door open for me. Careful not to hurt her, I place her in the front seat of the truck, the oxygen tank next to her on the floor. I caress her forehead.

"Shorty, you feel a little hot," I murmur, and she looks so pale.

"Not in front of Jay," she jokes, her voice barely a whisper, and coming out ever so slowly as she stares at her father. We smile at each other, and Jay slaps me on the back. I close the door and walk with him to the other truck.

"Should we stay home?" I sigh, leaning against the truck, shoving my hands in the pockets of my jeans.

He shakes his head, pulling on the lashing straps, checking if the boards are tightly fastened on the roof of his car.

"I don't know. She stays in bed all the time. Maybe a little fresh air will do her good," he mutters, turning to Marian for support, who smiles.

"She should be okay," she responds.

"All right, we will both keep an eye on her," I promise him. I get in the driver's seat and open the windows, hoping the fresh air will bring a little color to her cheeks.

I watch her from the corner of my eyes while we cruise along the highway to the beach. Her long hair sways in the breeze.

We're not going to have years of this.

No more drives to the beach. And they're just one thing on a list of many I would like us to do together. She lays her hand on my knee. Shaking my head I kiss her fist. We grin at each other. Sometimes you don't have to say anything. A smile is enough.

Pulling into the parking lot, I stare at the beach, and my mouth drops. "What the hell is this?"

She turns to follow my gaze and smiles. All my friends from racing and surfing are here. There's a barbeque and a bonfire. Jay gets out of his car and my father steps up and slaps him on the back, Oliver's new wife by his side. A blonde surfer babe in her forties. I know by the way he looks at her and the way she kisses his cheek that they're in this for life, and it fucking hurts knowing I'm never going to have that with Sky.

"What is this, Hunter?" Sky asks in slow motion, pulling me from my thoughts. Her voice sounds nothing like it did before, and I hate this fucking disease, the way it's slowly breaking down the woman I love.

I shrug, grinning at her. I need to stay strong. "I don't know," I say, turning the ignition off. Drew opens the door and rock music fills the car.

"Drew," she says, while he takes her into his arms.

"Come on. I got you." Timothy has already gotten her wheelchair out of the truck bed. Drew places her carefully in the chair and together they pick her up, and carry her to the beach.

I can smell the burning embers in the air from the fire, and everywhere around us are friendly faces. Some people are in the water, surfing.

I follow Tim and Drew along the sand. Drew softly places Sky on a large blanket. Even her mother, stepfather, and little brother, Stevie, are here.

"What is this?" I ask, and say hello to a few racing friends as they pass by.

"A little get-together me and Tim organized." Drew beams.

Sky smiles up at him. "I love it."

Her mother hugs her and sits next to Sky, kissing her hair. Jay and Conrad laugh while Jay motions to the guys already catching a wave. Tim helps me get the boards out of the truck. He slaps me reassuringly on my shoulder and we both smile through our tears. Jay and Marian have spread a blanket next to Sky to sit on.

Tim bumps fists with me, winking. "See you in the water?"

"Yeah." I smile, glancing at Sky who's wearing one of my black sweaters, and her favorite black skinny jeans with boots. She looks paler than normal, her hair flowing in the breeze.

After I catch up with a couple of friends, I head over to my father who introduces me to Debra, his new wife. We chat for a while before I plant my ass in the sand next to Sky. People stop and talk to her or sit for a while. She smiles and listens, sometimes laughing out loud. Even May and Clay from the diner come by. Sky has trouble speaking. Funny how the disease works; some people first lose all their motor function, their speech or the movement in their hands and legs. For each patient ALS works in its own way, this fucking disease.

Lydia and Ryan talk to Sky, and I spend some time with Chelsea.

"I'm going into the ocean," I tell Sky, kissing her forehead, I grab my board and make my way across the sand. The water is cold, but soothing. From the surf, I spot my father talking to Sky.

She nods and smiles. After a while, Ryan walks up to Jay and takes his seat next to him.

After a flat period, I catch a wave in and walk back up the shore. I clear my throat and set my board next to them, wiping the water out of my eyes.

"Hey, man," I say, tossing my wet hair out of my face. I haven't bothered to cut it these last few weeks; I've only shaved the side. Sky likes it like this so I keep it long.

Ryan stands and shakes my hand.

"Have you talked to Jay already?" I ask him.

"Talked to me about what?" Jay chimes in, eyeing Ryan.

Ryan swallows. "I wanted to ask if I could race for you?"

Jay's eyes shine as he checks him out, the side of his mouth twitching. "Have you got what it takes?"

"Yes, sir," Ryan answers, standing tall.

Jay laughs. "Wanna grab a beer and talk about it?"

"I would love to." Ryan beams. Lydia says goodbye to Sky, and I kiss my girl's lips, making myself comfortable next to her. I ask her many times if she wants to leave. Each time, she shakes her head and takes it all in.

Cody, one of the kids from BMX training, calls me and I wave at him. He has his board tucked under his arm. Quinn claps, standing near the waterline. "That was awesome, honey," she hollers.

"Mom," he groans, rolling his eyes, and I chuckle.

Grinning, she winks at me. Quinn's smile grows even more when she sees Sky sitting by my side.

"Hey, Hunt," Cody says, running up to me all excited. "Want to catch a wave?"

I turn to Sky, she nods and gives me her beautiful smile. She turns that same one to Cody and I see him puff out his chest, trying to appear bigger than he is. Sky's grin gets even bigger and Quinn laughs.

"Sure, why not buddy."

Sky

I stare out to the water. Hunter leans in and kisses me, and I close my eyes, savoring the touch of his lips on my own. "Catch you later, babe," he whispers.

"Are you ready, Cody?" Hunter asks, picking up his board and holding out his fist for his young friend to bump.

Cody smiles up at Hunter. "When I grow up I want to have as many tattoos as you," he states, not a hint of doubt in his voice.

Hunter shakes his head, smiling, and shoves him playfully in the shoulder. "First you have to ask your mother. My guess is she'll have something to say about it." He grins at Quinn who heads over to us, her thick red hair blowing in the soft breeze.

"About what?" she asks.

"About the tattoos, Mom," Cody says, all serious, looking from Hunter to Quinn, his eyes full of mischief.

"We'll talk again when you're eighteen," she says, smiling at me. I can't help but chuckle.

"Mom," he whines, "that's still eight years away!"

"I guess it is," she says, laughing and smiling down at her son, she makes a move to ruffle his hair but he ducks, and she winks at me. Hunter tries to hide his grin behind his inked hand, as he looks at Cody, whose cheeks turn a bright shade of red. My smile is just as wide as Quinn's. I love the way Hunter is around Cody, he adores him. Quinn keeps looking at her son and Hunter, while the little boy talks about BMX. I recognize her smile, and my heart feels full because I know he's not going to be alone.

"Come on, Cody," Hunter says, putting his arm around the little boy's neck. "Let's catch some waves."

"Hey, Sky," Quinn greets me, a hint of a Texas drawl in her voice.

"Hi." I say softly.

Hunter scrunches up his eyebrows, looking between me and her. "Go," I tell him, motioning with my chin to the ocean.

"Come on, Hunter. I'll race you," Cody yells, getting a head start.

"Kid is fast." Hunter snorts, running after him.

Quinn giggles, watching them sprint to the water's edge.

"Sit?" I rasp, talking slowly.

She nods, taking a seat next to me and pushing her Wayfarers on top of her head.

"Hunter really loves Cody," I tell her, struggling to form each word.

Quinn nods, grinning from ear to ear when Cody tries to pull Hunter underwater. "God, I'm glad he has a good male role model in his life. I'm forever grateful Hunt took Cody under his wing. Don't know where we would be if he hadn't helped us." She stares at her hands. "I'm so sorry, Sky, for what is happening to you." She sniffles, wiping away a tear.

I nod, flashing her a smile, focusing on the boys in the water.

Quinn talks for a while about her life as a single mom, as a nurse and I really get to know the person she is—kind, caring and funny as hell. She loves eighties music, has been riding a motorcycle all her life, and tries to take Cody on small road trips whenever she can.

She claps as Cody rides a big wave. I take a deep breath, smiling at her, trying to bring up the courage to tell her what she needs to hear from me. "You really love him, don't you," I say, taking my time to pronounce each word.

"Yes." She beams. "The kid is the love of my life."

"Not Cody," I respond, dipping my head in Hunter's direction.

Color creeps up her neck. "Sky, I ..." I lay my hand on hers and she takes it.

"Sky, I don't... I would never... he loves you so much. I

would never come between that." I keep looking at her. "I've known Hunter for years, I hope he's my friend, I respect his work with the kids, and I admire his career, the risks he takes."

We both smile at the same time, and she whispers, "I really do care for him, maybe more than I ever wanted to admit to myself. But I've never seen him look at anyone like he looks at you. He loves you so much, Sky, and I'm so grateful I've gotten a glimpse of what true love is. He's..." she stops talking, and looks at her son talking and laughing with Hunter in the water. "I... how did you know?"

I shrug and wink at her.

"I do love him," she tells me, a soft smile warming her face.

I nod, turning to Cody and Hunter, both catching the same wave. "Wait," I whisper.

"Wait for what?" she asks, gazing longingly at Hunter and her son.

"Hunter," I reply.

She hugs me. "I promise, Sky. I promise," she whispers, holding me in her arms.

And I know she will.

Hunter

We watch the sun set together. The bonfire warms us. "What did you talk about with Quinn?" I ask.

Sky smiles, watching people dance to a song by Post Malone.

"Shorty?"

She touches my face, her eyes meeting mine, her expression serene.

"You're not going to tell me, are you?" I ask with a smirk.

She shakes her head, closing her eyes and leaning against my chest.

"Want to head home? We've been here the whole day. You're probably tired," I say.

She nods, not opening her eyes.

"Let me give Jay a heads up." I move her gently to her chair, stand and walk over to Jay where he's talking with my father.

"I'm going to take her home," I tell Jay.

"Yeah, probably a good idea."

"Thanks for coming, Dad." I smile, shaking my father's hand.

"Anytime, son. Would you like to have dinner…"

"Call nine-one-one!"

I spin around. Quinn crouches next to Sky who's fallen on the ground. She pumps up and down on her chest, performing CPR. "Fuck, God, no!" I yell, running to Sky with Jay and my father in pursuit.

"Here you go, son," my father says, handing me a coffee.

"Thanks, Dad," I reply, sipping from the steaming cup.

"Any news?" he asks, taking a seat next to me.

Sliding my fingers through my hair, I glance around the hospital waiting area. Everyone I care about is here. Some are sleeping or talking quietly amongst each other. We have been waiting here for hours. Jay is with Sky right now.

Quinn kept giving her CPR. Luckily, Sky came to, thank God Quinn was there. She kept her stable and conscious until the ambulance arrived. The way she kept talking to me as the paramedics helped Sky kept me calm. Fuck, I don't know what would have happened if Quinn hadn't been there. According to the paramedics it is going to be touch and go.

"I don't know what is going to happen. It's all fucked," I groan, rubbing both my hands over my face.

Dad squeezes my shoulder. "I know, son. I know."

Jay walks through the sliding doors, and I glance up locking eyes with him.

"She wants to see you," he whispers, holding in his tears. I hand my father my coffee, and follow Jay to her room.

He pauses in front of her door. "Are you not going in, Jay?"

He lets out a strangled sob, embracing me. "No. She wants you. They just confirmed it's pneumonia. I knew this could happen, she's not strong enough to beat this son, but fuck I know she is going to try for you."

"What's going to happen?" I ask, brushing the snot from my nose with the palm of my hand.

He runs both his hands across his face. "They took her off the ventilator. She wanted them to, but she can't properly breathe on her own anymore; her lungs are too weak." He tries to hold in a sob.

My body shakes, and my vision blurs as I shut my eyes, leaning against the doorframe. When I open them, I ask, "how long?"

He shakes his head, and I take hold of his hand.

"How long?"

He locks eyes with me. "They don't know—days, weeks, they can't say. It differs between patients, they told me. But she's so tired, son. So goddamn tired. It's not fair."

I hold him before he collapses then step back, giving him space. Burying my face in my hand, I slam my foot against the concrete wall. We stare at each other, not saying anything.

When I finally enter her room, she is sleeping, the oxygen tube in her nose. I cup her face, staring at her. Every once in a while her breath stutters, and the machine beeps in response.

She opens her eyes. I smile. "Babe, you had us worried there."

She reaches out, and with her shaking palm she brushes the hair from my eyes, tracing my wet cheeks with her fist.

"Why aren't you on a ventilator?" I ask.

She shrugs then smiles, searching my eyes for something.

"Are you ready to go home?"

Her face sobers. I shake my head, frowning. She blinks rapidly, gasping for air.

"Yes," she rasps, as I bury my face in her chest lying next to her on the bed, silently crying. She kisses my forehead, her lips lingering, and I shiver as I close my eyes.

CHAPTER 31

Hunter

I haven't left her side the last couple of days. If she wakes, I make her drink something, take her to the bathroom, and help her shower.

Her mother, stepfather and little brother come to visit. I don't stay; I want them to be able to say goodbye alone.

I'm sitting on the porch, staring out to the track when they walk downstairs. Jay hugs them and goes up to her room himself, and they leave to walk around the track. He stays with her for a long time and then he comes down and takes his seat next to me, burying his face in his hands.

"I'm sorry, son," he says, sliding his fingers through his long hair.

"It's okay, Jay," I mutter, laying my hand on his shoulder, smiling as Drew and Timothy walk up to the house.

"Hey, Hunt." Drew hugs me.

"Hey, man," I whisper, embracing him tighter.

"Can we go to her?" Tim asks, leaning against the porch railing.

"Yeah." I nod. "You can try. She has been sleeping a lot the last couple days. She only stays awake for a few minutes before she conks out again. Maybe you guys could get her to drink something."

Tim nods.

"Can I get you anything, Jay?" Drew asks, motioning to the kitchen.

"No, I'm good," he answers, giving Drew a small smile. "I'll get dinner going. You guys staying here again tonight?"

They both nod before heading upstairs.

Later that evening we all have dinner together. Her mother, stepfather, and little brother. Jay and Marian. Mac, Drew and Tim. Even my father and Debra show up. When everything is ready, and I glance around the table, I know what I have to do.

"Want to set another plate?" Jay asks me, reading my mind.

"Yeah. I'm going to get her," I say, sliding my chair back.

I knock on her door. I push it open and she smiles weakly. I kneel next to her bed, "Want to come downstairs with me, Shorty?"

Those big beautiful brown eyes blink a couple times and shine as she slowly nods.

"Okay, baby," I say, kissing her lips. My mouth lingers on her skin. She closes her eyes. I help her sit up, pulling one of my black sweaters over her head and making sure her breathing tube is secure in her nose. She touches my jaw with her fist, then moves it over my hair. What I would give to have her fingers slide through my strands again. Her eyes are glistening with moisture. "You're tired, aren't you, babe?"

She nods, slowly opening and closing her eyes.

"I know. I know," I whisper, taking her downstairs.

Sky listens to the stories during dinner, the laughter and

the tears we share. Drew and Tim help her eat, feeding her little bites of vanilla ice cream, and get her to drink a little bit of water through a straw. Jay sits next to her and whispers something in her ear that makes her smile. He catches my stare and winks, tears rolling down his face. I watch her taking in everything happening around her. Our eyes lock from across the table, and everyone around us fades away. It's like we are the only two here. She smiles at me like she did the first time we made love, my cheeks heat thinking about all the beautiful moments we've shared together.

I wink at her. She parts her lips, giving me a full-blown smile and mouths *I love you*. I stand and walk around the table to her. She follows me with her eyes.

"Cross my heart, babe," I say. Her earth-shattering smile is all I need to know she feels the same.

After dinner I take her upstairs. She doesn't want to wear the oxygen tube anymore. I beg her, but I also understand we're almost at the finish line.

She falls asleep in my arms. Fuck, she is so thin, I feel her heartbeat hammering in her small chest. She's been wheezing and gasping for air the whole day. She's so sick, so god damn sick.

"My Shorty." I run my fingers through her hair, staring at her beautiful face. Memorizing every line, every freckle, and the laugh lines around her eyes. I memorize her neck, her collarbone, the swell of her breasts, her tiny waist, and those long legs. How can this body, how can something this beautiful, be so cruel? Pulling the covers over her, I notice how much weight she has lost in the last week alone. Her skin is covered with bruises. Despite all this, she's still as beautiful as she was the first day I met her. And I'm fucking thankful I get to love her, and she loves me just the same.

Sky sleeps through the whole night and well into the next day. Slowly opening my eyes I stretch, I'm still wearing last night's clothes. The midday sun beats through the open patio doors. I turn on my side; she is watching me. A soft glow illuminates her face, her blonde hair shining like a field of corn in the summer.

I reach out and kiss her lips, and she runs her knuckles over my inked neck, following the lines of my tattoos and stopping below my jaw. Pulling back, she smiles.

"Take me to the track," she whispers, her voice sounding stronger than it's been in weeks.

"You want to go outside?" I ask, brushing the sleep out of my eyes.

"Yes." She smiles. I pick her up and hold her in my arms.

Walking to the track, we never break eye contact. The wind picks up and blows her hair out of her face, the sun touches her cheeks, and she smiles.

"Why are you looking at me like that?" she asks, as I gently set her on the dirt track. Her speech is still weak and the words are broken up, but definitely clearer than they've been. Hope flares in my chest even though I know nothing is going to change. I smile, as I look around; we are at the spot where I almost ran her over with my bike months ago.

"I'm grateful, babe," I tell her, draping my leather jacket over her thin shoulders.

Smiling, she motions to the track laid out in front of us with her chin. "This is the spot, isn't it?"

I sit behind her so she can lean against me, my legs on either side of hers. I can't help but grin. "You mean the place where I almost ran you over, because you were taking a nap on the fucking track when the sun came up?"

Her body shudders as she laughs. It brings tears to my eyes. Leaning against my chest, she presses her cheek against mine. I catch her rolling her eyes. "I wasn't taking a nap."

Kissing her hair, I pull her close. "You feel better today?"

"I'm ready," she whispers, reaching out, her hands moving through the breeze. She smiles and turns in my arms, slowly running her shaking fingers through my long hair.

"Is this a dream?" I husk out. It's almost like she's doing better. Like the disease is gone, but that can't be. "Am I still sleeping?"

"No," she says, a soft smile on her lips while she caresses my face. She trails her hand along the lines of my brows, my nose and my mouth. "It was a beautiful dream," she tells me. "God I'm going to miss you."

She kisses me, then pulls back and smiles at me with a look of wonder in her eyes. The sun is sinking lower, shades of yellow and orange painting the sky. She is engulfed by light. It takes my breath away.

"Don't cry, babe," she whispers, her thumb moving across the wet streaks on my face.

"I can't help it. I don't understand how this is even possible," I say, shaking my head.

"Does it have to make sense for it to be real?" she asks.

Those were the same words I said to her when I told her I loved her. I swallow back the lump in my throat. "No, babe. I guess not. This is it, isn't it? This is what true love is. It hurts like fucking hell but makes you feel alive in the best possible ways."

"That's it," she tells me, without breaking eye contact.

"I never thought anyone would take me for the man I am. The man behind the mask. But, Shorty, you see every color, every shade, every part of me I tried so long to hide."

"And I always will." Beaming, she gazes up at the sky. "There," she says, her voice strong like it used to be. I turn and look out across the track, taking in the colors, the red, pink and yellow casting a beautiful glow on her face.

"That's where you'll find me," she says, and we lock eyes.

Sitting back, I wrap my arms tighter around her waist. Slowly, she leans forward and puts the necklace she always wears around my neck. I hold the silver bird with its wings spread out in my hand, my chest tightening.

"Babe, I can't. This is yours," I say, my voice hoarse and husky.

"It's yours now. Jay told me yesterday to give it to the man who has my heart," she tells me, tucking my long hair behind my ear. "You will always have my heart." Her palm moves over my cheekbone to the scruff on my jaw.

"Don't go looking for me in places where you lose yourself, Hunter," she says, her hands on either side of my face. "I'll always be right here." Her fingers move to my heart.

I take her palm in mine and skim her knuckles over my mouth. She closes her eyes, and I kiss her neck, her cheeks, her eyelids.

Opening her eyes, she whispers, "You have given me your heart, Hunter, and I will always love every part of what you gave me. The good, the bad and the ugly."

I grin, fighting the tears burning in my eyes. "It was good, wasn't it?"

She smiles up at me and says, "It was everything."

"I'm still so angry," I confess, leaning my forehead against hers, brushing my lips over her skin.

Her voice is soft when she tells me, "Don't be. I wouldn't want to change a thing. Because it led to this moment. It led me to you." She caresses my cheek. "You have given me the greatest gift anyone could ever receive in this life. You have given me unconditional love. Don't close your heart because I'm gone," she says, turning my chin to her. "Promise me you'll never do that."

"I c-can't," I stutter.

"Promise me, Hunter," she says.

I close my eyes in pain. Opening them, she is still waiting for my answer.

"I promise." My voice trembles.

Her fingers trace the line of my lips, as rays of sunlight hit her beautiful face.

I kiss her fingertips, wanting this moment to last forever, but I know it can't. "I promise."

I wrap my arms around her while her breathing slows.

Closing my eyes, I brush my lips over her temple. "I love you, Shorty," I whisper as she slowly drifts off while I hold her.

Burying my face in her neck, I feel her faint pulse against my lips when her heart takes its last beat. "Fuck forever, babe," I whisper, gently turning her lifeless body, I caress her cheek, and softly kiss her lips. "Thank you for loving every broken part of me," I say choking on my words. "I'll miss you so damn much. I love you, Shorty," I cry, rocking her in my arms. "Cross my heart."

CHAPTER 32

Hunter

Eight years later

Time is a mean son of a bitch. It doesn't heal a single fucking thing. But the hole in my heart is getting smaller with each sunrise. Not a day goes by when I don't cherish every single moment I spent with her. She taught me how to live, to forgive, but above all, she taught me how to love. Not only love another person, but love myself. With all my flaws and my regrets, the time I wasted and the moments I can never return to.

It is funny what you remember, and what you don't. I only spent a summer with her but it could have easily been fifty years.

I don't think it really matters how much time you spend with someone; love doesn't need to have a time stamp on it for it to be real, for it to define the rest of your life. Still, even eight years after she died, I love her. Although now, it's a different kind of love. A love that opened my eyes.

It's crazy—if you'd asked me how I wanted to live my life before I met her, before her love changed me, I would have told you I'd rather kill myself than give my heart to a girl.

Now, I smile every time I remember the little things, her laugh, the way she'd put me in my place, how we fought, the way we loved each other without anything left unspoken between us.

Sometimes when the sun is about to set and I'm done teaching the kids for the day, I head over to the track. I sit there and close my eyes, remembering how I held her in my arms one last time.

The day we spread her ashes in the ocean was beautiful. The moment I walked into the blue water with Jay, Drew and Tim by my side is etched in my mind. I was there with my friends, Ryan and Lydia, my father, Debra, Marian, Quinn and Cody. And with Sky's mother, Chelsea, Conrad and her little brother, Stevie. We all stood on the beach with "Free Bird" playing in the background while the sun set. They said time will heal. I pray to fuck it does. First came anger, then pain, then numbness and rage, but now, thinking about that day and holding the necklace of the bird she gave me, I'm slowly becoming whole again. Sky will always be part of me, like I'm always going to be a part of her.

The month after she died, I rode the last race of my life. Standing there, waiting for the gate to fall, I knew it was time to stop chasing the ride on the tracks.

I bought an empty plot of land next to Jay's, and built my own house. We opened a brand-new training facility in Sky's name so we could train more kids. We couldn't have done it without her help.

Ryan has been riding full-time for our company, and has defended his number-one position for the better part of the last seven years. We have a dozen promising young riders, even a couple who tried out for Nitro Circus. Drew is managing all of them; he's needed to turn kids away or put them on a waiting list. Work is good.

Kneeling in front of the plaque next to the track, I smile, reading her name. *FREE BIRD. In loving memory of Sky Alexander.*

"Today is a big day, Shorty," I whisper, taking out the last letter she wrote to me. I don't know how many times I read those words before I could let them in. Taking a deep breath, I trace my fingers over her name on the plaque. "Today is the day," I tell myself. "I'm keeping my promise, Sky." I kiss my fingertips and let them glide across the engraving. Kissing the letter, I fold it, and put it back in my pocket.

"You ready?" Drew asks, walking over and handing me a coffee.

"I am." I slap him on the back and follow him toward a group of kids already waiting for us on the track.

"How's your dad doing?" he asks.

Grinning, I roll my eyes. "He's good. You know, Debra and him actually go on double dates with Marian and Jay."

"Old people." Drew laughs.

"Hey, I have dinner with you and Tim almost every week and we're not old."

He winks at me. "Face it, Hunt. We're ancient in their eyes," he jokes, and points to the kids.

"Fuck, I know," I say, shaking my head and laugh. "Feels like a lifetime ago when I was sixteen like them and racing for the stars."

Drew laughs and takes a sip from his coffee.

We watch Cody pedaling down the track with Jay shouting pointers to him, and the other riders wait their turn. Cody's the best and they know it. Drew heads over to Jay, handing him a coffee too. Jay waves at me and winks before shouting at Cody for missing his mark.

Quinn is talking to Debra, and my half-brother, Danny, sits next to them in the stands, and I smile.

My father was right; Danny is a light in the darkness. Every time I visit him at the amazing care facility where he lives, his innocence teaches me something new. I even helped him ride my bike. Debra and my tough-as-nails father brushed away a couple tears.

Quinn walks over to me. "Can't believe Cody is traveling the world doing what he loves," she says, watching her son balancing on his bike before the beeper goes off and he's flying down the track.

"Better believe it. Cody has the drive to be great. Be even better than I ever was." I grimace, giving her a wink.

She bumps her elbow in my side. "It's all because of you."

Smiling, I turn to her. I don't know when it happened; it wasn't an exact moment. My love grew for her over time. We started out as friends, and she never pushed me for something more when I wasn't ready to be the man she deserved. But I'm ready now.

My hands start to sweat, and something swells inside me that I haven't experienced for eight long years. Something I've longed for again, but thought would never happen after losing Sky.

I read somewhere the heart will always want more even if there is nothing left to give. Sky made me reach for something. Something I thought would never be in the cards for me. Not once, and certainly not twice in my fucked up life.

"What?" Quinn asks, tucking her red hair behind her pierced ear. I swallow hard. She smiles even wider, blushing a little. "Hunter, why are you looking at me like that?"

I glance over at the track. Cody grins at me. I give him a chin-tip he returns. He knows what I'm about to say.

Reaching out, I take her hand in mine.

"Hunter." She frowns, cocking her head.

"Honey, I know we've known each other for over ten years now." My voice shakes. Her green eyes calm me. I take a deep breath before I continue. "You have stayed with me at my worst, and when I tried to be my best. And you were there for me after Sky died."

She closes her eyes for a brief moment. She blinks back her tears, and locks her gaze on me.

"You never asked for more than I could give. You have been my best friend. You held me when I cried, when I relapsed, and when the darkness took over. And you forgave me when I took it out on you," I tell her.

"Hunter," she whispers.

"No, Quinn. Let me say this before the lump in my throat chokes me."

She swallows hard, holding my hand, tracing little circles with her fingers over my knuckles and across my *free* tattoo.

"I don't know when it happened but I fell in love with you. And I think you somehow always loved me, through all the hills of my life," I say. She nods, smiling up at me. "You know I gave a piece of my heart to her, but I'm asking you right here, right now—damn, this is going to sound fucking lame." I chuckle and she does the same. "I wanted to ask you if I could give this other piece to you?" My hand moves over my heart.

She bites her lip, her eyes hazy with unshed tears.

"Fuck, I'm not really great at these grand gestures. What I'm asking is ..." I take a deep, shuddering breath. "... would you like to spend the rest of our lives together? Will you marry me?"

She reaches up and traces the line of my jaw, her fingers running through my short hair.

"I thought you'd never ask," she says, grinning.

I burst out laughing. "The worst line ever, isn't it?"

Winking, she stands on her tiptoes, her plump lips inches away from my own. "The worst," she says, beaming up at me.

"I knew it." I hold her against my chest, my hand travels into her hair. "Are you going to kiss me now, woman?" My voice is thick with emotion.

She nods. "I plan to kiss you for the rest of our lives."

"Fuck, that is way better than what I said." I bite on my lip.

Quinn laughs. She touches my cheek, and I know this is not the end of my story, this is only the beginning, and I have *her* to thank for it.

There isn't going to be a day I won't stare at a sunset and see Sky's face in the bright colors. Sky opened up my heart so I could walk this road with someone who loves me for who I am, the man I was, and the man I'm going to be in the future.

"I know it won't be easy, but, Hunter, I love every part of you. The parts you were with her and the parts you are going to be with me."

My lips find hers, and I lose myself in our embrace. Applause breaks out, and someone whistles from the track. Quinn chuckles.

"Those would be your boys," she snickers.

I flip them off, and yell at them to get a damn move on. It's followed by more laughing.

"Teenagers," I say, smiling, caressing her cheek and sliding my thumb back and forth over her bottom lip.

"I love you, Hunter. I've always loved you and I always will," she whispers.

"You keep me in the light, honey," I tell her, brushing my fingers over her wet cheeks. "I love you too, Quinn."

"Always," she beams.

I close my eyes, the rays of sunlight warming my face. Opening them, I see myself reflected in her stare. "Always," I whisper, before my lips find hers again.

For the love of my life,

There are so many things in life I took for granted. Every hour, every minute, every damn second. I barely made it through the day without feeling like shit.

I was scared to fail, scared of success. Love and happiness were some distant dream I couldn't remember when I woke.

You changed everything. You remind me every day to live life in the moment. You make me remember; you give me strength I didn't even know I possessed. Babe, you inspire me. You see everything every color, every light, and every shade. The best and the worst. You see all the pieces I lost along the way, the pieces you helped me put back together.

I never met anyone who lived his life exactly how he wanted, screw the consequences, until you. You don't care about other people's opinions, or what they say or think about you. You face life head-on with a big "fuck you" smirk on your face. You live life with no regrets.

You take credit for every success and every failure that's led you here. How many people can say that? Truly say they did it all? You can and you will.

You once told me you were a mistake. If that is the case, babe, then you are the best mistake I've ever made.

You made me lose myself, and helped me find what was missing.

True and unconditional love is messy, and sometimes it's as dirty as the races you ride. It's the kind of love that brings you back to life, that lets you reach for the light.

The joy of being exactly where you are meant to be with your best friend, the one who will race with you till the end. That is what you gave me, Hunter.

You promised me your heart, but babe, you still have so much left to give. Don't hold back, love her with everything you've got. Open your heart for her, and she will love every part of you.

You are my home, my life.

My love.

My once-in-a-lifetime.

Promise me you'll love her with everything you have to give. To love her for all she is.

Fuck forever, babe.

Promise me you'll live, baby. Just live.

I will love you always.

Cross my heart.

Shorty

ACKNOWLEDGEMENTS

First of all, I would like to thank my fantastic editors Lauren Clarke, Sali Benbow-Powers, and Sarah Plocher for making this book what it is today.

This was a difficult book to write, not only because it involved describing ALS and the impact it has on those living with this awful disease, but also what it means for the people in their lives. Please forgive me for the liberties I took when it comes to the timeline of the symptoms and the progression of this disease. Each person is different—some live with ALS for a decade, and others only two to four years. I hope I have given everyone the respect they deserve and shown what true fighters you guys are. If you want to know more about ALS and how you can help end it, visit: www.alsa.org/donate/

I want to especially thank Ady Barkan for sharing his courageous battle with the world, not only in fighting this disease, but also in shedding light on the United States healthcare system. I hope this story will inspire people who are fighting their own battle no matter how big or small, to take a chance. Buy that motorcycle, travel the world, fall in love, and never stop believing in yourself. We don't know how much time we are given, let go, and enjoy the ride.

A big heartfelt thank you to Twan van Gendt, BMX world champion and Olympic medalist, for taking the time to answer my questions about the world of BMX.

Most of all, I would like to thank you, the reader. Without you guys I wouldn't be able to live out my dream. Thank you to all the bloggers and readers who post kind words about my stories. I can't thank you enough, so I'll keep doing it ;)

Thank you Michelle Lancaster for shooting the beautiful cover picture. And Chase Cassels for bringing Hunter to life.

"So Far Away" by Agust D was the song that kick-started this story. Thank you 민윤기. You make me want to be a better writer when I sing along to the lyrics of your songs. They inspire me to keep going without fear or regret, to enjoy the ride, and most of all to dream.

X My Heart is dedicated to every single one of you who is fighting your own battle. Take a chance on love. Be proud of who you are, and don't fucking apologize for it. Love is love. Let's keep fighting for it!

xxx

ABOUT THE AUTHOR

L.A. Wayward is the author of *Make It Burn,* the first book in The Nashville Outlaws series, *Ranger Danger* and *Thirst.* A self-declared nomad, '70s and '80s music-lover, motorcycle enthusiast, film buff, and music addict, this wayward rebel likes to take the road less traveled. Pretending to be a rock star in her downtime, she wears mostly black, and loves to tour the world when her bank account allows it, while plotting her stories on the road. Wayward has interned as a script reader, and sold a treatment for a movie. She's written for a music magazine, which was a ploy to collect backstage passes and listen to some good music for free. Writing about hot alphas and badass women in search of a happily ever after is a dream come true. Because let's face it—who doesn't like to spend their time fantasizing about hot guys?

Drop me a line at lawayward.com, and don't forget to sign up for my newsletter.

-XXX-

Thank you for reading *X My Heart*.
If you have the time, please leave a review on Amazon, Instagram, TikTok or Goodreads. You'll get a sparkly unicorn, and my virtual hug in return!!! ;)

If you'd like to be alerted to my new releases, you can subscribe to my newsletter

I have more books coming out this year. Head over to my website at www.lawayward.com to drop a line, I would love to hear from you.

Instagram:
www.instagram.com/lawaywardauthor

Twitter:
twitter.com/authorlawayward

Facebook:
www.facebook.com/lawaywardauthor

Goodreads:
www.goodreads.com/author/show/20129154.L_A_Wayward

Amazon
www.amazon.com/L-A-Wayward/e/B08KQH1Z4W/ref=dp_byline_cont_pop_ebooks_1

Printed in Great Britain
by Amazon

43299939R00209